Nathan Woolford is a newspaper journalist, sub-editor and writer.

Born and raised in Swindon, Wiltshire, his journalism career began while he was still at school, with a weekend job at BBC Wiltshire Sound. He also wrote articles and features for various local papers and magazines.

Nathan graduated from University College Falmouth, with an honours degree in journalism, and has worked as a writer and copy editor for more than 20 years.

He lives in Hounslow, south-west London, with wife Lisa, twin boys, Will and George and dog, Waggy.

Nathan Woolford

TRAIL DUST

AUSTIN MACAULEY PUBLISHERS™

LONDON * CAMBRIDGE * NEW YORK * SHARJAH

A CIP catalogue record for this title is available from the British Library.

ISBN 9781398420373 (Paperback)
ISBN 9781398420380 (ePub e-book)

www.austinmacauley.com

First Published 2022
Austin Macauley Publishers Ltd®
1 Canada Square
Canary Wharf
London
E14 5AA

Chapter 1

Carlton County. Northern California. 1958

Home sweet home.

The truth was, for a man like him, there was no such place. Just the next stop on the road. The next town, the next crowd. But, for four months a year, home was just one safe place. And this was it.

The old turquoise Delta jeep turned off the highway and ascended a dirt road that led up a hill and into the surrounding countryside.

Speeding through woodland, the jeep turned again and cruised along a lane until it came out at the top of a huge hill that provided a magnificent view of the Carlton County countryside, with endless meadows spreading out below in all directions.

And there it was.

Kal Klondike pulled up and climbed out of the cabin. With a mesmeric gaze and a childlike smile curling the corners of his lips, he took in a sight he could only describe as breathtaking. And one he would never get tired of. It inspired him now, just as it always did. This was the magic he lived for.

A seemingly endless community of tents, marquees, trailers and stalls covered the fields like a city of playgrounds. There were small wooden cabins littered throughout the ensemble, and tiny figures could be seen roaming between the various constructions. He could see the stables and cages, where a host of animals were being cared for and treated like the kings and queens they undoubtedly were. Beyond that sat a remuda of transport – tractors, trucks and low-carriers. And, even from high up here, he could make out the giant banners and signs, covered in brightly coloured paint. Some were being carried around the site, while others were being worked on by bill writers. It truly was a sea of activity.

His stare moved north, and he caught sight of the railroad siding that would transport them all – everything – to the main line. And then, the magic really started.

Klondike shook his head in awe as he watched the proceedings from the top of the incline.

There it lay. Klondike's Circus Winter Camp.

Everything was set. The season was almost upon them. The circus train was heading north to greet them after weeks of renovations down south. He'd finalised the schedule, agreed all the bookings and closed a whole bunch of deals.

But, as was the case every year, a whole new series of problems and episodes had emerged as he'd tried to put together the new season.

He sniggered to himself as he looked over his empire. He was a tall man in his late forties, powerfully built and sporting a mighty mane of wavy jet-black hair and sideburns. His tanned, rugged features were matched by his equally rough-looking, virtually ever-present attire of desert slacks and a buckskin shirt, topped by a battered brown leather jacket. The ensemble was completed by another favourite, his old oak fedora. As he often proudly proclaimed, it had been given to him by the legendary John Ringling North.

Kal Klondike did not look like a businessman, an entrepreneur and a builder of empires. But he didn't consider himself any of those entities. He was a circus man. Period.

With a sigh, he got back behind the wheel of his jeep and started up the engine again. As the old Delta surged on down towards the endless sea of activity below, he reflected with mixed emotions on his meeting in San Francisco earlier that morning.

It had been a make or break set-up, as usual, and had set in motion the season that lay ahead.

He had felt an almighty surge of anticipation as he entered the banker's office…

"Ah, Kal, there you are. Come on in."

He breezed into the executive office of Daryl Addison, co-owner and founder of Addison and Lee Merchant Banking. The office was on the top floor of the firm's downtown San Francisco headquarters. It was a giant, spacious affair, with a large desk in the corner by the window and two couches enclosing a round conference table in a more informal area.

Addison, a small, lithe figure with short brown hair and a moustache, rose from behind the desk and shook hands with Klondike as he entered the great room.

"Good to see ya, Daryl," he boomed, crushing the man's hand in the process.

"Has it been 12 months already..." the banker mused.

Klondike smiled. He was dressed in a tanned suit with necktie and carried a large leather satchel under one arm. "I always look forward to our get-togethers."

"As do I," said the smaller man. "Can I offer you coffee? Tea?"

Klondike grinned. "Anything stronger?"

Addison grimaced and moved to a cabinet, where he poured a small pitcher of dry brown whiskey. He handed it to his guest and made himself a glass of soda water.

"So," he proclaimed grandly, "what news from the midway?"

Klondike forced a smile. "We're about all set, I reckon. I've been at the camp since end of fall. Everyone's rested. Spirits are high. Hell... It's circus season!" He laughed enthusiastically.

Addison stared back. "I see."

Klondike looked at him. Theirs was a peculiar relationship. Addison's loans had helped bankroll Klondike's Circus for years, in return for repayment, interest and a small cut of the profits. Klondike often wondered why he bothered, for such an insignificant return. Sure, his company got free advertising all across the big top and the midway and a mention in the programme. But the risk was vast, and the only collateral was a company of circus animals, a whole heap of performers and an ocean of cotton candy.

Addison motioned to the couches and they sat opposite each other. "OK Kal, let's cut to the chase," he said. "I was a touch surprised and a little bemused when I received your telegram last month. 75 thousand! That's a steep jump from our normal arrangement." He studied the circus boss shrewdly, sipping his soda water. "You realise the enormity of what you're asking? I mean, this is unprecedented. I've had to give this a lot of thought. Truth is, I still am." He fixed a stare that cut through his guest. "Tell me, what is the meaning of all this?"

Klondike gave the banker a big smile, eyes alive. "This is going to be the greatest season yet, Daryl."

"What...since the last one?"

"Come on, Daryl, wait till you see what I got lined up."

Addison seemed to shrink into the sofa. "OK," he sighed, "come on. Give it to me."

Suddenly, as if an ignition switch had been turned on inside him, Klondike threw himself into action. Opening the satchel, he placed upon the table a swathe of printed documents, all neatly filed. A logistics sheet, a collection of press releases on headed paper, a flyer, a poster and a large map.

As Addison surveyed the collection, Klondike stood and paced the room.

"1958, the year of Klondike's Circus," he began grandly. "Five months across the west coast, the usual gig, only this time 24 cities. California, Arizona and Nevada. We start as normal in Santa Cruz at the end of the month. We'll follow the usual route to begin with. But we head south once we reach Los Angeles to San Diego, then back up country until we hit our grand finale in Las Vegas. The entertainment capital of the world… Playing host to the greatest circus spectacular of all time. At the Golden Dune casino."

Addison looked up, shocked. "The Golden Dune?"

Klondike smiled. "That's right, Mr Banker, the Golden Dune. I've brokered a deal with Claude Hershey, the big casino king, to put on a show at the grandest hotel/casino on the strip. We're going to set up the big top on the parking lot, right next door, so the gaming floors and the circus will be conjoined," he chuckled. "It will be like a licence to print money. Folks can walk from the casino floor straight into the big top."

Addison looked confused. "Parking lot?" he blurted. He chewed it over. "Well, it's ambitious, Kal, I'll give you that."

Klondike, the great showman, continued loudly, still pacing before the banker like a hungry lion. "The roster is first class. And I'm delighted to announce that all the Klondike stars are signed up and ready to return." He pointed at the poster lying on the table. "Gino Shapiro, the world's most fearless flyer. Corky, beloved clown to thousands, the most multi-talented performer I have ever seen. My two most valued treasures… Both will be headlining the forthcoming season."

Addison looked underwhelmed. "So you're still relying on these two to generate ticket sales? Again? I thought you were going to freshen up the roster. Bring in new people." He held the poster aloft. It contained a picture of the famous red and white big top with a host of figures photo-spliced onto the shot. Gino Shapiro and Corky were placed at the front, surrounded by trapeze artists, lions, tigers, elephants, chimpanzees and various other performers. "What about all that scouting you did in the fall?"

Klondike swiped a hand through the air. "I've found and signed more talent. But the stars are my regular guys. Emile the animal trainer. Amanda's elephant acrobatics. Cathy and her dancing chimps. The new guys are introduced in that last press release."

Addison picked up the copy. He read aloud. "Goliath. The world's tallest man. Gargantua. The human blob. All 500 pounds of him. Rumpy Stiltskin. The man with ten-foot legs." He looked up, bemused. "Where the hell do you find these people?"

Klondike laughed. "It's what I do."

"What about the pay scale? Wages?"

"We figured all that out last season. Everyone is on a pay freeze this time round, but with a bonus if we double our take by the end. So a lot will be riding on the Vegas show."

"Jesus…" Addison mused. He glared down at the circus poster, then stared at Klondike incredulously. "These people…" he breathed, "the roustabouts. The hawkers. The goddamn talent. How do you keep them in this? What makes them keep coming back?"

Klondike smiled mesmerically, looking every inch the charismatic maverick. "They're circus folk," he whispered. "They've got sawdust in their shoes and—"

"Yeah, yeah," the banker interrupted moodily, "I know the damn line. They've got sawdust in their shoes, and sawdust in their hearts."

Klondike laughed heartily. "You said it, partner!"

Addison merely stared at him. Then he waved a hand. "All right, Kal, sit down for Christ sakes." When the taller man was seated, he continued. "I have to tell you, I have mixed thoughts about all this. Twenty-four cities, compared to your usual 18. This whole Las Vegas idea. It's a big risk. Guaranteeing that old train of yours is going to get you and your troupe up and down the west coast. Are the public going to go for it?" He rubbed a hand through his slick hair. "And then there's our old friend Eric Ribbeck to worry about."

Klondike froze. Ribbeck. His arch nemesis. Owner of the Ribbeck's World Circus. Arguably the biggest set-up in America today. And it was due to tour the west coast during the peak summer months. The rivalry was an annual dogfight, but Ribbeck had the good fortune of being backed up his old oil baron buddies from Texas, some of the wealthiest families in the state.

Klondike stared at his poster ruefully. He had been a trick shot artist and knife thrower for Ribbeck in his youth, before becoming deputy circus manager. His flair for the business and knack for talent spotting had seen him climb the ladder fast. But he had also seen corruption and gross indecency at the highest levels, with Ribbeck keeping the largest share of the profits for himself and his cronies and skimming money throughout the operation for his string of mistresses, many of whom worked in his troupe. He had also mistreated more employees than Klondike cared to remember. All these instances had led to Klondike leaving Ribbeck's World Circus, breaking away to form his own troupe. Many performers had left with him, including Gino and Corky, who were key to the company's success. Ribbeck had never forgiven him.

"Can you really compete with the old man?" Addison's question brought him back to the present.

He snarled. "We've competed with him before. And we'll do it again."

Addison smiled for the first time. "You've always returned a profit, Kal, I have to admit." He shifted in the couch. "I've given all this a lot of thought. A hell of a lot of thought. And I've made a decision. In fact, I made it several days ago."

Klondike leaned across the table eagerly.

Addison stared at him directly. "You've got your 75 thousand…" He held up a bony hand as Klondike made to celebrate. "But I have several terms."

"Just name them, Daryl."

"I want you to bring along two people. My people."

"What?"

"Don't worry, they're not performers. Firstly, I'm sending one of my principal accountants along with you. Richie Plum."

"Richie Plum?"

"That's right. He will be your finance manager for the season. The terms are any decisions Plum makes regarding money are to be obeyed. He will be my inside man, if you like."

Klondike baulked. "What does this Plum know about the circus business?"

Addison chuckled. "He's reading up."

"I dunno, Daryl, that's a lot of responsibility for a newcomer."

"Plum is a good man. He will bring your operating costs down without you even knowing it. If I'm putting in all that dough, I want a man with you overseeing my investment. It makes perfect sense. Perfect business sense."

Klondike looked downwards. "I guess so. But, er, you said two people."

Addison grinned. "That's right," he proclaimed, "and I'll also be sending along your new secret weapon. Lacey Tanner!"

Klondike stared dumbly. "Lacey? What kind of a name is that?"

"With a name like that she ought to fit right in with your colourful cast of characters."

"Who the hell is she?"

"Lacey Tanner is a publicist we work with on big projects. She will be in charge of all your publicity for the season."

"Now hold on," Klondike fired back. "I happen to do my own publicity. And, damn it, I've done a pretty good job down the years."

"You have indeed. But Lacey will take your circus to a new level." He leant back on the sofa. "Kal, you do realise that Addison and Lee is a major national investor? We put up for movies, Broadway shows, hotels, television. We have a wealth of experience in the entertainment sector. And Lacey has conducted PR campaigns across the board. We put her on the books a few years back after she generated huge press coverage for some of our projects. She has… I dunno, the Midas touch. You'll see."

Klondike looked less than impressed. "I'm not convinced, Daryl. You're asking me to bring in two newcomers, and in senior positions. I've got a business to run."

Addison folded his arms smugly. "Those are my conditions. We're not going to sign on the dotted line without them." He paused. "You're asking for a big investment, Kal. You've got to expect a little leeway here. Besides, Lacey and Richie are going to enhance your product. They're going to ensure greater profits for us. Now what's so bad about that?"

Klondike looked down at his paperwork. There were no options, and he knew it. He'd always enjoyed a free reign, but the stakes were higher this time. The season he had planned was bigger than anything they had ever put on. And there was no backing down now. He needed Addison's money. He needed the bank's support. He had to dance.

"All right," he muttered, before downing the rest of his whiskey.

Addison smiled brightly, rising from the couch. "The contracts are just about all set. I'll get them now."

And that was that.

The jeep cruised through the entrance to the winter camp, leaving a rampaging trail of dust in its wake. The entire ensemble was protected by a man-made oak fence, and Klondike felt a strange sense of relief as he drove through the front gate.

He wound the Delta through the meandering jungle of tents and stalls, that were positioned in place ready for the arrival of the train.

As he drove, he waved enthusiastically at the various workers under his employ and honked his horn several times in greeting. Everyone he passed as he drove down the trail path waved and shouted a warm welcome.

He passed Amanda Hart and her assistant Hans, who were walking one of their troupe of four elephants.

"Welcome back, boss," Amanda called out in her dry, husky voice as he passed.

Cathy Cassidy was also present, sat on the steps of her trailer with her hoard of beloved, disciplined chimpanzees sprawled all around as she handed out treats. As the jeep passed, Cathy and the entire brigade of simians all looked up and waved as one.

He also drove past Emile Rance's enclosure. Most of the staff stayed away from this area located in the far corner of the camp. A miniature pen was set up protected by a makeshift wall of wooden decking. Within, Emile worked with his family – two magnificent Namibian lions and his most prized possession, the white tiger, which had come from Burma.

As Klondike drove past, he slowed slightly. There was Emile, a short, athletic South African with rich, curly blond hair, dressed as always in safari attire, directing the animals in the pen. At this time, he was addressing the two lions, making them roll over and then stand on their hind legs.

"Keep 'em busy, Emile," he called out as the jeep rolled by.

Emile looked up and grinned. "Just get us under that tent, boss, and they'll do da rest."

Klondike threw a wave and wound the jeep down as he approached a large wooden cabin at the far end of the camp. His office and quarters.

Henry 'Heavy' Brown, his right-hand man and ringmaster, was waiting for him. As befitted his nickname, he was a burly figure, medium height but brawny, a mixture of fat and muscle. Balding and blessed with a cherubic, almost childlike face, he was without his beautiful scarlet ringmaster's jacket and black Stetson, and was instead dressed in a lumberjack shirt and jeans.

"Welcome back, Kal," he said dutifully.

"Thanks Heavy," he replied as he pulled up. As the dust settled all around them, he jumped from the jeep and grabbed his satchel and bagged up suit from the rear bench seat.

"How'd it go?" Heavy asked as they fell in step in the shadow of the cabin.

"Good news and bad, old buddy," he said as they reached the front door. With a weary sigh, Klondike opened the door and led the way into the office-cum-living quarters. The cabin was basically one large room featuring a desk, a bed, a couch and a kitchenette in the far corner. A closet bathroom was adjoined to the cabin via a swinging saloon-style wooden door.

Heavy followed him in and watched as he dumped his belongings on the couch. "Do tell."

Klondike threw his jacket onto the back of a chair. "We got the dough," he began, "but old man Addison had two provisions. Two people, in fact."

Heavy stared at him dumbly. "What people?"

"He wants us to take along two of his stooges for the whole tour. A publicist and an accountant."

"But…but we do the publicity. Everyone knows that."

Klondike grimaced. "It seems not quite everyone." He moved to a drinks cabinet and poured them both a shot of whiskey. Then, handing his old friend one of the glasses, continued: "The important thing is we got the cash. Without the loan, we were screwed. No amount of contingency planning can cover over that. These two newcomers, we'll deal with them when they turn up. Day after next, so Addison said. But, listen, the old banker gave a green light to everything. The whole season. So…" he pulled a cigar from a box on his desk. "We may as well celebrate, for now. There's a lot to be thankful for."

Heavy baulked. "I guess." He thought for a moment, his large, buggy eyes lost in thought. "There were always going to be some demands. For a price that large."

"Exactly." Klondike lit his cigar, blowing a great waft of purple smoke towards the ceiling. "Now listen up, Heavy. The first thing I want to do is call an executive council meeting. Let everyone know how this is going to work. I saw most of the guys outside while I drove in. Where's Gino? And Corky? And Jim McCabe?"

Heavy sipped his drink. "Gino is still in Hollywood. Due back tomorrow of course. Corky is doing his last class at that college in Oakland. And Jim has been rounding up roustabouts in Santa Cruz all week. But they should all be here in the morning. They know the schedule."

Klondike nodded, dragging deeply on the cigar. He moved to the window and gazed out at the melee of activity going on all around them. It was like a sea of people, animals and motion.

He placed an arm around his old friend. "Good," he said, as if in a trance. "It's time to blow some trail dust."

Chapter 2

In a plush bungalow high in the Hollywood hills, Gino Shapiro awoke to the sound of beautiful, soft Spanish singing. The soulful, sensitive voice came from the shower and drifted into the bedroom like a luscious wave of pure charm.

He was lying on his back on a giant four-poster bed, wearing only his shorts. He blinked several times, listening to the singing, before sliding off the silk sheets and padding across to the wall-length mirror by the dresser.

He was a tanned, swarthy character with slicked back ebony hair and the classic build of a welterweight boxer. He studied himself in the mirror.

"Not bad for a veteran," he told his reflection. He stretched his arms out high, then grimaced slightly, cursing.

He made for a portable refrigerator in the room's corner and pulled an ice pack out of the freezer shelf. He placed the pack against his shoulder and held it steady for several moments before rubbing it across his flesh.

"Another tweak there, champ?"

He turned and saw Rosalita, the Mexican B movie actress he had been dating all winter, standing in the bedroom doorway, draped in a fluffy white towel. They had met when he had come out here in the fall, as he usually did at the end of the season. She was a former dancer from Mexico City. Shapiro, a third-generation trapeze artist of Mexican/Italian heritage, had been instantly drawn to her. They had met on the set of the movie he had found work on as a technical consultant, The Biggest Show in the West.

"It's getting worse," he stammered, moving the pack across his shoulder blade. "Stinking joints. They always told me this would happen. Too much swinging on the rings."

She looked at him as he slumped onto the edge of the bed. "Shouldn't you get that checked out, Gino?"

"What!" he gasped, "and be told I can never fly again? Uh huh, mamacita. As long as I have ice, I am in shape."

15

"If you say so," she said doubtfully. She came over and perched next to him on the bed. "So this is it, huh? Our last night together." She looked around the room. "I guess we will always have the memories."

Shapiro frowned. "We knew it would be like this when we started, Rosalita. That was the deal. You knew my schedule."

"Can't it still work? Hell, I could join the circus."

He gazed at their reflections in the mirror ruefully. "No," he said, "it's over."

She slumped, but then nodded understandingly. "It… It must be nice. Going back there. To friends. Family. A home. People who love you."

He looked at her. "It's what I do. My act is everything to me. You know that." He stood and looked out the window at the setting sun, slanting over the hills. "The crowd. The fans. The people. That electricity of performing in front of a live audience. Nothing… Nothing can touch that."

"Your brother… He is waiting for you?"

"Sure. Me and Nicky are the flyers, along with young Jenny, our apprentice. We are the stars. We are the superheroes. When we fly, we… We reign!" His eyes were wide now as he paced around the room, like a bull ready to charge.

She sighed, gripping an idle hairbrush. "The studio man is driving you up to Carlton County?"

"Right." He began pulling a pair of chinos on, followed by a silk shirt.

"What can I say, Gino?"

He smiled beautifully at her. "How about… See you next winter!"

Rosalita looked up glumly. "How about one last kiss?"

Shapiro laughed. "We'll make it last seven months!"

With that, they embraced for one final time.

"Once you can take your eyes off the pins, you've got it made!"

The man known to the world as Corky the Clown was juggling six pins with subtle ease as he addressed the small classroom of youngsters. They stared at him in utter bewilderment as he wandered in a circle before them, turning his head away from the juggling pins and looking at the back of the room. Gasps gushed from their excited faces.

The clown, with his white face paint, bright yellow and red striped suit and purple top hat, paraded before them jovially.

He had been born John Lone in Cleveland, Ohio. After a difficult upbringing in an orphanage, he done what so many youngsters of that era had longed to do and had run away to join a circus. Taken under the wing of a group of traditional clowns, he had excelled at all elements of the art and had quickly become a top draw with his all-consuming clown act. An old school performer, he only removed his make-up at bedtime and never went around in public out of character or without his costume. The Corky persona had saved his life, and he owed everything to his comic creation.

Now, as a guest lecturer at Oakland Art College, he was giving a troupe of young students a masterclass in how to create a circus act.

"So remember," he was saying, "practice, practice, practice. And, when you can juggle without looking, without even thinking, then you have got it. You'll be a master."

Finally, he threw each pin high in the air as they passed in mid-spin and eloquently caught each one in the front of his pants.

The students applauded merrily, with a few shouting out 'woos' as Corky gathered the pins and placed them in his kit bag.

He placed his hands in the air and smiled mischievously at his audience. "Thank you, thank you friends. Now, any questions?"

A flurry of sentences were thrown at him from the floor as he stood before the youngsters.

"How long have you been a clown?"

"Haha. Forever!"

"When did you join Klondike's Circus?"

"I joined Klondike about six years ago."

"In the newspapers, it says you are unique because you can perform every clown discipline there is. Juggling, uni-cycling, balloons, even the human cannonball act. Is that really true?"

"It is true. I was very well trained. When I was even younger than you. By a legendary clown troupe called the Trumbo Clan. They were all-rounders. I think it's the best way to perform."

"Are you always so cheerful?"

"Ha! I try to be, a circus is a very happy place y'know."

"Where did you grow up, Mr Corky?"

He looked up suddenly. This had come from the only girl in the room, seated towards the rear. His live wire eyes took on a sad look, shocking the class.

He held up a gloved hand. "OK, OK, I think I'll leave that one for next time, guys."

Then, with an exuberant flourish, he pulled a small wallet from his pocket and cried out to the students: "Now, who wants some tickets to the first show of the season?"

Everyone stood and rushed towards him, many hugging him and embracing him as he handed out the free passes.

Even the college administrator, who had watched the proceedings from a doorway, moved towards the melee. "Thank you, Corky, that was truly breathtaking."

The clown smiled, his face paint showing no cracks as it glowed immaculately. "My pleasure. Y'know, I think you may have some budding clowns right here in this room."

Everybody laughed.

Darkness had settled over the winter camp as Klondike ducked out of his cabin and lit one of his crisp, Virginian cigars. All was relatively quiet now. The animals had been put to rest, and most of the guys were in their quarters, be that a trailer, van or cabin like his.

He wandered out towards the gate that enclosed the entire camp and gazed at the railroad branch line that sat just yards away. There was a full moon tonight, and its beam lit up the tracks perfectly.

He stood there, watching as great puffs of greenish purple smoke obscured his view of the line. *It ain't cold at night no more,* he thought. *That means it's the start of the season.*

He felt a presence lurking behind him and turned suddenly. When he saw who was approaching, he winced inwardly.

Jenny Cross. One of his flyers. She occupied ring one in the trapeze act, alongside Nicky Shapiro on ring three and his brother, the great Gino, in centre.

Klondike sighed as he studied her. They had been lovers once, two seasons ago, for an entire year. When he had called it off, due to the relationship damaging his sense of moral duty as manager, Jenny had taken it badly. In fact, she had virtually ignored him for the last few years. Their few meetings were awkward, angst-ridden affairs. He sometimes wondered why he had taken the action he had, but knew he had broken a golden rule by dating talent.

Jenny was slight, lithe and with the toned arms and thighs of an acrobat. Her long blonde hair was straight and shiny. A California native, she had been brought into the show by Gino as an apprentice some years back. He'd found her on a movie lot, or so he claimed. She was barely 30, far too young, as Klondike often told himself.

"A lonely night?" She purred as she approached him. She was wearing a cloak over her blouse and looked almost angelic in the fading moonlight.

"It can be lonely at the top," he replied, puffing on the cigar and gazing out at the prairies.

"You've been alone your whole life," she mused conversationally, "everyone knows that. People, they come and go. The talent, the crowds. Friends, lovers, family. All you care about is that damned circus."

He sighed heavily, looking down at her. "Is there something you wanted, Jenny?"

She floated about him airily, annoying him more and more with each step.

"Oh," she said, "I haven't seen you over the winter. I just wanted to know if there were any changes this season. There usually are."

Klondike frowned. "We're having an executive council meeting day after tomorrow. Gino will be there. He'll report back to you and Nicky."

She smiled teasingly. "Can't just tell me yourself, huh boss man?"

"That's not how it works. You know that."

"How about any other changes?"

He glared at her, cigar in mouth. "What?"

"Changes between you and me, Kal."

"What changes? What the hell are you talking about?"

She stared straight at him. "I know you still want me. Hell, it's obvious to everyone here."

"You're crazy!"

"Am I?" She looked him over slowly. "Don't you ever think about what might have been?"

"Nope!" he said bluntly. "Why the sudden interest again? What is this?"

She frowned at him. "You broke my heart once, Kal. I think about it all the time. I just wanted to see if you do. And, I guess it's fairly obvious you have no such feelings. And why should I be surprised? As long as the circus keeps on rolling, you've got all the happiness you'll ever need."

"Dammit!" he snapped. He glared at her. "Why are you still here, Jenny? Why don't you go and join the Coleman's Circus or Ringman's? Be a star in your own right? What's keeping you here?"

"I'm not quitting," she shot back. "You'll have to fire me."

"I'm not doing that."

"Because I'm too good a flyer." She laughed seductively, tilting her head back. "Of course, Mr Klondike. We all know how your mind works. Talent." She threw her cloak hood back, her blonde hair tumbling out like a tidal wave. The effect was astonishing. "I'm like a reminder of a bad day for you, hanging around with your troupe. But you won't give up top talent. What a trauma it must be for you, boss man."

He took a gentle drag on the cigar, moving away from the fence. And her.

"Listen," he drawled, "do me a favour and stay outta my way, will ya? I got enough on my plate without your nonsense."

As he walked away, Jenny called after him. "You're a cold man, Kal Klondike. A cold, ruthless man. One day, you're going to learn from your heartlessness."

He turned angrily. "Just work your magic on the rings, Jenny. Do your job. Please!" He seemed to calm suddenly, and stood in the doorway of his cabin. "Look, we were sweet on each other once. I'm sorry if I ever led you on. It was not my intention. I made a mistake. We never should have dated. It was breaking the workplace code. We've been through all this before. I feel bad for what happened, you know that. Now," he looked at her softly, "can we just put all this behind us and get on with our work? I'm begging you, Jenny."

She stood still in the moonlight. "Why Kal," she mused with mock concern, "for a minute there it almost sounded like you had feelings."

He looked at her. "What's the use," he muttered to himself. Then, he wandered idly into his cabin. Once inside, he ripped off his hat and threw it angrily onto the couch. Hands on hips, he cursed to himself.

Outside, Jenny still stood in the same spot. Glaring at the closed cabin door, she remained perfectly still. She could have been a statue out there in the night, but for a slight, unmistakable trembling around her eyelids. The eyes were like stone, and their look was one of pure venom.

Chapter 3

The giant marquee in the centre of the camp was buzzing with noise and commotion as the principal players and staff from the circus, or as Klondike liked to call it "the executive council", all gathered in the tent for the first meeting of pre-season.

Inside the marquee was a large conference table, which had been hastily set up amidst the various dinner tables and chairs that surrounded the chow line. This tent was where the staff ate their meals, but also served as a meeting point and communal area.

Klondike and Heavy had arrived early and sat at the head of the table, watching with amusement and interest as the talent slowly assembled.

As expected, Emile Rance had shown up first, followed by the circus foreman, Jim McCabe.

Gino had burst in, laughing loudly, with Amanda and Cathy on one arm each, both desperate to hear the latest news from Hollywood. He was dressed in some kind of leather jumpsuit like nothing anyone had ever seen before. He embraced Klondike and Heavy warmly, then sat at the opposite end, with Amanda and Cathy either side.

Corky walked in quietly, offering a firm handshake to everyone. He wore a business suit, with his ever-present face paint up top, and a bowler hat.

Then came Suzi Dando, a young singer who performed the circus's anthem, 'Can You Feel the Magic Tonight?' during the closing parade.

Klondike looked around expectantly as the general chitchat died down. His team finally assembled, he felt relief flooding through his every pore. There would be no hold-ups, everyone was here. He noticed with a grin that Corky had sat next to him, at the other end of the table to Gino. Despite sharing a mutual respect for one another, the clown and the flyer were rivals over who should have top billing. Although Gino's name was at the top of all bills and posters, Corky seemed to have a greater fan base and drawing power.

"All right, all right," said Klondike, raising a hand. "Welcome all. Welcome back. It's good to see everyone under one roof again, and good to know there's no need for any search parties. This time!"

They all laughed.

"OK gang. This is the usual drill. I lay out the season plan. Everything you need to know. Then, after, I want to hear any problems, issues, difficulties, and I'll take care of them. OK? So…"

He then proceeded to tell the assembled talent about his meeting with Daryl Addison, the money loan, the addition of two new faces, the new bumper route and a summary of each town they would visit. The big Las Vegas idea had been announced to the troupe last year and so was merely confirmed during the meeting.

After he had finished speaking, the usual deluge of questions followed. Klondike remained standing as the talent spoke up.

As expected, Gino was first. "An excellent appraisal, chairman. I applaud your grand vision. Las Vegas is perfecto for a showcase of my talents. I want you to know that when we hit Los Angeles and Montecito, I have arranged for several movie stars to make guest appearances at the shows."

Klondike frowned. "Have you now? OK, let's discuss that in private."

The Latino flyer continued: "And some of the studio executives have agreed to shift some tickets for me in Hollywood."

Klondike sighed. "That's just wonderful, Gino. Now, you just make sure you, Nicky and Jenny are ready for Santa Cruz at the end of the month."

Gino smiled beautifully, looking like a million dollars. "Always ready, chairman."

Cathy Cassidy was next to speak. "Is the circus train going to be clean this time? My chimps got infected last season. The whole thing stunk!"

"Rest assured," said Klondike, "the train has undergone a refit and has been cleaned to an industrial standard. It's been reconstructed in Frisco and will be here in a few weeks so we can roll."

"I'm worried too." This from Amanda. "My girls were exhausted by the end of last season. I don't know that they can handle so many shows."

"Your elephants will be just fine. They'll have the best of everything. Food, water, luxurious quarters."

"Luxurious!" Amanda squealed. "In a hold on a train?"

He sighed. "Listen, if there ever comes a time when you think they ain't up to it, we'll pull 'em out and come up with something different."

Amanda nodded slowly. "OK, boss."

Emile spoke next. "We all agreed to pay freezes last year, Kal. Now you tell us this banker of yours wants a greater hold on us. Is he getting more of da profits?"

Every face turned to the front of the table. "No," Klondike replied calmly. "Same quota. But he is expecting bigger profits all round due to the fine touches we've added. The better publicity, the finance manager, the Vegas gig. So that means we all have to do our damnedest to put on the best damn shows we can. Then, we'll generate greater profits for all of us. Addison's percentage is the same it's always been."

Suzi raised her hand, an unnecessary gesture, and spoke in her quiet, angelic voice. She was a child among the guys around the table, barely out of her teens, her innocent little face and bobbed hazelnut hair making her seem even more youthful. "Is the grand finale going to change, Mr Klondike?"

He smiled. "No, Suzy, it will stay the same."

She flushed excitedly and sat still.

Jim McCabe was next. A squat, bullish man, he wore his standard attire of a polo shirt, slacks and a pork pie hat.

"These new stops," he wheezed, pulling a small cigar out of his mouth, "it might be hard finding hands in em. We got our usual people in the cities we been to before, but this is something else completely. What if there ain't anybody to help when we get there?"

This was an annual problem. McCabe retained about 20 roustabouts, who lived on the train for the entire season in the bunkhouse. But most of the workforce was obtained on arrival in each new town, with workers signing on with McCabe once the train had docked in. He employed the same people each year in the cities and towns they played at, but the new route could prove a dangerous one in terms of finding hands.

"I hear that, Jim," said Klondike. "What can I tell you? Word has spread, the towns know the circus is coming. The people will be ready. Look at it like this… When we started out, we had no one in any of these places. We built up a temporary workforce then. Who says we can't do it now?"

McCabe chewed on his cigar. He seldom smiled and looked permanently disgruntled. "OK Kal. I'm just saying it's a gamble is all."

23

"It's all a gamble," said Klondike grandly. "That's the world we have chosen. And the one we live in." He looked around and noticed a few nervous faces.

Beside him, Heavy saw his hesitation and addressed the table.

"Listen, people," he bellowed, "all we have to do is stay in the black and we are rolling. The doughs in place, we just have to show a profit. And we will."

"Right," Klondike seconded. He looked around the table with a grin. Then he looked down at the clown beside him.

"How about you, Corky? No questions?"

The beloved clown chuckled before pulling out a polka dot coloured handkerchief and pretending to dab his forehead. "Yeah... When do we start, boss?"

The females all laughed and Klondike cracked a big smile.

"That's the spirit. Now, listen, we got under two weeks, then we got —"

He broke off abruptly at the sound of chattering and cheering outside. A crowd had gathered beyond the tent and people were cheering and whistling. The honking of a car horn followed.

Klondike stared at Heavy, who shrugged in puzzlement.

"What the..." said Klondike, before heading to the flap door.

The rest slowly rose and followed as he flung the tent door open and stared in dismay at the sight before him.

A whole squad of circus helpers and roustabouts were excitedly following in the wake of a beautiful silver Cadillac convertible, so shiny it looked like it had just come off the production line. They were all cheering and calling out exclamations as the exotic automobile manoeuvred its way up the old gravel path in the camp's centre. The horn kept honking as the car tried to find a clear route.

Klondike stared dumbfounded, Heavy joining him at the flap. No one had ever seen such a flashy motor, especially in a circus camp. If the car was impressive, the woman at the wheel cut an equally dashing picture. She appeared to be wearing a bright yellow blazer, with giant black sunglasses covering her honey skin and beautiful flaming red hair blowing gracefully in the breeze.

A small, plump, balding man with glasses and wearing a suit was seated next to her. He appeared to disprove of the fanfare.

"What's all this?" cried Heavy excitedly.

"I think I have an idea," said Klondike gravely.

He stepped out of the tent, with the rest of his troupe gathering up behind him in the gravel.

The Cadillac came to a stop, and the excited group all stood around it, gawking at its sparkling lines and decor.

The woman got out, shook her hair grandly, and pulled her sunglasses onto the top of her forehead. She looked around idly, taking in the rows of trailers and vans all around. She wore a yellow skirt to match her blazer, and even her high heels were the same colour. She trudged carefully across the gravel and came face to face with Klondike.

She looked up, revealing a pair of sparkling violet eyes.

"Kalvin Klondike, I presume?" she gushed.

Klondike smirked. "Right."

She extended a leather-gloved hand. "Lacey Tanner. I'm your new publicist. What a pleasure to meet you."

They shook hands gamely.

Her small male companion exited the vehicle and shuffled over uneasily. "Richie Plum," he blurted to no one in particular. No one even noticed him. All eyes were on the glamorous woman in yellow, both male and female.

"That was quite an entrance, Miss Tanner," said Klondike coolly.

"Lacey," the dazzling newcomer squeaked. "And I believe in doing everything in style. Grand entrances leave lasting impressions. Everything is designed for impact. Mr Addison paid for this car in order for me to travel around making people like you look good."

Klondike was already lost for words. "Well, er, that's just great Miss, er, I mean…"

Suddenly, Gino was all over the newcomer, standing almost on top of her and flashing his widest smile.

"Gino Shapiro," he squawked, kissing her hand, which she hadn't offered. "The debonair king of the air. Star of the show. And what an immense pleasure to meet you, Miss Lacey."

She gave him a half-hearted glance. "Ah yes, Gino Shapiro. I've heard a lot about you. The man with the star billing, huh?"

"Quite right." He made an exuberant gesture. "I am ready for your debriefing, Miss Lacey, we have much to discuss. I have many ideas on how to promote our show, and my act, in Hollywood. I am all yours."

The gathered ensemble groaned as one at the Latino flyer's outrageous flirting. But Lacey merely shrugged, offered her thanks, and moved towards the tent. "This is incredible," she breathed, looking around her, "the circus all set to roll."

Then, she studied Klondike, and addressed only him. "We have much to get through, Kalvin. Can we get started in here? This looks like a place of business."

Klondike strode towards her. "It's Kal, and we were just in the middle of a meeting, dammit."

Lacey looked around, smiling beautifully. "Well, you'll have to reschedule. There's not a moment to lose here, baby. We need to go through all your publicity campaigns for the tour. I understand the train rolls in under two weeks. That's a tough deadline."

Klondike glared at her, incredulous, his temper rising. "Baby? Campaign? Deadline? What in San Hill are you talking about?"

The gathered crowd were loving every minute. Here was this uptown dame talking like a movie star, ripping rugged old Kal Klondike to pieces. Laughter blurted out from most of the onlookers. Even Heavy was trying not to chuckle.

Lacey merely shrugged, then inexplicably placed her arm through Klondike's and led him into the marquee. Like a child being forced into a dentist's, Klondike begrudgingly followed. Plum, shifting nervously by the circus people, followed them inside.

Everyone stared at the door flap in astonishment. Heavy, struggling to know what to do, made his way to the door and closed the flap shut. Then he addressed the assembled crowd.

"All right, folks, you heard the lady. Meeting adjourned. Now let's all get back to work. Nothing to see here."

"I'd say there's plenty to see here," Emile growled, hovering by the door.

"Yeah," said Amanda anxiously. "Is that really the publicist? She looks more like a contessa from Europe."

"I'd say," Gino added. He looked at Heavy. "So this is the new deal, eh, fat man? The chairman gets to spend all the time with the publicity lady."

"Buster," Heavy blurted, "I don't know what the hell the new deal is. Things are changing too fast around here for me to comprehend."

Corky tried to lead the group away. "Why don't we just leave old Kal to it now?"

Slowly, the group dissembled, each going about their own business.

"Let's go through my file on you first, Kal."

Lacey had seated herself on the edge of the conference table, legs crossed, with a pile of papers set out to the side of her frame. She lit a cigarette and surveyed a thin file on her lap.

Klondike grudgingly sat in a seat to the side of her, while Plum wandered about the tent, studying its structure. He had still hardly said a word.

"You have a file on me?" Klondike said in shock.

"Of course." She looked over the top of the papers she was studying, and removed her sunglasses, shaking her flaming hair again. She inhaled deeply and smiled a winning grin at him. "You're too important not to have a file. Now please."

She read aloud, as if addressing an audience in an arena. "Kalvin Klondike. Born Terry Calder in Hell's Kitchen, New York. Parents unknown. You were raised in an orphanage. The Westley Boys Home. As a youth, you ran with a street gang. Called yourselves... The Cobras." She looked up, smiling. "Cute." She continued: "At 18 you joined the Marines. Served in World War Two. France. Italy. The fall of Berlin. You requested an honorary discharge following the court martial of one Max Drago." She looked up. "Can you elaborate on that, Kal?"

He had sat there obediently, but now squirmed under her gaze. The giant violet eyes seemed to bore right through him.

"I can't see how it's relevant," he began, "but Drago was a drill sergeant. A no-good son of a bitch. He was bullying new recruits. Drowning them in a training pool. I reported him. The top brass nailed him. After that, I'd had enough and came home to New York."

She tapped a pen against the table. "Whatever became of this Drago?"

Klondike shook his head. "He became a private contractor and died peddling guns in, er, Brazil, I think it was. I had friends who attended his funeral."

"Hmmm," Lacey breathed, still tapping the pen. "So, you left the services and joined the circus. You were a crack shot in the marines and were invited to audition for Ribbeck World Circus as a sharpshooter. Eric Ribbeck labels you the greatest marksman he has ever seen. You join his troupe and quickly establish yourself as a businessman. Within two years, you're working in admin as a booker and talent scout." She put the file on her lap and looked at him sceptically. "Now, I'm sorry, Kal, I don't mean to sound rude and I know I'm no circus expert. Yet. But it seems unlikely that a circus sharpshooter with no experience

27

of the business and no experience of corporate affairs can suddenly be left in charge of talent affairs." She pretended to whisper, "Did you sleep with his daughter?"

"Jesus Christ!" Klondike roared. "What is this? I didn't realise I was going to have to justify my life story with you."

"She's right." They both turned in shock as Plum finally spoke.

"What?" Klondike blurted.

Plum wandered over to them and took a seat beside the circus boss. He continued: "You have very little experience in actual circus management, Klondike. Rising to the top that fast is very unusual in this business."

"How would you know?" he shot back. "What are you even doing here, little man? I thought you were supposed to be making decisions on keeping costs down."

"I'm your new finances manager, Klondike," the smaller man replied matter-of-factly. A smug look appeared on his sweaty, fleshy face. "You must comply with me, or else Addison will change his mind about that loan. About your funding."

"So that's the deal, huh?"

"Just share with us your story. Please."

Klondike gave an almighty sigh. "All right. It's simple." He looked around, as the other two waited patiently. "The circus...it's my calling. All my life I was amazed and entranced by its wonders...its beauty. As a kid I would go down to Coney Island every summer to watch Ribbeck World Circus. Even in the services, I went along when I could. The sharpshooter act was my talent, that got me in. I learnt knife throwing and showmanship. But my true mission was to be involved at the top. To run my own troupe. And run it properly. Not like that snake Ribbeck. When I was under him, I went to so many shows, scouting for talent, that I became an expert in what a show needs to succeed. An expert in knowing what people want. In what entertains everyday folks. That, you see, is my true skill."

The two newcomers remained silent for several moments, the sound of the elephants chortling in the background punctuating the silence.

"A pretty story," Lacey finally mused. She stubbed out her cigarette in an ashtray. "Richie, get us all a coffee, would ya, baby?"

The little man baulked, but duly obeyed, moving to the coffee pot in the corner and pouring there cups.

28

She continued. "In fact, it's beautiful. A life under the big top."

"It's my home. I belong here."

Lacey removed one of her leather gloves and waved it through the air. "So, I understand Ribbeck now wants your blood."

"You could say that. He never forgave me for leaving him. And taking Gino and Corky too."

"Understandable." She leaned over, eyeing him up with her mesmerising eyes. "But you don't have to worry, kitty cat. You want to know why? Because we're going to trump him. We will have the bigger crowds. We will be number one on the West Coast. You'll see."

Klondike finally smiled. But he was still mystified by the beautiful, beguiling woman who had marched into his camp as if she owned it. "Now you're talking, lady," he stammered.

She looked at him soberly. "Quite." She pulled another file up from her pile. "So Ribbeck hits the West Coast in August? So we'll be in direct competition for the second half of the season?"

"Well, yes, but our dates are slightly different. We will only be in the same town at the same time once."

She closed her eyes. "Las Vegas."

"Right."

"But, still, we will be in competition in terms of attracting out of town audiences. For example, if you live in San Remo, you will go to shows in Los Angeles and Sacramento. We will be in Sac. He will be in LA."

He shrugged. "It's an annual fight. We go through it every year. And we ain't done too badly down the years, considering the vast resources Ribbeck's got at his disposal."

She nodded thoughtfully. Plum returned with their coffees and they all sat and sipped in silence. Plum began going through some of the papers for himself. He seemed happy to play a supporting role to the publicity queen.

Lacey had picked up yet another file. "So, your line-up for the show is settled? It'll be the same for every show?"

Klondike nodded. "Barring any unforeseen incidents."

She smiled devilishly. "Like my arrival." She laughed gaily. "So, you open with Cathy Cassidy and her chimps. Then Corky's act. Followed by bareback horse riders…whatever that is. Then Amanda with her elephants. Then the clown revue. Then what you call the freak show. I can only imagine. Then Emile the lion trainer. Then, of course, the trapeze artists. And then, the grand finale…a parade of all the stars on floats around the tent, with Suzi singing that song you like so much."

"That's about the whole of it. We've kept the same formula for three years now. Everyone is happy with it."

"That's why we must change it!" Lacey threw the papers onto the desk.

"What!" Klondike raged. He had heard just about enough from this glorified glamour puss. She was pushing way too far for his liking. "Listen, this is my circus and…"

"And we're going to make it better," she said placidly. She raised a hand to calm him. "Change is good, Kal. Trust me. Just a few tweaks. I know I can make your circus better. More audience friendly."

Klondike was aghast. "But you've got no experience of circus shows at all. What in hell do you propose?"

She smiled sweetly, and despite himself he felt his anger cooling off, with those giant eyes imploring him to play along. "It's OK, Kal," she said quietly. "First, I want to see every act perform right here. You've got practice areas? Good. I'll make a decision after I've seen everyone. But, already, I'm warming to the idea of having that singer, Suzi, play it out with the clowns. They can make a mess of her as she tries to perform a ballad. It's a classic routine, people love it."

"Listen," Klondike snarled, "I thought you were here for publicity. You can't just run the whole show."

"Yes, she can," Plum put in from the corner.

"Damn the pair of you," Klondike moaned in despair. He got up and began pacing inside the great tent.

Lacey joined him, like a faithful hound, and again clasped her arm in his. He didn't like it, yet for some reason refused to wriggle free. It was like she was toying with him.

"It's OK, Kal. You'll have the final say. After all, you are the boss."

He shook his head as they walked to the chow line. "That's right," he said through gritted teeth. He looked back at Plum, studiously going through the papers, and then at Lacey again. In a few short minutes, everything had changed. His authority was being brought into check.

"Listen," he began, "if this is going to work, we've got to work and act like a team."

Lacey nodded. "Absolutely. But, Kal, trust me when I tell you, this can get better. I know what I'm doing. My track record is second to none."

"Yeah, Addison told me." He removed his hat and ran a hand through his thick black hair. "OK, smart lady, so what are your big ideas for publicity, anyway?"

"Ha!" she barked, moving quickly back to the table. She perched again, holding yet another sheet of paper before her. "I have already sent a press release to every newspaper, TV and radio station that reaches each town we play in. My office sent out more than 100 releases in all."

"What!" Klondike visibly shook. He towered over her. "Jesus, you don't waste time. Can I actually see the press release?"

"Sure, tiger." She handed it to him.

He read it slowly, circling the table. After a few minutes, he looked up, and actually grinned. "Not bad, lady. Not bad at all. It sounds more like a movie preview in some fancy LA tabloid than anything I've come up with. I kinda like it."

She smiled beautifully at him. "You see, just trust me with this. That'll run in every paper on the west circuit. I'd bet the farm on it." She paused. "Kal, I know what I'm doing. I've written releases for major Hollywood movies. This will sell, sell, sell."

He nodded, somewhat staggered by it all. "All right. What else?"

She barely caught breath. "I've arranged a press conference at the Leopold Hotel in Santa Cruz for Tuesday morning."

Again, he shook his head in bewilderment. "A press call? Why, we ain't never held one of them before."

"I know, and it's time to go for it now. Present will be me, you, Gino, Corky and Emile. That's it. Three talent. They will field questions from the assorted press. I've invited 30 journalists from TV, radio and the press. Hopefully at least 15 will be there."

Klondike was staggered. "How, where, how on earth did you organise all this? I can't believe it."

She smiled at him. "It's what I do. I can arrange a press call during a lunch break. It's…my calling, baby."

"All right," he replied, head still spinning. "What else?"

"We're hosting a VIP party the night before the train rolls. This marquee will do as a venue. All we need is a temporary bar in the corner. All the bigwigs are invited. Daryl, his fellow board members at Addison and Lee. The mayor of Santa Cruz. The parish chaplain. Newspaper editor. You get the idea."

Klondike sat down again. "You really did think of everything, Lacey. Tell me, can you really make all this happen?"

She smiled her beautiful smile yet again. "It is happening, Kal. Don't you worry about any of it. I have it under control. Your job is just to get everyone ready to put on the greatest show of their lives. Then with my public relations, the people will come out to the circus."

He nodded. Slowly, methodically, he thought out everything she had put to him. He had to admit he was impressed, albeit slightly blown away and flabbergasted. Finally, he looked up. "OK, Lacey," he proclaimed, "get to work!"

"Not until you've shown me to my quarters."

"Er, yeah, well we have a few spare trailers out back."

She smirked. "Good job I've brought my furs and cosmetics along. It's been a long time since I stayed in a caravan park."

Klondike ignored the remark, and instead looked down at Plum, who had sat through the whole exchange.

"And what about you?" he bellowed.

Plum looked up and smiled thinly. He spoke like a pre-programmed robot. "I'll need to see all your books. Everything."

Klondike growled slightly. "All right, follow me to my cabin."

The trio all left the tent together. Lacey linked her arms through those of the two men and skipped along happily.

"You know boys," she said gaily, "I think this could be the start of a beautiful partnership."

Chapter 4

The Amtrak West Coast Special rolled into Santa Cruz station, a huge cloud of steam descending across the platforms as the great locomotive came to a rest. As the engine took on water, doors up and down the carriages opened and a wave of passengers departed and stepped into the bright California sunshine, making their way along the station concourse towards the exit.

All except one. Roddy Olsen carefully left the train, carrying a large Navy-style tote bag on one shoulder and clutching a hefty leather suitcase in his right hand. He looked about his new surroundings earnestly and grinned to himself.

He was a small man, barely over five feet tall, but had movie star looks. His long dusty blond hair flowed alongside a tanned, youthful face, with sparkling green eyes. He was still a teenager, but carried himself in a confident, assured manner, comfortable in any environment.

Olsen wandered along the platform. His thoughts were interrupted by an announcement on the station's public address system, with a metallic voice booming overhead: "Would the controller please report to front desk immediately. The controller. Front desk. Thank you."

He noticed a large heavyset man on the other side of the line rushing from inside a work booth towards the nearby stairwell that led to the bridge connecting the platforms.

He walked towards the station exit. By the doors stood another official, dressed in rail workers uniform, with the words 'foreman' emblazoned over the left breast.

Olsen noticed a group of three children sat on the ground nearby, playing marbles against the station wall. He chuckled to himself.

"Hey kids," he exclaimed, "want to see something real funny?"

The youngsters looked up, uninterested. Finally, two of them nodded.

With that, Olsen put his tote bag and suitcase on the ground. Then, to the children's dismay, he moved his hands to his mouth and made a curious cupping motion.

He started talking, but the children looked up, as the noise sounded exactly like another public address announcement.

"Would the foreman please report to front desk immediately? The foreman. Front desk. Thank you."

Olsen let his hands fall and they all watched in bewilderment as the station foreman, standing barely 20 feet away, sprang to attention and made his way down the platform, walking straight past them.

The children watched in amazement as the official walked away, their eyes popping. Then, as one, they all laughed wildly.

"That was the craziest thing I ever saw!" said one. "What did you do, mister?"

Olsen smiled down at them. He picked up his belongings and made to leave.

"You kids have a nice day."

With that, he walked down the platform through the big double doors, and headed for the adjoining taxi rank. There was only one cab waiting. But that suited him just fine.

Jenny Cross drained the contents of her cocktail glass, looked about impishly, and left her position at the bar. With elegance and poise, she exited Marcy's Lounge, a downtown cocktail joint, pulling a thin cardigan over her flowery blouse as she moved. With relish, she felt the eyes of several male patrons following her as she left. Many had never seen a woman on her own, sitting at the bar, at this time of day. All alone.

She walked out into the bright afternoon haze. Downtown Santa Cruz looked fairly dead, as various old motors rumbled down Main Street and townspeople wandered around, keeping to themselves, glancing in shop windows. As in most western towns, desert dust seemed to cloak the streets and sidewalks, and everything seemed subdued.

Jenny crossed the street and headed for the giant indoor market and general store, which dominated the main drag like some kind of territorial fort overlooking the grounds.

Once inside, she walked down a flight of steps to the underground parking lot. In contrast to the sun-drenched streets, this tomb-like enclosure was dark, dingy and devoid of life. A small hole of light at the opposite end of the lot signalled a way back out into the sunshine.

She walked for several moments and then located her rented Ford. It was due back at the centre tomorrow. She fished for her keys in her handbag.

"Are you still in?"

She froze all over, veering in shock as the rasping voice from behind made her heart miss a beat. She spun round, looking with wide, frightened eyes.

"Who's there?" She gasped.

She could see no one, just a smattering of cars and trucks and scraps of garbage littering the concrete ground.

"You know who it is," the rasping voice spoke again. It sounded pained, as if its owner was being strangled.

Now she nodded with vague understanding. She whispered into the dark: "It's you, isn't it? Mercer?"

"No names." The voice still frightened her.

She stared dumbly into the shadows, still stunned. "How in god's name did you know I was here? Right at this moment. Oh god... Are you... Are you following me?" Her panic was all too evident.

"Quiet!" the stranger's voice snapped. "I asked you a question, Miss Cross. Are you still in? Answer me."

She nodded dumbly, still trying to ascertain where the mysterious voice was emanating from. "Yes."

Suddenly, she sensed a movement behind a pillar about ten yards away. She gasped, almost choked, as a tall figure emerged from behind the brickwork, like a ghostly apparition in the night. The figure was dressed in a long green trench coat, pulled up at the collar, with a fedora hat worn low over the face. In the shadowy light she could barely make out any of the man's features, but once again thought she could detect scar tissue on what little of the face she could see. The mystery man had been dressed the exact same way on their previous two meetings.

Now he just stood there in the shadow of the pillar in the deserted lair.

"Good," came the croaky reply. "Then we are all set. Our deal is still on."

Jenny's mind whirled. She had been told she would be contacted before the season began. But never when or where. Now she realised this was the appointment.

"Why down here?" She rasped, angrily. Her fright was subsiding with each second.

"Quiet." The figure took a step closer, and she saw an unshaven jawline under the fedora's shadow. "All you have to worry about is one thing. The directive I gave you last time. Don't let Klondike get to Las Vegas."

She nodded, shivering slightly. "I remember."

"Succeed... And that new life you want so bad... It's all yours. I will make it happen, just like I said. You know what you have to do."

She took a step forward herself. "I want a new life. But that's not why I am doing this."

The shadowy figure tilted its head slightly. "Of course. He scorned you. He broke your heart. Made you feel like a cheap hooker. I remember. That's more than enough motivation for this. Excellent, Miss Cross, excellent."

"Listen," she blurted at him, "where are you going to be once the circus rolls? Not down here I take it?"

"You have the number I gave you. Call me with any updates."

"And when shall we next meet?"

The mystery man stood perfectly still. "I will always be watching, Miss Cross. You'll never know when and where, but I'll be around. One way or another."

Suddenly, she was frightened again. "If you double cross me, or harm me in any way, Gino and Nicky will not stop until they have you cornered."

The man laughed, a sickening sound that sounded more animal than human. "Do not be afraid, Miss Cross. I am a man of my word. A man of honour. We are partners. Just keep your end of the bargain."

The figure produced a large Manila envelope from behind the pillar and tossed it onto the ground between them.

"Consider that a down payment. Now go get yourself some frilly dresses."

She gawked, before tiptoeing over to the envelope, bending, and retrieving it. Subconsciously, she walked backwards as she peered inside. She gasped. There must have been close to a thousand dollars in loose clips bundled within.

"Where did you get this?" She hissed.

She looked up. He was gone. All was deathly silent again in the underground domain. Dark and silent. She wandered towards the pillar, and checked behind. Nothing. It was as if the man with the terrifying voice had never been there.

She looked around nervously, shaking a little. Then, with a determined shake of her head, she roughly squashed the envelope into her bag and quickly made for her car.

Sixty seconds later, she was on the highway, racing away from the scene.

The palace-like pavilion stood at the head of a pier among the endless waterfront boardwalks of Atlantic City.

A giant plain white structure, it had an air of Arabian Nights about it, and looked somewhat out of place amid the fairgrounds, newsstands and walkways that dominated the waterfront.

A giant board placed above the entrance conveyed the words RIBBECK WORLD CIRCUS in bright red paint, screaming down at all who breezed past.

The inside was like some kind of circus museum, with apparatus and memorabilia associated with the big top scattered everywhere, and promotional posters covering the walls. Several offices littered the ground floor, with a spiral staircase leading to the executive rooms.

If the building felt like a castle, then its master most certainly felt like a king.

Eric Ribbeck was sitting at his desk in his office on the top floor. The large room, like the entranceway, had old circus posters all over its walls, promoting all sorts of stars and attractions.

The son of a Texas cattle baron, Ribbeck represented an intriguing blend of East and West. His ripe southern accent was somewhat nullified by his eccentric, colourful attire. He was a slim man, with leathery skin and a magnificent pompadour of thick white hair that made him look his sixty years.

At that moment, he was dressed in a crimson robe, smoking a thin cigarillo, as he studied a collection of enlarged photographs and several pages of notes.

He looked up at the man seated opposite. "Looks like our boy has a few tricks up his sleeve," he drawled in his Texan accent.

Luca Marconi, a hawkish, oily character, all slicked back hair and shiny suit, shrugged in his chair opposite. "I think the two newcomers were forced on him by Addison."

Ribbeck grunted, squinting at a picture. "The publicist is a real looker." He raised an eyebrow at Marconi. "Are you sure this is Lacey Tanner?"

The man nodded. "I was right there, boss. That's Tanner all right. I heard her introduce herself to our boy."

The older man nodded, studying the woman in the picture. "That is a blow. Lacey Tanner is one of the best in the business. I've heard of her. Worked out of Hollywood, no less." He waved the photo through the air idly. "I don't know what he's up to but I don't like it." He looked back at the image. "Who's the gimp?"

"He came with Tanner. An accountant. Name of Plum."

Ribbeck laughed with contempt. "Forget him. It's Tanner I'm worried about."

Marconi leant forward excitedly. "You want I should lean on her, boss? Get her to come join us and water down Klondike?"

"Forget it." Ribbeck sighed and grimaced, his old leathery skin showing creases and lines in abundance. "You're in the enemy camp. Any funny business, it'll be the Alamo for you. No, just continue as you are, Luca. You're an observer. For now." He suddenly glared at the man opposite. "You're sure you're on the inside? No hitches? Hell, you don't exactly look like no roustabout."

Marconi nodded smoothly, lighting a cigarette. "I'm in. Jim McCabe came to Santa Cruz looking for hands a few days back. I signed up with a few other guys. Farm hands, so they said. Ain't no one suspects anything, boss."

"Are you sleeping in the bunkhouse with the rest of the men?"

"You betcha."

"And you'll be based in the train bunkhouse once they roll?"

Marconi smiled. "Like I said, I'm in."

Ribbeck looked his man over. "Don't wear any of these fancy clothes, for Christ sakes. They'll make you in a second."

"I dress like a bum."

"And what excuse did you give for this trip?"

"Aunt Joan's funeral back east."

Ribbeck laughed, but without humour. He puffed on the cigarillo, and sat back, feeling warm and smug once more. He glanced idly at some of the posters covering his walls. They depicted another era. The glory days. When no one could ever touch him. Or even dream of it. Now, he was in a war. A ticket sales war. For some reason, though, he actually liked it.

He addressed Marconi once more. "Observe, Luca. Take in everything. Watch for outsiders, newcomers, anybody who acts out of turn."

Marconi dragged on his smoke, intrigued. "What are you expecting, boss?"

Ribbeck gazed into nothingness, turning in his chair and taking in the endless tides of the mighty ocean behind. "A man like Klondike is a man who attracts unrest, danger, even violence. He is a man of honour, old fashioned, and such a man is one others will always be keen to exploit. Take advantage of. Maybe even unsettle. He has taken a dangerous path. Yes, he comes across as a saint... But every saint has his demons."

"So what are we gunna do? When do we hit him?"

The older man leant forward. "When the time is right. And you, my inside man, will know when that is. Circus season is coming... And all kinds of twists and turns lie ahead."

Marconi studied his superior. "You really hate him, don't you, boss?"

Ribbeck looked down in disgust. His temper was rising. "That yahoo was the best damn circus man we had. His eye for talent was beyond parallel. He brought to me some of the best acts we ever showcased. He knew what the people wanted. We were making money like never before. Then, one day, he decided he could do it better on his own. Leading his own troupe. Cutting me out... The man who made him. When he first came to me he was nothing but a two-bit street punk. Out of the army, heading for a life of crime. A bum!" He jabbed the air with his cigarillo. "And now... Now we're going to blackball him out of this industry."

Marconi grinned sadistically. "That's the part I like, boss."

Ribbeck looked back ruefully. "Now you just stay in touch now, boy."

Chapter 5

"Merchandising is paramount. We're really missing out here."

Lacey was at the head of the conference table in the marquee, making her point. Opposite her, Klondike, Heavy and Plum all sat, listening obediently.

She had turned the giant tent into a makeshift office and media room, with contacts books, manuals and various papers strewn everywhere, even on the tarpaulin floor.

Klondike was taking it all in. "But we already do merchandising. We have a stall where we sell the programmes."

Lacey nodded vigorously. "Yes, yes. The pictures and the posters. That's all just dandy, Kal. But I'm talking about branded merchandise. Official Klondike's Circus t-shirts. Gino t-shirts. Corky t-shirts. Toys. We could even sell replica costumes, so kids can dress like Gino and Corky and the others. That will be a major add-on for our revenue."

Klondike nodded. "But how the hell do we manufacture all that stuff? And pay for it?"

She smiled her winning smile. It had become a familiar sight to all assembled. "Can you guess what I'm about to say?"

He rolled his eyes. "You'll take care of it."

"Always."

Heavy was deep in thought beside Klondike. "Maybe the programme stall could become the merchandising stall. Where customers can get everything."

Klondike gave him an irked sideways glance. "Wise guy."

Lacey laughed at them girlishly. "How about you, Richie?"

The accountant shrugged. "Let me know the figures."

Klondike grimaced. "Listen," he drawled, "there's something missing with all this. I think that…"

He broke off abruptly as the door flap swung open and Suzi Dando ran in excitedly.

"Mr Klondike, Mr Klondike…" she cried. She slowed down on realising she had interrupted a meeting. She was grinning from ear to ear as she skipped along. "I'm so sorry, but you have to see this guy, Mr Klondike. He was throwing his voice like nothing I ever saw. It's incredible."

She turned to the door, and all eyes followed.

Roddy Olsen strode in, carrying the tote bag and large leather suitcase. Everyone stared at the youngster with the long blond hair and suntan and the spring in his step.

Klondike came round. "Er, Suzi, I'm sorry, we are in a meeting here. Can this wait, dear?"

Suzi shook, clasping her hands excitedly. "I know, Mr Klondike, but I just met this gentleman out by the gate. He's looking for a job here. And… And… Well, I really think you need to see him."

Klondike frowned. "What the hell is this?"

Olsen stepped forward and gently placed a hand on Suzi's shoulder, easing her to one side.

"I'm sorry, sir," he said gracefully. "Allow me to explain. I don't mean to barge in when you're busy, but I was hoping you'd give me an audition. I think you'll like what you see and I'm just sure you'll want me to be part of your show."

Lacey addressed the youngster. "Who are you and what do you do?" She looked him over. "And, for god's sake, how old are you?"

He smiled warmly, and bowed slightly. "My last name is Olsen. Roddy Olsen. I'm 19. And I'm a ventriloquist."

They all baulked. "A what?" Heavy stammered.

"A ventriloquist. Y'know, like Edgar Bergen."

Heavy shook his head. "You mean you prat around with dolls?"

Olsen grinned. "We call them dummies, sir. Or puppets."

Klondike's head was spinning. "All right, all right," he breathed. He addressed the teenager. "Listen, I'm sorry kid. You got it all wrong. We don't audition talent here. If I hear of you I come and watch you in a show somewhere and we go from there. We don't have any 'opportunity night' here. Besides, this is a circus. Edgar Bergen's act isn't exactly what I'd call circus material."

The kid was completely unflappable. Confidence oozed from him and he eyed Klondike squarely, as if in a trance. "You haven't seen my act, Mr

Klondike. Y'see… I'm going to be a big star. This is your big chance. Surely you believe in taking chances."

Klondike shook his head. "When did things get so complicated around here?" Again, he addressed the kid. "Listen, son, the circus is no place for a nice young man like you. Go to college. Go to school. Be a doctor or a lawyer. Change the world."

Olsen laughed. "I intend to sir."

"Confident, ain't ya?"

"Confidence is everything. Ambition is critical."

Lacey stood and walked around the table, perching on the edge almost on top of Klondike. She whispered: "Let's do it, Kal. Hell, look at him. He's gorgeous. Confident. Can't hurt to give him five minutes and see what all the fuss is about."

Klondike groaned. "What fuss? Suzi goes nuts for a school choir. It doesn't mean I'm going to hire one."

She batted her giant eyelashes. "I have a feeling."

He sank into his chair and cursed. "All right," he called out, "all right, kid, let's see what you got, god damn it." He glared at the youngster. "You're on. Give us your act."

With that, Suzi walked over to join the four figures at the table. They all moved their chairs into a row so to create a mini audience.

Olsen had his stage.

He removed his blazer to reveal a bright purple shirt. Then he placed the suitcase flat down to his left, propped open.

"Ladies and gentleman," he said to the assembled group. "My name is Roddy Olsen. I'm a singer. A comedian. And tonight I'm going to entertain you all with my —"

"Let me out!"

Klondike and the others all looked about them at the sudden interruption. No one could ascertain where the new voice had come from.

Olsen smiled. "I'm sorry, my little friend is very impatient and —"

"Get me out of here Roddy! Now!" said the mystery voice.

"OK," said Olsen, moving to the suitcase, "but you've got to promise to be good."

He bent down and reached into the suitcase, and then emerged carrying a comedic-looking fox puppet, that looked like a child's cuddly toy that had somehow come to life.

"That's better," the puppet said. It was wearing a black leather jacket and jeans. The accent was like a juvenile Brooklyn drawl.

The onlookers stared in shock. The voice had been Olsen's all along, in the role of the puppet.

"Man," the little fox continued, "it sure is uncomfortable in that case. And it really stinks."

"Now, Rusty," Olsen told the puppet. "Why don't you introduce yourself to our friends."

The fox character stared at the audience and laughed. "Good evening, folks. My name is Rusty Fox, and I am a rock n roll star. A teen idol."

"And what do you do, Rusty?"

"I sing, man," replied the puppet. He then broke into a chorus of Amazing Grace.

"That's great, Rusty. What else do you do?"

"Impressions. Here's my impression of Vice President Nixon." The puppet somehow picked up its foot and placed it in his mouth. They all laughed.

"And Robert Mitchum." The fox slowly fell over backwards until it was horizontal.

"And California governor Alan Beck." This time the puppet put its foot into its mouth and fell over backwards. Everybody laughed boisterously.

"Tell us a joke, Rusty." Olsen prompted to the puppet on his arm.

"Hell, I should work in politics."

"Why's that?"

"The White House is full of dummies."

"Are you going to sing then, Rusty?"

"I sure am, Rod." The fox cleared its throat. "I'm going to perform Bobby Darin's hit Rock Island Mine. Just don't tell him. He's still mad at me after I ate his budgie."

Rusty Fox cleared his throat. But suddenly another voice erupted from the suitcase.

"Attention! Stop that singing." This voice sounded like an old man, and was harsher.

"Uh-oh," said Olsen. He dipped into the suitcase and miraculously emerged with a second puppet. Now he had a figure on each arm. This model was a dummy of a grey haired old man in army fatigues. He scowled.

"Don't let that good for nothing punk kid sing! I've told him his singing days are over. No more juvenile delinquency. It's time for this kid to join the US Army. And that's an order!"

Olsen spoke next. "Ladies and gentleman, please meet Napoleon."

The new puppet saluted. "US Army. Retired."

The five seated onlookers could only stare in fascination, completely taken in by the youngster and his characters. The dialogue was sharp, and perfectly orchestrated.

Rusty spoke next. "I'm not joining no army. I've got to conquer the music charts. And Hollywood. I'll be famous. Then I'll get all the chicks. To eat by myself!"

"You need to learn respect and discipline first, you slimy little maggot." Suddenly, the Napoleon puppet stared at Klondike, pointing a finger. "Kal Klondike! You were in the army. Maybe you can talk some sense into this punk."

Olsen spoke again. "There's only one solution, guys," he said, smiling. "We're all going to sing. Come on, Napoleon, it'll be fun."

The army man puppet shook its head, but Rusty had already begun singing Rock Island Mine, a track known for its speeded-up chorus.

Like a mini choir, Roddy and his two creations took it in turns to belt out the tune, a few lines each, getting faster and faster.

Klondike stared in rapt fascination at the young man with the dummy on each arm. They all did. Never in all his years of talent spotting had he seen anything quite like this. He felt like he was having an otherworldly experience. Olsen's lips hadn't moved while he made the puppets talk, and his voice manipulation skills were extraordinary. The two characters were completely engrossing. The comedy was original and funny. The singing was high class… How could one man sing as three?

The song came to an end and the set was over. Suzi and Lacey both jumped up and began applauding wildly. Heavy clapped too, looking bewildered. Plum just gaped at the younger man before them.

Klondike clapped slowly and spoke as the excitement died down. He stood and approached Olsen, staring at Rusty Fox and then Napoleon, then back at Olsen in the middle. He thought for a moment and finally spoke.

"Son, I've been watching talent all over America for 12 years. And I have never seen anything quite like that. Ever. I always thought ventriloquism was a wooden puppet sitting on a guy's lap telling stories to kids. But you've turned the art into something else. That was hilarious." He stared at the fox closely. "Your dummies are like cartoons come to life."

"Thank you, sir," Olsen said. Rusty then gave his thanks. Napoleon cursed. More laughs.

Lacey spoke up from behind him. "You are sensational, young man." She glanced idly at the suitcase. "Is there, urm, anyone else in there?"

"Why sure," came a smooth voice.

They all turned to Olsen, who deposited Rusty and Napoleon into the case and pulled out a third dummy. This one looked like a toy version of Dean Martin – tanned, tuxedo clad and with black bushy hair and eyebrows.

"This is Tony Tan," said Olsen. "A Las Vegas lounge singer."

With that, the figure sang the first few lines of 'That's Amore'.

Suzi shrieked and applauded some more.

Klondike smiled. "You're something else, kid." He rubbed at his stubble-ridden jaw, perplexed. "But I have to tell you, this act of yours, original as it is, just isn't circus. I... Er, I just don't think you belong here. Comedy clubs. Kids' clubs. Maybe kids' parties, even. Why don't you try to crack that market?"

Lacey pounced before Olsen could reply. "Where have you been working lately, Roddy?"

The youngster placed Tony Tan back in the case and closed it. He had an air of utter grace about him.

"County fairs. University of Santa Fe. College shows. And I supported Johnny Rex on tour. The singer."

Lacey frowned. Her stare was impenetrable as she studied the newcomer. "Where do you want to get to? What do you want to achieve?"

There was no hesitation. "I want my own TV special. That's how the nation will notice me. Then, all the top shows will come. Like Ed Sullivan."

She nodded approvingly. "Excellent." She studied his youthful appearance. "What does your mother think of this way of making a living?"

Olsen shrugged. "My mother's dead. They both are. Long time ago."

She looked down. "I'm sorry."

Klondike looked from one to the other. "Like I said kid, I'm very sorry but I just don't think there's any place for you here at—"

Again, Lacey interrupted. "Good heavens, Kal, stop talking nonsense. Our young friend here is a sensation." She stopped, before motioning to Suzi. "Darling girl, would you mind escorting Mr Olsen here for a quick tour of the camp? We are just going to discuss what we all just witnessed, and I don't think it would be polite to do it in front of him. Please."

Suzi nodded obediently and walked over to Olsen. The young man made to leave, before turning and approaching Klondike. He extended his hand.

"Thank you, sir. For the audition."

Klondike nodded soberly and shook the hand. Then, the two youngsters left the tent, Olsen leaving his case and bag behind.

Lacey marched over to Klondike and glared at him. "Good god in heaven, Kal," she shrieked, making no attempt to hide her feelings. "Did you just see that? That young man is a genius. He's just taken the art of ventriloquism fifty years into the future. That was impossibly original. He should be on TV already, dammit!" She stepped close to him, so close he could smell her honey-scented perfume and see her nostrils curl. "And you... You don't even see a golden opportunity when it lands on your doorstep. He chose us, Kal. He came here! He wants this!"

Klondike held up both hands at the excited woman. "Hold it. Now, everybody just calm down. Yes, I admit, what we just saw was something else. But, like I keep telling you all, it ain't circus."

Lacey was unrepentant. "We're a show! That kid is a natural entertainer. Can't you see that?"

He snarled back. "It takes a certain kind of entertainer to hold their own under my big top, lady."

"So... Why not him?"

"Damn it all to hell, woman! You're a publicist. This is my show. What makes you think you can dictate how I run things?"

"Just give me one reason why we shouldn't hire that boy?"

Klondike moved a step closer to the publicist. Their faces were inches apart. Both were more than riled. "How will he handle a circus audience? Can he live on a circus train? This isn't Hollywood. It's a way of life. A calling. We know nothing about him. He could've made all that stuff about Johnny Rex up for all we know." He thought for a moment. "And what in hell will people think of him?"

Lacey seemed to cool. She stepped back, and placed her hands on her hips. "OK," she breathed. "I understand those concerns. But we just witnessed a raw performance. Out of nothing. And look at our reactions. He blew us all away. Doesn't that tell you something?"

Klondike thought about it and nodded. "Heavy!" he barked to his right-hand man. "Let's have it, man."

Heavy Brown sat back in his seat, hands cupped in front of him. "If you ask me, that was a terrific performance. We've been to hundreds of auditions, Kal, but never one here on our doorstep. With that in mind, you have to hand it to the kid. To come in here like that and hit us with his act like that…"

"But it's puppets and voice skills, Heavy," Klondike shot back.

The big man gazed around the tent, pondering the predicament. "The circus world is changing, Kal. We all know that. Hell, Ribbeck now has a rock singer, a magician and that damn bird man in his shows. Everyone is branching out. Who knows, an act like this could be an ace in our pack."

"Oh, Jesus. You too?"

Heavy chuckled. "Come on, Kal. I saw your face when that kid was singing Rock Island Mine. In three voices."

Klondike nodded slowly. He glanced at Plum. "Dare I ask, Richie?"

Plum looked like he had been hypnotised. "I don't know what that was we saw, but all I know is I can't stop thinking about it. Don't let that kid outta this camp. I want him."

And there it was. They all looked at each other. Finally, Klondike wandered around in a half circle. Then, to everyone's dismay, he chuckled boisterously.

"The kid was something wasn't he?"

Lacey clapped her hands in delight. "I knew it."

"OK, OK," Klondike said rapidly, "let's get him signed up. But I'm putting him on the midway to begin with. He's gunna be a walk around talent. Ain't nobody come out of the cold and straight into the show if I ain't heard of em. You want to perform under my big top, you got to earn it."

Lacey looked drained. "The midway?"

"Those are my terms." He glanced over at Heavy. "Can we get a contract ready, big man?"

"Leave that to me," Lacey snapped. She rushed over to Plum and sat next to him. The pair began conversing in low terms.

Heavy got up and ambled over to where the boss stood.

"Good move, Kal."

Klondike squinted at him. "I guess we'll see who the real dummy is!"

Suzi Dando eased open the door to her trailer, and led the way inside. Roddy Olsen followed, taking in the small cabin with his wide, inquisitive eyes.

It was identical to the rest of the camp's trailers, featuring a single bed, table and couch and a tiny restroom at the far end. A living space of barely ten yards by five.

Pictures of Suzi singing at various joints across California adjourned the walls, along with posters advertising her appearances. In every one, she was far down the bill, underneath other, more accomplished performers.

The trailer was neat and tidy, with a suitcase half-full of clothes sitting on the table and various magazines and journals littering the couch and floor.

She poured them each a glass of lemonade from a pitcher sitting on a sideboard and they both sipped away quietly.

"Thanks for the tour," he said simply.

"What do you think?" she squealed, enthusiastic as ever.

He thought. "Well, I ain't never been backstage at a circus before. But I've been to TV studios, theatres and concerts. And I felt the same here as I felt there… Electricity. Excitement. And a lot of heart."

She gazed at him queerly. She had never met anyone who talked like him. It felt like he was from another world entirely. They were about the same age, yet Roddy oozed confidence and charm, a quality that belied his youthful years.

"Do you think you'll like it? Circus life, I mean?"

He shrugged. "I have to be offered a place on board first."

Suzi finally nailed him with something she had wanted to ask him all along. "Roddy, your voice skills are incredible. Where… How on earth did you learn to do that?"

He sipped his lemonade and looked away. "It's been in me my whole life. I was an only child, then an orphan raised by…others. Growing up, I had no real friends. Most of the time, it was just me in my room, alone. So I created friends, in my mind, and then out of puppets. Being alone soon became like a warm protective blanket to me. Then, one day, I saw Edgar Bergen's show at a picture house in Fresno. Then it all came together. I knew I wanted to be a ventriloquist, and starting practising."

She stared at him, her wide youthful eyes looking like they might pop out of their sockets. "Do you really want to be on TV? Do you think you'll make it to the Ed Sullivan Show?"

He grinned. "Sure I will."

"Y'know this circus is a long way from Ed Sullivan and his world."

He looked around. "I got to keep performing."

She laughed suddenly. "Oh, Roddy, your Rusty Fox is so cute. That was the most amazing act I ever saw."

He grinned. "Thank you, Suzi. That means a lot. Old Rusty has been with me since the beginning. Since I performed at my old high school prom."

She peered at him. "Have you more puppets? Or just those three?"

"There are more to come. Suzi, I have so many ideas. New characters, new material. I just need some capital to bring them along."

She smiled impishly. "I thought you were just a sensation."

"Thank you," he replied, putting his glass down. He turned to the posters and images on the walls. "Maybe we will perform together one day?" He studied a picture of Suzi standing in front of a velvet show curtain, clutching a microphone. "How long have you been singing?"

"All my life," she blurted out eagerly. "Ma and pa wanted me to join a convent. Maybe become a missionary." She smiled. "Strict upbringing. But I knew singing was my calling in life. At high school, I was always cast in the lead. Every show. I took out on the road. Played various nightclubs." She smiled ruefully. "I always thought that one day a man in a suit would come up to me after a show and offer me a recording contract. Ha! Some dream. No, instead, I took on this job here as an in-house singer." She looked around, then winked at him. "I got to keep performing."

"What do your parents think about all this? Taking off and all?"

She looked down and trembled slightly.

"It's OK, Suzi," he said gently. Suddenly, he rushed over and had her in his arms. She hugged him earnestly, and he let her stay nuzzled against him. "I'm sorry," he whispered.

At that moment, the door to the trailer burst open and the tall frame of Kal Klondike filled the entrance. He frowned at the pair embracing each other.

"Hell," he snarled, "you don't waste much time, kid. Looks like you found something you like about the circus and want to stay on, huh?"

Roddy moved away from the girl and made to speak, but Suzi beat him to it. "I'm sorry, Mr Klondike, I was just thinking about back home and got upset. Roddy here was just comforting me."

Olsen nodded. "That's the whole of it, sir."

Klondike gazed at them, dismay clouding his rugged features. "Whatever," he snapped. He moved inside, looking like a giant in a broom cupboard. "Well, kid, we all had a chat about your act. We liked it. I took some persuading, I gotta tell ya, but we made a decision. And there's just one thing I want to tell you."

The two youngsters stood perfectly still, and tensed up. Suddenly, the little trailer was filled with an eerie silence.

Olsen looked at the circus boss. "And what's that?"

Klondike glared at him. Then, inexplicably, his face broke into the most beautiful smile Suzi had ever seen, and he chuckled to himself.

"Welcome aboard!"

Chapter 6
Klondike's Circus Press Call
Leopold Hotel. Santa Cruz

The assembled media gathered in the grand lounge of the Leopold, where several rows of chairs had been arranged directly in front of a long rectangular table that sat at the front of the room. A beautiful red tablecloth had been draped over it, with several microphones connected to a sound system sat in place on the surface. Behind the great table an enlarged Klondike's Circus poster sat mounted on the wall.

There were between 20 and 30 reporters in all, professionals from press, magazines, TV, radio and a smattering of freelancers and stringers. They all sat expectantly as the big clock at the rear neared 10am.

Finally, the circus people entered, with the assorted press gang offering hearty applause.

Klondike sat in the centre of the table, with Gino Shapiro and Corky on either side of his frame. Emile Rance and Heavy sat at the two ends, with Lacey stood to the side, dressed in an immaculate white trouser suit.

As the gathered crowd offered their welcomes, Lacey held up a hand and uttered a loud introduction.

"Ladies and gentlemen of the press," she squawked, "thank you for attending our press call. Please state your name, outlet and question for the panel, one at a time. There are press packs on your seats, which include free passes to the opening show right here in Santa Cruz. If you require more information at the end, please see me. I will do all I can to help. I am Lacey Tanner, Head of Publicity for Klondike's Circus. My business card is in the packs."

She came up for air, looking about excitedly. The turnout was better than she had hoped for. "And now," she announced, "I give you the stars of Klondike's Circus."

A second fainter round of applause followed. Klondike held up a hand in thanks. He was wearing his standard attire of brown leather jacket and fedora, and the press gang were lapping it up. He looked more like an adventurer than a businessman.

"Thank you," he began, "I'd like to thank all you people for coming." That was as far as he got.

"Thank you, thank you friends," Shapiro exclaimed, standing up and holding out his arms in some kind of celebration. This time, he was dressed in an exotic fur coat, over an expensive-looking silver suit. "The circus embraces you, good people. I hope you are all ready for the greatest show on earth. We are here, my friends, and the show is ready to roll. Now, please field your questions."

Everyone stared at the strangely dressed figure in near-shock, including those at the table. Lacey, on the sidelines, stifled a laugh. Klondike merely shook his head as Gino sat down again.

A sea of hands shot up from the press pack. Lacey pointed and orchestrated the questioning.

A suited man in a flat cap opened the proceedings. "Alan Blake, San Francisco Sentinel. What were you doing in Hollywood, Gino? And is it true some of your movie star buddies are making special guest appearances in the circus?"

Gino laughed out loud, but no one knew why. He smiled angelically. "Beautiful question, my friend. Ladies and gentlemen of the press, I can exclusively reveal that Hollywood stars will be guesting for the Los Angeles show. Cowboy actor Jason Lash, a close personal friend of mine, will be joining us for the grand parade. Also, beautiful Linda Schneider, from TV's Cabaret Hour, will be along. Comedian Larry Lassiter will also be there. I can confirm that I have arranged for all three to appear as my guests." Shapiro swept a hand before him. "As for what I was doing all winter in Hollywood, I was working as a technical adviser for The Biggest Show in the West, the latest blockbuster from Maverick Studios. The story concerns a young Mexican immigrant who dreams of joining the circus. He meets a —"

"Do you prefer movies to the circus, Gino?" the reporter fired over impatiently.

"Well, er, I like both," said Shapiro, slightly irked at the interruption. "But this movie will be a smash hit and I am glad —"

"Laura Ashby, Sentinel features department," said a demanding female voice from the press pack. "Will you be performing again with your brother Nicky and Jenny Cross?"

Shapiro tried to see where the voice had come from, unsuccessfully. "Er, yes, madam. That is correct."

"Is it true you will attempt the devil drop this season?" This from a new voice.

"Who said that?" Lacey demanded from the side.

"Sorry," the voice said again, emanating from the back. "Sidney Hackett. Daily World." A general disgruntled muttering rose from the gathered audience. Hackett was renowned as a sleazy tabloid journalist, in league with scores of underworld figures.

Shapiro and Klondike stared at each other. Then Shapiro answered. "I don't know about any devil drop," he said weakly.

"But you're keeping the triple, the tightrope walk and the leap of faith, right?" Hackett prompted.

"Er, yes, of course. Gino Shapiro is the debonair king of the air. No man alive can match my act. In one week, right here in beautiful Santa Cruz, you will all see for yourselves how my work is unparalleled in show business."

A new speaker rose. "Ben Sharp. Oakland Star. Is this the greatest line-up Klondike's Circus has ever assembled?"

Klondike spoke. "Yes, I think so. I have travelled far and wide these past few months, and have signed up some intriguing new players. The Klondike Showcase has some interesting new faces, as I'm sure you have read about in your press packs."

"Is it true Goliath is eight feet tall?"

Klondike grinned. "Last time they measured him."

"And what about Gargantua? He's 500 pounds?"

"Not any more. He just ate breakfast."

The press pool laughed. "Joe Walker, Daily Globe. You say Klondike Showcase. Isn't that commonly known as the freak show?"

Klondike sat pensively. "I don't know what you're talking about. These people are performers. Stars."

He looked discreetly at Lacey, who nodded subtly.

"When do all these guys turn up?"

"Any day now, son."

"Are you ever going to start performing again, Kal?"

Klondike laughed merrily. "Hell, are you kidding? I haven't fired a gun or thrown a knife in years. I might kill somebody if I start again! I don't think our paying fans want to see a death in the circus. No, I am happy in my role as manager. It's all I ever wanted."

"Jerry Langdon. Sacramento Courier. I have a question for Corky. Do you have anything new planned for this season?"

Corky, dressed in his clown attire, featuring a yellow checked suit and brown bowler hat, began to answer. "Well, I have a few surprises up my sleeve, folks..." at that moment a chain of handkerchiefs shot out of the sleeve of his blazer, exploding into the reporters seated in the front row.

"Oh, I'm sorry," he said playfully. "Let me give you hand." With that, he threw a pink prosthetic hand to one of the journalists now covered in hankies. The man laughed heartily.

Lacey smiled smugly at the comical exchanges. This kind of publicity was golden. The media pack would not forget this conference in a hurry.

"How many other clowns are in this year's show?" asked the same reporter.

"Well," Corky replied, "we are all clowns in this circus. But, only a few of us wear face print and dress like we're from another planet. Besides me, there are four other guys on board. So expect plenty of mischief!"

"Sarah Tweed. West Coast Life. I have a question for the animal trainer. Sir, aren't you ashamed of yourself being a lion tamer in this day and age? Exploiting those poor animals for your own personal gain, keeping them in captivity like that. Don't you think you're living in the past?"

Rance practically exploded out of his seat. The jovial atmosphere in the lounge turned decidedly dark.

"What is da meaning of this?" Rance boomed. He stood up, his face a mask of crimson. "You do not know what you're talking about, woman. How dare you suggest such nonsense! My lions get the best of everything. They are treated like kings wherever they go. They eat only the finest raw meat. Sleep on silk cushions. Bathe in a bathtub. What the hell do you know about any of this? My white tiger, Cicero, is a god in this circus. Where he goes, people stand back and admire his beauty." He was breathing heavily now, glaring at the female speaker. "You damn animal rights activists are all da same. You know nothing! Yet you preach of what you know."

"You're holding them against their will!" the woman shot back.

"All right," Lacey screeched from the corner. "That's quite enough of that." She looked at the defiant reporter. "Miss Tweed, if you would see me at the end, I will gladly debrief you on how we treat our beloved animals. I think you will be very surprised to hear of our welfare work."

The woman looked far from impressed, but sat down slowly. At the table, Rance glared at her for a few more seconds, then seated himself.

The Oakland Star journalist said: "Have you ever had any nasty injuries working with lions and tigers?"

Rance still looked riled, his red face seemingly inflaming his fair hair and beard. "No. Never. I am a professional. Those animals are my family. My life. I have raised dam since they were all cubs."

The mood gradually changed to one of general pleasantness once again.

"Chuck Starkey. San Juan Gazette. What else can we expect from the season?"

Klondike leant forward. "Oh, there will be a few surprises. New faces. Guest stars, like Gino said. And then, of course, the grand finale in Las Vegas."

"Are you really going to put the circus in the parking lot of the Golden Dune?"

"We sure are, son. It will be a first in the history of our industry. A circus adjoined to a casino. It should be a sell-out, and we're hoping to create circus history on that night. It will be the biggest show in the history of the big top."

The whiny voice of Hackett emanated from the back. "An ideal time to do the devil drop?"

Again, Klondike glanced at Shapiro. The two men looked confused. "Well, I don't know about that," Klondike finally muttered.

The press call drew to a close amid a prolonged, hushed-up murmuring among the media gathering. The words "devil drop" could be heard within the whispers and muted conversations.

Lacey walked in front of the head table and thanked everyone for attending, before conversing with some of the journalists seated at the front.

Everyone stood and made to leave. Klondike and his crew all left the table and made their way towards the rear exit, which led to a private briefing room and then onto gardens and a swimming pool. As they all moved away, Klondike put his arm around Shapiro conspiringly.

"How in hell did that pigeon know about the devil drop?" he whispered savagely.

Shapiro was equally aghast. "I have no idea, chairman. Hardly anyone knows about it, even within the company." He thought for a moment. "That Hackett is a slippery one. A snake. He must have been watching me. Following me. Sniffing for a scoop."

Klondike grimaced bitterly. "Not likely, pal. Someone blabbed."

"Impossible!"

"Well, there's nothing we can do now." He thought about it. "In one way, if it's advertised in advance, it might generate more interest. The great Gino performing the devil drop."

Shapiro frowned. "Yes...until Dirk Tempest or one of the others gets wind of my plan and then tries it first, leaving me out of the limelight. It was to be a secret, chairman, but now it's out."

Klondike left him and watched as his team exited the building and filtered out towards the pool, and an outdoor bar area.

He stood there for several minutes, feeling strangely despondent.

After a while, Lacey joined him, skipping out of the grand lounge. She beamed at him. "Well, how about it, Kal. What a tremendous success!"

He ignored her. "Who is that guy Hackett? And how does he know our plans?"

She waved a hand. "Forget it. Sid Hackett is the biggest drunk in the West Coast press corps. And the most corrupt reporter in California. No one will believe a word he says, much less trust him."

"That's not what it sounded like to me. All the press were talking about afterwards was the devil drop."

"Relax." Yet again, she played her arm through his and tried to guide him away. "Even if the story does run, it will only add interest and more publicity to your circus."

Klondike slowed her down. "He knew," he said bitterly.

Lacey decided against trying to soothe him anymore, and tugged him out to the poolside. "Come on," she murmured. "Snap out of it, tiger. We've got a party to plan."

ROLL UP, ROLL UP... IT'S TIME FOR SAWDUST, STARS AND COTTON CANDY!

By Laura Ashby, San Francisco Sentinel

Spring is in the air and, as far as this correspondent is concerned, that means only one thing: its circus time!

That's right, the big top season is all set to swing into action, with seven months of thrills, spills, laughter and delight ready to grace fairgrounds, fields and parkland all over America.

Up and down the States, circus companies have been busy all winter putting together their shows, assembling their talent, and preparing new feats of awe and amusement to keep us, the adoring audience, keen and ready to snap up tickets. Now, with the season traditionally set to open on April 1, fine-tuning is underway as the talent rehearses, routines are perfected…and the animals come out of winter hibernation.

I give you the circus, beloved readers. What is it about this mystical, carnivalesque art that makes us all go misty-eyed and star-struck, bringing out the inner child in our being? On an artistic scale, the circus with its clowns and feats of derring do is about as nutritious as the cotton candy sold by the shedload out in the midway.

Yet still, last year's circus returns ran to the millions, with more than half the American population visiting a big top at some point during the summer.

America simply loves the circus. A combination of traditions, heritage, nostalgia and the new age acts that a circus embraces, such as magicians and variety performers, has ensured that big top entertainment is not just still here…but here to stay.

How PT Barnum would chuckle if he could see how a medium he helped create had flourished in the years since his death. This summer, a circus will embrace almost every major town or city in the country at some point. Children, grandparents, the young and the old, will flock to see the show. Thousands will sign up for temporary work, helping to erect the great tent and various midway stalls. The people will come…of that you can be sure.

The big players in this mystic medium will be rolling out their tents within the next two weeks. Who will visit your town?

Of all the major circus players in America, two stand alone at the head of the pile: Ribbeck World Circus and Gonzo's Circus.

Much has been made of the great entrepreneur Eric Ribbeck, who runs his huge international business out of Atlantic City. The Texan, who hails from a family of cowboys, learnt the circus trade as a bareback rider in El Paso, before forming his own company before the war. Ribbeck built his circus into a million-dollar enterprise, and now runs a nationwide schedule, taking in the north, south, east and west of America. Trapeze king Dirk Tempest, motorcycle stunt riders The Wild Bunch, acrobats Jurgen and Lucinda, loveable clown Fireman Fredo and, of course, circus mascot and wild bird trainer Walter Read are among the stars of Ribbeck's world. His shows will be seen by Americans everywhere, with a schedule promising a new extravaganza in a new town every four days.

Gonzo's Circus was founded and built up by Michael Daly, aka Gonzo the Clown. Now retired from performing, Daly these days oversees a sprawling operation which, unlike Ribbeck's set-up, is routed much more in the traditional circus arts. Expect elephants, giraffes, monkeys, zebras, ponies and even a bear. The trained beasts are surrounded by clowns, midgets, dancing showgirls, human cannonballs and a plethora of trapeze artists, who hang over the action from high above, as if trying to stay out of the way.

These shows are magical, but for this correspondent, a California native and proud advocate of all things West Coast, there is only one circus troupe worth cheering for this season.

Klondike's Circus is a three-ring show that combines both tradition and modern-day glamour and excitement. Run by Kal Klondike, real name Terry Calder, the programme runs more like a variety show. Klondike knows his stuff. For years, he was a trick-shot artist and knife thrower under Ribbeck, before becoming a booker and talent spotter for the big top giant. He learnt from the best. When he decided to try his hand at running a show for himself, he managed to persuade two of Ribbeck's biggest stars – trapeze artist Gino Shapiro and Corky the Clown – to come with him. A new empire was born.

Klondike has been operating for the past eight years and has gone from strength to strength. The shows have an emphasis on old school family entertainment, and the roster has an intriguing blend of the old and the new.

There is Cathy Cassidy and her chummy chimps. Lion tamer extraordinaire Emile Rance, who hails from South Africa. The Range Riders, a team of cowboys who ride horses bareback across the arena. Amanda Hart introduces her team of trick-loving elephants. This year, the always popular Klondike Showcase, known as the freak show, promises a giant called Goliath and a gentleman known as Gargantua due to his immense girth. What tricks they will bring, we can only guess.

And at the heart of it all will be Gino Shapiro, who performs with his brother Nicky and apprentice Jenny Cross, and the beloved Corky, a multi-talented clown who excels at juggling and fire-eating.

I can promise you, just talking about it gets me excited. Klondike is set to run dates in Frisco, Oakland, San Pedro, San Jose and Sacramento, so there are plenty of opportunities to check out the action in our local area.

I will be at all five. I never miss it. See you on the midway!

CIRCUS KING: GET READY FOR THE SHOWS OF SHOWS!
By Brian Ringerman, New York Daily News

Circus tycoon Eric Ribbeck insists this year's travelling extravaganza will be his greatest creation yet, labelling it "the show of shows".

The veteran showman, 60, has invested a small fortune in recruiting fresh talent for his forthcoming offering, and now firmly believes he has created the ultimate in big top entertainment.

The show is set to roll on Monday, with a grand schedule that befits such a spectacular card.

Ribbeck has promised more than two shows a week in a near 50-city tour, that will take in all corners of America.

The fun begins in Atlantic City, where his company is headquartered, next week. From there, Ribbeck World Circus will visit everywhere from New York, Los Angeles and Chicago, to Memphis, Houston and New Orleans.

The schedule is harsh and taxing. But Ribbeck clearly wants maximum bang for his buck, having splashed the cash assembling a world class team of performers.

The circus king, who started out as a bareback rider before buying his own troupe in 1936, said: "Everybody get ready. Grandmas, grandpas, mums and dads, boys and girls, juveniles, spinsters and bachelors. Nobody will want to miss Ribbeck World Circus's 1958 season…the greatest show in the history of the circus. The most expensive roster of talent ever assembled. The most incredible collection of exotic animals seen under one roof. The showcase of the immortals. The arena of the superstars. The show of shows."

He continued: "I guarantee that anyone who visits my circus this year will be mesmerised by the talent on show. I have taken the art form of the circus and catapulted it into a new world. This show offers a glimpse into the future…a new world of entertainment and magic. Do not miss it."

Ribbeck hit the headlines earlier this year when he agreed a huge fee to obtain the services of motorcycle stunt team The Wild Bunch. The performers were previously tied down to a contract at Rancho Deluxo casino in Las Vegas, before Ribbeck bought it out and signed them to his tour for an unreleased sum. The team's daredevil antics represent the "changing face of the circus" that Ribbeck refers to. Clowns, tightrope walkers and exotic animals still have their place in his grand vision, but stuntmen and super heroes may well be the way ahead.

Ribbeck added: "I have invested a great deal and brought in advisers and marketing people to ensure that my circus remains as number one. There are many pretenders, a host of contenders, but there's only one original, all-action American circus. Ribbeck World Circus. Don't miss it."

The fun gets under way next Tuesday at Davenport Promenade, Atlantic City.

Chapter 7

The grand marquee in the centre of the winter camp was the setting for Lacey Tanner's VIP pre-season party.

The tent had been decorated with clean sheets and red and blue tinsel, with a new floor tarpaulin hauled in. Tables and chairs were spread about neatly, and various tropical plants, obtained from nobody knew where, were installed around the perimeter.

A temporary bar had arrived in a crate with Lacey's name on it. The roustabouts had erected it in a far corner and the PR woman had ordered in various spirits and bottles of beer from a wholesaler in town. On top of that, one of the bar stewards from the Leopold had agreed to moonlight for the evening as their barman. As if that wasn't enough, the chow line had been turned into an extravagant-looking buffet.

Kal Klondike simply did not know how she did it. But he had to admit, she truly delivered on everything she promised, every outlandish idea. And she was right, he told himself. The circus, the product, looked better and much more professional thanks to her 'little touches', as she so aptly put it. Everything felt classy and glitzy, as show business should be. This corporate gathering was indeed a splendid idea, a perfect way to raise their appeal.

He smiled to himself as the notions went through his mind. The party was just getting started, and Klondike was working the room, shaking hands, laughing at idle jokes and thanking everyone for attending. He was dressed in his 'official' attire of the tanned suit, but Heavy, who had joined him for the walkabout, had gone all in and worn his scarlet ringmasters jacket and top hat. The effect was priceless, inspiring awe and excitement among the guests.

It was quite an ensemble gathered at the marquee. At a centre table sat Daryl Addison and his board members, all stiff-looking suited types sipping cocktails. The tables to their left featured Santa Cruz's great and good. The mayor, chief of police, newspaper editor, chamber of commerce heads and the chairman of a local mining firm. All stood mesmerised by the dazzling beauty of Amanda Hart, dressed in her circus leotard, who held them all with various tales of life under the big top. Several reporters who had attended the press call were also present, as was the host of a local radio talk show.

Klondike did the rounds, before heading to the bar with Heavy. They both looked up as Lacey finally entered the marquee, looking resplendent in a velvet cocktail dress. Every head seemed to tilt her way, and she gushed out thanks to the many compliments that flooded over. Like Klondike, she worked the room, shaking every hand, already knowing every name.

"You gotta hand it to her," Heavy was saying as they leant against the bar. He had removed the top hat. "Lacey sure knows how to put on a show. Look at how she transformed this tent. And this crowd! It's like a country club in here."

Klondike nodded. A glass of scotch landed before him and he downed it instantly, nodding for another. "I can't deny it," he stammered. "She has the Midas touch. No one can argue. Not now." He studied her as she moved among the guests. "She did what she promised. She moved us to another level."

Heavy picked up a bottle of beer. "And just look at her. That dress. That personality. Hell, we should put her in the show, Kal. She'd probably steal the whole thing and be the star of it all."

Klondike leant back as he surveyed the gathered crowd. "I reckon you're about right, big man."

At the entrance area, Gino Shapiro had just entered, flanked by Nicky and Jenny. He wore a silk shirt with tight pants, while his brother dressed identically. Jenny wore a ballroom gown. Eyes turned their way and there was faint applause as they entered. Gino waved charismatically.

"Enjoy the party," he told Nicky. The younger Shapiro was taller, lankier and less muscular, with short black hair and a large protruding nose. He had lived in his brother's shadow since they were infants, but enjoyed playing a supporting role. Gino's business sense and trapeze skills had brought them wealth, fame and a lifestyle that seemed a million miles removed from their childhood in Lagunas.

"Not my scene," Nicky murmured, to which Gino laughed.

Jenny was glaring at Lacey in the centre of the room. "What do you make of our glamorous hostess?" She said icily. "They might as well call it Tanner's Circus."

Gino just kept on laughing. "A grand addition," he stated. Then, with a nod, he added: "OK guys, mingle. Promote the act."

He wandered away from them. Almost instantly, he was greeted by Corky. The clown was carrying two champagne glasses, and offered one to Shapiro. He accepted.

"To the season!" Corky proclaimed, raising his glass. He was wearing a tuxedo and straw boater hat. Shapiro thought he looked ridiculous but followed the toast.

"The season," he muttered idly.

Corky grinned, the white face paint glimmering in the lighting. "I was wondering when we might get the chance to talk."

Shapiro stared at him. "And why's that?"

"Listen, bub, we go back a long way. Atlantic City. Ribbeck. Now here."

"What's your point, clown?"

"I know we haven't exactly always seen eye to eye. But, I want you to know, I've always respected you. And your act. You're as vital to the success of this circus as anyone. And, listen, I want you to know there's no hard feelings. About star billing, salaries, that sort of thing."

Shapiro studied him. "All those things," he breathed, "are same in reverse. You... You are very talented. Almost more than a clown. Multi-talented, indeed. I salute you, clown." He looked about idly. In the fluorescent lighting, he looked almost like a plastic mannequin, with his perfect tan, gelled hair and shiny shirt. "Just remember this, amigo. Diamonds last forever. And so does Gino Shapiro."

With that, he strode forward, leaving a bemused Corky staring after him in confusion.

Emile Rance and Cathy Cassidy entered the marquee next, quietly making their way towards Amanda's group, where they were warmly greeted by the excited townsfolk.

Roddy Olsen and Suzi Dando also joined the party, looking significantly younger than anyone else amidst the gathering.

Olsen wore simple white shirt and slacks, and Suzi a flowery blouse. No one looked up as they entered, and Olsen guided her to a table in a far corner.

"Wow, a show business party," he exclaimed.

Suzi's eyes widened. "We've never had anything like this before."

As conversations flowed and laughter rolled across the great tent, Lacey made her way over to Klondike and Heavy at the bar.

"Looking radiant, Lacey," Heavy said as she approached. Her flowing red hair was worn long, draping across her bare shoulders. Klondike smiled. "The belle of the ball," he added.

"Oh, boys," she giggled. "Stop it." Then, all serious, "Listen, Kal, it's speech time. You ready?"

He nodded. She immediately began hammering a knife against her champagne glass. Slowly, the conversations ceased and a general hush descended over the room.

Klondike stepped forward and spoke. "Ladies and gentlemen, may I offer you my eternal gratitude. Your support and enthusiasm has been more than welcome at this time, and on behalf of everybody here at Klondike's Circus, I would like to extend my warmest compliments to you all." A faint applause rippled across the tent floor. He smiled. "We could not run this show without you people. So I say to you now, enjoy the party, have some chow and, of course, come see us as we tour California." He raised his glass. "God bless America."

Everyone echoed his words in a grand toast.

As the party swung back into motion, Daryl Addison joined Klondike in the far corner.

"Well said, Kal," the banker began. "I can see that my old pals Richie and Lacey have made a real impact around here."

Klondike smiled. "You could say that."

Addison looked around happily. "It was nice to get everyone together here. We all believe in you, Kal. Nobody on the board at Addison and Lee doubts that this is going to be a big success. Yet again."

"That's very kind of you, Daryl," Klondike began, "and I want you to know —"

He was cut off by a terrifying sound as the primal scream of a woman in peril shattered the jovial atmosphere. Everyone stared at the spot where the high-pitched noise had originated. A newspaperwoman, seated near the far wall. She had one hand clasped over her mouth. The other hand was outstretched, pointing towards the entranceway.

Every head turned in the direction she was indicating. Then, as one, every mouth dropped open.

There, walking through the door flap with an angry poise, was one of Rance's lions. Snarling, it had wandered into the marquee, and was eyeing up just about everybody within.

Several more screams rang out, as all the guests leapt out of their seats and made their way towards the rear. Chairs crashed to the floor as a stampede commenced. But, as everyone flocked to the rear, the realisation that there was only one way in or out – and this was behind the lion – seemed to provoke paranoia. Shouts and wild exclamations filled the tent as a sea of bodies writhed around in panic.

Klondike and Heavy fought their way through the crowd towards the front. The lion was pacing back and forth, watching the rampage, as if ready to pounce at any moment. Its nostrils flared savagely.

Rance suddenly appeared in front of the mighty beast. It stared up at him. Without hesitation, he reached out and placed his palm in front of the snarling animal.

"Apollo!" he shouted. The lion made to sit.

Then, inexplicably, someone raced forward and hurled a wine bottle at the animal. It smashed into the beast's face. "That thing will maul us, you fool!" he cried.

"No!" Rance roared in horror. It was too late. The lion leapt up at its master in shock, blood pouring from its head. Rance made a gutsy snarl and somehow caught both of its paws as it lunged. The power of the animal's thrust knocked him over backwards. He rolled over, looking up in desperation. Apollo watched him. Then, with a venomous roar, it hurled its entire frame at the South African in a full-blooded attack. Everyone watched in shock as the lion smashed into the fair-haired animal trainer, their heads seemingly colliding. The impact sent Rance flying through the air and he crashed into the buffet table, breaking it in two.

Klondike and Heavy finally made it to the front of the tent. They both crouched low. The lion was skulking around its master, snarling in shock and anger. They moved to within a few yards of the beast, both stunned at the sudden turn of events. The entire group had assembled at the back of the marquee, and now all stared dumbly as the lion pondered its next move. Nobody spoke. Men in suits, women in ballroom gowns. All looked on, petrified.

Klondike thought fast. Then, from out of nowhere, a familiar voice snapped him to attention.

"Chairman! Follow my lead!"

He turned as Gino Shapiro ran behind them both, carrying a bright red tent sheet in his wake. As he accelerated, it ran out behind him like a streamer. He cried out in a high-pitched wail. They all watched. The lion turned and, noticing the bright red juggernaut, made off at full speed after the crazed runner. In a second, Shapiro was out the door, with the lion galloping in hot pursuit.

"Go!" Klondike cried, racing after the wild beast. Heavy followed, with Corky and Olsen not far behind.

Shapiro charged through the camp like an Olympic sprinter. He could hear the lion bearing down on him, could sense its wrath. Without even thinking, he entered Rance's enclosure and immediately saw an empty lion cage, right next to the ones containing Apollo's partner, Cassius, and Cicero the tiger.

With a sudden burst, Shapiro threw himself into the empty cage, the red sheet flowing in the breeze as it followed him inside. He moved to the rear, then turned and looked back.

The lion slowed as it approached his cage. Seeing an intruder within, it walked steadily to the door before moving inside with stealth, intrigued. It saw the red material, and growled.

Finally, Klondike and the others reached the enclosure. They saw the lion enter the cage, then noticed with horror that Shapiro was trapped inside.

"Gino!" Klondike cried.

"OK, chairman," Gino stated, remarkably calm but with a disturbed look on his face. "Distract the lion. Get its attention. Then, I move. OK?"

The group understood. Moving around the cage in the darkened enclosure, they tried to get the lion's attention. But the animal's gaze was only on the red.

Suddenly, a high-pitched, drilling noise emanated from the group. They all turned. Olsen had made another strange cupping motion with his hands, and had uttered the unusual cry.

Instantly, the lion sprang forward towards the bars at the far end of the cage, following the direction of the loud shriek.

Shapiro sprang forward like a rampant cat, performing a neat forward roll on the cage floor before spinning out of the door. Jim McCabe, who had appeared out of nowhere, sprang forward and slammed the cage door shut. He rapidly tied it closed with a leather strap.

Everyone let out an almighty sigh of relief.

Shapiro led on the gravel, breathless. Cathy ran up from the main tent and wrapped her arms around him, shaking.

Klondike looked around, making sure everything was in place. He turned to Olsen, who was glaring wide-eyed at the cage. He nodded at the youngster in thanks.

Heavy and Corky went to check on Shapiro.

Incredibly, as if the whole incident had never happened, Apollo the lion stretched out in its cage, lovingly chewing the red sheet. Wide-eyed and tail up, it had never looked happier.

The party guests slowly made their respective exits. Many were still in shock, some looked completely dishevelled. But all were relieved beyond words. The inside of the marquee, a picture of class and glamour just a half hour earlier, now resembled the aftermath of a cattle stampede, with upturned furniture everywhere and spilt alcohol covering the floor mat.

Lacey pleaded with the assembled press not to report on the incident, but knew it was futile. An escaped lion was big news, even if it was rounded up within minutes. Deep down, she told herself no publicity was bad publicity, and could sense that the notoriety of the lion would likely add to the circus's appeal with a fascinated public.

The most important result of all though was that nobody was seriously hurt, or worse.

The immediate aftermath of the incident was not without its awkward exchanges.

The chief of police, who had cowered with the rest of the dignitaries at the back of the tent when Apollo first appeared, now swaggered around the camp, asking questions and demanding answers.

However, he soon called it a night, satisfied that the danger had been equalised pretty fast. He left with the line: "Wait till the boys at the station hear about this!"

Klondike and his crew stood scattered around the enclosure, everyone making sure others were all right. Rance appeared, a large plaster covering a gash in his head. He looked stunned still and a trifle estranged, but quickly shook hands with everyone before embracing Shapiro with a large bear hug. The fiery South African then moved towards the cages, and stood there staring at Apollo, as if in a trance.

Shapiro accepted an endless stream of plaudits and thanks from both talent and roustabouts, before wandering back towards his executive trailer. He spotted Olsen sitting on the steps of a holding booth and smiled.

"You did good back there, kid," he said, holding his shoulder in pain.

Olsen looked up, still in a state of shock. "No, you did. That was incredible, man. Real fast thinking."

Shapiro laughed to himself. "You are the boy with the dolls, right?"

Olsen rolled his eyes. "Ventriloquist."

"Whatever. I hear they are putting you on the midway?"

The teen looked up curiously. "For now."

Again the older man laughed. "I think that is where you belong, boy."

Olsen was aghast. "You almost got eaten by a lion back there. What do you care where I perform?"

Shapiro leaned in close. "I take an interest in all talent." He winced as he massaged the shoulder roughly, twisting his arm several times. "Because everyone is measured against me. That's what I have to live with. When we hit the big cities, we will see what you can do, doll maker."

With that, Shapiro surged off into the night, still holding the shoulder.

"It was nice meeting you," Olsen called after him.

Back in the animal enclosure, Klondike was conversing with Heavy and Lacey. Everyone had calmed down.

"Kal!" It was Rance, who was crouched down studying the cage door. "You need to see this."

Klondike wandered over, taking up a similar squatted position to the animal trainer. They both studied the cage door, with Rance pointing to the padlock. As they looked, Apollo simply sat at the far end, chewing on the endless red sheet.

"Look," Rance was whispering. "Just look at the padlock."

Klondike ran his eyes over the small steel contraption. It had a brutal looking dent at its head. He looked down at the locking clip. The free end was hanging limply and looked crooked and misshapen. The whole thing was hanging from a wire on the edge of the door, with McCabe's leather strap now acting as the lock.

"Jesus..." Klondike breathed. "This has been hit with a sledgehammer. Or worse."

Rance nodded gravely. "I know. Someone broke this lock on purpose. From the outside."

A thousand notions seemed to hit Klondike's conscience at the same time. He looked up, stunned. "Who would do this? What the hell is going on here?"

Rance's eyes were fixed on the busted lock. "This could have caused untold carnage. Apollo could have escaped into the wild. Just imagine…"

Klondike rose slowly, a pensive glare locked into his features. He realised Heavy and Lacey had joined them, overhearing everything.

"All right," he murmured, "we need to keep this among ourselves. That is essential. Then, privately, speak to the roustabouts. The performers. Ask if anyone saw anything. Somebody must have an idea on this."

"Kal!" Lacey shrieked. "What are you saying?"

"I'm not saying anything… Yet. But whoever did this did it for a reason. And I want to know what that reason is." He eyed the lion, lying peacefully in its cage.

"Something tells me I'm not gunna like what I find."

Chapter 8

TERROR AT THE CIRCUS

By Sidney Hackett, Daily World

A lion ran wild in a circus camp last night, terrifying guests at a VIP launch party.

The wild African beast escaped from his holding cage and raced into the party tent, causing visitors and staff to run for their lives.

The incident occurred at Klondike's Circus's winter holding camp in Carlton County, Northern California.

The near-tragedy was a personal disaster for circus boss Kal Klondike, real name Terry Calder, who had hoped to use the evening to promote his event to distinguished local businessmen and executives, not to mention members of the California press.

Instead, the VIP guests were left frightened and disturbed at the sight of a runaway lion rampaging through what was supposed to be a secure area.

Little is known about how the beast escaped, but the incident asks serious questions about Klondike's security…and whether punters will want to come to his show, knowing they might get mauled by a lion.

One terrified member of the media told your correspondent: "It was just awful. That horrible lion came at us, meaning to kill us all. What a disgrace of a circus company… To allow something like this to happen. We could've all been killed. It was supposed to be a party."

After several minutes running wild in the party tent, the lion was eventually tricked back into its cage by a passing hired hand.

Circus staff were left thinking about what might have been after this horrifying spectacle, and could only speculate as to…

Eric Ribbeck placed the newspaper back on his desk gently. With a warm smile, he stood up and walked idly to the balcony of his great boardwalk office. Standing against the railings, he took in the mighty Atlantic Ocean beyond, before glancing sideways towards Davenport Promenade to the south.

If he squinted he could just about see his own circus tent being raised on the far horizon. A giant purple apparition, blotting out a whole chunk of sky. It looked otherworldly. He could vaguely make out trucks and vans milling around, and knew that a sea of people would be in motion on the deck. His opening show was tonight. The circus's hometown show. Atlantic City.

Then they headed west. First New York, then everywhere. The big cities formed in his mind. Washington. Chicago. St Louis. Denver. And, of course, Los Angeles.

He was grinning like a child as he relaxed on the balcony, casually lighting one of his thin cigarillos. The gentle sea breeze was cool and refreshing.

He was awoken from his reprieve by the ringing of his desk telephone. Only a handful of people knew the number, but he knew who it would be.

He returned to the large cushioned chair and picked up the receiver.

"Talk to me."

"It's me, boss, Marconi."

"What goes on, boy?"

There was no hesitation. "Did you hear about the lion?"

"Sure as hell did," Ribbeck drawled, placing the cigarillo between his lips. "What the hell happened out there?"

"Sabotage."

Ribbeck stared into nothingness, his emotions a mixture of fear and desire. "What's the story?"

Marconi spoke rapidly like a machine. "Someone smashed the lock apart on the cage door. Probably with a sledgehammer or pick axe. Nobody knows the whole story yet, boss. But the lock was smashed all right. The lion apparently found its own way into the party tent."

"Was anyone hurt?"

"Only Rance. And it wasn't exactly serious. The whole thing was all over in two minutes."

Ribbeck thought earnestly as he pictured the scene. Then, he glanced down at the newspaper.

"Have you ever heard of Sidney Hackett?"

"Sure," came the blurted reply. "He's that writer for the Daily World. Asked some awkward questions at the press conference."

Ribbeck's eyes froze. "What's that you say?"

"Yeah, something about Shapiro doing a devil drop. I think it was supposed to be a secret. Kinda riled old Klondike some that it was out in da open. At least, that's what the guy from the Santa Cruz Herald told me when I got talking to him."

Ribbeck stared at the receiver in disbelief. A puzzle was being formed in his head, with the pieces slowly coming together to form a very disturbing picture. But one he intended to exploit.

"Good work, Luca," he spat out. "Now, listen to me very carefully. If there is a saboteur in Klondike's ranks, you have to find out who it is. This could be our inside man. This... Could be our big chance, the one we've been waiting for."

"But what do I —"

"Silence! Listen to me. I don't care how you do it, but find this bum Hackett. He'll show up on the road, I guarantee it. Why? Because he is involved in all this. He has a stake. Get to him, Luca, and find out who fed him the information on the devil drop. Make this yahoo talk. Then, we will know more about this so-called sabotage. They must be in league with one anoth⌄. It's a beautiful set-up."

"But, but..." Marconi was babbling on the end of the line. "I thought I was gunna lean on 'em all. You hired me to hassle the circus folk. You reckon these guys are gunna do it for us?"

"Don't you see? That's beautiful, boy." The older man smirked to himself. "You can lead them to me. It won't be hard for Klondike to make that connection. But...now one of his own might be causing the unrest and damage we so facetiously desire." He laughed out loud, sounding like a hillbilly yokel riding a bronco bull. "Now all we have to do is make the connection and help them along. Confederates. All with a common goal – putting that son of a bitch Klondike out of business."

Marconi was still flapping on the other end of the line. "But, Mr Ribbeck, sir, we don't even know there is a saboteur yet. And how do I make contact with this Hackett fella?"

"Just keep doing what you've had so much practice doing, Luca. Observe. That way, you'll find Hackett and you'll find the rotten egg."

Marconi, standing in a phone booth 3,000 miles away, sounded sceptical. "I dunno, boss, sounds like you got it all figured out already. I'm out on my own out here. I don't know what's going on."

"Snap out of, sonny," Ribbeck drawled menacingly. "You've exceeded all expectations so far. Your information is excellent. Now keep it up. Find out what goes on, and you can expect that big fat bonus we talked about in the fall. How d'ya like them apples, boy?"

"Yes, boss. I'll be in touch."

Ribbeck simply put the phone down. He toked on the cigarillo. The smoke that wafted over his desk was a brownish grey colour. He smiled to himself.

Gazing at the various mementoes of circus life that adjourned the walls of his private domain, he leant back, feeling his aching joints creak and tremble.

His steely grey eyes locked onto an old Ribbeck World Circus poster from the 1940s. He thought of his old foe Kal Klondike. As if hypnotised, he glared at it and said one line:

"It's time to blow some trail dust isn't it, you rotten son of a bitch!"

Chapter 9

There's nothing quite like roll out day, Heavy Brown thought to himself as he left his trailer and swaggered merrily towards the far end of the camp.

As always, the whole place was a beehive of activity. Bodies were in motion everywhere, their calls and cries drowned by the endless vacuum of exhaust spewing from a sea of vans and trucks that motored around in zigzags everywhere. There was a conveyor belt of new arrivals at the circus, and a string of departures. At the front gate, a long queue of automobiles of all shapes and sizes filled the old highway.

Heavy grinned to himself as he made his way past the final few trailers and enclosures at the back of the camp, nodding his greetings to various roustabouts and helpers who passed. Everyone seemed to be in a hurry.

Finally, he made it to the rear gateway, where scores of people were walking to and from a momentous sight. There it was. The circus train.

Forty-eight carriages of tungsten steel and oak wood, all decorated in traditional red and blue paint. The words Klondike's Circus were emblazoned on giant billboards on every carriage. The paintwork shone, the roof beams were freshly varnished and the huge iron wheels looked like they had just come off the assembly line.

Heavy stood there admiring the mighty train. It would be their principal home and headquarters for the next five months. Their church, sanctuary and mess hall.

Not only did the circus train contain staterooms for all the staff, along with a bunkhouse for the roustabouts, but it would carry everything involved in the construction and maintenance of the circus. Holding pens carried the animals, open carriages held the midway stalls and freight coaches carried tractors and trucks needed for the construction of the big top.

Heavy nodded with approval. The train certainly had been renovated over the winter. It looked stylish, classy and brand new.

He chuckled as he saw Klondike climb onto the roof of one of the carriages. He knew what was coming. The boss stood proudly atop the train and called out to everyone in earshot.

"All right people," he bellowed from his podium, "this is it. Now let's blow some trail dust!"

A mighty cheer went up from the gathered crowd and then, as if a whistle had been blown, everyone got to work, loading up the carriages and sorting through supplies.

Heavy greeted Klondike as he climbed down from the top of the carriage.

"Y'know, Kal," he mused, "I don't think I'll ever get tired hearing that line."

Klondike grinned. "Heard it once in a western. The trail boss said it just before a cattle drive. Seems somehow apt."

They walked to the end carriage, which held the final run of staterooms. Klondike's and Heavy's individual quarters occupied the very end of the final carriage.

Klondike leant against the final connector, folded his arms and merely watched the melee all around him in sheer wonder. He squinted into the early morning sun. A strange looking assortment of folks were wandering through the camp in his direction. Heavy was laughing, and had met the group as they neared the railroad siding.

"OK, boss," said Heavy as he led the new group over. "Allow me to introduce your top draft picks for 1958."

Klondike smiled as his chief lieutenant welcomed the newcomers.

"Here's trouble," Heavy bellowed comically. "All 500 pounds of it!"

With that, an obese man breezed past Heavy and laid out a puffy, sweaty palm for Klondike. He was dressed in a tracksuit and looked soaking wet. His round, red face looked cherubic and his short brown hair was thinning. Klondike looked down at the tracksuit. One word was printed across the chest in spiked letters. Gargantua.

Klondike greeted him warmly. "Can you still do that stunt I saw you pull in Kansas City?" he said after pleasantries were exchanged.

"Sure," said the giant newcomer in a high-pitched whine. With that, he stunned them both by throwing himself into a back somersault, before cartwheeling several times in the gravel. Then, with a childlike grin, he wandered back to the train, to hearty applause.

"Unbelievable," Klondike breathed.

"Where's ma place?" Gargantua asked.

"Third carriage along, your name is on the door, pal," said Heavy.

Klondike turned as a new figure emerged. He towered over them all and was wearing a denim dungaree with a sun hat. A surreal sight, the giant looked painfully thin and strangely dishevelled.

"Good morning Goliath," Klondike called up to the head.

"Morning mister boss man, sir," the giant said in a rasping voice. Everyone seemed to gather round and stare at this new figure. He was just impossibly tall.

"How many midgets can you carry these days?" Klondike quipped.

"Still the same. It ain't changed none. Eight midgets." Goliath looked and sounded sad and weary. In a way, it was all part of the act.

"Let's see, eh?" Klondike said mischievously, pointing behind the giant. They all turned.

There stood together one of his favourite old acts, an annual treat to anyone who saw them. The nine midgets were known as Percy Pringle and his Dancing Dwarves. Pringle, the tallest of the gang, was always dressed in a white suit and acted as a director and manager for the ensemble, who all wore performance leotards.

The little group all greeted Klondike and Heavy. Then, following a wink from the circus boss, Pringle clapped his hands and yelped: "OK boys, let's welcome Goliath into the act."

With that, the eight other midgets jumped at the giant and clambered up his frame in one odd-looking scramble. Within seconds, the entire group were hanging off the giant, clinging to his arms, legs, neck and back.

Klondike applauded heartily, and the performers all made their way onto the train.

The final man to greet them was the one they called Rumpy Stiltskin. He walked over expertly in his six-foot tall stilts, dressed in bright clown clothes.

"Rumpy," Klondike greeted, "good to see you again. Still got the legs for all this?"

The man on stilts shook the offered hands, squatting obscenely on his long pegs.

"Wouldn't miss it for the world, boss," he said heartily. He eyed the train suspiciously. "You got beer on this war wagon?"

Klondike laughed. "All you can drink. But not on show day."

Rumpy nodded and manoeuvred himself down the railroad towards the next doorway.

Klondike was still laughing. He looked at Heavy. "Now that's what I call a showcase."

Heavy nodded approvingly. "The crowds are gunna love it."

Lacey Tanner was struggling to walk as she carried a plethora of bags and trunks towards the train. Richie Plum bounced alongside her, carrying his single suitcase and several more of hers.

They boarded the circus train on the third carriage, and squeezed through the companionway until they found their staterooms, which were next to each other.

Lacey virtually collapsed into her quarters, the bags and trunks falling out on the carpeted floor. She looked about idly. "Well, at least it's comfortable," she murmured.

Plum opened the door to his room. He looked downwards. "No TV. No double bed. No bath. No morning paper. No secretary..."

Lacey looked up from her muddle. She jumped onto her bed, and waved excitedly. "Welcome to circus life, kiddo. It's just us and the open road. Or railroad, at least." She looked around, Plum marvelling at her constant sense of enthusiasm. "It's so quaint," she breathed huskily. "I can almost smell the sawdust and cotton candy."

Plum leant against the doorway. "I think I can smell horse dung. Still!"

Lacey laughed. "Listen, this is one assignment you'll never forget."

He didn't have an answer.

Gino Shapiro, his brother Nicky and Jenny Cross all made their way to their staterooms on the second carriage. Their usual berth.

The trapeze artists all unpacked their belongings privately and quietly.

Two carriages up, Corky led the circus's small team of clowns towards their usual carriage.

Corky occupied the first room of the coach, and each of his small team had their own, smaller room further down.

Amanda Hart used the stateroom at the end of the first accommodation carriage, because it was next to her elephants' pens. Cathy's chimps had a room of their own that represented a play hall. Emile Rance's lions and tiger lived in their private pens near the train's central coaches. Several stable blocks carried the many horses used in the show. They were attended to by the bareback riders, who worked the winters as wranglers and horse breakers at ranches in the southern states.

The heavy machinery and equipment supplies filled the front carriages. Even Klondike's jeep had a place among the packed freight holders.

Roddy Olsen hopped aboard the train, found his appointed stateroom and smiled as he checked the companionway. He was not entirely surprised to see he had been placed next door to Suzi. The young songstress had been his guide, friend and meals partner since he had walked through the gate of the winter camp ten days ago.

Olsen gently placed his trusty suitcase and tote bag on the bed and took in his latest surroundings. He caught his reflection in a mirror above the washbasin and smiled charismatically at himself. "Next stop Las Vegas," he whispered. "Hollywood. TV land. Ed Sullivan. The Tonight Show." He laughed good-naturedly.

"Don't forget Santa Cruz recreation ground," came a squeaky voice from the doorway.

Olsen turned as Suzi hovered in the aisle. They smiled at one another.

"Welcome to the circus train. What d'ya think, Roddy?"

"It's incredible," he answered.

"Who knows how the season's going to play out." She laughed gaily. "Every year, there are new surprises. Shocks. Twists. I remember Cathy telling me when I first joined the year before last."

Olsen sat back on the room's solitary chair and looked up at her with glee. "Bring it on!"

Jim McCabe rounded up the floating myriad of roustabouts that were scattered around the railroad siding overseeing the last of the loading details.

He walked along the side of the train, checking each carriage's contents with a clipboard held before him.

Finally satisfied, he let out a mighty cry of "All aboard" and began ushering his team towards the bunkhouse, located towards the centre of the behemoth.

Men of all shapes and sizes, wearing cheap clothes and looking largely rugged and unwholesome, all made their way towards the middle carriages.

McCabe noticed one of the men standing on his own, further back from the railroad siding, staring at the train suspiciously. There was something about this character that didn't sit right with McCabe. He had slicked back dark hair, olive oil skin and beady eyes, and his clothes were spotless.

"Hey you!" he called out. "What's ya name? Marconi! What ya doing? Get on board."

The man shook himself out of his reprieve instantly. "Yes sir, Mr McCabe. Right away." He jogged towards the others and followed them to a large door that led to a double carriage, basically two coaches that had been welded together to form a giant travelling hall.

McCabe watched the man climb on, shook his head, then continued to walk to the far end of the train, where the staterooms were located.

Marconi followed the others into the double carriage, and looked around in near disgust.

The bunkhouse. One long dormitory-like room full of bunk beds. Some kind of shower room was found at the far end, and a small table with couches and armchairs scattered around could be seen at the end of the bunks.

Marconi paced down the room, staring at the bunks. It reminded him of a shelter he had stayed in when he'd first run away from home in Albany, New York.

Nodding to various familiar faces, men he'd come to know on the roustabout detail, he chose a bunk, a top one, and climbed onto the soft linen sheets.

A copy of the Holy Bible had been left on the bed. Idly, he began reading.

Back in Klondike's stateroom at the very end of the train, Klondike and Heavy sat down at the table, all set for their annual season-opening tradition.

While in transit on the mighty train, the two old friends spent a great deal of time playing poker, when they weren't discussing the show and the many different strands of the business.

Klondike poured them each a shot of scotch, pulled two cigars from a desk drawer, and handed one of each across the table to Heavy.

Then, with a big grin, he pulled a pack of cards from his valise and placed them theatrically on the deck between them.

"I believe it's your cut, old buddy."

Heavy nodded, impressed with his pal's memory. He cut the pack, and held up the broken pile so Klondike could see the bottom card.

"An ace!" Klondike cried. "Let's hope that's a sign. Of success… This year." He idly picked a card from the remainder of the pack. He looked at it, then showed Heavy. "A king. Well, I guess it doesn't get much better than that."

Heavy nodded. "It's definitely a sign, pal." He raised his glass. "To the season."

Klondike followed suit. "To the season."

They clinked glasses, looking each other firmly in the eye.

McCabe slammed shut the final carriage door after completing his rounds. The train was full. They were all set at last.

A conductor walked the length of the train, before finally reaching the driver's box. With a happy thumbs up, he leapt aboard and helped the driver and engineer with their final checks.

Then, the driver pulled on a hand chord and a deafening toot reverberated all across the surrounding countryside. The wheels were in motion and the train slid down the siding.

Everyone on board let out a cheer, and suddenly the winter camp was left behind, an abandoned fort not to be seen again until fall. The only figures to grace its grounds for the next five months would be watchmen and the odd maintenance specialist.

The train slowly picked up speed as it wound its way down towards the main line.

The branch track was barely three miles long. Once on the railroad proper, it was barely 30 miles to their first stop of Santa Cruz, a gentle introduction to the new season for all.

Due to its heavy load and mix of animals and machinery on board, the train cruised at just under 40mph for most of its journey time.

It represented an awe-inspiring sight for all who glimpsed it as it wound its way through the countryside, heading to the next town. A dazzling liner of red and blue, transporting entertainment, glamour and razzle dazzle.

Everyone who saw the train pointed and smiled. Many followed in its wake. For the circus train promised a welcome escape to many from their everyday lives and routines. It offered hope, excitement and enchantment. It was a glimpse into another world.

And it was coming.

IT'S HERE! SANTA CRUZ WELCOMES A GIANT ATTRACTION AS BIG TOP ROLLS INTO TOWN

By Lester Jones. Santa Cruz Herald.

There's a new show in town… And it lives under a giant red and blue tent.

That's right, the circus is back in Santa Cruz. And the townsfolk couldn't be happier.

The big event occurred yesterday, as the great Klondike's Circus arrived on board its impossibly long, never-ending train.

Hundreds of fans were at the railroad siding at Santa Cruz recreation fields to greet it and welcome the stars of the show, both human and animal.

The show may be on Saturday night, but the gathered fans enjoyed a true spectacle to behold throughout the day yesterday as Kal Klondike's team began setting up their circus world.

What a sight it was! An army of men transported tents and equipment onto the fields, as trucks left the train and began unloading everything imaginable from the train cars.

Elephants were herded from the train into temporary pens, and caged lions were lifted into their new lairs.

Circus fans young and old hung about the fields all day to witness the excitement.

And then there was the raising of the big top.

The giant, larger than life tarpaulin was led flat on the field, checked over and over again by spotters for holes or cracks that could prove disastrous. Then, lynching poles were erected in place at the designated raise points, filling holes in the flat tent that were set out at pre-determined points in the patchwork. Lines were attached and secured tightly.

Then, as an expectant crowd held its breath, forty roustabouts all pulled together on the lines. The giant tarpaulin slowly rose up the poles and, before our very eyes, a circus tent materialised, rising above us like a new build skyscraper, covering the horizon and dominating the fields all around. Its glorious red and blue colours told us, though, that this was no place of business, but a world of fun and glee.

The cheer that went up as the tent was pulled to its full height said it all. The waiting was over. The circus was here.

Roll on Saturday night. Let's hope there's room in there for everybody.

Chapter 10
Santa Cruz. Opening Show

The crowds began pouring into the midway at about five, ready for the start of the show at seven. There were plenty of attractions to keep everyone entertained until then, and families and people from all walks of life had descended upon this new little city that had taken over the recreational fields.

Setting up had gone to plan, without even the slightest hitch. The big top now sat proudly at the end of the fields, with a settlement of smaller tents, stalls and mini-cabins pitched up all around it.

An orderly line of patrons queued up by the entrance, waiting outside a ticket office made up of a small portable trailer.

Once inside, the paying public roamed the midway, with some even entering the big top early to get a decent seat.

Inside the giant circus tent, all was quiet at this stage, with rows of bleachers fixed on wooden blocks rising higher and higher into the upper echelons of the tent's mass. A six-foot wall made of solid oak wood separated the elevated front row from the performance area which was, of course, draped in sawdust.

Kal Klondike walked idly through the midway, exchanging pleasantries with excited fans and watching as the various stalls sprang into action and accepted their first business of the season. There were shooting galleries, pitching games and various other games of chance, as well as confectionary stands and hot dog shacks. The programme stall had indeed been turned into a merchandise store, as Lacey had suggested. Patrons could pick up signed pictures of Gino Shapiro and Corky the Clown, as well as replica versions of Gino's famous firebrand orange tights and top.

Klondike smiled happily as he walked the midway. Finally, the season was up and running. The waiting was over. As he paced around, he inspected the many stalls, glanced up at the imposing big top beyond, and greeted his many workers.

The circus's clowns, minus Corky, who only performed in the main show, also patrolled the midway, performing tricks for the spectators and handing out free posters.

As more and more people funnelled past the ticket booth, Klondike was joined by Lacey and Plum, who were also wandering about, gazing wide eyed at the attractions.

"Well," Klondike said, "what do you guys make of it all?"

"It's so wonderful," Lacey blurted with her usual enthusiasm. "Oh, Kal, it's just what I imagined."

Klondike shook his head at her gushing melodramatics. He looked at Plum.

"Well done, Klondike," he said with vague excitement. He pointed at the ticket booth near the main entrance, where scores of people were pouring through the gates. "It's going to be a hit. The public haven't stopped buying tickets and coming in since five."

Klondike chuckled. "What I tell ya?" He looked about, soaking up the laughter and jovial atmosphere. "Everyone loves the circus."

Lacey nodded gamely. "Richie, baby, why don't you buy me some cotton candy now." She pulled some notes from her little purse. "And one for yourself and Kal."

Klondike stared at her. She smiled impishly. "I'm in the circus business now, my friend. I might as well look the part. And feel it."

Plum shrugged, taking the money and moping away. She called after him. "Large for me, Richie."

Klondike laughed and they began walking round the big top.

"I must say, Kal," she began, "you've done a wonderful job. I kept thinking how this was all going to play out, how you'd suddenly have a circus ready to go in a small town, on the recreational fields. Just like that. But there was no drama at all. Everyone knew their role, and this whole thing was a seamless transition. From the train to the fields."

Klondike nodded. "We're a well-oiled machine," he explained. "We've all been doing this for so long. It's what we do. But remember," he looked down at her with widened eyes. "The golden rule is... You're only as good as your last show. The key to success is to keep this whole enterprise rolling. From town to town. Every few days. It's got to look fresh. Everything. When the people see the show, they want to see something no one ever saw before, not a re-run of something that's played out ten times before, in ten other towns. Every time, we need to go all out to entertain the crowds as best we can, and not look like we've done this show a hundred times before. All my guys have changed their acts for this season, but they've got to make it look fresh in every show."

Lacey was nodding thoughtfully. "They will. Your performers are like something from another world. A different planet." She pointed to a nearby poster of Gino that was stuck to an ice cream stall. "And there's your planet's prince!"

They both laughed. Then, walking on, they spotted a large gathering of people at the far end of the midway. They all seemed to be crowded into a circle, with someone in the middle. Their laughter and gasps of delight aroused the attention of both Klondike and Lacey. Curious, they wandered over as the gathering broke into a loud applause.

As they made the edge of the crowd, they peered through the bodies and saw what everyone was so excited about.

There, in the middle of the group, in his own private performance space, was Roddy Olsen. He had mounted a temporary mini-tightrope the roustabouts had assembled for performers to practice on, and was striding across, with his Rusty Fox puppet on his back. Incredibly, the two were having a conversation as Olsen paced across the wire, six feet off the ground, joking and bantering as Olsen expertly manoeuvred himself along.

When he reached the other end, he dismounted and held Rusty Fox in the customary position as the crowd applauded warmly. They both bowed.

Yet again, Klondike and Lacey found themselves staring dumbly, open-mouthed, at the blond haired youngster.

"How the hell did he make that puppet's mouth move?" Klondike demanded. "He was walking a wire!"

Lacey looked on in awe. "There seems no limit to this boy's talents."

They both watched as more and more patrons joined the crowded circle. Olsen was now engaging in a comedy monologue with Rusty, to more laughs and applause.

Klondike studied his poise and delivery. "He's a natural showman," he said at last, "his interaction with an audience, his confidence, his timing. It's all faultless." He shook his head. "He may look like a kid better suited to surfing in Santa Monica, but he works a crowd better than a 20-year veteran."

Lacey nodded admiringly. "He's terrific." Then she gazed up at Klondike in mock smugness. "And... I told you so."

They continued watching the act until Plum reappeared beside them, carrying three giant sticks of cotton candy. He handed them out and tucked into his portion happily.

Klondike calmly passed his stick onto a passing clown, then reached for a cigar from a breast pocket.

"Say," said Plum, "where are we going to watch the show from? Do you have a director's box or something, Klondike?"

The circus boss laughed, the cigar hanging limply in the corner of his mouth. "I'll be at the stage door, watching everything. You two ought to join me. It's quite a sight from down there."

Lacey nibbled at the cotton candy. "Like a baseball coach in the dugout?"

Klondike grinned down at her. "Lacey," he drawled, "you're finally getting it."

"Ladies and gentlemen..."

Heavy Brown's booming announcement, enhanced by a microphone and sound system, reverberated around the big top like a clap of thunder. A general hush descended across the thousands of paying patrons crammed into the bleacher seats, stacked high and encircling the round, sawdust-covered stage below. More than ten thousand people got settled and stared down at the man in the scarlet red jacket and top hat.

Heavy looked around at the endless arena of humanity. Every eye in the house was fixed upon him. Holding one hand aloft, the other clasped on the microphone, he bellowed out his traditional greeting.

"Welcome to the most incredible, the most fantastic, the most mesmerising show on earth. Once seen, never forgotten. The show of the hour. The show with the power. Always great. Never faked. The all-American jamboree. The bash that will leave you full of glee. It's here, it's live and it's ready to blow you all away!

"So, ladies and gentlemen, sit back, relax and prepare to be enchanted. My name is Heavy Brown, and I give to you... Klondike's Circus!"

The crowd broke into a rapturous applause, with screams of delight and wild cries breaking from the bleachers.

Then, from the big top's stage entrance behind Heavy, Cathy Cassidy ran into the arena, followed by her eight chimpanzees.

"Behold," Heavy announced, "Cathy Cassidy and her dancing chimps!"

The applause continued as Cathy began her act. She was quickly joined by five of the circus's clown revue. This had been one of Lacey's ideas, to mix up the acts some.

Cathy, dressed in a red and blue leotard, firstly ran around in a wide circle, with the monkeys all following expertly. Then, she led down, with the animals following suit. The chimps completed various tricks and routines, with the grand showpiece seeing them all create a 'monkey pole', where one carried the rest on its shoulders in sequence and then paraded around the sawdust. The clowns then gathered around the pole and caught each of the chimps as they jumped down into waiting arms. As they exited the floor, the chimps took it in turns to leapfrog one another, before all joining hands with Cathy and the clowns for a collective bow.

Next up was Corky's act.

"And now," bellowed Heavy from the entrance area, "it gives me great pleasure to introduce to you all, one of Klondike's Circus's star performers and a hero beloved by all who see him in action. Ladies and gentlemen, please welcome the world's greatest clown, Corky!"

The beloved clown entered the big top to wild applause. The other circus clowns followed in his wake, clapping also. Corky was dressed in his usual attire of yellow chequered suit, crooked tie and brown bowler hat.

He began by riding a six-foot tall unicycle, catching various items as the other clowns threw them up at him. An iron, stool, imitation ham and basketball were all dispatched, with Corky catching each one. He then threw each piece back at one of the others, before hoisting himself up, twisting in mid-air, and riding the cycle with his hands while balancing himself vertically. The crowd whistled and cheered as he did a lap of the floor.

Then, as the cycle was led away by the other clowns, he was handed an opening set of six juggling pins. This was where Corky truly excelled as an entertainer. He began juggling, gaining more momentum, going faster and faster until the red pins were a blur of motion. One of the other clowns tossed another pin into the mix, then another. Corky moved them around expertly, never pausing or even blinking.

Watching from the entrance, Klondike grinned. He turned to Lacey, Plum and Heavy, who were all stood next to him watching the incredible feat.

"He told me he'd got even faster," said Klondike in dismay. "I didn't believe him. Now, I believe him all right. I didn't think it possible."

Plum was staring at the clown, transfixed by the flashing pins. "Jesus!" he blurted. "He must be the fastest juggler in the world!"

"You bet," Klondike answered.

Finally, Corky rounded up the pins in his customary manner, catching them in the front of his pants. Bowing gamely to the applause, he handed over the pins and then began one of his customary tricks. Holding an imitation bowling ball, that was really made of soft rubber, he juggled the black ball, a tennis ball and a marble. As he kept the items floating, the revue clowns took it in turns to throw small dough balls into his mouth, which he duly ate.

Next, he juggled four small rubber balls in the 'high juggle', sending the items up to 12 feet in the air. As he kept going, he mounted another clown's shoulders and was paraded around the floor.

His juggling finale was a stunning sight. A backstage helper set alight four pins with a gasoline feeder and a lighter. Corky again jumped up onto the unicycle. The lit pins were handed to him and, as a drumroll sounded on the public address system, he juggled the flaming pins while riding the cycle. From any kind of distance, it looked as if he was juggling fire.

The audience screamed as one as Corky finally dismounted the unicycle, with the on-fire sticks all tossed high into the air and caught by the clowns.

"And now," came Heavy's voice, as the ringmaster moved towards the star clown, "we come to the piece de resistance. Corky will now perform for you his most daring feat of all…the human cannonball!"

A giant old-fashioned cannon was wheeled out from the back into the near side of the big top. The clowns pointed it at a huge net on the far side, that was tilted at about 45 degrees.

The cannon was in fact a giant catapult, with a huge spring inside that could fire a human 50 yards through the air. Corky donned a pair of airman's goggles and a pilot's cap and climbed into the cannon via a ladder.

As the drum roll returned, a clown lit an imitation fuse at the rear of the cannon. This was done purely for effect. The coiled spring was activated by a switch underneath that the clown pressed with his foot once the flame reached the end of the fuse.

With a bang, Corky shot out of the cannon's mouth and flew across the circus floor, shaping his body like a dart, arms crossed over his chest for safety. His body slammed into the tilted net, and the clown bounced several times in the lining before manoeuvring himself onto the ground.

"There he is, Corky the Clown!" Heavy roared as Corky and his assistants offered a bow, gave a wave and headed for the entranceway again. As he passed, Klondike shook his hand heartily and slapped a giant hand onto his back. "One of these days I'll start listening to you," he cried.

Corky winked at the circus boss, before hovering by the edge of the nearest grandstand, and producing a bouquet of flowers from his sleeve, which he gave to an old lady who was cheering loudly at him.

"Like I said, boss," Corky said, returning to the backstage platform, "I'm always looking to improve my act."

With that, he trotted away.

"And now," came the booming voice of Heavy, "brace yourselves for the wildest ride in the circus, as we give you... The Bareback Riders of the Big Top."

A team of 12 horses ridden bareback by riders dressed as cowboys all raced into the big top, passing either side of Heavy and descending on the circus floor, before beginning a galloping circle round the arena. Round and round the bareback riders went, performing various tricks on their mounts as they moved.

Some stood on the horses' backs, one short rider performed a headstand on his mount, before all performed vaults over various wooden jump obstacles laid in the circus's centre. One rider then held on to two horses' manes and was pulled along in-between them as they gallivanted around the floor, while another ran at the flying triumvirate, before ducking between the rider's legs.

Four of the horses then laid down, while the others took it in turns to jump over the group.

At the conclusion of the act, each of the riders made their horses stand on its hind legs and perform a bow. The stallions then trotted backstage, with the riders waving their goodbyes.

"Ladies and gentlemen, please welcome the enchanting Amanda Hart and her incredible elephants."

A customary gasp broke out as the four jumbo elephants, wearing red and blue dress sleeves, all waded onto the floor.

Amanda, dressed in her usual leotard and a red top hat, was seated on the neck of the lead elephant, with her assistant Hans walking between the group.

Amanda's feats were extraordinary. At a quickly erected see-saw, she pivoted on one end while one of the elephants jumped onto the other, propelling her into the air. She performed a somersault and landed, sitting down, back on the elephant's neck. She performed the same feat with the other three.

Then, she directed the lead elephant to lie down, with each of the others propping themselves up onto the previous one to form an arc.

Next, Amanda led flat on the ground, with the elephants all marching towards her but avoiding stepping on her, to the horror of the watching crowd. She remained lying down as another of the beasts, the largest, was led over by Hans before raising his front leg and making to stamp on Amanda's head, before stopping at the last minute and leaving its foot hovering over the brave woman's face.

The four elephants then lined up, four feet between each. Amanda was hoisted up by the first animal's trunk, before being passed through the air by each trunk, going from elephant to elephant, until the last trunk deposited her back on the ground again.

As the adoring audience cheered, each of the elephants managed a bow, before being led on a lap of honour around the circus floor by Amanda and Hans.

Heavy patted each elephant as they exited the arena. "And now, please welcome the Klondike Clowns!"

The small group of brightly dressed clowns then burst onto the floor. They had assisted Corky with his act earlier, but this was their time to shine. Essentially, this part of the show was just silliness as the clowns messed around and interacted with the audience.

There was a custard pie fight, a host of magic tricks, a balloon animal making contest – that never had a winner but ended in a mock fistfight – and a trampolining segment.

The clown revue was a perfect introduction to the "freak show". As the clowns went about their acts, the circus's more unusual characters were slowly introduced.

"Ladies and gentlemen, please give a large welcome to the human blob. All 500 pounds of him. You'll never see anyone quite like... Gargantua!"

Gargantua entered the fray, immediately launching himself into his back-flipping, somersaulting and cartwheeling routine, before chasing after a clown who was carrying a tray of custard pies. On catching his prey, the fat man began eating the pies with delight. The crowd lapped it all up with laughter.

"And now…the world's tallest man. I give you… Goliath!"

The giant wandered onto the floor, dressed in a red and blue jumpsuit. A stunned gasp was audible from the watching thousands as Goliath moved menacingly towards the clowns. Reaching the melee in the middle of the floor, he picked two of the clowns up by the collar, one in each hand. He then hoisted them up and down, as if lifting weights.

"But, what's this? The world's smallest army!"

Percy Pringle and his Dancing Dwarves then raced onto the floor. Surrounding Goliath, they performed the climbing routine until all eight were clinging to Goliath, hanging onto the giant and suspended in the air. Goliath dropped the two clowns, before proceeding to walk across the floor, with the midgets all in tow.

The dancing dwarves then completed their main routine, performing a flurry of acrobatics as bluegrass music played on the tannoy.

Rumpy Stiltskin joined the showcase, performing his stilts handstand routine before hoisting himself onto Goliath's shoulders.

The whole group performed a lap of honour together, with Gargantua and the midgets performing more acrobatics as they all moved round the floor.

As the showcase ensemble exited the big top, a deafening roar sounded on the public address system. All eyes were on the entranceway, as Emile Rance, dressed in his safari costume, led out two lions and the beautiful white tiger. The wild beasts followed him out of their transit cages as if in a trance, and stood alongside him as he held out his arms and soaked up the applause.

"Ladies and gentlemen," Heavy was crying into the microphone, "all the way from the continent of Africa, please behold the lord of the jungle, best friend to lions and tigers, the master, Emile Rance, with Apollo, Cassius and the white tiger, Cicero!"

As the applause faded, a deadly hush descended on the big top. None of the crowd had ever glimpsed a lion, let alone seen one loose before them on an arena floor.

Rance produced a bullwhip from his belt and cracked it once on the floor. The two lions produced a barrel roll, as the tiger watched.

Two cracks were followed by a double roll. Another crack saw the lions stay grounded, before Cicero ran forwards and leapt over both.

Rance then formed a crouching position and uttered a high-pitched command. The lions began running around him in a dizzying circle, before

Cicero padded between them and gave Rance an unexpected hug. The stunt drew rapturous applause.

As the lions stopped running, they awaited further instruction. Rance uttered another command. Cassius roared aloud and held its mouth wide open, stretching its jaws and baring a deadly set of razor-sharp teeth. To gasps of horror from all present, Rance bent down and placed his head into the gaping mouth, holding it there for a full ten seconds.

The fearless Rance then stood tall, extending both arms out wide. The two lions moved towards him and stood on their hind legs, resting their front paws on his arms and letting their weight fall on him. As Rance stood rigid, Cicero moved behind him and delicately placed its head between his legs before slowly lifting him onto its shoulders. The four forms – three beasts and one man – stood aloft in an absurd myriad that defied all belief. Everyone present – audience members, stewards, circus staff, even Klondike and his cohorts – all stood rigid, staring in utter disbelief and muted shock at the surreal sight. No one had ever seen anything quite like this.

The feat earned a standing ovation that thundered through the massive tent.

Rance dismounted with care. His every movement was painfully slow, never moving his arms or legs with a jolt, and he continually whispered to his prized animals as the applause drowned out all other sounds.

Next, he sat cross-legged in the centre of the floor and placed his hands out before him. The three animals then began running round him in a circle, before taking it in turns to leap over him.

Standing, he then walked in a long straight line, with the lions following directly behind and Cicero a little further back. This time, all three mirrored his actions exactly. They stopped when he stopped. Led down when he led down. Turned when he turned. Then, all four performed a running leap together.

Rance then performed his usual finale. He produced a bicycle from the back stage platform and began riding around the edge of the circus floor, with Apollo, Cassius and Cicero all following playfully, at a slight gallop, as the crowd applauded the extraordinary performers. Rance waved as he rode round, before guiding his animals into the waiting cages by the entranceway.

"Let's hear it for the animal trainer extraordinaire, Emile Rance!"

Heavy's call was met with another deafening roar, as Rance appeared again by the tent flap and held his arms aloft. Then, he slowly paced backstage, following the freshly locked mobile cages.

He was embraced by Klondike and Lacey as he neared the doorway. "That was some trick, Emile, the group hug," Klondike said, breathless.

Rance merely looked back at the grandstands all around and shrugged. He rarely smiled, and spoke now in a soft tone. "It's good to be back. Back out there." He padded out of the big top.

Then, as everyone caught a collective breath, the familiar sound of dramatic opera music roared over the PA system. This was the signal for the final act of the night, the theme music for the performer many had come to cheer tonight. It was synonymous with his daring acts of bravery and defiance. As the loud tenor voice boomed all around, the crowd rose expectedly.

"And now," Heavy began, building up the drama, "ladies and gentlemen, behold one of the premier attractions in world circus today. Direct from Hollywood, California, Klondike's Circus proudly presents the daredevil sensation…the debonair king of the air…the one and only Gino Shapiro!"

The big top erupted as a lithe, musclebound figure, with tanned skin and swept back, jet-black hair walked onto the arena floor. He was wearing his legendary firebrand orange tights, vest and cape. Holding his arms wide, he soaked up the heavy applause, before nodding towards two figures behind him.

"And let's hear it for our fellow high-flyers, Nicky Shapiro, and the beautiful bombshell, Jenny Cross."

Nicky Shapiro and Jenny Cross stepped forward and joined hands with Gino. They were clad in similar orange clothing, and the trio looked like comic book characters as they raised their hands aloft. Then, with a whirlwind flourish, Gino removed his cape and hurled it back towards Heavy. Klondike watched the jazzy entrance from his post just behind. "They love you, Gino," he called out.

The charismatic Italian/Mexican offered him a wave, then all three trapeze artists jogged towards the centre of the floor.

Klondike and Lacey glanced up, high above, to the rigged trapeze lines. This was the part of the show where they might get neckache.

The act was underway. Gino, Nicky and Jenny made for three ropes that dangled from the big top ceiling and led to their rings. Gino, of course, took centre ring, with Nicky on one and Jenny on three.

The flyers shot up the ropes like wild cats. As they slithered high above the arena floor, looking smaller and smaller as they rose to the stratosphere, the trio finally reached their rings and sat in place. In unison, they each started rocking back and forth. Then, Nicky and Jenny both dropped backwards, held upside down by their legs over the seat, and let their arms fall into place. With that, Gino stood, somersaulted through the air towards Nicky, who caught his hands, swinging his brother back and forth, before propelling him over to a turret on a circus pole on the far side. Gino landed expertly, waved to the crowd as they applauded, then repeated the feat in reverse, with Nicky helping him onto the centre ring, from where he swung around twice before diving to Jenny, who performed the same support act, propelling him towards a turret at the far end.

As the audience applauded, Lacey, way down at the stage entrance, looked from the three flyers to the arena floor. "Er, Kal," she muttered, glancing around at the sawdust. "Where is the net?"

Klondike laughed. "With these three, there is no net!"

Lacey baulked. "Surely this is too scary for children. Jesus… I can hardly look myself. If they fall, they will die."

Klondike was impassive, gazing up at the flying forms above as they broke into a new routine. "They won't fall."

Lacey glared at him, shocked. Suddenly, she felt she had glimpsed a different side to the great Kal Klondike. She sensed ruthlessness and authority. The whole scene made her shudder.

High above, Gino performed a solo run, vaulting onto each ring to propel himself across the air from turret to turret. After a return flight, he stood gallantly on his perch, looking down at everyone and soaking up the applause with more flourishes and waves.

Jenny and Nicky were now on the other side of the turret. Now both dived back and manoeuvred their way across to their respective rings. Gino jumped towards Jenny, was spun back and forth twice, before being hurled wildly into the air. Placing his elbows into his knees, Gino performed the revered triple roll, sending him spinning through the atmosphere until he was headed for Nicky, who grabbed his hands, and duly propelled him to the safety of the turret again.

Barely pausing for breath, Gino nodded at his little brother before diving for the support rope. His immense upper body strength sent him hurtling five yards up the rope in a second. Then, as the rope swung wildly, he built up momentum and completed the vaunted leap of faith, flying vertically through the air and catching the ropes to Nicky's ring, before holding them firm and landing in a standing position, directly above his brother, who now sat on the ring seat.

As the cheers and applause continued, Gino swung back and vaulted across to his centre ring. Three objects had been tied to each of the support ropes at the bottom by helpers. Now, the three trapeze artists pulled at the ropes to bring the suspended items up to their perches.

Gino had a wooden chair, Jenny what looked like a cosmetics bag and Nicky a blindfold. The three took it in turns to perform their specialty act. First, Nicky tied on the blindfold before performing a handstand on the ring.

Then, Jenny sat delicately in her ring seat, let her hands leave the ring ropes, and balanced herself. She opened the pouch, and began applying lipstick, mascara and eyeliner. She then pretended to fall backwards to a gasp from the crowd, before again letting her legs support her as she swung upside down and blew kisses to the audience.

Finally, as a drum roll sounded from the speakers, Gino balanced one front leg and one back leg from his chair on the ring seat before moving himself onto the chair itself.

Slowly, he put both feet on the chair base, rose to a standing position and, finally, let go of the ring ropes. He balanced like that for a full ten seconds, wobbling absurdly, but remaining elevated on the chair. When he finally grabbed the ropes again, he picked up the chair with his legs, before swinging into a sitting down position on the ring again, with the chair falling onto his lap.

The applause was thunderous as the three flyers waved and held their arms aloft as they swung from their positions.

"And now," said Heavy into the microphone from far below, "hold your breath and rub your eyes in disbelief as Gino Shapiro performs that most daring of feats… The high wire."

Smiling and waving to all around, Gino had descended his support rope by twenty feet until he reached a piece of apparatus that had been assembled during his routine high above.

The high wire. Two platforms rising fifty feet off the ground, with a slim ten-yard line of metal cable covered in welded plastic shooting between them. Below, a clean drop to the circus sawdust.

As Jenny and Nicky watched from the rings above, Gino sat on the far platform, and took a pre-laid bowl of powder onto his lap. Covering his hands in the gunk, he rubbed it all over the soles of his feet. Then, a helper ascended the stairs that ran down the platform and handed him a long metal pole.

The drum roll sounded again. A collective hush fell over the floor. Gino held a hand high to acknowledge the silence. Then, he drew the pole horizontally across him and held it lightly in the palms of each hand.

Every pair of eyes in the behemoth tent was fixed on the man in orange, suspended in mid-air, as he began the walk, moving slowly, his footsteps joining up one after another.

At the stage entrance, Lacey found herself looking away. Plum was holding a hand over his eyes. Klondike stood, arms folded, studying Gino's poise and posture. As often happened at this time, various other performers had gathered at the platform to watch the incredible high wire act.

Gino never once faltered, never swayed and never broke his rhythm or his stride as he walked, trance-like, straight across the high wire, reaching the other end in about ninety seconds. As his feet hit the opposite platform, he held both hands aloft in celebration and punched the air.

Every patron in the house was on their feet, clapping and cheering and staring in disbelief. The applause lasted a good two minutes.

"See him, love him, never forget him," screamed Heavy as the show reached fever pitch. "That's Gino Shapiro."

Gino blew kisses in all directions, before slowly descending the stairs, and a return to the ground at last. Nicky and Jenny slid down their ropes and joined him at the bottom for a group bow.

The three then jogged to the backstage platform, where they were greeted by Klondike and Lacey, who embraced them warmly.

"Gino, you're the greatest," Klondike was saying, hands on the flyer's arms as he shook him. "You nailed every one of them. Hell, this will be the talk of the west coast."

Shapiro smiled back at him, the sweat giving his tanned body a sheen. "Of the world!" he said, still slightly breathless. His chest was heaving, and he gripped his left shoulder. "I am going to make you the envy of everyone in this industry, chairman. You just wait and see."

Klondike laughed boisterously, slapping the trapeze artist on the back. He locked eyes on Jenny, stood just behind. "Well done, Jenny," he said weakly.

"Oh," said the blonde in the wet make-up, "don't mind me, boss man. I'm sure there's money to be counted. Contracts to be drawn up. You better run along."

With a pout, she waltzed past him after Gino and Nicky. Lacey watched the whole exchange with interest. She caught Klondike's eye, and whispered. "The whole story. Later."

Klondike shrugged, annoyed. Then, listening to the endless applause in the grandstands all around, he smiled and waved his hand through the air.

"Just listen to that," he said, mesmerised, "that's all I want to talk about."

Lacey looked up at the crowds, and smiled. "Incredible."

Plum seemed transfixed as he stared up at the cheering thousands. They were all around him, a cascade of noise and excitement. "Just listen to these people," he said dumbly. "They're going crazy. This show… This show is a sensation!" He looked at Klondike in shock. "We can take this show everywhere. Look at the people. Everyone will pay to see this. We… We need more dates. More venues. More merchandise. A fan club. TV appearances…"

"Hey, take it easy Richie," Klondike said, grinning. "Let's just see how the season pans out before we start planning to take over the world."

Lacey watched the exchange. "He's right," she mused, "we need to expand." She smiled at Klondike. "I'll take care of it."

He chuckled. "Of course!"

The trio were stirred from their backstage discussion by the thundering voice of Heavy, stood just before them.

"Ladies and gentlemen, we hope you have enjoyed your evening. We now present to you the finale of our circus spectacular, the grand parade. Please show your appreciation for the stars and sparkle of Klondike's Circus. And let's hear it for our very own singing starlet, Miss Suzi Dando."

It was time for the show's big ending, the grand parade. The finale saw all of the circus stars paraded around on eight sets of giant float trucks, that had been decorated in the traditional red and blue colours, with plenty of tinsel and bright banners.

It was also Suzi's time to shine. As music filled the public address system, the first truck of the parade motored in through the entrance flap. The back canvas was decorated to look like an old-fashioned royal crown room, with Suzi seated in a giant throne in the centre.

As the vehicle entered the arena floor, Suzi broke into song, her beautiful high voice singing the circus's trademark anthem, 'Can You Feel the Magic Tonight'. It had been written years earlier by Heavy, and its lyrics suggested circus performers brought dreams to life, and that the big top was a land of magic and make believe.

As Suzi sang, the procession of float trucks followed the lead vehicle, with all travelling around the floor in one final lap of honour.

The second truck carried the midway workers, who all waved enthusiastically. Roddy Olsen was being carried on the shoulders of several backstage helpers in the centre, with Rusty Fox and Napoleon on each arm. All three bowed as the applause rang out.

The next truck featured Amanda Hart and Hans, along with several clowns. The four elephants walked alongside the truck as it roamed round in a circle. The applause continued.

Then came the showcase performers, who continued their earlier act on the back of their truck as Gargantua, Rumpy and Goliath all tried to fight off Percy Pringle's midgets as they climbed on them and vaulted away.

The bareback riders were next, riding between trucks and performing more stunts on their horses as they waved and acknowledged the cheers.

The next truck had a jungle theme and carried Emile Rance, all on his own. The South African cracked his whip several times as the vehicle motored along slowly, bowing professionally.

Behind the jungle-themed truck came a lorry carrying a red and blue gazebo, with Cathy Cassidy and her chimps all dancing together, arm in arm, to Suzi's song.

Next up was a bright yellow truck, which carried Corky and the rest of the clown revue. As Corky juggled a set of balls, several of the clowns passed balloons to junior members of the audience.

Finally, as the motors went round and round the big top, a large orange truck joined the ensemble. This one featured what looked like an Olympic medal podium on the back, with Gino, in the middle of course, flanked by Jenny and Nicky on the elevated platforms. Gino was now dressed in a pink-feathered robe, and held his arms high as the cheers grew louder and louder.

On the platform, Lacey shook her head. "I was right," she whispered to Klondike, "he is a prince from another planet. What planet, I'm not entirely sure."

The trucks all turned into a formation in the centre of the arena floor, as Suzi reached the climax of the seemingly never-ending song. As she finished with one last high note, she waved excitedly in a 360-degree arc, entranced by the packed grandstands full of screaming fans.

Then, with a final growl, the parade of trucks all headed in a line for the flap in the tent. The show was over.

"Ladies and gentleman," Heavy began again, "on behalf of everyone here at Klondike's Circus, I would like to thank you all for joining us tonight. There are many pretenders, many wonders… But there is only one Klondike's Circus. We hope you can feel the magic tonight. Please join our west coast tour. Next show is Wednesday at Eureka. Until then, goodnight one and all. And God bless America."

Heavy bowed before following the trucks and horses off the arena floor.

And that was opening night.

Chapter 11

The following day, after the mammoth task of clearing out the field and returning everything to the carriages and freight holders, the circus train was back on the rails.

The next stop, Eureka, was barely 80 miles away, and the locomotive adopted a smooth, steady pace as it headed south through a pathway surrounded by rich, rolling countryside.

In the rear, Heavy had joined Klondike in his stateroom for their usual debriefing session as the train got underway.

Both men were grinning like hyenas as they sat around the central table, scouring through the morning's newspapers, which were scattered across the surface alongside plates of sweet rolls and sandwiches and a pot of coffee.

The day after a show, Klondike and Heavy would go over the various printed reviews, exchange thoughts and observations and, vitally, go over the returns books, provided by their cashiers from the ticket booth and midway stalls. Plum was now responsible for the books, so the two men busied themselves with the reviews.

"Listen to this," Klondike drawled, pulling an unlit cigar from his mouth. He held aloft a copy of the Santa Cruz Herald and read the text aloud: "I have no hesitation in declaring Klondike's Circus as one of the greatest spectacles ever to land in our town. A perfect show in every respect. From the stalls outside and the friendly hawkers, to the majesty of the big top performers, many of whom took the breath away from the watching thousands."

Heavy nodded, sipping at his coffee. He motioned towards a copy of the Santa Cruz Gazette he had been reading. "How about this: 'Klondike's Circus was a joy throughout. There was old-fashioned circus tradition, with mischievous clowns, bareback horse riders and monkeys and elephants. There was a freak show, with giants and midgets. And there were individual acts that proved astonishing. Lion tamer Emile Rance stunned the audience with his act, which included an extraordinary sequence where he endured a group hug of sorts with his two lions and white tiger. The beloved Corky the Clown also drew gasps of disbelief with his impossibly fast juggling skills, including one set piece in which he juggled pins that were on fire. And, of course, the legendary Gino Shapiro brought the house down with the show's finale, as he twirled through the air high above the floor with his famous trapeze act and high wire walk. What a star! The only question now is can the stars of Klondike's Circus maintain this incredible high standard for a full season? We will see, but one thing's for sure – circus fans will lap up this showtime spectacular.'"

Klondike nodded approvingly. "That's how we like it," he said, pouring more coffee. "So," he added, "what did you make of it all, old buddy?"

Heavy lent back. "I got to tell ya, Kal, I can't think of any faults. Everything, everyone, looked fresh. The guys killed it. McCabe's team did just fine. No hiccups. No hold-ups." He ran a hand through his thinning hair. "If it weren't for my sore throat, I'd say I feel on top of the world."

"It's only sore cos it's your first time yelling like that for six months," Klondike consoled him.

Heavy rubbed at his Adam's apple, grimacing. "How about that so-called group hug Emile pulled off?"

Klondike gazed out the window at the rolling countryside as the train cruised along. "Something else. Frightening. Breathtaking. Y'know, I don't know who's scarier… Rance or those lions."

Heavy nodded. "Well, I think it's fair to say all the new routines paid off…and then some."

"I couldn't agree more."

Heavy studied his old friend and boss. "And, er, Lacey's ideas really did the trick, don't you think, Kal?"

Klondike smiled knowingly. "It's OK, Heavy, I am with you. That crazy woman… I tell ya… I don't know where she came from, or what goes with her, but she is a natural at this. Her plans going forward are gold. Merchandising. The fan club. TV. She has contacts everywhere. She's already ordered hundreds more publicity pictures to be with us in San Francisco."

"How?"

Klondike shrugged. "She just says she'll take care of it and that's all she wrote, as they say."

Both men shook their heads.

At that moment, there was a brief knock at the door, and Lacey herself marched in, closely followed by Richie Plum.

The publicity ace was wearing fashionable purple trousers and a white woolly sweater. She looked like she had just walked out of an episode of Lifestyles of the Rich and Famous.

"Congratulations boys," she roared, motioning towards the papers on the table. "The reviews are out of this world. Fabulous! You did it, Kal, you put on a master show." She circled around the table, helping herself to a cinnamon roll before lighting a cigarette and perching herself on the dresser. Plum sat at the table, placed a pile of books on the surface and reached for the coffee.

"OK boys," Lacey said, finishing her roll and toking on the cigarette in one fluid motion. She leant forward, all business. "Let's have a debriefing session. There is much to discuss." The three men stared at her, almost standing to attention. "I want to begin with you," she said teasingly but sharply, pointing at Klondike.

The circus boss rolled his eyes, knowing exactly what was coming. He raised both hands, palms out. "First of all, I plead innocent of all charges."

She ignored him. "What's the story with Jenny Cross? I saw how she spoke to you. She can't talk to you like that, dammit."

Klondike grimaced. "All right. We were an item once. Two seasons ago. It lasted one summer. I called it off because it was wrong. It just took me a while to figure that out, I guess." He shook his head. "She…she didn't handle it well. She hates me now. Big time."

Lacey's beautiful violet eyes were wide in fright and alarm. "Why in heaven's name didn't you fire her?"

Klondike stared at her. "Why do you think?"

She nodded. "Of course. She's integral to the show. How many people can have that telepathic understanding with Gino and do all those things in the air? As well as looking like she does. You can't replace all that."

"Not to mention Gino trusts her and has looked after her. He was her mentor for years. They have that bond. All three of them. Gino is the star, and you don't mess around with your top guy."

Lacey seemed lost in thought. "Kal, did you love her?"

He squirmed in the chair under her powerful gaze. "Hell, no. Well…it's complicated. It never should have happened."

She persisted, sensing danger. "And Kal, this is very important…how did she feel about you?"

Klondike shrugged awkwardly, glanced at Heavy, then spoke weakly. "She was crazy about me. In awe of me, I guess. Hell, it's like the starlet falling for the director. She looked up to me. That was the…the…"

"The dynamic," she finished for him. She toked at her cigarette. "And how is Gino with all this?"

Klondike looked more comfortable. "The consummate professional. It hasn't affected him at all. He's barely even mentioned it."

Lacey pondered this. "Interesting." She thought for a moment. "So what we have is an uneasy alliance. But everyone does their thing for the good of the circus, huh?"

Klondike nodded. "That's about the whole of it."

She nodded, rose, and paced around the stateroom, fidgeting with the cigarette. She walked to a wall mirror by the door and examined herself for several moments, touching her hair. As the three men stared at her, strangely transfixed, she suddenly walked over to the table and stubbed out her smoke.

"All right," she cried, making them jump, "on to business, boys." She poured herself a cup of coffee, and returned to perch on the dresser, clutching the cup close to her. "My immediate observation. We need to make more of Suzi Dando. That beautiful child can sing like an angel. She looks terrific. I say let's include her with Cathy and the chimps, like I said before. We're paying her well…but all she's doing is one song. Let's get her more involved."

Klondike nodded thoughtfully. Heavy seemed to like this idea. He had always been fond of Suzi's singing. "I think that's a great plan," he mused, "Suzi is popular and brings in the youth crowd. Her and Cathy would go well together. But what will she sing for that routine?"

Lacey didn't even pause for thought. "Monkeying Around." She laughed aloud. "I'll get the backing track on record."

Heavy stared at her. "How? Where? That'll take weeks."

She smiled down at him, as Klondike spoke for her. "She takes care of things, Heavy. It's what she does."

"Let's just say I know a guy," Lacey put in.

"What about the kid? Roddy?" Plum finally spoke, and sounded like he had been aching to ask this question all morning.

Lacey looked questioningly down at Klondike. "Well, boss man?"

Klondike smiled, gnawing at his still unlit cigar. "Hell, I just don't know. I think for now let's keep him on the midway. He's just embarking on a whole new way of life. Let's steadily drive him into it."

Plum was unusually adamant, his red skin glowing. "He deserves a place on the bill, Klondike! Come on!"

Klondike didn't rise to the angry response, but held up his hands. "I know. And I think he'll get it. But we have to come up with the best way to utilise his talents. We can't just throw him in headfirst. If he drowns, it could destroy him. We must be careful."

"Well," Lacey said in shock, "big Kal Klondike does have a heart after all." She smiled down at him sweetly. "Bravo, Kalvin, bravo. A perfect response. And I couldn't agree more. The kid is ready, I think we all agree on that, but accommodating him is a new dilemma." She thought for a moment. "Let's dissect the show in Eureka, Kal. Act by act. We need to note audience responses, where there's drama and where there's calm. I want your thoughts on all the reactions."

"Right," Klondike grunted. He waved a hand through the air, sipped his coffee, and looked across at Plum. "Now, if nobody else has any wise guy ideas about transforming my show, I think we'd all like to hear from good old Richie here, and what our takings were." No one objected. He continued. "How about it, Richie?"

The smaller man cracked a rare smile, opening the first book on his small pile. "Everything is better than I expected."

Heavy leaned closer. "Are we in the black, pal?"

Plum nodded studiously. "We are."

"How much?" Heavy barked.

"Well, it's thousands, as opposed to hundreds. I just need to —"

Heavy was laughing aloud, clapping his hands in delight. He grabbed Klondike by the sleeve and shook his head. "I knew it! I knew it! We were raking it in. A sell-out crowd. The queues in the midway. The gross is out of sight. Ha ha, it's a smash!"

Klondike smiled at him. "What else, Richie?"

The accountant looked through the returns books, put off by Heavy's loud boyishness. He continued quietly: "The takings were very impressive. Every ticket sold. Ten thousand spectators. The midway returns were also way over what I predicted. I had no idea paying customers would go for all that carnival gaming." He adjusted his glasses shyly. "I guess I'm a bit out of my depth." He got back on track. "But these figures are all above any predictions I calculated. However, to get a true confirmed number I need to go through all your spending over the winter, find out how much all this costs in total – the train, maintenance, equipment, all spending, including everyone's salary – then divide that by 21, for each show, and obtain a spend average. Then, I'll compare the average, or mean, with how much each show brings in on average. That will give us a final figure."

Klondike and Heavy stared at him dumbfounded as Lacey giggled in the corner.

"Can we leave all that to you, pal?" Heavy mumbled.

"Yes. I have it all under control."

"Thank god."

Klondike shook his head at the comical exchange. Finally, he lit his cigar, and waved it around triumphantly, the thick smoke forming a dark purple cloud above the table. "OK. We keep this up and we got us a healthy profit. I want sell-outs in every town now. There's no reason we can't recreate what we did last night at every stop along the way. Starting with Eureka."

Lacey clapped excitedly. "Wait till you see my press release for the Eureka Daily News! I'll be quoting those reporters from the Santa Cruz papers. We'll whip everybody up into a frenzy."

Klondike cocked his head. "What about these TV and radio people you keep harping on about? Let's get Gino and Corky into the studios for promotions."

She held up a hand. "All in good time, tiger. When we near Los Angeles, there will be plenty of exposure on air. That's TV land."

Klondike chuckled, taking it all in. He looked from the glamorous Lacey, to the deadpan Plum, to the wisecracking Heavy.

"Roll on Eureka!" he roared.

The circus train duly arrived in the small coastal town of Eureka later that afternoon.

The crowd that greeted the dynamic red and blue locomotive was not as large as that which had cheered wildly in Santa Cruz, but was still an enthusiastic ensemble.

The circus was pitched up at the Rosemont Gardens, separated from the railroad by a short promenade. Once again, the locals were impressed by the smoothness and military-like operation as the roustabouts and local helpers unloaded the endless masses of equipment and slowly manoeuvred everything into place.

As the big top was erected and the stalls and booths were driven into position, many of the performers took the time to enjoy an afternoon of recreation in the charming small town.

Amanda and Cathy headed straight for a coffee shop they had remembered from previous visits. Both happily chatted with locals as they walked the streets.

Corky headed into town in full clown attire, joined by several members of the clown revue. The group handed out flyers, performed tricks to passing children and families and essentially completed a mini publicity tour as they roamed the town centre, generating interest in the show.

Roddy and Suzi, who were becoming inseparable, headed for the beach and took in a leisurely stroll along the sand. As they walked, they sang softly together, attracting plenty of glances from the townsfolk with their faultless harmonies.

Emile remained in his stateroom back on the train, eagerly reading a newspaper from his native South Africa that had been mailed to him before the train had departed the winter camp.

Jenny Cross, who never mixed with anyone outside of Gino and Nicky, headed for a cocktail bar, making sure she wasn't followed.

The Shapiro brothers merely walked around the playing fields, stopping to chat to excited passers-by, and acting as if they didn't have a care in the world.

When Nicky headed back to the train, Gino excused himself and set off on a brisk stroll towards the town centre.

As he reached a promenade of shops, the lithe trapeze artist pulled up the collar on his long leather jacket and ducked into a side street, before slipping through a door next to a fire escape stairwell.

He looked up, studying the inside of the building, before consulting a small scrap of paper he pulled from his wallet. Then, with renewed vigour, he mounted a stairwell and stopped outside a door. He looked at the number. 10.

With a grin, he knocked gently.

Seconds later, the door cracked open an inch and a woman dressed in a robe peeked out cautiously. One look at Shapiro and she broke into a gigantic, childlike smile.

"Gino!" she squealed in delight. "You made it! Oh my god, it's really you."

"Of course I made it, mamacita," he said softly.

She opened the door wide. He looked at her. She was just as he remembered. Thick, short auburn hair, green eyes, freckles. "You look even more beautiful than I remember."

"And you," she gasped, eyeing him up and down, "I... I could just eat you up right now."

He laughed. "What's stopping you?"

She pouted. "Shock. Has it been a year already?"

He smiled. "Si."

"I saw the circus was coming, but I didn't know for sure if you'd come. I had no idea what had happened to you."

"Baby," he said teasingly, "of course I come. Coming here, to Eureka, is a highlight for me. All because I get to see you."

She raised a tiny eyebrow. "Do you even know anything about me?"

He looked hurt. "Baby, you insult me." He took her in his arms in the centre of the woman's apartment. "My darling's name is Pamela Shields. Age, 33. Occupation, waitress at Ringo's. Likes, movies, rock n roll music and, of course, going to the circus. Dislikes, jazz, dominoes and that lousy film star Tab Hunter."

She laughed. "You're incredible, Gino. But you forgot one important like."

"And what is that, baby?"

"You!" She jumped at him and they kissed passionately.

Chapter 12

The following morning, disaster struck.

Klondike was shaving at his washbasin, stripped to his waist. As he whistled an old country tune merrily to himself, the door to his stateroom burst open without a warning knock, and in staggered Heavy.

Klondike froze, and studied his old friend in shock, mouth agape.

Heavy was in his dressing gown, and looked terrible. His face was pale, his eyes bloodshot and he was holding his throat in agony.

"Heavy! Heavy!" Klondike cried in alarm. "What the hell? Are…are you OK?"

The big man swarmed over, collapsing into a chair at the table. Klondike, still with half a face of stubble, wiped his skin with a towel and rushed over, putting a hand on Heavy's shoulder.

"What happened, buddy? You look awful."

Heavy clutched at his throat and tried to speak. A vague wheeze came out, but was inaudible. Klondike watched in dismay as his friend snatched a notepad and pen from the table and began to write. His face dropped completely when he read the resultant message Heavy wrote on the paper.

HAVE LOST MY VOICE. THROAT IS ON FIRE.

Klondike ripped the sheet from the pad and stared at it in shock. He looked down at Heavy. The ringmaster was grimacing, shaking with every breath and swallow. He looked up and just about managed to wheeze: "I'm sorry, Kal," the words came out in a tiny, strangulated voice.

Klondike patted the meaty shoulder, studying the man's appearance. He looked like the life was draining out of him. He thought fast, rubbing his friend's shoulders comfortingly.

"It's all right, old buddy," he said weakly, looking around as if trying to find a cure. "It's OK, just try to breathe normally now. We'll get you fixed up, you bet we will." He walked in front of his seated companion. "Is it tonsillitis? Or worse? Any idea?"

Heavy held up both hands and shrugged. "Back of throat," he wheezed coarsely.

Klondike stared down at him. He was thinking desperately. His eyes caught hold of his clock on the wall. 48 hours. That's all they had until the show. He looked again at Heavy, who was still clutching his throat, a strange gurgling sound emerging from his lips as he tried to speak again. Klondike poured him a glass of water and watched him drink. Then, with a curse, he admitted defeat.

Moving to the door, he pulled it open and yelled at the top of his voice: "Lacey! Get in here!"

The publicity expert was in the room in less than 30 seconds. She too was dressed in a robe, though hers was bright pink with feathered edges. Klondike ignored her appearance as she breezed in, looking alarmed.

He showed her the note. She studied it, before looking at Heavy with motherly concern.

"It's OK, Henry," she said soothingly, pulling up a chair next to him and gazing gingerly into his big blue eyes. "It's probably just a sore throat. You haven't roared like you did on Saturday for some time." She reached over and moved his hands aside before opening his mouth with her fingers. After a brief examination for god only knew what, she let the mouth close. "Can you talk at all, Henry?" she whispered.

He shrugged and swallowed hard. "Just," he breathed in that coarse whisper. "It's killing me to get anything out…" Klondike and Lacey could barely hear his muffled tones. Finally, they looked at each other, their eyes locking in a mutual understanding that reflected defeat and concern.

Lacey patted his fleshy hand reassuringly. "Don't worry," she said, "we'll get you to a doctor in town. Right away. Go get changed next door and one of the boys will run you down to the surgery."

He looked up hopefully, before nodding and scuttling out of the room.

Once the door closed, Lacey leant against it and folded her arms. She looked Klondike over coolly. He had pulled on a vest and was rubbing at his leftover stubble.

"So," she began quietly, "we now have a ringmaster who cannot talk. An announcer who cannot announce. A host who cannot introduce anyone." She rolled her eyes, tugging at her loose red hair as it fell across her shoulders. She looked somehow out of sorts, caught off guard. The flaming hair was wild, not styled, and her skin looked raw and paler than usual.

He looked at her, and their eyes locked together again for several moments. "Time for a big decision, circus boss," she mused.

"We've got 48 hours," Klondike replied nervously, pulling on a sweater.

"Indeed." She caught her reflection in the mirror, and shuddered. Then, she turned to him abruptly. "Think fast, baby. We need a plan. And we need one now." She walked over to him, almost jovially, as she fiddled with her hair. "It must be tonsillitis. Or worse. A sore throat wouldn't just knock his voice out like that."

Klondike shook his head. "Thank you, Dr Tanner."

She frowned at him. "You really need a doctor to tell you he's in a bad way? Kalvin, your ringmaster is sick. Sick! We need to figure out what to do. Now!"

Klondike nodded ruefully. "I'm thinking."

They both paced around sullenly. Lacey sat at the table, and Klondike fiddled nervously with his shaving gear. They locked eyes yet again. When it happened for a fourth time, moments later, they both smiled queerly at one another.

Klondike pretended it hadn't happened. "Well?" he barked.

Lacey smiled girlishly. "Oh, Kal. Are you thinking what I'm thinking?"

"What?"

"Come, come. I think you are."

Klondike nodded. "All right, I think I am."

She was grinning broadly now. "Well?"

He shook, almost convulsively. "Oh god," he stammered. He caught his reflection in the shaving mirror above the washbasin. "What am I getting myself into? God damn it, how has it come to this?"

"Fate. Doors close. Doors open. And round and round we all go." Now, she sounded like a ruthless PR shark.

Klondike stared at himself again. "God help me."

Roddy Olsen slowly looked up, his eyes wide and bright. He had been washing at his basin, and now leant against the wall in his stateroom, a towel draped around his shoulders over a vest.

"You want me to be the host?" he said, as if mesmerised.

"No," Klondike snapped. "We want you to be ringmaster. But only while Heavy is sick."

Olsen gazed at him in awe. "That's perfect," he whispered, as if to himself.

Klondike frowned. "Perfect? For what? For you? For us? What do you mean?"

The youngster smiled back. "For them. The fans."

Klondike and Lacey had entered his room moments earlier. They had broken the news about Heavy immediately, before pitching their offer to him. Olsen had continued washing, until they had got to the part about him taking Heavy's place in the big top.

Now, both stared at the ever-confident youngster as he folded his arms and gazed into nothingness, as if in a dream.

"Roddy," Lacey began in a warm, motherly tone, "we have total faith in you. We want you to know that. We have both been enthralled by your talent. Your performance on the midway only underlined that. And now we want to give you this chance...this honour. The role of ringmaster is very important, one of the biggest roles in any circus, and we believe you deserve this opportunity."

Klondike nodded, still studying the teenager. "Yes, yes. It's a massive opportunity for you, kid. It's come quicker than I thought it would. Now, the question I have for you is...are you up to it?"

Olsen smiled beautifully, looking as relaxed as a patron in a bar. "You bet, Mr Klondike," he said boyishly. "This is the big opportunity I've been waiting for. I won't let you down, I swear to god. I've been waiting for a new challenge. A gig like this. And I want to thank you for giving me the chance to shine."

Klondike shrugged awkwardly as the youngster walked across the room and shook his hand sincerely. He then offered a hand to Lacey, who joyfully rushed forward and hugged him. Both laughed. "You can do it, Roddy!" Lacey was squealing. "I know you can. Kal and I have such faith in you. Ever since you first entered the tent. This is your moment!"

Klondike glared at the embrace. "All right," he murmured. Then, he addressed Olsen directly. "This is my decision, kid, and I've got to live by it. I've just elected to appoint a new ringmaster. A 19-year-old with no experience. Nothing! If you stink the place up, people are going to be reminding me of this for years. And you'll be finished in this industry."

Olsen was still smiling. "I can do it, Mr Klondike."

"OK, there are strict rules. I'll get you Heavy's script. Basically, you must memorise the introductions for each act. Er, outside of that, you can just go along and…er, you can…"

"I can do my act?" he exclaimed.

"Well, yes, you just do your thing. Like you have been all this time."

"Do I get creative control?"

Klondike frowned. It was all happening too fast. "Up to a point. Listen, kid, we got 48 hours. I'll be back tonight. Then we'll go through how you want to play this. I imagine a small skit between each act will be adequate. You just have a think, go through your repertoire of sketches, and let me know later what you'll be saying and when. But my decision is final, got it? If I don't like your material, it's out. You got a problem with that, and you're out!"

Olsen nodded enthusiastically. Lacey patted him on the back. "Perfect," he said again.

Lacey giggled. "You will give Eureka a real show, Roddy. It can really work. A little touch of your act between each of the circus performers."

"I love it," Olsen said, beaming. He looked down at his beloved suitcase. "I will be the host, but Rusty will think he is the host and will ultimately introduce all the acts. Before I can. Then Napoleon can take over. He should introduce Emile for sure. Maybe Tony Tan can sing High Hopes before Gino goes on." He looked up at Klondike. "I can do songs, right? Maybe I can work something in to sing with Suzi at the end!"

Klondike looked about vaguely. "To be honest, I'm not sure about any of that." He paused. "But the people seem to like you and your puppets, kid. There's no doubting that. But this is your big test now, sonny, make no qualms about that."

Olsen didn't seem to hear him. "I can interact with the performers. Corky will love it! I just know he will."

Klondike shook his head. "Listen," he barked, "just have a plan for what you want to do by eight tonight. Coz that's when I come knocking. We'll go over everything then." He made to leave the room, exhausted already and it wasn't even nine. He paused at the door, and finally smiled at the youngster hopping excitedly before him. "Well done, Roddy."

He left, wandering into the corridor. Lacey patted Olsen again on the back, and made to follow the circus boss. She blushed at Olsen and said gaily: "This is your chance, Roddy. Show everyone what a star you are."

As the door closed, Olsen stared at it dumbly. Then, as if activated by some hidden device, he sat at his desk and began furiously scribbling notes. He didn't stop for some time.

Out in the train corridor, Lacey caught up with Klondike at a joiner doorway.

"OK, what next, tiger? Things are moving at a lightning speed already this morning. Hell, I can't wait for tomorrow's show."

Klondike kept on moving. "I'm calling an executive council meeting for noon. I need to tell the guys about all this. This is a major change to the show. They may not like it."

Lacey touched his arm. "Shouldn't Roddy now be in the executive council?"

Klondike grunted. "I know you're his number one fan. But first he has to prove himself. If he pulls it off tomorrow in my big top…then he can earn a call-up to the executive council."

Lacey laughed. "And just where is this meeting taking place? In the dining car?"

"The hell with that! McCabe's crew erected the tent yesterday. So we're meeting in the big top!"

The so-called executive council gathered in the bleachers by the tent entrance and backstage platform. Everyone sat on the wooden bench seats as Klondike explained Heavy's ailment and the subsequent elevation of Roddy Olsen to ringmaster.

The empty circus tent looked forlorn and barren without any spectators inside. The endless rows of wooden benches seemed to stretch into the heavens, reaching up to the lofty tarpaulin roof hanging high above.

As was common practice with such meetings, everyone remained silent until Klondike finished speaking. Then the inevitable questions and, in this case, exclamations followed.

As usual, Gino Shapiro was first off the mark. Seated on the third row in the strange, eerie quiet of the spectator area, his sharp Latino accent echoed around the big top like a tenor in a concerto.

"Chairman, I must object to this development. The doll maker is an outsider. He is an amateur. He works on the midway. There is no place for him in our show." He narrowed his eyes. "I have seen his tricks. He will use this chance to throw those damn dolls in everyone's faces. Is that you want for your show?"

Klondike, standing before the group on the circus floor, opened his mouth to speak but, predictably, Lacey beat him to it. She was sat on the front row, on the edge, and turned to face Gino at the back.

"Actually, Gino," she said shrewdly, "Roddy has performed in all sorts of shows. He is only 19, but he is already a veteran in show business."

Shapiro frowned down at her. "He has you fooled with his tricks, madam publicist." His stare returned to Klondike. "Do not let him be the host, chairman. He does not deserve it!"

As Lacey pouted, Klondike nodded at Shapiro.

Emile Rance, seated slightly away from the group in the middle bench, spoke next. "I agree with Gino," he said gruffly. "You can't just give a kid off the street the ringmaster's mic. Not like that. We don't know anything about him."

Cathy Cassidy nodded. "Listen," she began, "he is cute. And I mean real cute. I know he looks like a star already and everybody seems to love him. But ringmaster? Come on, Kal. Let's get serious."

Klondike kept nodding, looking about the group. To his surprise, Corky spoke next, rising to his feet and addressing the gathering as one.

"You know what I think?" he said, smiling widely as usual. "I think maybe you all don't know talent when you see it. That kid is a gem. I tell ya, he's a gem. And I should know. I've toured in comedy clubs and variety acts for 20 years. His form of ventriloquism is light years ahead of anything out there. On TV. In Hollywood. Possibly in the world. Like Cathy says, he looks like a movie star. His confidence is beyond equal. He can work a crowd. I say…bravo, Kal, bravo. A brave move. But I like it. His act is ideally suited to the role of a host or compere."

"That's all very well," Cathy said, taking an interest in the clown's overview, "but we're talking about suddenly putting him in the sawdust. As ringmaster! He came here from nowhere. Just walked right into the camp."

Rance nodded vigorously. "He has no experience!"

Lacey stood and glared at the lion tamer. "How the hell is anyone supposed to get experience if no one will give him a shot?"

"This is too big a gig," Cathy said, taking a firm interest in the proceedings. "We should put him with the clown revue or the showcase to begin with. Not throw him straight into this!"

"No, no, I have seen the kid perform," Corky was saying, almost poetically. "I say he is ready."

Shapiro glared down the rows of seats. "Come off it, clown. We're talking ten thousand people. An arena crowd!"

Klondike interjected at that moment. "Actually, we never sell out in Eureka. This is our smallest town, and possibly our smallest crowd. There simply aren't ten thousand spectators out there, even if we were to go door to door raising interest. And therein lies the key to this move. I'm giving Roddy the gig here, in Eureka, as it's probably our most uninfluential gig of the season, with all due respect to the residents. Listen, if we're going to do this, we might as well do it here. If he does bomb, no one will ever hear of it. No one important, anyway."

Shapiro was adamant. "I still don't like it, chairman. Who cares about this funny kid and his stupid dolls?"

Lacey answered again. "Well, I guess we'll all find out tomorrow, won't we?"

Everyone seemed to agree with that. Klondike glanced over at Amanda Hart, seated in the middle. "What say, Mandy? Are you a fan of our boy?"

The blonde smiled broadly. "I sure am, Kal. And what a nice kid. I say let him bring the house down!"

Finally, he turned to the strangely quiet Suzi Dando, who was sat next to Lacey. She had remained silent throughout the exchanges, aware that everyone present knew she and Roddy had become close friends.

"It's OK, Suzi," Klondike said softly. "You can say your bit. We're all friends here."

The youngster looked up shyly, her large bunny eyes bright and alive. "Everyone knows how I feel about Roddy," she murmured. "Yeah, we're tight. We're pals. We're the same generation." She looked around at the performers seated all about her. "I might as well tell you guys what I think. What I really think. I think Roddy Olsen is the most talented man I have ever met. And I think he's going to be a smash hit. A great discovery for you, Mr Klondike."

Klondike smiled down at her and nodded. Her comments were dismissed by Shapiro at the back, who made a grunting noise and cried: "The nonsensical ramblings of a child! I plead with you, chairman. Do not give the doll maker the gig."

"I'm sorry, Gino," Klondike said gently. "The decision has been made."

Shapiro sat back, folding his arms. "As you say, chairman."

With that, the meeting was concluded. Klondike made a few announcements about the weather and some of the VIPs who would be attending the show, before the executive council slowly sank off the bleachers.

All except Lacey and Richie Plum, who joined Klondike on the arena floor. Lacey looked back at the departing performers as they left the tent.

"Tough call," she said, "but I guess that's why you are the boss."

"You've played a winning hand," Plum said with no emotion. "This kid's going to be a hit with everyone."

Klondike looked from one to the other, then wandered around the circus floor idly. His empire had been transformed in a few short weeks. Now, he found himself reporting to a dour accountant with a bloodsucking mentality, and a publicity expert who acted like a high society countessa. On top of that, he was handing over the ringmaster's mic to a 19-year-old ventriloquist.

He scratched at his chin. "OK, PR queen," he said to Lacey. "We need to think fast. How do we market Olsen? What do we call him? Gino is the debonair king of the air. Corky is the world's greatest clown. Emile is the lord of the jungle. How about this kid? The boy who can make everything talk?"

Lacey stepped forward, spreading her arms wide as if the tent was full of cheering spectators. "Roddy Olsen," she proclaimed, "the puppetmaster!"

"I like it," Plum cried.

Klondike nodded in acceptance. "I can see you've been working on that," he said dryly. He looked around the empty big top, bending and grabbing a fistful of sawdust. "This is a different kind of ringmaster routine. We've got to work it differently. It ain't a traditional run like Heavy does. This is talent calling talent."

Lacey followed him on the circus floor. "You're absolutely right, Kal. Why don't we call him host instead of ringmaster? A new term for…for a new image."

Klondike just gazed at the sawdust as he let it filter through his fingertips. "What else?"

She smiled, knowing he guessed she had plans in motion. "Let me dress him, Kal. This isn't a red jacket and top hat gig. This is something new and exciting."

Klondike held up a hand and sighed. "Lacey," he drawled, "you haven't let me down once since you rolled into camp in that fancy motor of yours. You go ahead and do what you got to do. Make that kid shine. I trust you completely." He looked up towards the 'nose bleed' seats high above them near the tent's ceiling. "Hell," he mumbled, "have you got anything that will make him look taller?"

Lacey merely smiled emphatically. "He won't need it. True talent stands out on its own."

Suzi Dando ran excitedly back to the train, climbing aboard the fourth carriage and racing down the corridor until she reached the door next to her own.

She was about to knock, but heard Olsen talking aloud. She smiled. Practice.

She listened, hand over her mouth, as the unmistakable tones of Rusty Fox and Napoleon, then Roddy again, rang out, going through another of the comedy routines.

Finally, the voices stopped, and all was silent. With a gasp of delight, she knocked lightly at the door and breezed into the stateroom.

Olsen was seated at his desk, furiously making notes on a pad, while his puppets sat neatly on the bed.

He looked up and smiled as he saw Suzi enter, jumping up to greet her. She rushed into his arms, not even pausing to think about what she was doing.

"Oh, Roddy!" she cried. "I just heard the news. Mr Klondike held an executive council meeting in the tent and told us all. My god Roddy, you're going to be the ringmaster. I can't believe it."

Olsen smiled down at her as he held her arms, feeling her vibrancy coursing through into him. They stared at each other for several moments, both laughing in a surreal fashion.

"Well," he finally said, "they're calling me the host. It's a different kind of gig to Heavy's."

"It's fantastic!" she panted. "Oh my." She looked at his notes, sprawled all over the desk. "Do you know what you're going to do? What you're going to say? How it will work?"

"Of course," he said softly, "it's perfect. Even Mr Klondike said that. This role suits my act perfectly. I can do brief skits, as we call it. And, well, you know, Suzi, I've got so many brief skits in my repertoire, I can go on all night."

She sat on the bed, her brilliant blue eyes looking innocent and alive at the same time. Coupled with her tidy bob of hazelnut hair, she could have passed for 15 right there and then, such was her youthful vigour and enthusiasm.

"Roddy," she whispered, "you'll even be introducing me."

"I know. Just like we planned. We can sing together. Live, under the big top."

"You can join me on my float. We'll sing 'Can You Feel the Magic Tonight'. Oh boy, what a moment." She looked down at the puppets, and gently stroked Rusty Fox's comical quiff hairdo. "It'll be a perfect showcase for your puppets. Your guys, as you call them." She fiddled with Rusty's imitation fur. "He's so cute. I love him, Roddy."

"Thank you," he mused. "For inviting me onto your float, I mean. That is an honour."

She could not stop smiling up at him. "You deserve it. I can't believe we found you. You found us. And now…this."

Olsen turned and looked out the window at the playing fields beyond. "I can't wait. Can't wait to experience that live, raw feel of an audience again. To be under the spotlight. To soak up the applause. The acclaim. Nothing can match that feeling of live performance. You know that, Suzi."

She shook her head. "You're so confident. So assured. I've never met anyone quite like you."

He chuckled shyly. Then, with a theatrical flourish, he picked up a white box from the dresser, pulling out a shiny, glitzy silver waistcoat. He pulled it on over his white buttoned shirt. "What do you think?" He twirled round in a circle. "Miss Tanner bought it me from town earlier. She wants a new look for her…er, host. No more red coat and top hat."

"Oh Roddy," she purred, "you look like a star."

He studied himself in the mirror. "I guess the good people of Eureka will be the judge of that."

Chapter 13

Eureka. Second Show

To the welcome surprise of Klondike and his staff, the big top was virtually a sell-out for the second show of the season.

Newspaper articles, fed by Lacey's exciting press releases, had galvanised the townsfolk and whipped locals into a frenzy. This feeling had only been enhanced when the circus train rolled into town.

Now, on show night, as Klondike held his customary vigil backstage by the flap and looked around at the packed grandstands, he had to admit he was stunned. He could see not a single empty seat in the arena, and a warm, vibrant atmosphere gripped the big top.

He took a deep breath as the clock reached seven. Time to dance.

Tonight, everything would run a little differently. To begin with, Klondike had elected Lacey to make the opening announcement.

As the crowd cheered and the lights dimmed, he wiped his brow and nodded to the publicist beside him.

Lacey had gone to town, and was dressed in a feathered red and blue showgirl dress, loving every minute of her stage debut.

Now, she walked elegantly towards the microphone stand at the end of the arena floor and waved at the cheering masses. Then, in her rasping, authoritative tone, she spoke into the mic.

"Ladies and gentlemen, boys and girls, this is Klondike's Circus. And now, please welcome your host, the puppet master... Roddy Olsen!"

The audience cheered, though many baffled expressions could be seen among the endless sea of faces. Many of those broke into wide grins when Olsen appeared from the flap, carrying Rusty Fox on his right arm.

Olsen was dressed in the glitzy silver waistcoat Lacey had given him, with his favourite purple shirt beneath. Rusty wore his usual leather jacket.

Watching on as the youngster approached the mic, Klondike and Lacey held their collective breaths.

"Thank you," Olsen cried into the mic. He put one foot onto a high stool next to the stand, and rested the puppet on his lap. "Good evening, and welcome to Klondike's Circus. Thank you for joining us. My name is Roddy Olsen and I am your host for this evening's show and —"

"No, I'm the host!" Rusty barked, interrupting. "How many times have I got to tell you, Roddy, these people are here to see me." The fox puppet looked all around the grandstands. "Thank you for coming out folks, I appreciate it."

"Now, Rusty, we talked about this. No interrupting."

"I'm sorry, Roddy, I'm just so excited." The puppet let out a high-pitched squeal.

Roddy smiled. "Ladies and gentlemen, I'd like to introduce you to my good friend, Rusty Fox."

The crowd, who all sat staring in wonder and surprise at the young man throwing his voice, applauded happily.

"Thank you, thank you," Rusty cried, bowing wildly. "That's Rusty Fox, teen idol. Rock n roll superstar. Yeah!"

"Now, you're a singer, Rusty. But I'm afraid we haven't got time for you to sing any songs tonight. We have acts to introduce. Some of the most amazing performers in the world."

"What!" the little fox blurted. "But I'm a singing sensation. First, I'm a recording artist. Next, I'll be a Hollywood actor. Then, I'll get all the chicks. And you know how foxes like chicks!"

The crowd roared with laughter.

"No!" Roddy said firmly. "There is no time. You can't sing any songs for these people."

The puppet held its head and, right on cue, a sympathetic "ahhh" emanated from the spectators.

"You stink, Roddy," said Rusty Fox. "Get your hands off me!"

"That's impossible...how would you talk?"

"I'm not gunna talk...because, I'm gunna sing!"

With that, Rusty broke into the 'Johnny Cash hit Walk the Line', accompanied by a backing track that played on the PA system. This was a surprise to even Klondike. He glanced at Lacey beside him, who winked slyly. *Incredible,* he thought.

The audience were lapping up the song, clapping and whooping at the end of each verse. Again, Olsen's voice manipulation was stunning, with everyone in the tent watching the little fox puppet as it seemingly belted out the lyrics.

At the song's conclusion, as the crowd applauded, Roddy shook his head. "Well, you can sing, Rusty, I'll give you that. But what else can you do?"

Rusty sniggered. "Well, this is the circus. And I can do this…"

With that, Olsen manoeuvred the puppet's right arm into a beckoning motion. A clown appeared silently behind them, and handed Rusty a custard pie. As Olsen looked around innocently, waiting for something to happen, Rusty slammed the pie into his face.

The audience burst into hearty laughter.

At the flap, Klondike smiled. It was working. Olsen had blended traditional circus slapstick into his act, just as Klondike had suggested. Lacey smiled too, clapping wildly, while the stoic Richie Plum, who had again joined them backstage, was laughing merrily. That had to be seen to be believed.

Olsen, with Rusty Fox on his arm and pie mix covering his face, smiled at the applause. "Thank you," he cried. "And now, ladies and gentlemen, please welcome our opening act – Cathy Cassidy and her dancing chimps!"

As Cathy and her chimpanzees erupted onto the sawdust, everyone cheered. Cathy and Olsen high-fived as he left the arena.

As Cathy began her routine, Olsen joined Klondike on the backstage platform.

"Way to go, kid," the circus manager drawled. "That was excellent."

Olsen took the moist towel offered by Lacey, and wiped the white pie mix off his face. He looked up and smiled. "Thanks, boss."

He placed Rusty Fox back into his suitcase momentarily, and rubbed the last of the mix from his skin.

"They love you, Roddy," Lacey was saying warmly, hovering around him like an excited pup. "Just keep it up."

Plum, as animated as anyone had ever seen him, slapped the youngster on the back and took the towel from him as if he was a butler.

Klondike was surveying the audience all around them. He squinted against the bright lights. "Everyone's smiling and laughing. The tone has been set."

Lacey smirked next to him. "Just as we knew it would be."

After Cathy's act, Olsen returned on his own, carrying the suitcase up to the mic. This time, he performed his favourite routine, the one he had shown Klondike on his first appearance at the circus camp two weeks ago.

The crowd cheered Rusty Fox's reappearance from the suitcase. They then reacted with shock as Napoleon joined the fray, before lapping up the banter between the two puppets as Olsen struggled to control them.

Then, of course, came the singing of Rock Island Line as Olsen, Rusty and Napoleon all belted out the lyrics to the fast-versed hit.

The audience applauded emphatically at the song's conclusion, as Olsen introduced Corky and the circus clowns for the next act.

Each of the clowns shook hands with the two puppets on Olsen's arms as they rushed onto the arena floor. Corky gave Olsen a pretend kiss on the lips, before repeating the action on Rusty and Napoleon.

And so the pattern was set.

Olsen performed a brief sketch with a puppet before introducing each performer. The new format seemed to be working a gem, with Olsen's appearances garnering a stronger reaction from the fans each time, with the ventriloquist greeted with cheers and whoops.

His skits were varied. He introduced Emile Rance using Napoleon, who called the lion tamer a "respected fellow professional. Like me, he shows discipline and poise. A man we could use in the US Army. Hell, we have enough animals there that need taming!"

The tuxedo-clad crooner Tony Tan appeared to introduce Amanda Hart and her elephants. During this routine, Olsen had Tan sing O Solo Mio, to a standing ovation.

Rusty returned to introduce the bareback riders, with the comedy revolving around his fear of horses.

For the skit proceeding the clown revue and the Klondike Showcase, Olsen stunned everyone – both spectators and backstage staff – by making his bare hand come to life and talking to it. The bizarre exchange, going back and forth, had many shaking their heads in dismay. As he addressed his own limb, Olsen added a sock to the hand, two small sticky beads for eyes and a tiny bowler hat. Suddenly, a new character had been created, but all the youngster was doing was talking to himself and moving his hand in perfect speaking mechanisms.

As he watched this unusual offering, Klondike frowned in disbelief. It was like watching a magician pretending he had an invisible assistant. But what he didn't bank on was the reaction of the crowd. Gasps of shock and hysteria rumbled through the tent as Olsen addressed his sock-covered hand, which replied in a high-pitched feminine squeal. Lacey and Plum were roaring with laughter at the comical exchange, and Klondike had to admit, once again, that he had never witnessed an act quite like this. He shook his head yet again.

For the final act, Gino Shapiro's trapeze performance, Olsen followed up on the previous day's promise and had Tony Tan perform the introduction. Tan sang the Frank Sinatra classic High Hopes, and then gave Shapiro's traditional welcome speech, which Heavy had supplied earlier. Olsen's smooth Dean Martin persona that he had created for Tony Tan was ideal for the Shapiro introduction.

However, when the glorious triumvirate of Gino, Nicky and Jenny made their grand entrance, there was no interaction at all with Olsen this time. The three flyers ignored him, jogging to their ropes in the big top's centre.

For Roddy Olsen, on this most dramatic of circus debuts, there was one final act. He introduced the grand parade, alongside both Rusty and Tony.

As the first truck rumbled onto the arena floor, Suzi Dando began belting out 'Can You Feel the Magic Tonight', sitting on her throne on the royal-themed float. To everyone's surprise, she beckoned for Olsen and his puppets to join her at the throne. He duly obliged, and Suzi threw her arms towards Olsen, signalling for the audience to show its appreciation. A raucous ovation followed as Olsen, Rusty and Tony bowed. Then, in the now customary manner, Olsen performed his three-man singing trick as all three joined in with the song in sequence as Suzi wowed the crowd, whirling the mic around like a pop diva.

Everyone applauded grandly as the float parade made its way around the floor. As with the Santa Cruz show, everything had run smoothly, with the acts all flawless. It was as if the audience had spent two hours cheering non-stop.

At the backstage platform, Klondike, Lacey and Plum stared in awe at the grand parade. Klondike couldn't stop gazing up at the cheering fans all around.

"Jesus," he mused, "I can't remember an audience reaction like this. Look at these people. They've been clapping non-stop for the whole show it seems."

Lacey, still in her feathered dress, surveyed the grandstands. "Small town folk. None of them have ever seen anything like this in their lives. Many will probably speak of this day for years. The night they saw the world's fastest juggler. Dancing monkeys and elephants. A lion tamer performing a group hug with lions and a tiger. A trapeze artist flying 100 feet in the air with no net beneath. And…" she smiled devilishly, "a man who could make anything talk!"

Plum was nodding behind her. "Damn straight. Oh man… I can't get enough of this kid." The little accountant with the dour manner had transformed into a being resembling a teenaged bubble gum pop fan. "I can't wait to see more. More sketches. More songs. Hell, more characters!"

Klondike and Lacey stared at him, dumbfounded. "Well," Klondike finally rasped, "the brave new world has worked. No one can deny that. Our new show format has been a success. I'll be damned."

Lacey grabbed his arm softly, and nodded towards the front row of bleachers just in front of them.

There, on the very end of the front row, next to the exit way, sat Heavy Brown, watching mesmerised as the float parade rolled round the circus floor. He was dressed in thick woollen winter clothes, despite it being spring. He still looked pale, his wide head topped off with a black fedora, while a scarf was wrapped around his neck.

Klondike stared in shock. He thought Heavy was still with the doctor in town, and hadn't realised his old friend had returned. He presumed Heavy would have gone to his room on the train, and not ventured into the circus itself.

He wandered over to the bleachers, for once ignoring the wild cheering as it spewed from the stands.

"Heavy!" he cried, putting an arm around the big man's shoulders. "What in the hell are you doing here? I thought you were holed up in the Eureka town sick bay!"

Heavy laughed mirthlessly. His voice had apparently returned, but came out in a low, painful-sounding rasp. "I saw the doc in town. Young fella. He gave me a few tests. Truth is, he didn't know what was wrong. Ruled out tonsillitis. So that's a mystery." He grimaced as he rubbed at his Adam's apple. "I'll be damned if I know what's wrong with me. My throat is still on fire, that's for sure. I managed to speak again about four hours ago, so left the surgery and came back here. Everyone was busy getting ready so I didn't want to distract y'all, so I just got a ticket from the boys and came on in. What a seat I got me!"

Klondike nodded absent-mindedly, his face a mask of concern as he looked his friend over. "How do you feel, old buddy?"

"Still awful. And cold, too. Like I'm shaking. It was baking out there this afternoon in that sun. So, go figure that one out."

Klondike wore a grim expression. "That's not good, Heav."

"You're telling me!" Heavy coughed roughly, and looked up at Klondike seriously. He was slouched in the bench seat, looking as if he might roll off into the sawdust below. "But I ain't none the wiser for seeing this small town quack. Listen, if this feeling doesn't go away, I'll see me a proper big city doctor when we hit Frisco. I need an answer."

"Is it flu?"

Heavy shrugged. "I guess I hope it is. But nothing hurts, except my damn throat. Hell, at least I can talk again."

They halted the conversation as the float parade completed its lap of honour and the trucks headed towards the flap, passing them both as they watched from the front row. All the performers bar none saved a special wave for Heavy as the floats rolled by. Heavy and Klondike both waved back as the parade came to an end.

Then, Lacey, in her new role, stepped out to the microphone stand and delivered the closing announcement.

"Ladies and gentlemen, on behalf of everyone here at Klondike's Circus, we would like to thank you all for joining us tonight. There are many pretenders, many wonders…but there is only one Klondike's Circus. We hope you can feel the magic tonight. Please join our West Coast tour. Next show is Saturday at Sacramento. Until then, goodnight one and all. And God bless America."

Lacey bowed and returned to the platform.

As the spectators slowly exited the grandstands, Klondike helped Heavy from his seat and ushered him gently to the flap, where he accepted the well wishes of Lacey and Plum. They all watched as the people moved as one towards the designated tent exits.

With a grunt, Heavy slipped a small hip flask from a pocket on the mighty cardigan he wore and took a pull.

Swapping concerned looks, Lacey and Plum excused themselves and went out the flap door, joining the swarms of people outside in the cool night air.

Klondike leant against the tent and looked Heavy over. "Are you sure you're OK, Heav? I mean, being here, at the circus."

Heavy coughed slightly, and took another sip from the flask. "Sure. I just can't roar like before. For now." He looked around him feebly, before eyeing Klondike with a sudden laser-like intensity. "We need to talk."

Klondike nodded. "You saw the whole show?"

"I saw it all right. And, boy, what I saw. That was as good as it gets, Kal. You know it, I know it."

"The kid?"

"Damn right!" Heavy took another pull, then put the flask back in his pocket before rubbing at his forehead with a handkerchief. He kept his gaze fixed on Klondike. "He was a sensation. Just like we all knew he would be. I was sat with the fans. The people. I heard their reactions, saw their amazement. He created all that on his own, through his own ingenuity, his own creations." He glanced around at the now virtually empty big top. "Jesus Christ. A puppeteer. A doll talker. Who would have guessed he'd have an effect like that."

Klondike folded his arms. "Well, he was a good stand-in, nothing more. Once you're back to full health again we're —"

"Ah, come off it Kal!" Heavy roared, taking them both by surprise. He lowered his tone. "Come off it, man. That kid can do the job a hundred times better than me. He is talent, not some loafer belting out introductions to everyone. He brings an act to the role. His little bits were the highlight tonight. It was perfect for the role of ringmaster. Can't you see that?"

Klondike nodded, concern clouding his features. "He was excellent. A unique perfumer in every way. But the ringmaster's role is yours, Heavy. It always has been. I'm not changing things around, not in a role like that."

Heavy was repugnant. "I never thought I'd say this, Kal, but the kid is a better bet. We both know it deep down. I watched his act. I was blown away, like all these other people out in the bleachers."

Klondike looked around awkwardly. "What are you saying, Heavy?"

Heavy walked over to him, so that their faces were inches apart. His pale skin, bloodshot eyes and dry, cracked lips made Klondike shudder. "I'm saying I'm going to take a bullet for the good of the show."

"No!" Klondike rasped. "You don't just walk away from this. All right, maybe you don't want the announcing gig anymore, I can take that. But you're my eyes and ears out here, Heavy. I can't do this without you, you know that!"

"Relax," Heavy said, placing a hand on his friend's shoulder. "Who said anything about quitting? Hell, I could never do that. All I'm saying is I think Roddy should be our new ringmaster…or host. He brings so much more to the role. Besides, this is a revolutionary move on behalf of Klondike's Circus. We're making it more like a TV variety show. It appeals to a mass market."

Klondike came back round. "That's exactly what Lacey said. And she knows about such matters. She's been championing the kid from day one."

Heavy nodded solemnly. The tent was empty now, and they were all alone on the platform, as the crowd emptied the fields outside under the light of a full moon. "Maybe it's time to hang up my top hat and coat. For good."

Klondike frowned. "Do you really want that?"

"No. But more than anything I want the circus to succeed. I want it to excel. I want it to make us both rich, ha ha! It needs someone like Roddy. A unique performer. He can help us move to the next level. I just know it."

Klondike nodded thoughtfully. "Righteous words, my friend. You..." he eyed Heavy directly, "...you are one in a million. You know that?"

The big man laughed. "Come on," he wheezed, "let's go see the kid. I want to tell him he's got the gig."

They left the tent, Klondike wrapping an arm over Heavy.

Roddy Olsen was sat at his dresser in his stateroom, still in his costume. His youthful face was bathed in sweat, the gel was still sparkling in his hair, and his chest still heaved following the adrenaline rush of the show.

As he took a giant swig from a water bottle, he relayed the entire performance through his mind, like a re-run. He grinned at his own reflection in the mirror, before closing his eyes and slipping into a dream-like trance.

A loud knock at the door woke him from his own private world.

"Come on in," he called.

Klondike and Heavy marched in, both wearing grins nearly as large as the kid's. In an usual show of affection, Klondike hugged the youngster, before patting him on the back. Heavy also embraced the teenager, offering glowing praise.

"You did it, Roddy!" Klondike was saying, "That was a sensation. Well done, and many congratulations."

Olsen nodded. "Thanks, Mr Klondike, I sure appreciate it. I owe you everything for giving me that chance." Then, taking everyone by surprise under the circumstances, he turned and enquired about Heavy's health.

The big man gave him a summary of what the doctor had said, describing how he could only communicate in a rasping wheeze for now.

Olsen listened, full of concern, then offered some encouragement. "I'm sure you'll be just fine, Mr Brown. It probably is tonsillitis. Like you say, wait till we hit San Francisco, then I'm sure you'll get a proper diagnosis from a big city doctor." He grinned impishly. "Then you'll be back behind the mic before you know it."

Heavy looked at Klondike, then smiled paternally. "I'm not going back behind the mic, Roddy."

Olsen froze. "What do you mean, Mr Brown?"

Heavy chuckled, the effort paining him. "I was out there with the crowd, Roddy. I watched your act. It was incredible. I never saw nothing like it. Your skills are exceptional. But seeing you introduce the acts, the way you were interacting with each performer, making it one long continuous show, that was extraordinary." He took a long swallow, grimacing again. "And I've made the decision. I want you to have the job, kid. Full-time. We both do."

Olsen's eyes enlarged as he stood there gaping at the two older men before him in the stateroom. "Are you serious? But...but Mr Brown, you're the ringmaster. You've done this job for years. You know it better than anybody. You can't quit. I'm a performer...but you are the face of Klondike's Circus."

Heavy looked at Klondike and chuckled. "I ain't no face of nuthin, kid. Besides, yeah I like the job, but I only took it on in the first-place cos the real guy didn't turn up. Remember that, Kal?"

Klondike laughed ruefully. "How could I forget? 1953. The summer of mishaps."

"Well," Heavy continued, "I thought a whole lot about it while I was sat among the paying public. I had a feeling that I was glimpsing the future tonight. The future of circus entertainment. And, like I told Kal, I want this circus to succeed...to excel. And you, Roddy, you can help make that happen. I know it."

Olsen stared at him dumbly. "You're really serious, aren't you? You want me to take over from you. Just like that?"

Heavy smiled, despite the pain in his throat, and put his hands on Olsen's shoulders. "I'm deadly serious, son. This circus needs you. I have no qualms about stepping aside. It would seem —" he coughed violently, "— that I am getting too old for this gig."

"Maybe I could have my own separate appearance," Olsen said desperately, "and you can carry on announcing."

"No," said Heavy, "me and Kal both agree your style of, as we say, hosting, is something special. It works, kid, it really works. It blends the show together, holds everything in place. Like one continuous performance."

Olsen looked on in shock. He turned to Klondike. "Is this real?"

Klondike nodded resolutely. "Listen, kid, I'm still not sure I get your act. The puppets, the voice throwing. And I still don't know what brought you to me in the first place. But, there can be no doubt. Your comedy and singing is outstanding, your characters are popular, the way you get them all to talk without moving your lips...it's something else. Those voice skills are like nothing anyone has ever seen before. Anywhere!"

Olsen smiled boyishly. "I don't know how to ever begin to thank you, Mr Klondike. Mr Brown, it's an honour to follow in your footsteps, sir."

Heavy and Olsen shook hands as Klondike watched. "Like a passing of the torch," he uttered dryly.

"You know I won't let you down," Olsen said proudly.

Klondike slapped him on the back. "Damn right! You can show me how grateful you are by keeping up that level of performance for the whole season. That's all I want."

Olsen looked from Heavy to Klondike. "You got it!"

And so the new pattern for Klondike's Circus was set. The show's variety performance feel became the new norm and, for the first time in years, Klondike nurtured a major change to his beloved and recognised format and an all-new show graced the dust trails of the west coast.

That second night outing in the small town of Eureka changed everything. The audience reaction, the smooth transition of the acts and, of course, the impact of the newcomer, Roddy Olsen, ensured that this new format became cemented. And the circus went from strength to strength.

The shows came thick and fast. Sacramento. San Jose. Santa Fe. Napa Valley. Oakland. Each time, the crowds cheered louder than anyone could remember. The lights seemed to shine brighter. The train ran smoother. Everyone was cheerful. And each show was a sell-out, to the glee and amazement of Klondike and his newfound brethren of Lacey and Plum.

The few weeks following the Eureka show were some of the most glorious anyone could remember.

Klondike, as ever, ran his crew hard. The executive council meetings were kept brief, but everyone seemed happy.

Lacey kept the local press enthralled with her exhilarating press releases, sent weeks in advance to the required newsrooms and TV and radio stations. Her eloquent, pulpish way with words helped fuel extraordinary previews in the media, helping whip the next local crowd into a frenzy. Before the train had even rolled into town.

And Plum became a model of efficiency. Each show made a profit, he insisted, and the crew could afford ever more high tech equipment as a result of the cash pouring in. His balance sheets were professional and delivered to Klondike the night after each show.

Gino Shapiro remained the consummate professional, as always. His routine barely differed from show to show. However, he largely kept himself away from his fellow performers, except his brother and Jenny. This was nothing new. However, many crewmembers speculated that the great Gino had kept himself to himself as a direct result of his jealousy regarding the kid, Roddy Olsen, who was drawing cheers as large as his and was becoming a celebrity as the circus arrived in each new town. He had already garnered as many requests for press interviews as Gino and Corky, and was greeted at every stop on the route by a crowd of excited teenagers, who had already read all about his unique talents thanks to Lacey's advance publicity burning a hole in newspapers and magazines.

But there was no doubt Olsen's stock was on the rise. His routines drew staggering applause, and his delivery and skills seemed to become more polished with each performance.

Lacey was masterminding his progress. By Oakland, she had insisted on redesigning the main circus poster to include his picture, which became superimposed between Gino and Corky's profiles. A new roll out of posters was ordered from Frisco, with Lacey again billing Addison and Lee. Olsen, and Rusty Fox, now sat equal between the two main figureheads of Klondike's Circus in the all-important poster. It took Klondike a few days to accept such a big change, but even he had to admit the kid had earned it. And he now had drawing power, so in some ways demanded poster presence and headliner status.

As the crowds rolled into the big top and the money flowed, Klondike was glad of one thing and one thing only. That he had listened to Lacey and brought along this kid from Fresno. This kid from nowhere.

And, to his immense surprise, as Olsen starred in each show, there sat in the front row every time, roaring with laughter, was a proud and understanding Heavy Brown.

"I am proud," Heavy murmured as he lay back on the medic bed. "I'm proud of all my guys. We've brought them up in a way. From day one. Now, sitting there, watching them flourish under the big top, it's a helluva feeling, Doc. Hard to describe really. But, I tell ya, nothing can beat it."

Doc Sampson nodded enthusiastically as he studied a chart. "So you don't miss being the ringmaster?"

Heavy laughed. "No, not really. Hell, it's a fun job, a lot of laughs, but this is better in a way. It's kinda like being a coach. Developing talent. That's what me and Kal do best."

Doc Sampson raised an eyebrow. "Not a player coach? Only last year, you said performing in the circus was your calling in life. The greatest calling of all. You remember that, Henry?"

Heavy looked at him and his smile dipped.

The circus train had arrived in San Francisco that morning, ahead of one of the troupe's biggest shows of all, in one of its major cities. The California Classico, as they all called it.

As he had mooted previously, Heavy had sought out his long-time doctor Earl Sampson as soon as they had arrived in town, after he and Klondike had scouted out their playing field.

The surgery was downtown, hidden away in another giant building off Union Square.

Now, Heavy lay back on the soft bed, buttoning up his shirt after a thorough, professional examination.

Sampson, his white coat spotless in the bright medical room, surveyed him with a gentle glare.

"Well, Henry," he began, "let's not beat about the bush. You have a bad case of laryngitis. One of the worst I've ever seen. Now, don't be alarmed, it will clear up. But the cause is over use of that beautiful voice box of yours. After years of shouting, or wailing, or whatever it is you do out there, you've caused severe damage to the larynx, the chords around the box itself. In other words, too much announcing to a crowd."

Heavy smiled ruefully. "Jesus... Why don't you quit sugar coating it and give me it straight, Doc?"

The doctor laughed. "We go back a while, Henry. You've got all the symptoms of voice box trouble."

His brawny patient slowly sat up, shaking his head. "Well, I guess that seals it."

"What?"

"The end of my days as a ringmaster." He looked up. "Right?"

Sampson nodded. "My goodness me, yes." He looked down at his patient. "I'm sorry, Henry, but we've just about nipped it in the bud. More of your bawling will surely result in permanent damage. Even a loss of voice."

Heavy baulked slightly. Then, slapping his hand against his knee, he rose. "Well, like I said, I don't do that no more."

"Right, you're a coach now, right?"

"You bet." He wandered past the doctor to the surgery door, acting sprightly. "Er, how much do I owe you for this, Earl?"

Sampson smiled. "Forget it, Henry. Just come back next year. With a healthy throat."

Heavy laughed, waved a goodbye, and exited the surgery.

But, once outside in the reception room, his face dropped and he felt an unstoppable wave of sadness and despair hit him. Head down, he left the building.

Chapter 14

A STAR IS BORN… UNDER THE BIG TOP

By Jock Rawley, Oakland Advertiser

The legendary Klondike's Circus roared into Oakland on Thursday last for its annual tent spectacular.

With its wild tigers, dancing monkeys and prancing elephants, local crowds have come to expect anything and everything from this surreal showpiece of live entertainment.

The king of the skies, Gino Shapiro, the world's fastest juggler, Corky the Clown, and lion tamer extraordinaire Emile Rance all returned to thrill the sell-out crowd.

But it was a newcomer to the troupe that stole the show. And how! He's young, blond and looks like a Hollywood teen idol.

Ventriloquist Roddy Olsen has picked up on an unusual, some would say outdated, variety act and catapulted it into the 1950s American psyche. With voice throwing and comedy singing unlike anything your correspondent has ever seen, young Roddy was a sensation in this, one of his first ever outings with the Klondike group.

The Puppet Master, as he is billed, acted as host for the evening, introducing the acts and joining in with some of the fun and games. But it was his skits between each new performance that gave this circus show a fresh, seamless feel. It almost felt like a TV variety series, with the young ventriloquist a vibrant, hilarious presenter.

His puppets – 'singing star' Rusty Fox (an actual fox), army veteran Napoleon and Las Vegas cabaret star Tony Tan (complete with super tan ala Dean Martin) – are a joy to behold. Olsen has crafted some fantastic personalities with his creations, and for that deserves endless praise. The idea is each puppet tries to take centre stage as their master attempts to introduce each new act, creating chaos and many laughs.

What a great idea to give the circus an actual host, and splitting from the age-old tradition of the ringmaster, complete with a tired velvet robe and top hat and...

"Who the hell is Roddy Olsen?"

Eric Ribbeck spat the words out as he chewed the end of his Old Grayling pipe and ran his eyes over the latest edition of Spotlight.

His executive assistant, Veronica Hunslett, was reading the same copy. She looked up.

"The word is this boy turned up one day asking for an audition. Klondike saw him, liked it and ran with it. When Brown got a cold, they gave him the ringmaster job. From there, they seemed to have stumbled upon this whole host idea."

Ribbeck remained impassive. "I don't like it."

Ribbeck's World Circus had arrived in Chicago that morning. While his endless army of workers emptied the carriages of his executive circus train ready for the following night's show, the boss had remained locked in his lounging carriage. A luxurious open plan room featuring an office, lounge and dining area, with his bedroom and washroom concealed at the back, the master's carriage was as comfortable a way to travel as any known to rail men anywhere. It also gave Ribbeck, the workaholic business chief, a permanent headquarters where he was always close to his beloved circus.

Veronica was equally impassive, thinking frantically as she sat opposite her employer at the large ivory desk in the carriage's far end. A plain, powerful looking middle-aged woman, she wore her blonde hair tied back in a ponytail and dressed in a business suit. She had been with Ribbeck for years, and had helped mastermind his superiority in the circus field.

She tried not to look concerned. "I wouldn't read too much into it, Eric. It's a fad, a shot in the wild. Who the hell ever heard of a ventriloquist being a circus star?"

Ribbeck blew a long cloud of smoke across the desk towards her. "I've read the headlines and I've seen the returns. Every show a sell-out! People being turned away! TV spots! Radio!" He visibly shook. "No... That snake Klondike is onto something. He has unearthed a new gem. God damn him to hell."

Veronica shrugged, tossing the magazine aside. "It's strange. If Olsen really did just show up like that. What are the chances?"

Ribbeck snorted angrily. "With Klondike? Good. That son of a bitch was always a lucky one. Had things fall into his lap. It sure sounds like that's what happened here." He gazed into nothingness, tapping the stem of his pipe on his teeth. "Ventriloquism..." he mused. "I would never have seen that taking off. We've auditioned a few over the years. Never took one on. Too unnerving. Haunting, almost. But this...it sounds like a child friendly form of comedy. Like a cartoon come to life." He thought again, staring blankly at his assistant. "Edgar Bergen. Jimmy Nelson. Them's ventriloquists who have become national stars. Hell, maybe this Olsen is the next one."

"What does your man Marconi make of it all?" said Veronica.

Ribbeck snapped out of his trance. "Luca said he's the real deal. Very funny, and an expert with his damn puppets."

She spread her hands out. "So get him to burn the puppets!"

The old man sniggered behind his desk, running a hand through his thick white hair. "No, Luca's position is way too fragile for him to be rumbled pulling a stupid prank like that. Besides, he has a more important mission right now."

"Like what?"

"Have you ever heard of Sidney Hackett?"

She straightened up. "Sure. He's that writer, works the west coast papers. He followed us one season on the rails. Sleazy guy from what I recall."

"Right. You nailed him. He's in league with a saboteur in Klondike's group. Together, they're planning to nail the circus and put ol' Klondike out of business. I've ordered Luca to find Hackett and help along whoever the mystery figure, or figures, might be."

Veronica stared at him in dismay. "What? A saboteur? Are you serious?"

Ribbeck nodded vigorously. "There can be no doubt. The lion incident was the smoking gun. Then this Hackett has been writing negative stories in the Daily World. The saboteur then told him that Shapiro plans to attempt a devil drop this season. But no one knows when or where."

"A devil drop? Surely not!"

"It was top secret, but our unknown confederate told Hackett on purpose to ruin their big surprise. Their big highlight of the season. No doubt it is intended for this Las Vegas spectacular we have heard so much about."

Veronica leant forward, eyes wide. "We have to get Tempest to perform a devil drop immediately. Let's beat them to it. The glory shall be ours."

Ribbeck laughed softly. "Are you serious? Dirk is brave, but he's not crazy. There's no way he will perform that kind of stunt. Not even for a retirement pay off and a ranch in Tulsa. No, we let Shapiro try his insane stunt, but we will let Hackett kill off all element of surprise."

"Will he really go ahead with it?"

The old man waved a hand through the air. "That's not our concern now. We need Luca to find who is controlling Hackett, so we can then turn the conspiracy our way."

"How is he getting on?"

"So far, nothing. But he will make contact sooner rather than later."

Veronica thought for a moment. "You know, there could be more to this than just a saboteur and Hackett."

Ribbeck eyed her suspiciously. "What do you mean?"

"Well," she began, "Hackett is, indeed, a hack. He is paid to write garbage by people who want to discredit their enemies. A pen for hire, if you will. I seriously doubt one of Klondike's crew is paying him to wreck the circus, from which they earn their living. I'd guess someone else is behind this, controlling the saboteur and the reporter. Someone with money. Someone with a big, big score to settle. The saboteur would be just a pawn, to be thrown away and discarded once the damage is done. But the big player will be lurking even deeper in these muddied waters."

Ribbeck's eyes enlarged as he thought it over. He gazed out the carriage window at the endless green pastureland all around them. "A boss man," he mused.

Veronica nodded. They stared at each other for several seconds.

"You are often right about such matters, Miss Hunslett," he finally proclaimed. "I have a feeling you may be again. But, the more I hear, the more I like it. I sense not alarm, but an opportunity." His eyes settled back on his assistant and he smiled. "Let's see what our boy Luca comes up with."

Klondike walked into the barroom in the heart of Nob Hill, squinting as his eyes adjusted to the gloomy interior after walking through the blazing San Francisco sun.

It was a jazzy uptown joint, full of mahogany tables and leather-bound chairs. The patrons were all suits, smoking pipes and drinking martinis.

In his leather jacket and Fedora, Klondike didn't exactly fit in, and drew several astonished glances as he waltzed through the bar. More of a beer and whiskey man, he winced inwardly as he spotted the tables of office workers and executives all toasting each other with their fancy crystal glasses.

He finally located Daryl Addison seated in a booth in the far corner.

"Hey Kal," the banker cried, uncharacteristically. "Great to see you."

He leapt down from the table and the two men shook hands. "Hi Daryl, how's business?"

"Just terrific," said the small, wiry figure. He gestured to another man seated in the booth, dressed like Addison in a pinstriped suit. "You remember my associate and partner, Robert Lee?"

"Sure," Klondike drawled, shaking Lee's hand. The bank's other senior partner was a tall, balding man. "It's been a long time, Rob. Good to see you." He winked at Addison. "Bringing out all the big guns, eh?"

"We both wanted to meet with you, Kal," said Addison. "You're doing very well. A sound investment."

Klondike chuckled as he took a seat next to Lee. A waiter appeared and he ordered a beer. They all settled down, Addison and Lee both lighting up pipes and Klondike whipping out a cigar.

"So," Addison began, as a behemoth smoke cloud suddenly engulfed the table, "the circus is rolling on and the money is rolling in. That's about the whole of it, right Kal?"

Klondike nodded, puffing on his cigar. His beer arrived and he took a long pull. "I'll give it to you straight, Daryl. This season…so far…has been unprecedented. Full house every show. And I mean a capacity crowd. Record receipts. The coverage has been out of sight. We're on TV for Christ sakes. It's unreal." He chewed on his cigar and eyed the two bankers in admiration. "And I gotta tell you, gents, a lot of this success is down to Lacey and Richie. Lacey's pressers and media contacts have propelled us into the mainstream. And Richie has kept the books straight and come up with a whole financial plan, dictating what we spend, what we save, it's… It's really something else." He bowed his head. "I don't know how to thank you, Daryl."

Addison laughed enthusiastically. "What did I tell you, Kal? They're professionals. Didn't I say they'd raise your organisation to a new level? I said

137

they'd be a boost for you, and now you're reaping the rewards. It's good business all round. And we'll all make greater profits."

Klondike nodded. "You were right. I'm glad you persuaded me."

"We were all right."

Lee spoke up. "You're on a real roll right now, Kal. Your projected profits and mean share are higher than our estimates. Plum tells us the merchandise sales have skyrocketed and that they're going to surpass even the current figures once these new, er, signed pictures are ready. He said Lacey has made the media portray your performers as heroes, like action stars, and that the public wants more." He leant forward. "This is fantastic. It could open doors to all sorts of merchandise and marketing. My god… Your circus could become our highest grossing investment if everything goes to plan."

Klondike remained cool, sipping his beer and eyeing the two bankers with an air of grace. "We may be moving to a new level. We have some great people behind us. But we're still a circus. Entertaining is our business."

Addison shook excitedly. "Kal," he blurted, "tell us about the kid."

Klondike chuckled. "The kid from nowhere. You wouldn't believe me if I told you everything that happened." He shook his head. "He came from nowhere… But he's heading straight to the top." He then told Addison and Lee the story of when Roddy Olsen first arrived at the winter camp, followed by an account of his antics on the midway and, finally, his triumphant circus debut.

"Incredible," Lee mused, almost in a trance. "We can't wait to see him on the sawdust tomorrow."

Klondike looked up. "You'll be there?"

Lee chuckled. "Kal, my boy, all our senior executives, office staff and, well, just about everyone we deal with in Frisco will be there. Nobody wants to miss this. Everybody is fascinated by your circus."

Klondike looked across to Addison. "Is this true?"

The wiry banker grinned. "Lacey got us executive seats in the centre of the grandstand. Best in the house, she told us. Free cotton candy and a meet and greet with Gino, Corky and all the rest. The ultimate VIP package."

"Well," Klondike drawled, "you guys made it all possible. You deserve it all."

Lee could not stop smiling, like an overexcited child. "We are so glad we are on board. So far, you have exceeded all expectations." He leant forward. "Tell me, Kal, can you keep this level of high performance going? Until the end of the season?"

Klondike looked at him straight. "You bet I can."

Lee shook his head in awe. "Where will it all lead, I wonder…"

"Well," Klondike said emphatically, "all roads lead somewhere." He stared into his beer. He had remained calm throughout the meeting, despite the bankers' undoubted and uncharacteristic glee. Everything was happening very fast. He looked up. "And our road leads to Las Vegas. And a date at the Golden Dune. For the greatest circus show of all time."

The two bankers laughed and the three men clinked glasses.

Chapter 15
San Francisco. The California Classico

Located on the north side of San Francisco Bay, beside Golden Gate Park in a recreation field known as Marina Place, the Klondike's Circus tent was laid at the perfect venue for one of its biggest shows of the season.

Just off the city centre, close to the beach and within a short walk of Fisherman's Wharf, Golden Gate Bridge, the Presidio and Pier 39, Marina Place was at the heart of the tourist region. The giant red and blue tent could be spotted for miles around, and acted as a beacon for young and old, rich and poor, who all flocked to this exotic and glamorous world of fun and excitement. For the tourists, the trip to the big top formed the climax of their day, after trips to Alcatraz across the bay, or guided tours of the waterfront.

The grandstands within the great tent were full an hour before show time. The crowd buzzed with a kind of steady excitement as the clock drew nearer to 7pm.

Unusually, and only because it was a big show in a major city, Klondike took a seat in the front row, close to the flap, where he was joined by Heavy, Lacey and Plum. He looked at each of them. *My team,* he thought idly, *on a coach's bench of managers and experts.*

Everyone had an air of deep professionalism and calm about them, from the roustabouts helping with last minute technical issues, to the stewards showing spectators to their seats. They all knew San Francisco was the money show. TV crews, radio commentators, a sea of press, all waited patiently among the masses in the bleachers.

After Los Angeles and the big finale in Vegas, this was the one that counted, Klondike thought.

He turned in his seat and looked up towards the centre of the stand. He could see Addison, Lee and their various associates and staff, all sat clutching cotton candy sticks, drinks and programmes.

Suddenly, the pre-recorded sound of trumpets thundered through the tent and the audience cheered, before all held their collective breath.

The circus had changed the initial introduction of Olsen to a pre-recorded greeting from Heavy Brown. Lacey had done a fine job in Eureka, but Klondike had become so dependent on her and her observations, he wanted her by his side at all times. With that in mind, he had tasked Heavy, despite his illness, with recording a brief introduction and closing line which would play out on the tannoy.

With the mention of Olsen's name, the crowd roared. And then there he was, the teenager in the silver waistcoat, with the fox puppet on his arm, strolling casually into the sawdust, waving to the audience.

The applause grew...and Klondike and his crew never looked back.

In the end, to the immense relief of performers, roustabouts, Klondike and his management team and Addison and his executives, the California Classico went without a hitch.

The whole show ran smoothly, as it had at its six previous stops, and each performance was greeted by a jubilant reaction.

Cath Cassidy and her dancing chimps. The Klondike showcase of surreal marvels. The Bareback Riders. Corky and the Klondike clowns. Amanda Hart and her elephants. Emile Rance, the lion tamer. Roddy Olsen, the puppet master. Gino Shaprio, the trapeze king.

All were greeted like international superstars, as the audience revelled in their dazzling exploits.

Sat in front of the patrons, Klondike could only smile at the reactions emanating from all around him.

Then, at the grand finale, as Suzi Dando began singing and the floats made their way onto the circus floor, the cheers and applause ran out in one continuous wall of noise.

The performers all took their bow on their respective floats, waving to their fans in the grandstands, that seemed to stretch to the summit of the great tent.

In that moment, they were kings and queens among the townsfolk, promoted to the highest of pedestals, adored and revered in equal measure.

On the final float, where Gino, Nicky and Jenny sat on their royal thrones while soaking up the applause, it felt like an earthquake, such was the intensity of the final cheers.

As always, Gino played the role of king, draped in his gold cape and throwing roses into the crowd while blowing kisses to the smiling faces. The constant showman, he continually whipped the patrons into more of a frenzy by cajoling them with waves and signals to cheer louder.

Nicky merely sat on his throne, smiling and waving, as the float rolled round the arena floor.

For Jenny, the grand finale was always a chance to check out who was in the audience, or at least try to. On this occasion, with the noise and excitement, trying to spot anybody familiar was a challenge. She had a string of male admirers known to follow her around the west coast during circus season. She even indulged many of them with dates during stopovers. Sometimes she spotted a known talent scout or publicity man who might be worth sounding out after the show. And then there were the scores of disgruntled wives she had incurred the wrath of down the years. She kept a close eye out for them.

As she scanned the endless sea of faces spread out like rocky outcroppings in a canyon before her, she found herself disappointed. It was impossible to recognise anyone.

Like Gino, a true professional, she continued to wave and blow kisses to the circus goers. She laughed to herself. *There are worse ways to make a living,* she thought.

Suddenly, Jenny froze all over. She felt like a lightning bolt had struck her, and she swayed slightly. Icy tentacles stung the back of her neck.

There. On about the eighth row. A long green trench coat and a fedora pulled down low over the eyes. She couldn't even make out any human flesh, just the coat and hat.

She stared at the figure, and realised he knew she had spotted him. The hat moved slightly as the figure nodded. Then, in a surreal, slow movement, he pointed to the back of the tent.

Absent-mindedly, as if in a trance, Jenny nodded. Dumbly, like a jack in the box.

The figure was seated at the end of the row, but now got up slowly and moved towards the exit. The first of the patrons to leave the show.

Jenny stared, her eyes feeling like they were popping out of their sockets, as she watched the mysterious man disappear behind the rows of fans.

Then, with a nervous gulp, she continued to wave to the crowds. But, this time, there was no glee in her appearance. Only a haunted, sombre look.

"Where?"

Jenny almost screamed as she scrambled around the various midway tents and booths, which had been left for the night now the show was over and the audience was slowly dispersing the big top.

She hurried along the path in the field, moving further away from the circus tent as her eyes scoured the various attractions that had been surrounded by paying punters just hours earlier.

The light of a full moon illuminated the midway, but it was hard to see much beyond 50 yards. Jenny was frantic as she searched for a sign, anything. She moved past the main shooting gallery, the eerie quiet and stillness deeply unnerving her.

The circus crowd were by now making their way towards Golden Gate Park as they left the big top behind. Jenny suddenly felt like she had been abandoned. Left behind by her team and deemed to walk through the darkness alone.

A lone steward suddenly appeared. Jenny guessed he had drawn the night watch. She smiled dumbly as he glared at her, then trotted along until she reached the circus's boundary fencing.

"Where?" She hissed again.

Suddenly, she noticed a slight movement by a ticketing booth to her left, just metres away.

She gasped in fright. There he was. The long green trench coat and fedora emerged from the darkness surrounding the bright red booth, and the figure stood by its side, hidden within its shadows.

Jenny scurried over towards him, sweat smearing her make-up and dust covering her shiny leotard.

"That's close enough!" the man rasped as she surged towards him.

She was about ten yards away, and again struggled to see the face, which was perfectly obscured by the fedora and turned up collar of the coat.

"What…" she blurted, "what do you want?"

"You know what I want," came the firm reply. The voice maintained its croaky, painful sound. It sounded like the man was struggling to breathe. "The next stage."

Jenny visibly shuddered. "No!" she cried. "We're not ready for that yet. Give me more time. Wait till you see Hackett's review. It will do so much harm..."

"Forget it!" the man snapped. "I am following the circus. I have seen what is happening. Your man Hackett has failed. Klondike is a success. We have to stop him."

She was breathing heavily, frantically now. "Listen, Mercer, we can still make this happen. There is a long way to go yet. We have done damage. It can work... Just like we said."

"No!" the figure roared, the word coming out in an animal-like groan. "I am running this show, Miss Cross. So I call the tune. That was the agreement." He moved out of the shadows ever so slightly, the moonlight revealing a trace of scar tissue around his exposed neck and jawline. As ever, it had a haunting effect. "Now, I said we are moving onto the next stage. Now, tell me the information I need. When will you hit Blackhawk Point? When?"

There were tears in her eyes now. She looked downwards. "You can't do it. The results will be catastrophic."

"When!"

She sobbed into her hands. "It will be after eight o'clock."

"What day, dammit?"

She wiped away her tears and suddenly felt very small and helpless. "Tuesday."

The figure stepped back. "Good," he stammered. He seemed to stare at her for a moment, then retreated into the booth. "You have done well, Miss Cross. If all goes to plan, you will do very well out of this. A new life. New identity. No more...er, jealous housewives stalking you around the countryside. Now, just sit tight, and I'll be in touch again."

She suddenly snapped. "Who are you!" she cried into the night.

The man was a shadow now, moving away from the booth and towards the gateway. He paused slightly, and whispered: "You will know...soon enough."

Jenny walked forward, peering into the dark. Then, a voice from behind startled her.

"Are you all right, Miss Cross? I heard shouting."

144

The night watchman had appeared, and was approaching from the midway, a concerned look on his face.

She glared at him, then turned back to the ticket booth. Now, she saw nothing but ghostly shadows and a slight gloom.

With a huff, she stormed past the steward. "I'm fine. Get on with your job."

CIRCUS OF STARS? MORE LIKE CIRCUS OF SHAMBLES…

By Sidney Hackett, Daily World

The city of San Francisco was last night victim to that tiresome, archaic entertainment medium, the circus.

As small children and the elderly gathered under a garish red and blue tent for an evening of loud and boisterous variety, nobody was left in any doubt that the glory days of the big top are over.

Klondike's Circus, a tired and nomadic travelling troupe, limped into Marina Bay for their annual thrill-fest. Unfortunately, so did this correspondent.

The main problem for circus owner Kal Klondike is that he has shown too much faith in his tried and tested roster of performers.

The headline act, so-called king of trapeze Gino Shapiro, looks like an ageing B-movie star struggling to impress the ladies. Judging by his dabblings in Hollywood over the years, that is exactly what he is. On top of that, his act has barely changed at all in each of the last seven years he has performed in Frisco.

Corky the Clown's antics are submerged in the same problem. Everyone knows he can juggle extra fast on a tricycle. Do we have to see it all again?

And does anyone really feel entertained in this day and age by a clown? With that white face paint and brightly coloured suit, Corky and his fellow circus clowns are an insult to intelligent patrons. Only those under the age of five were entertained by their clowning last night.

As if all that was not bad enough, Klondike seems to have placed his faith in the future of his circus on the shallow shoulders of a teenage ventriloquist. Yes, that's right, a ventriloquist. The kid's name is Roddy Olsen, and he seems to have taken on the role of ringmaster, introducing each of the main acts alongside his grotesque array of puppets, who do much of the talking for him. If this was 200 years ago, this youthful weirdo would have been burnt at a steak for witchcraft. What a mess!

But the biggest outrage of all continues to be the circus's brazen use of animals as entertainment for a paying public.

There was a lion tamer, an elephant trainer and a woman who made monkeys dance, all in the aid of getting laughs from a shocked crowd. Well, it did not work in this proud, modern city, and it will not work anywhere ever again if animal rights campaigners force the US government to ban such practice once and for all.

Shame on Klondike's Circus! Using animals in this way is a disgrace to humanity. Not only are these beasts paraded for the paying patrons' viewing pleasure, but once the lights go down the lions and tigers and elephants are caged away, locked in confined cells on that infernal circus train until they are offloaded in the next town for another dose of public humiliation.

A banning order seems the right move, and such a practice can only be a matter of time away.

In the meantime, this correspondent calls on all and sundry in California, and across the west coast, to shun Klondike's Circus, and avoid its outdated, some would say prehistoric, forms of entertainment.

This is the rock n rolling 1950s, after all. There are so many more exciting ways to spend an evening these days.

"What d'ya think?" said Heavy, looking over the top of the tabloid newspaper. He eyed the room.

They were all there, in the train's conference room. Klondike, Heavy, Lacey and Plum. A unit. A team. United.

Klondike and Heavy had invited the two newcomers into their regular newspaper review summits, and all four now sat sprawled around the conference table at the front of the train, poring over a sea of morning papers. Coffee mugs and pots and plates of pastries sat among the news stream.

Klondike sat thinking as his old friend finished reading out the scathing review. "He's up to something."

"Damn straight," Heavy replied.

They all sat staring at each other.

Klondike took the lead. "You all saw the reaction last night. Heard it. Just like all the other nights. We're a smash hit. This…" he gestured wildly at the copy of the Daily World, "…this smacks of something else. A plot. This son of a bitch is trying to take us down. But why?"

Heavy snorted in disgust as he bit at a Danish. "You can bet that cretin Ribbeck is behind it. He's probably paying this writer to do us over."

Klondike nodded. "That seems highly likely." He turned to Lacey, who sat with her feet on the table, dressed in what looked like a dressing gown over her purple jeans. "You're the press expert, Lacey. What do we know about this sucker, Sidney Hackett?"

Lacey huffed and rolled her eyes. "The lowest of the low. Like I told you at the press conference before we left, he will write anything…for anyone…at any price. A true sleaze ball. He used to work in Hollywood, catching studio executives in motel rooms with starlets and hookers. Can you imagine?" She took a sip of coffee, which she curiously drank from a tall glass. Ignoring the others' puzzled looks, she continued. "On top of that devil drop comment he made at the hotel, I'd say he's up to something all right."

"The son of a bitch is trying to skewer us!" Heavy suddenly wailed. "Negative press. He ruined our big surprise, now he's writing these god awful reviews."

Lacey sipped at her coffee. "The only good thing here is that, such is his standing in the press world, nobody is likely to believe him. Readers know he is full of garbage."

"And," Plum added excitedly, joining the debate, "the Daily World is at the bottom of the barrel. I checked its circulation figures with Addison. It is a gutter paper."

Lacey smiled at him. "That is true. I'd imagine the actual impact of all this nonsense will be minimal at best."

Klondike had been listening intently, rechecking the article. "He's still out there, though. And that's what bothers me. Sure, his articles in this rag might not stir up a hornets' nest. But what's next? What else has this bum got up his sleeve?"

"Maybe nothing," Plum said quietly.

"Maybe everything," Klondike rasped. "Everything that is needed to nail us for good." He thought for a moment, removing his hat and running a hand through his swathy black hair. He could feel the sweat forming. "Listen, at the next executive council meeting, I'm going to tell everyone to watch their step. One bad word to the press, one moment caught off-guard, this chump is going to be in there. I can feel it." He turned to Lacey. "I want all our interviews closely monitored. Make sure no one unauthorised is in the vicinity of the interview."

She nodded officially. "I am always thorough."

"Keep it up." Klondike stared at the by-line on the page. Sidney Hackett. The reporter's earlier line about the devil drop still bugged him. "What are you up to…" he whispered.

Plum, who had slowly and emphatically transformed into a devout custodian of the circus over the past weeks, stood up.

"Don't worry, Kal," he said sincerely. "We are on a roll here. We all know it. This pipsqueak hack can't derail us. So he writes a bad review. Who cares? He somehow overheard gossip about the trapeze act. No big deal. Let's just focus on what we are doing and on making our shows as good as they can be."

Klondike smiled with respect at the stubby little accountant in a shirt and tie. Plum had turned from an outsider, an unwilling player in his circus crew, to a valued and respected adviser. His opinion on outlays and investments was second to none. What surprised them all, though, was his sudden and apparent love of the circus life. Even now, he had a programme tucked under his arm along with a copy of Spotlight.

"Thank you, Richie," the circus master drawled.

Their thoughts were interrupted by the shrill sound of the train's whistles. The steam began to pour through the vents, as the engines came to life all around them.

The train was moving on.

As the behemoth circus train began to inch its way along the San Francisco Central track, Gino Shapiro watched from his stateroom window as the luscious green countryside and soft blue of the Pacific Ocean rolled by.

Dressed in his beige robe and carrying a cup filled with coffee and amaretto, he crossed the spacious room and left, walking down the narrow corridor until he reached the lounge he shared with Nicky and Jenny.

Nicky was still asleep, but Jenny was sat on the sofa in the far corner, smoking a cigarette. She didn't even look up as he entered, her eyes dominated by a faraway look.

Gino wandered over, and lounged on the arm of the settee. His young partner looked pale, gaunt and a little underweight.

"Jenny girl," he began, "I've been meaning to ask. Is everything OK with you?" He eyed her suspiciously. "I never seen you so quiet. So, er, withdrawn."

She looked up, disinterested. "I am fine thank you. How are you?"

He frowned. "And this. This attitude. It's not like you. Me and Nicky… We worry."

She baulked at this. "Really? You actually think like that?"

Gino stood, hurt. "Absolutemente! You are our teammate. We care sure." He sat again closer to her. "Come on, what's wrong, dear girl? You can tell me. I… I know it. We have been together too long, you and I. Now, come, mamacita, what is it?"

Jenny blew out a smoke ring and let out a long sigh. "It's nothing Gino… I'm just tired. Tired of it all. The training. The performing. The crowds. The endless travel. It's a lot to take on."

He nodded. "The price of being the best." He pointed to an old poster on the wall from a long-forgotten show, picturing the three of them on their rings. "It is the life we lead, Jenny. We have it in our blood."

"You love it, Gino, every second. The adulation, the fame, the girls. For me, it's different. It's a job. I do my time and get my money."

He studied her. "Has someone said something to you? The chairman maybe?"

She laughed aloud. "Him? Don't talk crazy. Why would he check up on me? Just as long as I'm up there, twirling away, like a damn rag doll."

"Somebody else?"

"Like who?"

Gino shook his head. He slowly got up and made to leave the lounge. The train was picking up speed now, and he placed a hand on the doorframe. "Jenny, I love you like a sister. Believe me. Now, you tell me if anyone ever bothers you. I protect you, yes? But you have to tell me first, baby girl."

They stared at each other and she nodded weakly. With an enigmatic smile, he left the room.

And then, suddenly and uncontrollably, she burst into tears.

As her eyes scanned the room, she unexpectedly spotted a framed picture on the mantelpiece. It showed a younger Gino and Kal shaking hands many years earlier. She gazed at it in a queer way, a malicious frown slowly clouding her features. Her pale face took on an eerie, almost sadistic look and then, wiping away her tears, she began to laugh hysterically.

Chapter 16

McGinty's Bar on Fisherman's Wharf was a hive of noise and activity as a curious mix of longshoremen, city dwellers and beatniks scattered the joint. The beer and whiskey ran freely as laughter and exclamations permeated the smoky air of the waterfront bar. Barroom stewards expertly poured round after round of drinks, while saloon girls moved between the tables, taking glasses and offering idle chitchat. In the far corner, an old man played the piano, though no one seemed to be listening.

Luca Marconi breezed into the joint. He was wearing a sack suit, with his oily hair slicked back. On entry, he had to admit to himself it was almost impossible to fit in at a joint like this, such was the eclectic mix of characters drinking and chatting. Still, he was a professional.

This was an important outing. He had been allowed a night off from his roustabout duties, on the proviso he caught up with the circus the following day, ahead of the next show at Orion Bay on Sunday.

With cold, expert eyes, he scanned the bar floor like a stealth assassin, taking in each face, each figure. Slowly, he crept through the smoke-filled merriment, as if afraid of what he might find.

Suddenly, he stopped dead, eyes narrowing. Then, he smiled. Bingo. He had found him. At last.

He was focused on a small, overweight man in a cheap suit, wearing glasses and a derby hat. He was seated alone in a booth, reading a newspaper and nursing a beer. He seemed oblivious to the incessant noise all around.

Marconi approached. "Buy you a drink?"

The man looked up. If he was surprised, he didn't show it. "Sure, pal. Make it a whiskey mac."

Marconi signalled a passing saloon girl and ordered two macs. Then he sat casually opposite the little man, a smug look on his face. The smaller man barely looked up and spoke idly.

"I like to know who I'm drinking with."

The newcomer lit a cigarette. "A friend... Sidney."

At that, Hackett looked up sharply. He accepted the offered cigarette and light, then studied his new companion as he exhaled a waft of smoke. "Do I know you, friend?"

"Not yet."

"You got a name?"

"Let's just say we have a common goal."

Hackett frowned. "And what's that?"

"Oh, well, how can I put it," Marconi said menacingly. He stared at Hackett with venom. "The destruction of Klondike's Circus."

Hackett glared at him, then shuddered slightly. "I... I'm sorry. I don't know what you're talking about. You must have the wrong fella, mister."

The drinks arrived and Marconi offered a toast. The smaller man nervously touched the offered glass with his own. They drank. Marconi continued. "No, I don't think so. You're Sidney Hackett all right."

Sweat was forming on the reporter's brow. "I'm Hackett. Right. But I don't know nothing about no circus."

Marconi smiled, nodding. His oily hair, tanned skin and shiny white teeth took on an unnerving quality. The alligator grin looked anything but friendly.

"Let's cut the formalities, little man. I just want the name. Nothing more." He leaned across the table, his face no more than a foot from Hackett's. "Who is paying you to give Klondike negative press? Who told you about the devil drop?"

Hackett shuddered uncontrollably. He downed the contents of his glass and rapidly made to leave. "Listen, whoever you are, you've got the wrong man. I don't know no Klondike. You've made a mistake. Now leave me alone."

Hackett visibly shook, almost falling, before darting away from the booth and racing across the bar floor.

Marconi stood, snarling. He watched the reporter head for the batwing doors and shook his head. "You made the mistake, pal."

Like a tired hunter, he walked across the floor.

"No, not the face! Please! I beg you!"

Hackett screamed as Marconi held him against the alley wall, raising a clenched fist and holding it threateningly over the smaller man.

"The name!" he rasped.

"Please!" Hackett was a mess. His suit was ripped and battered, his glasses had fallen and smashed and he had at least one broken rib.

Marconi had followed him out of the bar, across Fisherman's Wharf before expertly cutting him off via a back alley opposite one of the waterfront pontoons. Laying the shocked reporter out with a hook into the midriff, he had dragged the squealing Hackett into the alley before striking him across the rib cage and stomach.

Now, he held his quarry by the throat, pinned against the wall of a canning plant, the fist hovering above the terrified abductee's face. A light sea mist had rolled into the gloomy alley, almost covering the two figures as they scrambled among the garbage cans and fishing nets.

Marconi gave up waiting. "You asked for this!"

Without hesitation, he rammed his fist into the mouth of Hackett, ripping several teeth from the gums and shattering both lips. The impact actually jostled both men. But as Marconi held his hand and winced, Hackett wailed like a banshee, and slid slowly to the floor.

Dazed, he grabbed at his mouth, which was now a bloody, grotesque pulp.

"Damn you," he blubbered. He sunk lower into the hunkered garbage on the alley's grimy paving slabs.

Emotionless, Marconi shook his punching wrist, before hauling Hackett up once again, pinning him to the wall and raising the fist once more.

"Your right eye is next, Hackett. Unless... Unless you give me that name."

"All right!" the reporter blurted in a curious high-pitched emission. "Just let me breathe for Christ sakes."

Marconi loosened his hold and Hackett slumped into him before swaying slightly. He held onto a garbage can to keep himself upright, breathing emphatically. He held his ribs and turned, glaring at his assailant. Marconi almost looked away, such was the grim sight of the bloodied, swollen mouth.

Hackett tried to compose himself, but was shaking uncontrollably. "You son of a bitch," he muttered.

Marconi raised his right again. The two men glared at each other in the swirling sea mist, engulfing the dark alley. It was silent all around.

"Jenny... Jenny Cross."

Marconi's eyes enlarged as he stared at the bloodied man in shock.

"Jenny Cross! What is this? You can't be serious."

Hackett rubbed at his side and spat out a mouthful of blood. "It's true, dammit. She's got something going down. She gave me two fifty bills. Cash! She fed me the information. Told me to write the put-down reviews. Said I'd get two more bills when the circus is finished." He looked up at Marconi, then shook his head. "That's all I know, damn you."

Marconi was still dumbfounded. He massaged his knuckles. "Is someone paying her?"

Hackett tried to straightened himself, the blood pouring down his jaw and onto his dirtied suit. "How would I know? She's trying to sabotage her own company. God knows why. I just did what she paid me for."

Marconi took it all in, and merely stood there, gazing into the mist. Then, with a nod, he finally said something.

"Enjoy the garbage, little man."

Hackett, swaying on his feet, stared at him dumbly. "W-what?"

In one swift move, Marconi grabbed the smaller man by the lapels, turned him around in the alley and, with surprising strength, ran with him for five paces before hurling his prone form head first into a giant pile of rubbish that was overflowing from a collection of small skips on the opposite side of the enclosure.

With one final look down, he noted with satisfaction that all he could now see of Hackett was a pair of legs sticking out of the mass of garbage.

With a chuckle, he walked out onto Fisherman's Wharf, searching for a call box.

The circus train arrived at Orion Bay the following morning, after a slow and steady trek down the Barbary Coastal trail.

Klondike was in his stateroom, going through various logistics and paperwork, when Lacey burst in and grabbed his hand.

"Come quick, Kal, to the communal carriage. You've got to see this."

"What in hell!" he barked, glaring at her two hands as they held his, attempting to prise him from his desk.

"Just come!"

She led him hurriedly through the carriage, still clutching his hand. They made quite a sight as they raced through five carriages of the train. The lady in the turquoise pyjama suit, and the gruff circus master in his work shirt and slacks.

Finally, after passing through a run of accommodation carriages on the motionless train, the duo burst into the communal lounge in the train's centre.

Corky, Suzi and Plum were all seated in armchairs gazing at the circus train's one and only television set, which sat on a small round table in the corner of the room.

Klondike and Lacey breezed past the chairs, couches and tables that made up the communal carriage, until they reached the far end and joined the others.

"Look!" Lacey exclaimed, pointing at the small screen before them all.

Still disgruntled, Klondike stared straight ahead. Then, his jaw dropped.

A well-known TV newsman, Len Gould, was interviewing Roddy Olsen, with Rusty Fox on his arm.

The circus people all watched, entranced.

"Well, Roddy," Gould was saying, resplendent in a tuxedo. They were standing in front of the circus tent in a pre-recorded segment. "You sure captivated the circus fans of San Francisco tonight. What was it like being out there, in front of thousands of people in that tent?"

Olsen laughed. "Incredible, Len. Nothing can beat the feel of a live audience. The energy, the electricity, the excitement."

"And all the chicks," Rusty added mischievously.

Gould laughed. "You have put together a tremendous act here, young man. How did you do it?"

Olsen looked solemn. "Practice, Len. It's all about practice. Growing up, I had plenty of time to practice. And I've spent years working on my act. Polishing, experimenting. Trying things out."

"He had a very boring life," Rusty added. "Then I made him a star."

Gould laughed out loud. "You used to support another one-time guest of ours here on Bay City Revue. The singer Johnny Rex. Maybe we could get you two to perform on the same card again one day."

Olsen smiled. "Johnny was a great help in my career. Without him, who knows where I might be now. And the same goes for Kal Klondike and his wonderful circus. Mr Klondike has given me the platform to showcase my act to people all over the west coast. I won't let him down."

"OK, Roddy," Gould began, "it's been a pleasure having you on our show. We wish you luck with everything going forward. You're a very talented young man… That's for sure." He looked down at Rusty. "And now, I believe our little furry friend has something to say to close us out?"

Rusty Fox turned to face the camera. "That's right folks. Don't miss Klondike's Circus live as we tour the west coast. Next show is Sunday at Orion Bay. The curtain rolls at 7. Get your tickets from our box office from Friday at noon. I'll be there, along with a sea of stars, but the main attraction is me, Rusty Fox, teen idol. It's going to be grrr-eat!"

"Way to go, Rusty!" Gould proclaimed, patting the puppet's head as he leant down.

"One more thing," said the fox puppet.

"What's that, little fella?"

"Your mouthwash ain't working!"

Gould burst into hysterics and the picture changed to another reporter at the seaside.

In the communal carriage, they all stood gaping at the footage. Suzy leant over to turn the volume down then looked back at the others.

"That was incredible. Isn't he the greatest!" She beamed up at them, looking like a child as she shook excitedly.

"He sure is," Plum enthused.

"And that was the greatest bit of advertising we could dream of," Lacey murmured approvingly. "All thanks to a fox puppet."

"That show is seen by hundreds of thousands," Plum rapped, looking as excited as anyone.

They all turned to Klondike, who in turn glanced at Corky.

The veteran clown, dressed as always in his face paint, but wearing a dungarees over a red and black shirt, nodded. He got out of his seat and put an arm round Klondike.

"Kal," he mused, the mocked-up red lips making the others grin. "I don't care what you do further down the line. But do not let that boy go. Not for all the gold in Orion Bay."

Klondike patted him on the chest. "You could still teach him a thing or two. You've been making folks laugh for years."

"Not on TV I ain't!" With that, he produced a bouquet of red roses from inside his dungarees, and handed them to Lacey. Then, he removed his bowler hat and placed it on Suzy's head. "Now, if you'll excuse me, I got to practice."

The ever-loveable clown meandered out the carriage, leaving the others staring after him.

"Well," Lacey began, staring at the flowers, before handing them over to an equally bemused Suzy, "what did you think of all that, Kal?"

Klondike shook his head. "I'm running out of superlatives for our boy." He frowned slightly, running the TV interview back through his mind.

Lacey watched him idly. "What is it?"

"Something he said back there. A lot of what he has told us." He looked up quizzically at Lacey and pulled her toward him, out of earshot of Plum and Suzy.

"Listen," he rasped, "I think it's time you got that rich old contacts book of yours up to my office."

She stared at him, her giant violet eyes almost hypnotic such was their intensity. "My roll-a-dial? My, it must be important."

"It is."

Now, it was his turn to pull her out of the room, dragging her back down the train towards the accommodation blocks.

Orion Bay was a picturesque California town, with its main drag and residential overflow filtering back from the bay and beachside area. There was a beautiful seaside for tourists and getawayers and promenades full of nickel and dime games and other attractions.

The circus train had pulled up on a railroad siding just off the station, and was sat just yards from the town's recreation field, where the roustabouts and work crews were now going about the behemoth task of setting up the tent and midway.

Klondike was seated on a bench overlooking a lake to the south of the parkland where the field lay. In his usual leather jacket and fedora, he sat pensively, gazing out at the vast expanse of grey water that lay just a few feet before him. He waited.

"You wanted to see me?"

He turned and squinted through the sunlight at the ever-youthful features of Roddy Olsen. The youngster was dressed in jeans and a yellow windbeater jacket, and smiled amiably as he walked in front of the bench.

"Sure," Klondike breathed. "Have a seat, kid." He reached down and pulled up two takeaway coffees he had just purchased from a booth. Handing one to Olsen, he nodded to the lake.

"I always take time to come out here when we stop at Orion. It's a beautiful spot. So peaceful."

Olsen took the coffee and sat next to the boss. "It sure is." He took a sip, and looked about awkwardly. With a heavy gulp, he quipped, "Am I in trouble?"

Klondike laughed. "Trouble, you say! Ha! No. No, I just wanted a talk is all." He looked the youngster over and shook his head. "I saw the TV interview earlier. Lacey had kept it a surprise for me. You were fantastic, kid. Again."

"Thank you Mr K—"

"You're just a natural, Rod. And I can't stop thinking about that. You're 19. You act like a show business veteran. You look like a matinee idol. You came from nowhere. That first day back at the camp... Now, look at you. The host. How did it all happen so fast? I... I just can't stop thinking about it."

Olsen looked out at the lake. "Sometimes all the pieces just fall into place, I guess. Right time. Right choices. Right decisions. I'm just so glad I sought you guys out at Santa Cruz."

"Yeah..." Klondike stared into nothingness, looking almost sad. He took a deep breath.

"I talked to Johnny Rex."

Olsen glared at him, turning on the bench. "You what? Johnny? But how..."

"I know everything, Roddy."

Olsen's eyes glazed over. He suddenly looked like a child, a boy facing an authority figure for the first time, threatened like never before. He cowered slightly.

"What... What do you mean?" Gone was the super confident, professional persona that had amazed everyone at the circus. Now, the young entertainer with the quick answers and the movie star looks was a confused juvenile, eyes wide in fright.

Klondike just stared straight ahead. He spoke quietly. "Something just didn't fit. I know the backgrounds of all my guys. But with you, I just didn't get it. It was as if you were hiding your past. I need to know your past to help me truly understand you, Rod. You're partly my responsibility now."

"What... What are you talking about?" Olsen whispered, quivering.

Klondike took a deep breath, and finally turned on the bench to face the youngster. He looked him over softly. His voice was low and gravelly.

"The car accident. Your mother was an alcoholic. Your folks were always fighting. When you were ten years old, she stormed out of the house, drunk as a skunk. Your dad went after her, made it into the car, before she drove straight into a bus. The locals called it the worst tragedy to hit Fresno in years. You went into care. Then, they sent you to live with your Uncle Ray. Another drunk. He beat you. Tormented you. For years. So you ran away. Ended up living in a boarding house in Los Angeles. You were 14. Just 14 and living in a damn boarding house."

He stopped and looked Olsen over. The teenager had tears in his eyes, that flowed down his cheeks and around his mouth. Fluid oozed from his nostrils and mixed with the tears. He was shaking his head, as if trying to banish memories. Feelings he had forgotten existed. He felt as though he was in a dreamlike state.

Klondike eyed him thoroughly. "Does that all sound about right, Rod?"

Olsen quivered, rubbing at his eyes and placing his coffee on the floor. "Life was never meant to be easy."

"Jesus Christ!" Klondike stammered. "There's life and then there's this."

Olsen looked down. "You spoke to Johnny?"

"That's right. He told me the whole story. Your story. Told me how you met at that god-forsaken boarding house. Two boys who wanted to be entertainers. Then, a few years later, he started getting gigs as a singer with his band and wanted a warm-up act. Who did he call? His old buddy from the boarding house. Reunited as performers."

Olsen gazed into nothingness, remembering. "We finally made it. In our minds."

Klondike tried to smile. "You'd worked as dig ditchers, towel boys in bars, shoe shiners. And all the while you should have been in school. Scoring touchdowns, dating cheerleaders, having shakes and burgers at the diner." He paused, looking glum. "You missed out on all that Roddy. Your path was a different one."

The youngster took a deep breath. "From what I've heard, your path was different too, Mr Klondike."

The circus master nodded ruefully. "That's right." He gazed out at the lake. "We're both orphans, Roddy. I never knew my folks. I was raised in an orphanage. All… All I ever wanted back then was to be part of a family. I found that… First in the army. Then, in the circus."

It was an unusually sentimental emission from the gruff trail boss. Olsen looked him over in shock and something like awe. He noted the craggy face, rugged demeanour and harsh leather-like skin. It just didn't add up.

"Why are you doing this?" he whimpered.

Klondike laid an arm over the backrest. "Because I want you to know…you've found your family, Roddy. Just like I did. Here at my circus. We are your family now. We are all together on this. Performers, roustabouts, the guys in the back. We…hell, we got you, kid. We got your back. That's what I'm trying to say." He looked the younger man over. "God knows, you've done your time, kid. All that you went through growing up. Well, that's all in the past now. Now, you've got everything to live for, everything to be happy for. Because you're in the circus, god damn it, and that's the greatest calling on earth for any man."

Olsen finally smiled. He wiped at his tears. "It is something special."

Klondike roared like an ox. "You bet!" He placed a hand on Olsen's shoulder. "We got ya, kid. You won't ever be alone again. You've got all the friends you'll ever need right here." He winked and gave him a playful nudge. "And one special lady."

He looked up. "Suzy? Hell Mr Klondike, we're just friends. We hit it off, you know?"

Klondike laughed. "Yeah, I know all right, kid."

Olsen laughed too. "What… What can I ever do to thank you for all this? For taking me in? For caring."

Klondike frowned. "What you can do is keep it up. Keep this level of performance up for the whole season, Rod." He eyed him shrewdly. "Think you can manage that, son?"

Olsen grinned widely. "Just watch me, boss man!"

Chapter 17

THE BIG BAY SPECTACULAR!

Don Hanley, Orion Bay Review

Lions! Tigers! Elephants! And dancing monkeys!

These were just some of the attractions on offer to Orion Bay's citizens last night when Klondike's Circus returned to the region for its annual stage spectacular.

It's like the zoo, mixed with a Las Vegas cabaret show, with a touch of magic thrown in. And who could possibly resist that eclectic mix?

The big top was a sell-out for this raucous night of fun; a capacity crowd crammed into the giant circus tent in the bay, which could be seen for miles around, the joyful applause and calls of delight heard no doubt equally as far.

Kal Klondike (if that is his real name) and his team of entertainers have been stopping off at the Bay for years now, and never disappoint. Their fan base here must be alarmingly large, with the show reportedly selling out within hours of the box office being set up in the bay on Saturday morning.

The big headline act, trapeze artist Gino Shapiro, the 'debonair king of the air', is one of the most dynamic perfumers in circus history, sailing through the air from ring to ring with poise and grace...and a big smile. He propels himself above the circus crowd with no safety net beneath. Some would call it pure insanity, but the grand showman Shapiro merely calls it his art form, his calling. His tentpole act, a daring tightrope walk 20 feet above the sawdust arena floor, forms the circus's final act...and what a sight it is.

Also appearing was Corky the Clown, reputedly the world's fastest juggler, who truly sets the big top alight with his antics. The veteran comic has being wowing audiences for years with his high-speed juggling atop a unicycle, and also delivers a show-stopping human cannonball act.

Klondike's Circus has always set itself apart from the rest with its unusual array of human exclamation marks. And it doesn't disappoint this year, with

Gargantua the human blob, Goliath the giant, a gang of dancing dwarves and a team of cowboys performing acrobatics while riding horses.

The circus's animal acts have proved a controversial point with journalists this year. The growing animal rights movement is gathering steam in the capital, and one can't help but wonder if the end is near for such traditional acts.

But, until that day, this circus continues to thrill us all with its hyper-trained beasts.

Cath Cassidy and her dancing chimps are cute and funny. Amanda Hart's prancing elephants are a marvel. And the mysterious safari master Emile Rance had us all spellbound as he displayed his lions and tiger, deploying them all in some incredible acts of derring do.

Introducing the acts and providing plenty of laughs is the puppetmaster, Roddy Olsen, a young ventriloquist who acts as ringmaster. Along with his puppet pals Rusty Fox, Napoleon and Tony Tan, Olsen gained some of the loudest cheers during the grand finale, when he joined circus songstress Suzi Dando for the Klondike anthem, 'Can You Feel the Magic Tonight?'

Well, I certainly felt the magic and, judging by the rousing, almost hysteria-like ovation the troupe got during that final lap of honour, it's fair to say most of those going home, especially the youngsters, will feel the same way.

As for the Klondike crew, they have big shows ahead in Los Angeles and Las Vegas as they head south on their west coast tour. With their current roster of talent and avalanche of publicity, the sky could well be the limit for this circus. Only time will tell, but this correspondent is predicting big things for the Klondike stars.

"All aboard!"

Jim McCabe roared like a wild animal as the work crew finished loading up the train's storage carriages. As the big man looked up and down the line and length of the mighty express cruiser, he nodded in satisfaction as each of his roustabouts slammed coach doors shut and locked the holdings, making certain everything was secure.

The ramps leading up into each carriage were gathered by the train gaffer and his assistant and secured in the bulk carrier.

An endless swirl of dust whipped up around the rails as teams of men raced towards the bunkhouse, where rest and cold lemonade awaited.

McCabe watched gruffly as each sweat-covered train hand shuffled past, heading for the roustabouts' haven at the three-quarter mark. He was dressed in slacks, a vest, braces and his usual porkpie hat, and muttered words of encouragement to his team as they passed him. He continually looked about, down to the field and back to the rails, double-checking nothing – and no one – had been left behind.

The crews had been working all morning and most of the afternoon following the previous night's show. Everything was now stored aboard the train, the great tent folded down and placed in its holding carriage.

Now, as dusk formed, the train was ready to roll again. And his men were ready for their rest.

Suddenly, as he went to board the carriage nearest to him, he spotted a figure running towards him from out of the swirling dust.

The train guard, stood at the head of the locomotive some 300 yards to his right, was blowing a whistle frantically through the evening sky, clearly aiming his display towards McCabe.

The chief frowned at the approaching figure, and held up a hand at the guard at the other end.

He gradually recognised the swarthy, lithe demeanour of Luca Marconi, as the Italian raced towards him in a cheap sack suit.

Something about this character just didn't fit, McCabe thought once again. But he was a good worker, he'd give him that.

"You're late, pretty boy!" he spat out at the approaching figure.

Marconi, out of breath and a little dishevelled as he finally joined his manager, smiled craftily. "It would appear I'm in the nick of time, boss."

McCabe nodded irritably. "I guess." He looked at the man's suit, the valise he was carrying. "Did you get your business sorted back in Frisco?"

Marconi nodded, one hand on the carriage door. "Sure. My cousin Paolo now has all his chickens ready for market."

McCabe stared at him blankly. "Right." He opened the train door. "Well, I hope you got a bit of rest cos we got a tough schedule ahead, boy. Three cities. Seven days. That's the roll call."

"Where we heading now?"

"Saracen City."

The Italian shook his head. "Will it take long?"

McCabe grunted. "Yes, it's a tricky path. Across Colby Canyon, through the Calico plains and then over Blackhawk Point."

Another air-piercing whistle rocked the two men, and they hastily climbed aboard the train. At the head, the guard was finally satisfied and joined the driver and fireman in the cab.

In seconds, the wheels began churning and, once again, the great circus train rolled on down the line.

Blackhawk Point. It had been used as a Union army fort during the civil war, storing men, supplies and ammunition. The US army had maintained a presence up until the start of World War One, when the fort was abruptly abandoned, its stores cleared out, and all trace of any military presence evaporated.

The fort was essentially a giant trench cut into the plains, and had allowed Yankee troops to hide within its depths and await enemy patrols or marauding Indian tribes, who they could then ambush.

Now, Blackhawk Point was little more than a giant, square ditch measuring about two square miles, little more than a curious geological anomaly.

Its only point of interest these days was the railroad. When the tracks were first constructed almost 50 years earlier, the old fort was positioned directly in the path of the approaching line. In order to nullify the difficulty of the giant trench, a huge elongated mound was erected that ran straight through the middle of the fort, allowing the rails to be placed on top and the train line to continue unabated through the submerged land.

The mound ensured that the railroad travelled about 12 feet above the ground – an elevated platform that ran for little more than a mile. A transportation oddity, the unusual stretch of track was simply another quirk of nature to be found on the west coast rails.

"Blackhawk Point…" Mercer said the words dryly as he surveyed the barren trench before him in the dusky moonlight.

Dressed as always in his green trench coat and fedora, he was walking slowly along the track, studying the rails and sleeper blocks.

An old man with grey hair and a wispy beard followed. He carried a large toolbox. "You sure this is the place, mister?"

Mercer continued to look. "Sure, I'm sure, old timer." He stopped, looked up and down the line, then crouched down, feeling the old iron rails. "Here."

The old man looked down. "You want it now?"

"Give me the destabiliser."

The old timer carefully placed the box on the damp earth next to the line, then delicately pulled out an odd-looking metal contraption that resembled a giant hinge, only with various screws and attachments joined to its ends.

Mercer took hold of the heavy item, then studiously placed it, face up, onto the railroad berth. Then, with calculated poise, he clamped two teeth on either end of the contraption to the rails on each side. The metal object was the perfect fit and, by the time he had finished, it sat easily in-between the two rails, jutting out from the ground like a road block. He screwed two further attachments to the sleeper block beneath, then tested the destabiliser's stability by pushing on it. Satisfied with his work, he finally stood and looked down at the strange metal block, which jutted out about two feet from the track.

The old man watched curiously from behind. "Listen, mister, that piece of steel ain't gunna stop no express train. You need a clamp, a blocker. That thing ain't no stopper."

Mercer continued to stare down the line. "It's perfect," he muttered icily. "My train doesn't break 30 miles an hour. This destabiliser will derail it perfectly. It will direct the carriages away from the line. That was the idea."

His companion gaped at the object on the railroad. He rubbed his hands through the tattered rags he wore without shame. "I still say it won't work."

Mercer growled in his low, rasping tone. "I didn't pay you for your opinion, pops. I paid you to get me up here. You came through. Way to go. Now, let's get back to town."

He picked up the toolbox, sealed it, and made to climb back down the mound to the fort's surface below. The hillside was steep and muddy.

"I just don't get why you'd want to derail that train," the old man muttered. "The carnage you'll cause. The people…the mess!"

Mercer was negotiating the steep incline. "Like I said, that's not your concern. Now, do you want the rest of the money or not?"

Like an obedient child, the other man lurched after him and both figures soon melted into the shadowy gloom descending on the old fort.

The train was steaming through the Calico plains of mid-California as nightfall set in.

Klondike had just completed a walk-through of the entire ensemble, passing through every carriage from front to back, checking in with every performer and line manager.

He finally reached the end of the train and his lodgings. With a heavy sigh, he opened the door to his stateroom, removing his hat, and turned on the light.

"There you are, Kal."

Lacey was lounging on an armchair, dressed in a shiny pastel frock, and nursing a glass of wine. Her red hair was worn up and she looked like she had just come from a small-town beauty pageant. Klondike stared at her dumbly.

She smiled wickedly and, standing, offered him a full glass from the round table. "Cabernet Sauvignon?"

Klondike shook his head. "I'm not even going to ask what that is." He looked her over. "And what's all this?"

Lacey laughed gaily, still holding both glasses. "Oh, I don't know. A celebration, maybe? The season has been a smash hit so far, no one can argue with that." She smiled at him mischievously. "Why can't we enjoy it a little?"

Finally, removing his jacket, he stepped forward and accepted the glass.

"Cheers," she murmured as they clinked glasses. Her giant, entrancing violet eyes never left him. He began to find it overpowering.

"Not bad," he grunted, acknowledging the wine. He looked around his room awkwardly, then eyed Lacey queerly. "Y'know, Lacey, a celebration is usually held at the end of the season. When we have succeeded."

She rolled her eyes, sipping her wine. "Oh, come on, Kal baby. Just... Just try to relax. A little. I see how you patrol this train. Keeping everyone in line. It works, sure, but you're going to give yourself a heart attack, sweetheart."

He looked downward, awkwardly sipping the wine. "I owe you a lot, Lacey. You know that. Your publicity machine deserves a lot of the credit."

She smiled beautifully. "We make quite a team, you and I."

He laughed at this. "You know what, we really do."

Lacey raised a pert eyebrow. "Maybe this is just the start."

He frowned. "What do you mean? What are you taking about?"

Her eyes sparkled. "I'm talking about a partnership." She thought for a moment, watching him intently. "What if I was to come in with you? Invest. And become a partner. Then it wouldn't be a loan deal, like what we have now with Addison. It would be permanent. We could try and get a residency contract in

Las Vegas. Maybe Broadway. Atlantic City. Don't you see, Kal. We are a smash hit. The only way is up from here. We can get so much bigger."

Klondike felt his head reeling. "Woh!" he barked. He smiled slightly. "I hear that. And I agree with you. We can get bigger. But…but are you saying you would want to come on board full-time? The circus life? What about your old pals in Hollywood? The movie people? I thought that was your bag. Not this life."

She moved very close to him. "It was a different kind of life, I'll give you that. But, can't you see… I've embraced this experience with Klondike's Circus. It's brought me into this wonderful world I never thought I would enjoy. It's brought me into the lives of these incredible people. The talent is amazing. It's made me feel emotions and ambitions I didn't think existed." She suddenly seemed to shrink under his gaze, the confidence and bravado evaporating and her voice quiet and childlike. "And it brought me to you."

He glared at her in shock. With a dumbfounded look, he took her glass out of her hand and poured her some more wine as she watched him hypnotically.

He turned to her, holding out the glass. "Have another drink, Lacey."

An odd silence filled the stateroom.

Jenny Cross crept into the lounge in her carriage, taking in everything as she moved.

There on the couch sat Gino with Amanda and Cathy on either side of him, enraptured once again by one of his tales of Hollywood. It annoyed her when he entertained other performers in this room. As she saw it, this was the trapeze artists' lounge, and outsiders were not welcome.

The two women both laughed as the great entertainer unveiled yet another corny anecdote. Gino looked up as Jenny wandered in. "Ah," he cried in delight. "It is true, I really am the luckiest man in the world. Tonight, I get to enjoy the company of three beautiful ladies. No, the three most beautiful ladies in all the world. Come, Jenny girl, I was telling my darlings all about my next project in the fall."

Amanda and Cathy both giggled as they nuzzled up to him on the couch. Both wore pyjamas while Gino was dressed in his favourite red tracksuit, which he often wore during practice sessions.

Jenny frowned at the two females. "Why don't you two take a hike," she mused acidly. "I think Mr Ed is on the television set in the lounging carriage."

Amanda pouted. "What's the matter, flyer? Worried you're not going to get Gino to yourself?"

Cathy laughed. "Don't worry about her, Mandy. She's always got a bee in her butt."

Jenny breezed to the dresser and poured herself a cognac. She looked around idly. "Say," she addressed Gino. "Where is Nicky? I haven't seen him all day."

Gino took on a sudden sombre look. "Poor Nicky. He was feeling a little sick. I think he is upset about something. He went up to the observation deck about an hour ago. He said looking at the countryside helps him to think."

Jenny froze, and almost dropped her glass. The observation deck. It was at the front of the train. Just behind the cab and the fire room. She stared at Gino in shock, her hand flying to her mouth.

He looked at her in fright. "Jenny girl, what is —"

"Observation deck!" she gasped in horror.

She stormed out of the room in a whirl, slamming the door behind her and racing down the aisle leading to the carriage door.

Gino stared at the two women in stunned silence, then made to follow her.

"Leave her," Cathy said in a high-pitched whine. "She has to be crazy."

Jenny was now darting through the carriages in fear, her face a white mask of terror as she ploughed through the train.

"Oh, Nicky!" she gasped aloud.

But she was too late.

It is difficult to describe what happened next.

The circus train chugged into Blackhawk Point, the driver slowing slightly at the sight of the unusual trench that played out before him. As the locomotive rode the rails atop the elevated trackline, time seemed to stand still. The carriages rattled over the railroad, as more of the train crept across the giant opening in the plains.

And then something deplorable happened. As the driver navigated the great train across the old fort, he sensed rather than saw an obstruction on the track. Before he could react, an almighty bang reverberated around the cab followed by a walloping shudder that sent both the driver and his fireman flying to the floor.

Like an earthquake, the cab shook wildly, as the train inexplicably separated from the rails, surging upwards into the air as its front wheels struck the destabiliser and were sent on an upward course into nothingness. The cab rose grotesquely into the air and then, sickeningly, dropped like a rock over the side and down the mound.

A thunderous crash followed as the cab cartwheeled insanely down the incline. But even worse was the sight of the rest of the train as it followed on this deadly path of destruction. The fire carriage, supplies wagon, observation deck, and all the other carts followed, pulled off the tracks by the plunging earlier carriages and sent flying down the mound by the momentum of the falling train.

The front-end carriages all crashed down the incline and ended up in a shattered mess of debris on the ground, 20 feet below.

As the tragedy ensued, more and more carriages followed, careering off the tracks and smashing into the by-now immense wreckage of wood, metal and slate.

Finally, after what felt like an endless procession of carnage and a sound like an exploding gas tank, the remaining carriages stabilised on the track as the momentum slowed to a halt, the pile of wreckage now running right up the mound and across the tracks.

In all, almost half of the circus train had fallen victim to the obstruction and had gone over with the destabilised driver's cab – an incredible 18 coaches.

The rest of the halted train now sat perched on the railroad above the fort. Fortunately, all the accommodations carriages were located in the rear half of the train, although the sudden and unexpected halt had caused carnage everywhere.

The great circus train had been mortally bludgeoned. Cut in two. Its front half now sat shattered all around the still intact rear, taken off the rails and delivered a killer blow.

Several miles away, atop a bell tower in a nearby town, the crash had been observed by a man using binoculars. As the tumbling train finally came to a halt on the strange elevated platform above Blackhawk Point, the man had smiled. Removing his binoculars, he said one word.

"Bingo."

The sudden smash and breaking mechanism was felt right through the train to the rear carriages.

Klondike and Lacey were sent sprawling, both falling on top of each other as the rumble reverberated through the carriages. The wine flew through the air, spilling all over them as they hit the floor in an undignified bundle.

In the lounging carriage, Corky, Olsen, Suzi and Goliath had all been watching TV. As the sudden impact hit, all were sent tumbling out of their seats, the television set smashing into the wall. They rolled around in stunned exasperation as the train rumbled on wildly, the roar of the falling coaches giving all cause for severe alarm. The train lurched on another 100 yards or so, unsteady and barely on the rails.

Further back, in his lounging quarters, Gino had sensed the crash immediately and had gallantly plucked up both Amanda and Cathy as if they were rag dolls, shielding them and forcing them to the floor. He led down on top of them as the train shook wildly, raising his head as he tried to understand what had happened. The sound of the falling carriages gripped him, and he tucked his head down among the women.

Richie Plum had been fast asleep in his stateroom at the back, and was flung to the floor as the impact hit. Striking his head heavily on the bedpost, he rolled awkwardly to the carpet below, half unconscious and stunned into a form of hyper-real. His mind surged, but he could find no answers as he felt the train rocking beneath him.

Heavy had also been dozing in his cabin, the rocketing motion sending him sprawling off the mattress and head first into his laundry basket.

In the bunkhouse, near the centre of the train and barely three carriages away from the last coach to tumble over the side, it felt like a giant hand had picked the room up and shaken it angrily. Bunkbeds fell apart and men flew through the air as the giant housing block rattled like a giant dodgem.

And then there was Jenny. She had been running for the front of the train when the disaster struck. She was just about to race through the bunkhouse when the cab hit the destabiliser, her hand on the carriage door as she passed through the outdoor interchange. She was flung against the door to the lodgings, and then pinned there by gravity as the full impact of the crash halted the great train. As the carriages slowly continued to rumble, dragged further along by the carnage at the front, she clung to the door hopelessly, her flowery dress torn and dirtied.

The unnerving, unsteady motion of the train finally stopped.

Klondike looked up, his eyes wild with shock. He glanced at Lacey lying beside him in the cluttered room. "You all right?"

169

She nodded feebly, shaking. "I... I think so." She tried to stand, and Klondike helped her as they rose from the floor. "What...what happened?"

He shook his head and made for the door. Panic had overcome him and he would not be stopped. Lacey followed gingerly, as if in a trance.

Klondike sprinted down the aisle, before charging into the carriage door like a bull. It swung open, and he jumped onto the interchange platform and out onto the ground. The night was pitch black, only the lights from the train's coaches enabled him to see the ground below the mound. Puzzled, as if unfamiliar with the unusual surroundings, he sprinted down the side of his beloved train, careful not to plunge down the incline just beyond.

He slowed as he saw a carriage ahead of him lying half on and half off the tracks at a grotesque angle, as if it had been twisted.

His heart sank, and he felt a stabbing pain in his chest as he glimpsed for the first time the hell that had been unleashed before him.

Staring dumbly, his face a mask of despair, he quietly surveyed the damage.

Half of the train now sat in a giant, ragged, seemingly endless heap of debris below and ahead of him. Smashed machinery was scattered all around, covering the muddy ground for an acre. The carriages hardly resembled carriages, more a battered assembly of smashed metal boxes.

Squinting into the gloom, he made out the front coaches and the driver's cabin lying at the front of the mess. Steam hissed through the night air, as cries of despair and shock filled the scene.

Klondike gaped at the horror before him, swaying slightly. It was a sight he could never have imagined, not even in his darkest nightmares. His mind raced, but his brain was not functioning. For a moment, he felt he might pass out. Instead, he just stared at the destroyed front half of his train.

Then, Heavy and Lacey were beside him, both out of breath and extremely dishevelled.

Heavy wandered to the edge of the mound. "God in heaven," he said in shock. "The train... How...how is it even possible?"

Klondike was about to form a reply when he heard a terrifying sound that rocked him to his core. He had been dreading it, maybe expecting it, but it shook him all the same.

The roar of a lion. Then an answering snarl.

Klondike stared into the distance. Then he saw them. Cassius and Apollo. Both racing away from the wreckage, free from their shattered cages. Two lions running wild into the night. Gone.

Seconds later, Emile Rance was seen racing down the mound towards them, still dressed in his velvet robe and pyjamas. He screamed morbidly, calling their names over and over, before disappearing into the night, following the sounds of the lions' growls.

Klondike made to call out to him from the mound, but he was gone in an instant, swallowed up by the night. His screams penetrated the sudden silence of the crash site.

Seeing him race into the dark after the lions, still dressed in his pyjamas, was a surreal sight none of them would ever forget.

As if that wasn't enough, the lions' roars were met by a sudden stampede of horses as a deluge of animals broke free from the wrecked coaches.

Pandemonium reigned. Several elephants were loose, while the monkeys also broke free into the night, charging about the battered carriages like enraged demons.

"Oh god!" Klondike groaned. He turned slowly and found many of his staff had gathered behind him, all staring in stunned silence at the impossible scenes before them.

Klondike took a deep breath. He was finally able to think and his leadership skills came to the fore as he stood before his people. Duty took over, and he formed a plan in his head.

"Attention everybody!" he bellowed at the gathered crowd. "We have an extreme emergency. The train has derailed. This is what we are going to do." He looked at the ashen faces all staring at him on the edge of the track. "Heavy… Call an ambulance and the police. Tell them to get as much help down here as they can. McCabe… I need a casualty list. Get to the driver's cab now. The accommodation blocks are still on the rails. But I don't know who was up top. Lacey, Amanda, Suzy, Cathy… You are now nurses. First aid boxes are located in the lounge and kitchen. Use them. Anyone injured and walking, go to the lounge. Richie…round up some men and make stretchers. Then transport the injured to the lounging coach." He stopped, glancing out into the night. "Some of the animals are loose so, for Christ sakes, be careful out there and —"

He broke off as a female scream pierced the night. It was Amanda, running wildly toward one of her beloved elephants, that was limping badly through the old fort below. In the dim moonlight, the beast resembled a nightmarish apparition from a horror movie. Klondike made to stop her, but she pushed him away as she hurried down the incline beyond.

"My babies!" she screamed, racing for the elephant.

Klondike watched in despair as she raced down the mound. His mind was whirling as he tried to stop his crew reacting wildly to the tragedy.

McCabe and two of his men had raced towards the drivers' cab, but now Shapiro had appeared out of the crowd and was also running into the debris beyond them.

"Gino!" Klondike called out, catching Shapiro as he charged past. "Gino, don't go in there. It's too dangerous."

"Nicky," he cried. "It's Nicky. He was in the observation coach."

Klondike let him go, cursing. He looked around in confusion as bodies raced about the train and the wreckage, his vision beginning to blur. Looking about him in a blind panic, he took off after Shapiro, sprinting through the debris field.

"Gino!" he screamed. "Come back. Don't go in there."

Shapiro had reached the shattered observation deck, which lay on its side. With minimal effort, he pulled a pile of wooden planks away from the lopsided doorway at the interchange platform and, angling his body, lurched inside.

Klondike made to follow him but, eyeing the fallen carriage, he tripped over a grounded cash register and sprawled heavily to the floor, smacking his head on the interchange's steel footing.

Everything seemed to happen in slow motion for several seconds as he tried to stand again, his legs unstable and his thinking unclear. His forehead throbbed and he felt a wet smattering of blood soaking his brow. He supported himself unsteadily with the edge of the carriage.

Shapiro emerged, carrying an unconscious Nicky in his arms. He carefully guided the prone form of his brother to the muddy ground below, then felt him all over, looking for broken bones. Grasping the right arm, he froze and glanced up at Klondike.

"Broken arm and shoulder. Concussion. Possible internal head injuries."

Klondike stared down at them in shock. It was all too much. He studied Nicky's frame. The poor kid's face was covered in bruises and cuts.

Then, to his relief, two roustabouts arrived and helped Shapiro carry his brother up the incline and back to the train.

Klondike rubbed at his throbbing forehead, then saw McCabe make his way over.

"Talk to me, Jim," he barked.

"No fatalities," McCabe reported dutifully. "It's some kinda miracle. The driver has a broken pelvis. The impact threw him against his desk. The fireman was lucky. He had been looking out the side of the train and ended up getting thrown over the side and rolled down the hill. He's with the driver now. We can't move him till the medics get here."

Klondike shook his head. "Thank god no one was killed," he breathed.

"It's gunna be one hell of a clean-up operation, Kal," said McCabe.

Klondike looked at him, then staggered back towards the tracks, away from the carnage.

He felt like he was in a trance as he looked on helplessly at the pandemonium all around him.

The old fort had become a hive of activity as bodies busied themselves along the length of the second half of the train. It felt like one surreal sight after another greeted him as he wandered through the mud.

Amanda was chasing two of her elephants as they high-tailed it away from the railroad. Cathy was hugging her chimpanzees as they cried like new-born babies at the horrors that forced them out of their pens. Horses galloped blindly up and down the incline, neighing in distress and kicking out as the cowboy riders tried to steady them.

Makeshift stretchers made from bed cots were used by roustabouts to ferry injured men to the lounging block.

He saw Corky, his make-up all but washed away, his face finally revealed, running alongside the tracks, with cushions in his hands. Heavy was helping a limping worker down the mound.

And Richie, in a show of courage and positivity, was directing roustabouts and giving jobs to all the helpers.

As Klondike surveyed the response from his team, a high-pitched siren shattered the night air. He turned to the head of the train, where it had veered off the track, and saw a police car and two ambulances arrive on the scene, their bright lights setting a blazing trail across the crash site.

He climbed over the mangled wreck of the coach that was tipping over the edge of the mound, and jumped onto the track. There, to his surprise, he saw Jenny, sitting on the tracks in a ball and sobbing quietly.

He looked at her. Her flowery dress was cut to ribbons and she was covered in gashes, her hair a dishevelled mess. She glanced up, the tears flowing uncontrollably as she shook spasmodically.

He placed a hand on her shoulder. "It's all right, Jenny," he said softly. "It'll be all right. I promise."

She stared at him for a long moment, then buried her face in her hands again, the sobs becoming more fervent. She moaned uncontrollably to herself.

Klondike looked down at her, patted her shoulder again, and, with a heavy sigh, made his way over to the waiting police car.

Medics carrying stretchers jumped out of the ambulances as he approached the service vehicles.

A patrolman emerged from the squad car and stared in despair at the carnage all around. "What the hell happened out here?" he snapped at Klondike.

Klondike looked back ruefully and shook his head.

"The end of the world."

Chapter 18

CIRCUS TRAIN DERAILED! DEADLY ANIMALS ON LOOSE!

By Karen Wayne, Briscoe County Journal

Two lions were said to be on the loose in Briscoe County last night after a circus train was derailed at Blackhawk Point.

The old civil war fort, one of the most unusual stretches of railroad in the USA, was the scene of a nightmarish crash as the giant transporter was derailed.

Klondike's Circus, a popular travelling show based out of Santa Cruz, Northern California, had been passing through county lines en route to Santa Brava when the incident occurred.

It is alleged that the giant, 32-coach train came off the tracks after the front cab hit an obstruction on the rail line, sending the front end of the train hurtling down into the fort.

Police and railroad officials are today investigating the cause of the wreck. The entire Briscoe County main line is temporarily closed until the wreckage can be shifted.

Disturbingly, there were reports that two of the circus's lions had escaped from their cages following the smash. The deadly beasts are said to be on the loose somewhere in the Calico Plains desert region.

Miraculously, there were no fatalities in the crash. Four people are said to have been taken to hospital with serious, but not life-threatening, injuries.

A Briscoe County Police source said: "The train was derailed late in the night and officers and railroad officials are now trying to establish exactly what caused this catastrophe.

"The railroad will reopen after Western Union experts and train haulage specialists have removed the debris, of which there is plenty.

"Several circus animals were injured in the smash, and they will be treated by local veterinary surgeons. There are unconfirmed reports of two lions being loose in the wild. I cannot comment any further on these claims."

The train crash is a major blow to Klondike's Circus, which had enjoyed a sell-out West Coast tour prior to the disaster. The future of the circus remains unclear at this point.

The ensuing days represented a never-ending nightmare for the men and women of Klondike's Circus.

The train had derailed three miles south of the town of Munson, California, so the entire troupe headed there to regroup, recover and, for many, to forget.

Klondike booked up virtually every room at the Landmark Hotel, in the town's main drag. Everybody – staff, performers, roustabouts – was given a room, with the bunkhouse boys all sharing family quarters.

The novelty of having their township invaded by a travelling circus proved overwhelming for the folks of Munson, who flocked to the Landmark to see the cultural curiosities now among their neighbours. Many queued outside the hotel lounge for hours to catch a glimpse of Gargantua or Goliath.

The train wreck had slowly been cleared of everything. The circus's surviving horde of vehicles, machinery, support equipment and even the great tent had been transported across the plains by McCabe and his men, and now sat in an unseemly heap in a stable house behind the hotel.

The train itself was still being inspected by police and Western Union officials, with all journeys using the railroad being diverted. The shattered carriages still lay broken across the tracks and within the ditches of Blackhawk Point, days after the incident.

The clean-up operation was in motion, though, with an armada of recovery trucks and Pullman rail cars on standby at the scene to remove the carriages and clear the area.

The biggest worry of all remained the missing lions and, indeed, the fate of Emile Rance. While the white tiger Cicero had remained sealed within its cage after the almighty crash, Apollo and Cassius had been thrown about their respective homes, which had shattered after plunging down the steep incline. Enraged, the lions had bolted into the night and had seemingly disappeared into the wilderness. There was also no word on Rance, last seen charging after his beloved animals while dressed in a robe and pyjamas.

The elephants, horses and monkeys had all been rounded up by morning, though many carried worrying injuries. The Munson town veterinary surgery had been overwhelmed by the demands of the circus animals, and had sent for help from the neighbouring parishes.

For Kal Klondike, the fallout from the train crash represented a vast logistical abyss. Camped in the presidential suite of the hotel, he had barely slept in the 48 hours since the catastrophe, an endless sea of problems gnawing at his overpowered senses. He had another nine shows to deliver across California and Nevada, including one scheduled for the day after tomorrow in Santa Brava. And then there were the two moneymakers, Los Angeles and Las Vegas, just around the corner.

His train was now a disembodied carcass, his equipment sat in a stable block, and his performers were sitting around in a hotel, shaken and disorientated.

Nicky Shapiro, the train driver and two of the roustabouts, who had sustained concussions, were all holed up in the town hospital. Klondike thanked his lucky stars over and over that the incident had yielded no fatalities or life-changing injuries. He had visited all of the wounded in the hospital, and expressed his sorrow.

The thought of the lions still on the loose troubled him more than anything. He knew too well his responsibility for the animals that were hurt in the great crash, and knew that responsibility would result in the immediate closure of his circus if those lions were not caught soon. Privately, he imagined with dread what might happen if Apollo and Cassius stalked into a township like Munson. He prayed Rance would find them and tame them. If anyone could save the day, it was him. And he was still out there.

Klondike had already been visited by a local animal rights activist, and had taken a staunch reprimand on the chin, not having the energy to defend himself. He had simply promised to remove all animal acts from his show until further notice.

All in all, there was little light at the end of the tunnel for the boss of the big top, and he silently wondered if this really was the end of Klondike's Circus.

"Where do we go from here?"

Heavy kept repeating the line, but offered few answers to the dilemma they now found themselves in.

They were gathered in the presidential suite – Klondike and his lieutenants, Heavy, Lacey and Richie – all perching and pacing nervously around the reception desk in the giant room's centre.

The plush suite was on the top floor of the hotel, and a floor to ceiling window at the far end of the lounge offered panoramic views of the dusty desert town.

They had been sat around the big table for hours, deliberating and festering.

Klondike was draining a glass of scotch.

"For the first time in, well, a long time, I feel like I'm just about out of answers." He looked across the table at Heavy. "I just don't know, old buddy."

Heavy shook his head, shuffling and reshuffling a deck of cards. "Come on Kal. This can't be the end. After all these years."

Klondike's stare shifted to Lacey, who was sat at the table hugging her legs, wearing a black jumper-dress.

"Well, Lacey, you've been our saving grace so far this season. You've drawn in the crowds. You persuaded me to take Roddy on. You got us the media spotlight. You're our ace in the pack. Any suggestions this time around?"

Lacey buried her head into her knees, looking like a spurned cat. Her eyes were tired and, for once, she looked distinctly unglamorous.

"All I can say," she mumbled, "is the show must go on. We have to make it work."

"Ah come on, Lacey!" Heavy bawled unexpectedly. "Look at the state of our circus. How are we supposed to get around? We've got 20 tons of gear sat in a stable block. Our train is a write off. We can never use any animals again after what happened back there. We're holed up in this backwater hellhole with no way out and –" he broke off as a coughing fit got the better of him. Rubbing his throat, he glared across at Klondike.

"We've lost a small fortune with the train being out of commission," said Klondike. "The costs from all this will ensure our profits are shot to hell. We're in the red already. The hotel bill for this place alone will be enormous."

Lacey looked up at him, her face strangely pale and innocent. "But we must go on, Kal. We must find a way. We simply have to think of something. Or else…or else it really will be all over."

Klondike glared at her, before draining the contents of his glass and pouring another from a bottle on a side bar. He glanced idly at Richie Plum, who had wandered over to the giant window at the far end of the room.

"What's the matter, Richie?" he barked. "All too much of a financial nightmare for you?"

Plum stood by the glass, gazing out into the desert beyond.

"I don't get what happened to Rance. Why hasn't he shown up? Where are those damn lions?"

Klondike shook his head. "Emile will track them, right through the desert. He will follow their marks. And, for the love of god, let's hope he finds them and gets them somewhere safe."

Plum seemed lost by the window. "Or else…" he let the grim possibility hang in the air.

The heated atmosphere was suddenly broken by a sharp rap at the door.

Klondike wandered across, glass in hand, and pulled it open. A tall man in a suit and fedora stood on the other side, staring back impassively.

"You Klondike?" he snapped. When his host nodded, he continued. "Detective Nelson, Briscoe County Police. I thought you'd like to know the results of our investigation into your train crash."

Klondike stared at him. "You bet I do."

Nelson remained cool and unflinching at the door. "Your train cab was derailed off the tracks after colliding with a mechanical toll breaker, also known as a destabiliser. It's a small piece of equipment made of iron. They used to use them in the old days to ferry railroad cars off main lines and onto sidings. Going at top speed though, your train collided with it and was sent flying."

Klondike shook his head. "I don't understand, detective. What the hell was that thing doing on the line?"

Nelson's brow knotted. "Someone put it there."

"What!"

"That's right. There was malice and planning involved. That line is used by plenty of traffic in the daytime. Someone targeted your train and clamped the destabiliser in the tracks before you arrived."

Klondike stared at the detective in shock. "But that's insane. They could've killed us all. What in hell would make someone —"

"Like I said," Nelson barked, "it was planted. Enquiries have begun. Somebody had to have seen something. If not the culprits, then the destabiliser itself. Them things are hard to hide."

The detective eyed him shrewdly. Klondike merely shook his head. "Someone tried to nail us. Kill us maybe. And ruin the circus for good," he whispered.

Nelson frowned. "It sure looks that way, pal. Listen…you and your roomies have a good old think about who might do something like this." He smiled grimly into the room. "Everyone has their enemies," he said dryly. Then, he handed Klondike a card. "Any thoughts, you can reach me here."

Klondike took the card. "What happens to my train now?"

Nelson, set to leave, looked back, annoyed. "Why, the Western Union boys will haul it the hell outta the way. That mess has fouled up the line for days. You'll probably be able to reclaim the undamaged, back end of the train. At some point. But, let's face it, pal, the whole thing is fit for scrap now. Nothing more. Just accept it."

Klondike glared at him and swallowed hard. "Thank you, detective." He closed the door.

Turning back to the lounge, he was met by three shocked, pale faces.

"Well," he stammered, "how'd you like them apples, folks?"

Heavy had a knowing look. "Ribbeck!" he blurted, loosening buttons on his shirt.

Richie and Lacey turned to look at Klondike.

"No," he said, swishing his scotch. "That's not his style. That would be too much. Even for him. Eric runs one of the biggest circuses in the world. Getting involved in attempted murder…can you imagine if that got back to him?" He thought for a moment. "Besides, there's a bigger reason he'd never try a stunt like that."

"And what's that?" asked Richie.

"Because he'd probably do anything to have half of our talent on his roster." He shook his head. "No, he'd never pull anything like that. Circus is in his blood. He'd never try and destroy a performer."

Heavy smiled grimly. "Oh really, Kal? You ask me, I think he wants to see the back of us. Permanently. Eliminate the competition. You scare him, Kal."

Richie stepped forward. "There's something else going on here." They all looked at him. "Don't you see," he continued. "The lion let loose at the launch party. The journalist knowing about the devil drop. And now…now this! Our train derailed. Someone is systematically taking us apart."

Klondike gazed downwards. "My god," he blurted. "A saboteur! On the inside, using their knowledge to destroy us." He looked at each of them, as if an epiphany had just occurred. "Of course. Why didn't I see it? We have a rat in the camp. Travelling with us to bring us down."

Heavy looked bewildered. "But who, Kal? You're talking about someone on the inside."

Klondike snarled in disgust. "I don't know, Heav, but we sure as hell better find out."

Lacey suddenly held up her hands. "OK, OK, boys, we will get to the bottom of the mystery. But, for now, we need a solution to our current predicament. And fast."

They all looked about the room, lost in their thoughts. The temporary reverie was shattered by the telephone ringing.

Richie answered and, after a nervous exchange of pleasantries, called over to Klondike. "It's Addison."

Klondike downed the contents of his glass and looked down at Lacey. "Swell," he murmured.

He ambled across to the far coffee table and grabbed the receiver off Richie. The others fell silent, watching with dread.

"Hello Daryl."

"Kal!" Addison blurted down the telephone line. "Jesus Christ. It's all over the papers up here. How did it happen?"

Klondike thought for a moment. "The police are investigating."

"Is everyone OK?"

Klondike explained how four of his troupe were in hospital.

"Oh lord!" Addison groaned. "That's just awful. Thank god no one was killed. Or paralysed. Or anything like that. Listen Kal, the papers are saying your lions are on the loose. Please tell me that is not the case!"

Again, Klondike paused. Swallowing hard, he realised there was no way out. "I'm afraid that is the case, Daryl. Their cages smashed in the train crash and they got out. Rance went out after them and, well, that's all we really know."

"God in heaven, man," Addison cried, "that is a disaster. People could be eaten alive out there. Anything could happen, Kal. And if there is an incident, we are finished. For good. There's no coming back from something like that."

"Daryl," Klondike said calmly, "the lions are in a new and foreign environment. They will be lost out there, and more likely to search for water and shelter than a town full of people. Have faith that everything will be all right. Please."

There was an awkward pause. Then Addison continued, still sounding on edge. "Listen, Kal, I... I just don't know where we go from here. What do we do about the remaining shows? The money, the profits? We're advertised in nine more cities for God's sake. And what do I tell Robert and our senior partners up here? How will you meet the targets?"

Klondike breathed heavily. "Just leave it to me, Daryl. I'll come up with something."

"You better do," came the curt reply, "or else we're going to have to get Eric Ribbeck on the phone and sell our stars' contracts to him. That's the only way we will make any money. He'd pay handsomely to get Shapiro and Corky back, and I bet he'd give anything to land Olsen."

"That's not gunna happen!" Klondike snapped angrily, before slamming the phone down.

He just had time to take a deep breath, before there was another knock at the door.

"Come in!" he bellowed.

This time, Jim McCabe swaggered in, his pork pie hat squashed and his shirt dirtied and wrinkled. He approached the table and shook his head.

"Jim..." Klondike said weakly. "Please give me some good news."

McCabe stared back dumbly. He seemed to have aged ten years overnight, his skin pallid and eyes reddened. "I'm sorry, Kal," he mumbled. "The boys are getting restless. They can see what's going on and, well, they want their next pay envelope. It's due on Friday, but they're worried there's no money left now. Some are even talking about deserting. There's work available at cattle farms all around here, and they think they might be better getting work there now."

"That's unacceptable!" Lacey snapped. "They will work when we tell them to work."

McCabe frowned down at her. "Miss Tanner, with all due respect, these are honest, simple men. Many have spent large parts of their lives starving and living in boarding houses. They are scared they might have to go back to that after what's happened with the train. Being holed up in this fancy hotel...it's made them uneasy."

"Listen," Klondike said, glaring at him. "You tell your boys they'll get their pay on Friday as usual. Anyone wants to quit, they can quit. But they'll never be allowed back. They stick with me, they'll get proper wages, as normal. But the crash has changed nothing."

McCabe flapped his arms. "But what are they supposed to do?"

"Get them to check all the equipment. Make sure everything is working and ready."

McCabe was incredulous. "Ready! Ready for what?"

Klondike looked across at Lacey and winked. "The show. What else?"

Most of the talent had spent the day and, indeed, most of the previous night, laid out in the hotel lounge.

The comfortable room boasted a long, mahogany bar along one side and a collection of couches, tables and bar stools throughout. It was an elegant, well-furnished affair, with a crystal chandelier hanging high above the carpeted floor.

While Jenny sat morose at the bar, alone nursing one cocktail after another, Shapiro was seated on a stool at the opposite end, watching her curiously as he drank champagne. Amanda and Cathy, as always, were fussing over him, perched on neighbouring stools.

Corky was sprawled out on a leather couch in the centre, and was largely the centre of attention as he had continued to appear in public without his face paint. For many, it was the first time they had seen his features. He had continued on without make-up following the crash, having seemingly lost all humour in the aftermath of the disaster.

His companions had stared at him on and off throughout the previous two days. They had been shocked at his ageing, craggy features. He always moved and performed with the grace and athleticism of a younger man, but here sat a tiring figure of middle age, looking somewhat awkward in a yellow and black suit and pink tie.

Corky had even lost his sense of fun, and merely sat there drinking a beer, offering small talk as the group reminisced about what had happened at Blackhawk Point.

Olsen and Suzy were seated at a table just behind, drinking soda pops and looking on at the forlorn scene around them.

Goliath was sat alone at a table to their left, while the dwarf Percy Pringle sat atop a jukebox, knocking back a giant mug of beer.

"Look at you, clown," Shapiro called out to Corky, who appeared on the verge of sleep. "You look like you have performed your last show. This craziness has taken it out of you, eh?"

Corky looked up at his old colleague wearily. "That could be said of all of us, Gino."

"Bah!" Shapiro spat out. "Not for me, clown. The chairman will get us going again. If not, I go somewhere else. Movies, TV, Vegas. They all want me."

"Everybody wants you, Gino," Cathy said drunkenly.

Jenny looked up from the bar. "Why don't you go play with your monkeys, Cath!"

Cathy gawked down the bar at her. "What's the matter, weirdo, worried I'm gunna play with your boy here?"

Jenny slouched over her drink, her eyes glazed and her speech slurred.

Amanda looked her over with contempt. "You're a mess, Jenny."

"So are you!" she shrieked back. "You should be nursing your elephants in a pig sty out back. Not drinking at the bar with the top talent."

"All right," Shapiro cried, raising his hands, "that's enough, chiquitas. Everybody calm down." He waited a few moments, and sipped at his tall glass. "Now, don't worry guys. There's not a show or a circus in the land that wouldn't want to hire each and every one of you. You are all very talented. If this is the end of the road for the chairman, it is very sad, but it is not the end for you."

Corky eyed him from the couch. "Would you really work for another circus, Gino? After all these great years. I know I wouldn't. Not now."

Shapiro leant back, glass in hand. "Si, it is true. A tough proposition. I would not like, for sure. I have had the best years of my life here. Being the star of the show, the top billing, the main event... I wouldn't want to give that up. Not for anything."

"You didn't give it up, you lost it!"

Everyone turned to look at Suzy, who had levelled the remark angrily from across the room. She glared at him, her childlike features mean and feisty. "You're not the star of the show any more, Mr Gino Shapiro. You're not the one the crowds flock to see. You're not the reason behind our smash hit run this season. There's a new star under our big top." She turned to look at the man seated opposite her. Olsen squirmed slightly under her gaze, then smiled awkwardly as every face turned to him.

Shapiro looked enraged. Then, he laughed good-naturedly. "Of course," he exclaimed, still giggling. "Young Roddy. The dollmaker. The kid from nowhere, they call him. He was a hawker on the medway. Then he became circus master. On the poster, with me and the clown."

Shapiro rose from his bar stool, making his way to Olsen and Suzy's table. On the couch, Corky looked on hesitantly.

"He fools us all with his dolls and his voice tricks," Shapiro was saying, pacing like a cat before them. "Like a village fool at a children's party. Sure, the children all laugh, but this is not a goddamn high school talent show. This is the circus! I am the flyer…and you kids are on my undercard."

Suzy shook her head, glaring back at him. "Roddy was on TV. His photo out sells yours at the merchandise stalls. He has a crowd of people waiting for him in each town…"

"Enough!" Shapiro suddenly roared, marching to the table and staring down at them.

Olsen finally spoke. "It's OK, Gino. Suzy is just upset, like all of us."

The girl sipped her drink, unrepentant. "I'm just saying it like it is."

Corky stood and placed an arm around Shapiro. "We are all stars, Gino," he said soothingly. "Sure, Roddy is a big draw right now. But you've been in the spotlight for years now. We've all had it. And we can share it."

But Shapiro was eyeing Olsen with contempt. "You think you are better than me, Olsen?"

"No, not at all," Olsen said, still seated. "I have massive respect for you, for what you do. I am in awe of all you guys. Truth is, I owe you all. You've taken me in, given me this platform to perform. I couldn't be happier."

"You deserve it, Rod," Corky said calmly.

Shapiro shrugged away from Corky's hand. "You may think that, clown," he sneered, "but I still say he is nothing. Nothing but a boy playing with dolls."

Olsen finally stood and faced Shapiro. Gone was the boyish innocence, replaced with a steely resolve borne of years of fighting to survive. "You know something, Gino, you've got a big mouth!"

Shapiro clenched his fists. "Then why don't you come over here and close it, boy?"

Corky quickly stood between them and was glad to be joined by Goliath, who eased his immense frame up to the table. "Let it go," the giant said simply. "Don't make me mad."

No one wanted to argue with the hulking Goliath, and everyone seemed to move away from the table at once.

Just as tensions reached boiling point, the whole situation deemed to defuse with the intervention of the giant.

Shapiro returned to the bar, and Amanda and Cathy. Olsen and Suzy got up and left the lounge completely.

Corky, picking up his bowler hat from the floor, looked around, and then addressed Shapiro.

"Y'know, Gino, if you could just get that giant chip off your shoulder and learn to co-exist with the whole of the talent, and love and support the rest of us... Hell, we would have one hell of a show. The best in the world."

Shapiro grunted as he sipped champagne. "What is that supposed to mean?"

Corky smiled beautifully, and his aged features took on a mesmeric, almost whimsical look.

"We are all stars, Gino. But, collectively, we are the heavens."

Chapter 19

Dusk had settled over the mammoth circus encampment that had engulfed Elysian Fields, in Chicago.

The bright blues, reds and yellows of the stall tents and trailers blended into the coming twilight to form an eerie glow across the horizon. The stalls seemed to stretch into eternity, with the whole ensemble resembling more a colonisation than a travelling attraction.

None of it touched Eric Ribbeck as he strolled nonchalantly across the field, working his way around the now barren stalls. Dressed in an expensive silver suit, he left no one in any doubt that he was the ruler of this colourful kingdom. His troupe had just completed two sell-out shows, and was moving out at first light.

Veronica Hunslett hopped excitedly after him, clad in a long beige trench coat.

Finally, they reached the refreshments kiosk, where a tired-looking Luca Marconi sat against the counter sipping a black coffee.

Ribbeck and Veronica faced him, before the old circus boss spoke in a quiet yet firm voice.

"Luca…what the hell happened out there?"

Marconi shook his head. "I'm still working on it. The cops say it was a destabiliser…lifted the train right off the track."

"Sabotage?"

Marconi nodded. "Right."

Ribbeck's face wrinkled up. "But surely Miss Cross couldn't have orchestrated such a scheme! She would have been on the train." He thought for a moment, rubbing his bony hands together. "Dammit, Luca, you were wrong about Cross being the troublemaker. That writer Hackett has played you! None of this makes sense. How would that bimbo trapeze girl pull off a calamity such as this?"

Veronica was nodding. "No circus girl I ever heard of moonlights as a criminal mastermind."

Marconi remained impassive, sipping his coffee. "That's because Jenny Cross just does the leg work. She is an informer. She paid off Hackett. But there is another."

The other two glared at him. "Who, dammit!" Ribbeck snarled.

"That's what I'm working on," Marconi replied coolly. "I can see how this whole thing is playing out. She is the insider. The ringleader is on the outside, boss. There can be no doubt." He lit a cigarette, enjoying his control of the suspense. "I'm just going to start tailing her when I get back. She will lead me to whoever is behind this."

"You may be too late," Veronica said coldly. "It looks like Kal Klondike and his merry band of followers are through. How can they come back from this devastating blow?"

"Pah!" Ribbeck spat like an enraged mule. "You don't know the son of a bitch! He ain't through. He always finds a way. He will be back...mark my words. His season ain't over yet."

"But surely..." she began.

Ribbeck shook his head. "That boy always has an ace up his sleeve. He has too many contacts...too much influence."

Marconi nodded absently. "Listen, boss," he stammered, "do you have any idea who is behind all this? Who's controlling Cross?"

Ribbeck looked out across the circus grounds. "So many yahoos," he mumbled, "but none who would go at him like this. There's no one..." His eyes suddenly took on a haunted, faraway look as he gazed into nothingness. He stood silent as a new notion seemed to gnaw at him.

Veronica broke the awkward silence. "What is it, Eric?"

He looked up suddenly, and shook off his private thoughts. "Oh, nothing, dear." He gazed around, seemingly confused. Then, with sudden alertness, he stared at Marconi. "Listen, Luca. I think it's time I made my move. I'm coming with you to...where was this place? Munson, you say? Yes. I want to see what's going on down there for myself."

Marconi chuckled. "Want to see the ruins of Klondike's Circus for yourself, eh?"

Ribbeck frowned at him. "And maybe more. Especially where Miss Cross is concerned."

"Er, Eric…" Veronica began, shocked. "Aren't you forgetting something? We are moving out tomorrow. Who's going to run the circus?"

He glared at her, smiling wickedly. "I'll give you one god damn guess, doll."

She looked down. "I see. Er, where can I reach you?"

"You can't!" he snapped. "Just get these yahoos to St Louis."

Marconi finished his coffee and stubbed out his smoke. "I'll get us tickets on the Transcontinental Express for first thing tomorrow, Mr Ribbeck."

Ribbeck stared at him as if he had gone mad. "The hell with that, boy. Get us a cab to O'Hare right now. We'll fly to LA and get to Munson before the cuckoos start gathering."

Marconi fled to find the nearest callbox. Ribbeck pulled out a cigarette from an ornate silver box and smiled at Veronica by his side. "It's time to dance," he said idly.

Klondike eased himself into the hotel bar, a tired, haggard figure with a forlorn look on his face.

Still dressed in his trademark leather jacket and fedora, he drew plenty of curious glances as he ambled lifelessly across the floor. Meandering past one couple at a corner table, he picked up a faint "That's the circus boss" remark as he made his way to the bar. It was late afternoon, and the lounge was sparsely populated, with most of the custom consisting of couples enjoying a pre-dinner drink.

Klondike glanced around, checking to see if any of his staff were present. He thought he had detected none when, to his surprise, he saw Gino Shapiro seated at the edge of the beautiful mahogany bar, alone for once in his life.

Klondike half smiled and wandered over, plonking himself down on the stool next to his star flyer.

Shapiro, dressed in a woolly white cardigan and green slacks, looked across and nodded in greeting.

"Chairman," he said, in an unusually casual tone. "Welcome."

Klondike nodded back. "I thought I was the last drinker in town."

A barman approached them at the far corner.

"Beer!" Klondike blurted, "and one…" he stared at the pink milk-like mixture sat in a tall glass before Shapiro. "What is that? Strawberry milkshake?"

Shapiro smiled. "Sasparilla," he said proudly. "The beverage of the cowboy. A sharpshooter like you should know that!"

Klondike chuckled as the barman got the drinks.

"I didn't expect to see you down here, Gino."

Shapiro looked him over. "I'd say you didn't expect a hell of a lot of anything, amigo." He looked around the lounge. "We've all been sat around this place for days now. Thinking. Speculating. And, hell, drinking. All of us hoping that the great Kal Klondike will somehow save the day."

The barman served the drinks and the two men at the bar clinked glasses. Klondike watched as Shapiro took a long slurp of his Sasparilla.

"Listen...how's Nicky doing?"

Shapiro put his glass down. "I was with him earlier. Poor Nicky. Arm in a sling. His pretty face ruined by the gashes. And still sore from the concussion." He looked down. "The doc said he can't fly again for six months. Six months! You know what that means to an artist of the air?"

Klondike nodded grimly. "It might as well be a lifetime."

"Damn right." Shapiro supped at his drink. Then he became more animated. "What the hell are we going to do, chairman?"

Klondike let the question hang in the air. Slowly, as if the effort pained him, he pulled a cigar from an inside breast pocket and lazily lit it with matches placed on the bar. He gazed at Shapiro, as a vacuum of purple smoke filled the air around them.

"Look, I'm sorry about Nicky but —"

"Nicky will get better. He will return. It is unfortunate. But, dammit Kal, I need to know...can we keep going? Is our show over?"

"Over..." Klondike whispered as if in a trance. He studied Shapiro thoughtfully. "Remember when we started out, Gino? When I first told you my plan?"

Shapiro stared at him incredulously. "On Ribbeck's train. Sure, I remember. You...you showed faith in me. Like no one ever had before. You said you'd make me a star. I laughed...but went along with it. And then...then the most beautiful thing happened. You made good on your promise, amigo. You made a beautiful show. All these years...these memories. How can I ever forget them? And now..." he eyed Klondike sadly, "and now this. This...this devastation. I am just hoping you will tell me, our beloved chairman, that we aren't through."

Klondike wedged his cigar in the corner of his mouth. He looked deadly serious. "Don't you give up on me, Gino."

Shapiro looked him over as if in awe and placed his hand on Klondike's at the bar. His features looked youthful and fresh, despite his advancing years.

"Kal…" he breathed. "How could I ever give up on you?" He smiled and took a sip of his drink. "Just get us on the road!"

They both laughed.

Klondike drank and puffed at his smoke, gazing about wistfully and lost in nostalgia.

Gradually, his gaze fell upon the lounge television set, sat above the counter in the far corner opposite them.

The Steve Irving Show was playing. The nightly chat and comedy broadcast was one of the biggest hits on the ATV network, with its seemingly endless string of star guests.

Irving was just closing the show to rapturous applause from the studio audience. Dressed in a tuxedo and wearing his trademark large spectacles, the popular comedian earned his usual standing ovation as he thanked his guests and house band. Then, the closing theme music aired as the credits rolled.

Klondike watched the screen from the bar, as if spellbound. Slowly, as if he had been hypnotised, his eyes enlarged. Then the faint beginnings of a smile etched into the corners of his lips.

He gently removed the cigar from the side of his mouth. "Son of a bitch…" he whispered, staring at the television.

Shapiro barely heard him, but caught his trance-like gaze and followed it up to the screen. Puzzled, he grunted. "What?"

Klondike nodded slowly, then turned on his stool and smiled at Shapiro, his mood seemingly altered.

"I've got it!" he cried.

"Got what?"

He laughed. "A plan. What else?"

He leapt off the bar stool and stood there thinking for a moment.

Shapiro frowned and turned his attention back to the television. He studied the screen as a commercial for bath soap ran.

Turning, he said: "Chairman, what the hell are you…"

But all he saw was an empty bar stool.

Klondike was on the move.

Lacey Tanner raced through the hotel lobby frantically.

Looking through every open door, she hurried from one end of the building to the other, searching the bar, dining room and library. Reaching the bottom of the main stairwell in the Landmark's reception area, she glanced around at her surroundings, hands on hips.

A sudden roar of delight from an adjoining room followed by a harsh coughing fit grabbed her attention. It could be only one man. She found a small alcove next to the reception desk and entered.

There he was, engaged in a game of five card stud with three other middle-aged men, all seated at a small round table. By the look and sound of it, he had won the last hand.

"Heavy!" she hissed, glaring at the poker match in progress.

Heavy sat with his back to her, his cards showing face up as he gathered up a small pile of chips.

"Hey Lacey," he murmured, grinning as he counted his winnings. "Hell, it's true what they say. There's action going down in every corner of California."

She looked at him in despair. "How can you play...poker at a time like this?"

"Why," the big man said, still not turning, "I'm gunna win us enough dough that we ain't gunna have to do no more shows." He laughed boisterously.

Lacey rolled her eyes, ignoring the three others, who were eyeing her approvingly.

"Listen," she snapped, "where in god's name is Kal? I haven't seen him all day. No one knows where he is. The receptionist hasn't seen him leave the building. It's as if he disappeared. And at a time like this!"

Heavy finally turned, and looked up at her, a cigar wedged in the corner of his mouth. "Well, that makes two of us. I ain't seen Kal all day. Or last night, come to think of it." He thought for a moment, then his eyes widened suddenly. "Maybe he's thought of a plan! To save the circus."

Lacey looked down at him and shook her head. "Jesus...we are due for the show in Santa Brava tomorrow. Tomorrow! If he has a plan, it better be rich. What...is he going to fly us there!"

Heavy removed his cigar and made to give a speech. "Miss Lacey," he began, "me and Kal have been putting on circus shows since we were kids. Now, if there is one thing you need to know about Kal, it's that he gets the job done. One way or the other. His way, most a time. It's in his —"

"In his blood, yes, yes, I know the speel," she cut in irritably. She looked around in despair, her mind racing. The poker players all gaped at her as if she was from another planet.

Heavy studied her, then smiled knowingly. "Listen," he mumbled, fiddling with his chips. "Kal is a man with many partners. We've been in this business a hell of a long time. Met many other bosses and fixers along the way. Hell...maybe he's out there right now reeling in an old favour from some old salt somewhere down the trail."

Lacey folded her arms, suddenly feeling like a fish out of water in the main drag hotel in the backwater town. Everyone seemed to be staring at her.

She shook her head. "It's going to take something big to hit the profit margin now. And to save the circus..."

Chapter 20

The American Television Network backlot represented a vast ensemble of warehouses, bungalows and studio buildings spread unevenly about a giant enclave set within the foot of the Hollywood Hills in west Los Angeles.

Errand boys ran back and forth between the studios, executives walked and talked on the paved walkways, and hourly tour groups jostled across the grounds, all hoping to catch a glimpse of one of their favourite stars.

What no one expected to see was comedy legend Steve Irving racing across the backlot on a vintage bicycle, happily ringing his bell as he passed familiar faces and old associates.

He dismounted outside the main ATV headquarters building, idly leaving his bike against a wall, knowing an intern would instantly stash it away in a garage.

Dressed in a silver and red tracksuit, his trademark large spectacles dominating his face, Irving looked even inch the eccentric, which he was. A diminutive, somewhat hyperactive fellow, he was known for his comic catchphrases and warm demeanour.

Crossing the main foyer, he happily stopped to give tour visitors his autograph and even engaged in some idle small talk, dropping in comedic antidotes to his adoring fans. With a curt nod to a giant portrait of himself that hung above the main reception, he headed for a large double door at the end of the vast room and threaded his way around to his executive office.

"Good morning, Mr Irving," his secretary, Jane, greeted enthusiastically. "You are all good to go this morning. The papers are all in. The showreels are in the player. And…would you believe, you have a surprise visitor."

Irving had waltzed past the secretary's desk, but halted abruptly at the last remark. He looked at her. "Good. Good. And…wha!" He chuckled. "What surprise? This early!"

Jane winked. "I know. That's what I told him. He's waiting in the lounge."

"He? And who is he?"

She smirked. "Well, we let him in because he said he was an old friend. But he's got the worst stage name I ever heard. Calls himself Kal Klondike."

Irving stared at her. Disbelief and then confusion clouded his cherubic features. "Kal..." he said absently.

Jane frowned. "I'll have security throw him out if you like. Mind, he looks like he can handle himself."

The comedian half-smiled. "You better believe it." He stared at the lounge door, next to the entrance to his own office. He shook his head slowly. "Hold off security, Jane. And, er, I guess hold my calls for now."

She looked up, concerned. "Is everything all right, Mr Irving?"

He moved to the door. "Yeah. It's just a little early for a game of cowboys and Indians."

He entered the lounge, leaving Jane with a confused look on her face.

"Kal!" he exclaimed loudly, wandering dreamlike into the smart, comfy room that served as a waiting area and additional conference room.

Klondike was seated in a couch at the opposite end, dressed as always in his leather jacket and fedora. He rose steadily, dwarfing Irving with his tall, lean physique.

The comedian shook his head. He hadn't changed a bit. Like a gunslinger from the old West, all shoulders, jawline and ruggedness. The two men couldn't have looked more different.

"The king of comedy," Klondike mused with a laugh. "Look at you. Swanky office in the Hollywood Hills. Who would have thought it?"

They shook hands warmly, Irving placing a hand on the bigger man's shoulder.

"Jesus, Kal," he whispered, "you look terrific. Just like I remember you. What's it been? Seven, eight years?"

"Almost ten. I recall we went our separate ways after the Atlanta Bowl. Great times."

Irving could not stop staring at his surprise visitor. "Incredible," he uttered. He gestured to the couch. "Can I get you coffee? A soda?"

Klondike shook his head. "Your gal Jane saw to that."

Irving sat on an easy chair opposite the couch. "Hell, it's good to see you, Kal. What a surprise!" His face and mood suddenly turned grave. "I, er, heard about the train crash. I sure am sorry. The papers said no one was seriously injured. Thank god. That's a miracle, man, a miracle." He eased his small, wiry frame back into the seat. "I followed your progress, daddio. All these years. The circus life has been good to you."

Klondike shook his head. "Until now…"

Irving studied his guest, casually placing a cigarette in a holder and inflaming it with a gold lighter. "A tragedy, sure, but you've been doing great, man. I've been hearing crackerjack things about your show. Even up here."

Klondike smirked. "I had tried to follow your career as well, Steve, but must have lost track at some point. It seems you've become the face of ATV. The Steve Irving Show. An associate at the network. Hell…" he grinned at the smaller man in the tracksuit. "You've come a long way since you opened for Ribbeck."

"Speak for yourself," Irving shot back good-naturedly. "I never saw you breaking away from the old man and starting your own outfit. With Gino and Corky too. Hell, how are they all?"

"Just fine," Klondike replied casually, "all things considered. Like the rest of my team, they are wondering where we go from here. All hoping old Kal can come up with another gig that can save the day." He looked down, suddenly appearing forlorn and weak. His voice came in a quiet, quivering tone. "The train wreck has gutted us, Steve. We're like a naval fleet without a ship. Who could have foreseen this mess? This devastation. And all on the back of our richest season yet. We were flying. And now…now this."

Irving nodded slowly. An awkward silence filled the lounge as the two men, once colleagues amidst the same troupe, tried to read each other's thoughts.

Finally, with a deep breath, Irving got to the point. "What are you doing here, Kal?"

Klondike grinned sheepishly. "You'd never believe it's just a social call? I was in the neighbourhood."

"Come off it, daddio." Irving puffed nonchalantly on his cigarette, studying his guest shrewdly. "We were in the same show. Years ago. Yeah, we got on well and all that. But…all these years, you never once contacted me. You've been in LA every summer. I know that. Hell, I'd have loved to have had you on the show. We've got the best variety acts in America performing every night. Your sharpshooter and knife thrower routine is right up our street. And then there's your other performers. We would have paid good dollar to give them air time, Kal." Aggravated, he swept a hand through his wavy red hair. "And now, you just turn up outta nowhere. Like we's old pals."

He suddenly rose and crossed the carpeted floor to a drinks cabinet in the far corner. He quickly poured two glasses of scotch, added ice, and returned, thrusting one of the glasses into Klondike's face.

"I know you want that," he blurted. "Now, drink, and tell me what the hell this is all about."

Klondike took the pincher and sipped at the brown liquid. "I'll tell you what this is about. A deal."

Irving eyed him questioningly. "A deal? What, you and me? We don't have any deal." He sat down again, shifting slightly in his chair. "Don't tell me you've dug up some IOU from the olden days, Kal. My lawyers will shoot it down, cowboy."

Klondike shook his head. With a deep breath, he looked up at Irving, and the seriousness of his visit suddenly become apparent. "We've got nine shows left in our schedule," he explained. "Including one tomorrow in Santa Brava. Then there are the two moneymakers, here and Las Vegas. My team, equipment, stores, everything, is all holed up in Munson, about three hours' drive from here. We're stuck. If I don't make a profit out of this season and come out in the black, the credit line ends and the circus is, well, I… I don't want to say it."

He grimaced and emptied the contents of his glass. Irving just sat there, watching and wondering.

"I had to come up with a plan," Klondike continued. "Something to make us a profit, to meet the figures, and turn good on our loan and backing from our investors. What I've come up with is audacious, but it's all I can go on."

Irving sat perplexed, staring across at his former colleague. "Kal, I am sorry about what happened, but I'm not sure how I can help." He frowned suddenly. "What is this plan?"

Klondike looked up, and there was fire and a steely resolve locked into his deep brown eyes. "I'm rescheduling the rest of the season. The nine dates are to be condensed into two. Los Angeles and Las Vegas. All of our concluding shows are within a 200-mile radius of both cities, so the spectators can still come. Two dates. And the two biggest shows we've ever put on."

Irving stared at him blankly. "But, er, how will nine shows into two help you meet your profit targets?"

Klondike looked up, a devilish smile on his face. "Because I'm going to sell the broadcast rights to you and ATV. You can screen both shows and have creative control. But I get the gate receipts."

"Woh, woh, woh, daddio!" Irving flapped, his face incredulous. "Broadcast rights? To what? A goddamn circus in a field? You're way out of line, man. This is ATV. We are the fourth biggest network in the country. What would we want with a circus? And what in hell makes you think I have the clout to make such a decision?"

Klondike was still smiling. "You just said you wanted my guys on your show." He cocked his head at the comedian. "Come off it, Steve. I know you were there in the big top in San Francisco. I know ATV has guys watching us. At every damn show. Seems to me like your outfit wants a piece of the pie."

Irving held his hands up, his face reddening. "All right, Kal, all right. I was there. We've been keeping tabs on the show. But, dammit, that's our job as gatekeepers of national show business. It don't mean nothing."

"Oh…" Klondike said in a tantalising tone. "Well, Steve, now I'm offering you and your network the opportunity to screen our show to the nation. An historic broadcast…the first ever live circus show, beamed to every home in the country. It will be like nothing ever seen before. The folks in TV land can watch the show live in their front rooms. Can you imagine? It will be a spectacular, landmark TV moment. And it happens in three weeks' time."

Irving was staring at him incredulously, running a hand through his hair. His face was glowing red. Finally, he smiled back. "You've still got the gift of the gab, cowboy. I'll give you that. Like a true circus man. PT Barnum would be proud."

Klondike chuckled. "You haven't heard the funny part…"

Irving looked back in disbelief. He waited for the rest.

"The Los Angeles show will be broadcast here. From your television studios. What a truly unique concept it will be. You can be in it yourself Steve. It will be a landmark broadcast…the circus world meets the TV variety world."

"Jesus Christ, Kal!" Irving blurted, "What do you think this is? Opportunity night?" He tried to cool down, sipping at his scotch and fishing wildly for another cigarette. "OK, OK, you got the talent, man, but putting on a show like this doesn't just happen overnight. You don't just ramrod a studio and broadcast whatever you like to the country. I like the idea, I admit that, but there are commissions, executives, schedule-makers, ratings analysts…an endless conveyor belt of people at the top who make things happen."

Klondike was still grinning, like a bear cub smelling a stray picnic basket. "You like the idea. You know it can work. You know what I got in my show."

The comedian lit his cigarette frantically. Then, he seemed to calm down. "All right. I like it, sure. But what in hell makes you think I got the clout to make this happen?"

"Come on, Steve. I know what you are now. A senior executive here. Your show has transformed the ratings of the network. You're a god here." He leant closer, a conspirational look etched into his craggy features. "And just think…you can go to the board with this yourself. It will be your idea! A circus special to bring in big ratings after the sell-out run we've had. Think of how that will go down. You'll get all the credit."

"Unless the whole thing is a turkey!" Irving was thinking steadily now, analysing pros and cons in his head. He stood suddenly and paced the room, toying with his cigarette as he spoke. "But you got something here, Kal. I can feel it."

"You bet you can."

Irving looked out of the lounge window opposite, squinting at the famous Hollywood sign watching over them high above in the famous LA hills.

"You bring some big players to the table. Shapiro. What he does is incredible. Corky the Clown. The world's fastest juggler and one of the greatest variety performers on this planet. All those freaks…like the 400-pound guy doing somersaults. I mean, this is hot for my dinner plate, man. And then…" He stared mesmerically at his guest, as if in a trance. "And then there's the kid. The Puppet Master. Man, it does not get any better than that. We've had plenty of ventriloquists on the show. But this guy is like something from the future. He's transformed the art form." He eyed Klondike approvingly. "And the people love him. That I saw for myself in Frisco."

"Roddy Olsen," Klondike mused. "Our host and rising star. He has stunned us all with his talent. And the incredible thing is, nothing seems to faze him. He belongs on TV."

Irving fidgeted as he paced around in front of the couch. "But then there's the scandal of the animals. No more animal acts. I read your views on that in the paper. Your whole show has been gutted. The lion tamer disappearing. How do you get over all that, daddio? And, what's more, this ain't a whole show you're offering me!"

Klondike held up his hands. "What we do have are special guests, arranged by Gino. He has persuaded Jason Lash, Linda Schneider and Larry Lassiter to appear. They were advertised for the LA show right from the off. And then, of course, we have you. Steve Irving. The king of comedy." He sat back and folded his arms. "Now, that sounds like one hell of a bill to me…daddio!"

Irving chewed it over. "I heard about Lash. He'll be doing his horse and roping act, right? And Lassiter is a sound stand-up. As for Linda… I can only presume Gino and her were, at some point in time, an item." He thought it all over. "I can't argue, man. They are big names. For ATV. For you. For all this. Lash's last movie grossed 10 mill. He's a hero to little boys everywhere."

Klondike rolled with it. "It's a superstar line-up, Steve. Movie stars. Stand-ups. Circus acts. A TV chat show host in Linda. The great Steve Irving. Come on, how can you resist?"

Irving smiled mischievously, nodding. "All right, all right. This all sounds hot. But you said two shows, sucker! LA can happen right here. Yes, I can make it happen, Kal. But what about this Vegas show you mention? I ain't got no control in Vegas, man. At least, not yet. How will that work?"

Klondike nodded reassuringly. "Steve, you look ugly when you panic. That will all be taken care of. I've already spoken to Claude Hershey. He owns the Golden Dune casino, where the show is taking place. He loved the idea of the circus, and his beloved casino, being broadcast to the nation. Just say you agree to it, and me and Claude will take care of everything. All you have to do is turn up in Vegas with your camera boys and runners."

"You…you know Claude Hershey!" the comedian said absent-mindedly. "Jesus, Kal, is there anyone on the West Coast you're not in bed with?"

"Yeah… Marilyn Monroe."

"But I hear the circus is taking place in the parking lot!" Irving shot back. "The big top is being attached to the casino entrance."

Klondike smiled. "That's right. For the most spectacular circus extravaganza of our time. Of any time."

Irving scoffed. "Save it, man. I heard it all before." He thought for a moment. "Two shows. All that talent. That's a big sell, baby."

"There's something else," Klondike put in. "For Vegas, we are saving our crowning glory. The most daring trapeze act ever performed. For the first time in front of a paying public. Gino Shapiro. Performing the devil drop."

Irving frowned. "Devil drop? What the hell is a devil drop?"

Klondike stood, and spread his hands about like a mime artist as he described the feat. "The trapeze artist climbs to the peak of the big top, balancing in the tentpole loop, with all before him. The centre ring, 30 feet below, is then pushed, and left to swing back and forth. The flyer dives from the tentpole and free falls the 30 feet before grasping the loose ring and swinging to safety. It's the ultimate act of timing, precision and bravery. All that stands under the ring is an 80-foot drop to the sawdust far below."

Irving looked unsteady. "You, er, sure that kinda stunt is safe? For TV and the paying public?"

Klondike spread his arms wide. "It's all part of the appeal, Steve. Always has been. The thrill and excitement. What if something went wrong...?"

"Has Shapiro even attempted this so-called devil drop before?"

"Several times. But never in a tent of our size. And in front of a crowd of thousands. And in this country."

Irving raised an inquiring eyebrow. "And..."

Klondike swallowed. "And not in the last two years."

"Jesus Christ! Talk about looking for trouble. Man, put all these elements together and we've got a doozie of a show, Kal. A doozie!"

"Like I said, the danger and excitement are what turn the public on. It will be the same on TV. Viewers will want to see something like this."

An eerie silence engulfed the lounge. Klondike held his breath, trying to look cool but frantically flapping deep inside. He knew it all came down to this one last desperate gamble. Everything hinged on the outcome of this meeting. His future. That of his staff and performers. His whole world. Yet he maintained a strange, unnerving faith in his old colleague from Ribbeck's World Circus. Steve Irving had a natural feel for showmanship and bravado, and was ultimately being offered a unique opportunity.

The two men eyed each other nervously, like two prize-fighters at the top of the 15th round, wearily trying to figure each other out.

Finally, Irving spoke. "My production team will be behind this."

Klondike felt like bursting, but held it all together. "I couldn't think of anything better."

"And I get creative control."

"Yes, but with my input as a consultant. It will be your show, Steve, but go through me."

Irving nodded, his mind racing. "OK. I like it. I'll do my skit at the end. Just before Shapiro, your headline act, closes the show." He looked about idly. "I'll take this to the station manager at lunch. He can get some sponsors on board. Three weeks, eh? That ain't a lot of time. How are you going to sell tickets? I guess I'll speak to our box office people." He suddenly looked angry. "This is going to be a hell of a pickle, Kal. I hope it's all gunna be worth it."

Klondike placed an arm around the smaller man's shoulders. "Does that mean we have a deal, old buddy?"

Irving looked up at his former colleague. "Jesus, you talked me into it, daddio." He shrugged away from the large arm. "You better get to work, Kal. You've got to get your people, your equipment…hell, everything, down to the studio block. We need rehearsals."

"That sounds like a green light, Steve."

Irving looked at him almost sadly. "Yeah. Well, it's like you said. They all love me. If I suggest it, they'll love it. That's…that's what I am now."

"Can we talk a price? For the broadcast rights?"

"In time, Kal, in time. Don't worry, I'll get you some figures. You just be ready in three weeks."

Klondike nodded. He didn't want to pester his host about the money. He was happy he had a deal. "All right!" he roared. "Let's get this show on the road."

Without another word, he charged out of the lounge like an alarmed bronc, leaving Steve Irving standing there, confused and overwhelmed. He caught his reflection in a wall mirror and addressed himself.

"Now, Irv, did that actually just happen?"

"You did what!"

Lacey Tanner was incandescent as she strode briskly across the penthouse towards where Klondike sat by the mini-bar in the far corner. Beyond, the dusky desert landscape filled the giant window that dominated the large room on the top floor of the hotel.

Heavy and Plum were seated at the main table in the room's centre, while Lacey had paced the floor anxiously. Having already been irate at Klondike's disappearance for the bulk of the day, she was positively rattled by his unexpected request for a meeting between the four of them, having not heard from him all day.

Now, having heard his audacious plan, she was on the verge of a total meltdown.

But Klondike was cool and affable, like a cat toying with some kits. "I told you," he said in a tired voice, "I've rescheduled the rest of the season. Two dates. LA and Vegas. Both shows will be broadcast on ATV. I've sold the broadcast rights to the circus. Price to be confirmed. But it'll be big. The network don't pay less than 50 grand for anything." He looked Lacey straight in the eye. "It's the only way, Lacey. I've considered every other avenue and they're all dead ends. The TV world can save us."

Lacey stood there, glaring at him. Her face was flushed and her red hair seemed somehow inflamed as her violet eyes bore into him. Many a man would quiver under such a gaze, but Klondike remained impassive.

"So, you just waltzed into a Hollywood studio and struck a deal with ATV and Steve Irving? Just like that?" she said angrily.

He shrugged. "Pretty much. I knew Steve and his cronies had been following the show. I had no idea, until yesterday, quite what a big shot he was at the network though."

Lacey put her hands on her hips, standing over him. "And you thought you could authorise all this by yourself? Without consulting us? Without consulting Addison?"

He looked up angrily, pouring himself a beer from the mini-bar fridge. "Hell, it's my circus, god damn it. I still own the show. I have investors and Addison but, Jesus, they trust me to take the risks. It's my neck on the line. Without shows, I'm finished."

Lacey was unrepentant. "Why didn't you run this by us first, for the love of god? Why didn't we all go to LA?"

He frowned, anger rising. "There was no time, dammit. I need action, not a round of discussions. LA is three weeks away. We have to have a show there, no matter what."

As Klondike and Lacey glared at each other, Heavy chuckled to himself as he shuffled his obligatory deck of cards. "Who would've thought it?" he mused. "A circus on TV. Now, that ain't never been done. Why, oh why, did we never think of that before?"

Klondike, eyes still locked on Lacey's, smiled. "That's the spirit, Heav."

Lacey finally shifted her gaze, focusing on Plum at the table. "Richie?" she barked.

To everyone's surprise, Plum grinned cheerfully. "I haven't gone through the figures yet...mainly because we don't have the ATV price yet. But...well, I have to say... I think this move is genius."

"What!" Lacey hissed, turning on her heel and subjecting the smaller Plum to her electrifying gaze and pout.

Plum shuffled uncomfortably in his chair, trying to gain some composure. He looked up at Lacey nervously. "Well, Lacey, think about it. The circus is finished after this. We can't get the equipment to nine different locations in three and a half weeks. It's impossible. We have to cut our losses with the season. But we can make two shows. And the two biggest. But the profit line wouldn't be met with gate receipts, midway takings, merchandise and the like. However, selling control to ATV in this manner, the profit will be handsome. And the exposure will be off the scale. Oh my word…we will be on nationwide television! This will make our season!" He looked pleadingly at Lacey. "Surely, as a publicist, you can see that?"

Lacey chewed it over, but still looked irate. "That's all very well," she said in a calmer voice. "But did anyone stop and think about the paying customers in Santa Brava? The kids coming to watch their heroes tomorrow. Tomorrow! And the others…the others in San Diego, Williams, Phoenix, Flagstaff, Reno and Salinas. What about their shows?"

Klondike took a swig of his beer and held up a reassuring hand. "LA and Vegas are within easy reach of all of those towns. Anyone can still make it to the show. But here's the beauty of the plan…they can all experience the excitement of Klondike's Circus on television. Everyone will see the show now. No one misses out."

"But they will," Lacey shot back, "as every sell-out crowd we would have accumulated in each of those towns will never be able to sit in a studio in LA. Or at the combined casino entrance hall and parking lot arena we have planned for Vegas." She looked at Klondike sadly now, her voice lowered. "They want to see the circus, Kal. You're robbing them of it."

Klondike was deadly serious. He spoke in a quiet, firm voice. "I didn't rob them, Lacey. Whoever took my train off the rails robbed them. Someone…someone out there has been trying to rob our paying public of their circus since before we started out. And now it's come to this. An all or nothing gamble. But this way, the TV option, at least as many people as possible can see the show. Then, next year, when we come back on tour, they can come see us for real, like it should be. And we'll love them for it all the more."

Lacey seemed to soften with these words. She swept a hand through her beautiful hair, and relaxed her frame. "That's a good way of putting it."

Klondike nodded. "I had to do something."

She looked at him, pained. "I just wish you'd consulted with me first."

He moved forward and, in an unexpected gesture, took both of her hands in his own. She flushed. "Lacey," he barked, "you have been an inspirational presence here. Ever since that first day when you rolled up at camp in that fancy motor in your big city glad rags. You're right, dammit. You're right... I should have put it to you first. And I'm sorry. Sorry I didn't share my ideas. I guess I'm panicking as well. It's clouding my judgment. Made me irrational."

The two continued holding hands, staring into each other's eyes. Both seemed to nod at one another.

At the table, Heavy and Plum felt an odd sensation permeate the smoky atmosphere in the penthouse.

"Er, Kal," said Plum nervously, attracting the duo's attention at last. "Have you...have you told Addison yet?"

Klondike grinned devilishly. "Why, Richie, I thought I'd leave that honour to you. After all, the finances is your department. And he wants you to report back."

"But..." Plum began.

"No," Lacey said in a husky voice. She smiled at the men around her, and twirled towards the table with effortless grace. "Leave Daryl to me, baby. He trusts my word more than anyone's. When he realises his bank will be subjected to TV advertising, he'll be in heaven, regardless of the show cancellations."

Heavy looked sceptical. "You really think so?"

Lacey sighed in an exaggerated manner. "Boys, please...let me work him over. I'll tell him all the Hollywood studios were in a bidding war to show our circus. ATV offered the most money. And threw in the king of comedy to boot. How, oh how, will poor little Daryl ever know what went down?"

Klondike and Heavy laughed boisterously. "Lacey," Klondike drawled, fishing a cigar out of his jacket. "I've said it before, and I'll say it again. I like the way you talk. You know why? Cos you talk circus language."

She leant over the table and fluttered her giant eyelids. "That's one of my more subtle qualities."

Heavy clapped his hands boyishly. "Let's all have a drink. Hell, we've got work to do."

And that was the truth.

Chapter 21

ATV TO SCREEN CIRCUS SPECTACULARS!

By Gil Ransom, Spotlight

The magic of the big top is coming to prime time television later this month after ATV announced plans to broadcast two circus shows on its network.

The American Television Network is partnering up with Klondike's Circus to put on two mega shows featuring some of the most original acts on the planet.

The two shows – entitled Circus of the Stars and Circus of the Stars: Las Vegas – are a firm gamble for the broadcaster, as it attempts to win the Nielsen ratings war over rivals Sinclair Television and UBC.

The filming of a circus show is not something attempted frequently by any provider, with multiple camera angles and a sea of electrics needed to relay the action.

The first show will take place in the ATV studios in Hollywood, with the building usually reserved for gameshows and variety acts doubling up as a home to the circus.

The second entertainment extravaganza taken on by the network is the much-publicised show taking place at The Golden Dune, at the heart of the Las Vegas strip. The circus tent is to be attached to the casino entrance to create a unique performing ground, where additional seating will be available in the casino foyer, among the slots and crap pits.

Advertised as 'the greatest circus spectacular of all time', the Vegas show should be a big draw for the network.

Circus of the Stars has already released its line-up. Special guests Jason Lash, the western movie star, and Linda Schneider, host of TV's Cabaret Hour, will be appearing, as will the king of comedy and ATV golden boy Steve Irving. Fellow comic Larry Lassiter has also agreed to appear.

The stars of Klondike's Circus will revel under such an immense spotlight.

The headline acts are trapeze artist extraordinaire Gino Shapiro, veteran big top favourite Corky the Clown, and multi-talented ventriloquist Roddy Olsen, who will host the extravaganza.

Also appearing will be circus sensations Gargantua, the human blob, and Goliath, the world's tallest performer. Percy Pringle and his Dancing Dwarves are another top act, while Rumpy Stiltskin will showcase an act that has to be seen to be believed.

All this and more is promised during both shows, as the thrills and spills of the circus are projected into front rooms across the land.

But will this prove to be a ratings winner for ATV? Only time will tell.

Show details: Circus of the Stars – Saturday, September 14, 7pm, ATV.

Circus of the Stars: Las Vegas – Saturday, September 21, 7pm, ATV.

From the desperate depths of despair, which had set in among the minds and actions of all within Klondike's Circus following the train crash, came salvation and, with it, a new purpose.

From facing a miserable end to the summer and being stranded in Munson, California, the men and women of the troupe were suddenly looking at the biggest show of their lives, broadcast on network television.

Kal Klondike's bold move to sell the circus's broadcast rights – effectively giving ATV ownership of any footage showing the circus – meant that the show would indeed go on...and not just on, but onto two of the grandest stages imaginable.

Following Klondike's return to the Landmark Hotel after his meeting with Steve Irving, things began to take shape with a frightening velocity.

The very next morning, a convoy of stage equipment trucks lined the main drag of downtown Munson. The giant black vans collected everything that had been held in storage outside the hotel in the stable blocks. The midway stalls, support vehicles, tentpoles, bleachers and, of course, the big tent itself. Klondike halted a work crew attempting to load his beloved jeep into the back of a holding, insisting on driving it to LA himself.

A luxury coach stopped outside the Landmark's reception to transport the staff and performers. Lacey took charge of this escapade, having everyone report to reception after breakfast and allocating seats. She herself sat behind the driver.

The animals would remain at the veterinary surgeons in the town, with Amanda's elephants later transported to a nearby wildlife sanctuary, where they would remain until a decision could be made on their future. Amanda stayed with her beloved animals, and was joined by Cathy Cassidy, who looked after her chimps at the same location. Both had been told they would not feature in the upcoming shows due to the animal controversy, but that they would be paid their full seasonal fees. Neither woman objected, any jealousy or wrath overshadowed by their worry and sense of care towards their animals.

The Rough Riders also remained behind, travelling with the horses to a nearby cattle ranch where the stallions would be kept busy for now chasing longhorns and helping break some of their younger brethren.

By noon, the large black stage trucks – more used to patrolling movie locations and sound stages than backwater rustic towns – had rolled on towards western California. The coach followed in their dusty wake along the trail. Klondike and Heavy followed at the back of the convoy in the jeep.

As the ungodly caravan headed into the desert, the people of Munson realised they would never forget the few days in late summer of 1958 when a circus train derailed down the road and its eccentric performers holed up in the town's Landmark Hotel. Indeed, the following year the hotel would be bought out by a West Coast consortium, who quickly changed its name after consulting with public opinion. The opulent building in the main drag would soon be known as Circus Hotel.

In Hollywood, a whole new world of elegance and style awaited the circus folk.

The convoy decamped within the ATV lot in the rich Hollywood Hills. The reams of equipment and vehicles were all stored in a giant warehouse usually used for props. The staff and performers were all allocated rooms in a vast apartment block used by the studios to house talent and production staff.

Klondike was allowed the use of two offices in a bungalow just off the main performance studio, where the circus would appear on the big night.

The midway stalls and kiosks were actually set up in place outside the studio, where they would be put into operation on the day of the circus. All the ATV staff and runners would have to stare at them for two weeks before they were activated.

The roustabouts, or rather those that were left, went straight to work fixing broken equipment amidst the stalls and tentpoles, taking full advantage of the studio block's workshop and endless supply of fixtures and tools.

The men and women of the circus soon adjusted to their new, temporary lives in Hollywood. Meals were served in a staff canteen in the main headquarters building, and everyone was treated like a contracted player which, considering the circus was under contract as a forthcoming attraction, was exactly what they were.

Rehearsals would begin in two days, and everyone was braced to give it their all.

Gino and Nicky silently paced across the vinyl floor of Central Studio's main stage.

Despite their vast show business experience, neither man had ever seen such a large indoor recording studio.

The stage was larger than a basketball court, while the balcony seemed to hang miles above them. And then, before the stage, a massive auditorium of several thousand plush leather-backed seats jutted out into infinity.

Gino was waltzing along, eyes wide and mouth agape as he studied the stage and its accessories.

Nicky followed sheepishly. Discharged from hospital in time to make the coach at Munson, he wore his right arm in a sling and sported several plasters on his face and neck. He looked pale and withdrawn, but even he was impressed by the great stage before them.

"Jesus, bro," he gawked, "we ain't never played in a place like this."

Gino was lost in the moment, his large brown eyes seduced by the bright lights and vinyl flooring. "This is the place, Nicky," he whispered in a daze, "don't you see? The grandest stage of all. Think of who you have seen on TV perform in here. Roy Burns. Jackie Sampson. The Great Santoro. Frank Kearns and Jumbo the Bear. And now…it's our turn. The Shapiro brothers. Finally…finally, dammit, we fly on the big stage."

Nicky looked down sadly. "Well, you will, Gino. And Jenny. Not me."

Gino snapped out of his revere and glared at him. "You will be part of it, Nicky. Your name will be in the credits. You will be with us on the float for the grand finale."

"Credits…" the younger brother said flatly. He looked at the thousands of seats in the auditorium, trying to imagine them full of paying spectators. *It would be different performing in front of an audience, and not having them all around,* he thought. "This is some deal Kal has put together," he finally said.

Gino nodded, still looking around the stage with the air of a hungry gold prospector. "The chairman is el genioso. This plan is excellent. Excellent. Getting us on TV. When all seemed lost. Selling these...these so-called broadcast rights. No one ever knew such a thing existed. Kal has done it again. What a man!" He turned to his brother, and approached slowly, smiling widely and looking somewhat unbalanced. "The show will be a smash. And when it's all over, and the people at home have seen it, everyone will remember one name. Shapiro! I... Gino Shapiro, the debonair king of the air, will put the art of trapeze at the heart of worldwide entertainment. The Shapiro brothers will be beloved by all."

Nicky still looked sad and uncomfortable. "You really think?"

Gino got even more animated. "But of course, chico. Who do you think is at the top of the bill? The final act? Me, of course. Just like always. This show is no different."

"I heard that cowboy actor pal of yours, Lash, is doing his bit as part of the grand finale."

Gino shook his head wildly. "No. Kal told me. Lash is riding out on that godforsaken horse of his as part of the float parade. Just a few fancy horse and rope tricks is all he brings to the big top." He laughed. "Jason is an old friend. He would never upstage ME on my show."

Nicky nodded blankly. He then looked up. Right up. To the very top of the stage ceiling.

"Er, I have to ask, bro," he mumbled, "you want we should talk about the devil drop?"

Gino lost his composure momentarily. "Talk? What talk?" he snapped.

"You've only ever done that gaff with me swinging the ring. I ain't gunna be up there in Las Vegas, Gino."

"Jenny can handle it. It's a ring, for Christ sakes."

"Really? She's beginning to look like a zombie, you ask me. Like she's drinking too much."

Gino studied him for a moment. Then, he nodded. "OK. Let's go talk to her. We've all been through a lot. I don't want no shaky hands here or in Vegas. There's too much at stake. For Kal and for us."

The two brothers ambled back towards the stage exit, Nicky struggling to keep up with his taller sibling.

"Hey, kid. Over here. I saw your act at Orion Bay. You were terrific. Good luck for the TV special."

Roddy Olsen waved happily at the stagehand who had called out to him from a warehouse door as he walked through the ATV lot. He offered his thanks, exchanged pleasantries, then continued on his way.

The youngster weaved his way around the various bungalows and store huts that surrounded the gravel path up the hillside, away from the studios and sound stages and up into the Hollywood Hills themselves. As he walked further uphill, the buildings became less frequent, and the constant buzz of chatter and machinery that filled the backlot seemed to fade away. A forklift truck drove by him idly from the top of the hills but that was the last sign of humanity he saw for some time.

Striding up the path, he reached a small stonewall that signalled the boundary of the ATV properties. With a chuckle, he leapt up and over the wall and waded into the longer, more unkept grass that sat beyond. With nervous trepidation, he climbed the slight grassy incline that sat before him. Reaching the top, he peaked over the soil mound and let out a gasp of disbelief.

There it was. All before him.

HOLLYWOOD. The most famous sign in the world. The iconic white letters sat there, barely 500 yards away, directly in front of him, glistening in the afternoon sun.

Olsen sat on top of the small incline and gazed in a dream-like state at the word. In a strange, surreal way, he felt justified. Any performer who found themselves set to star on any stage so close to the heart of American show business was entitled to tell the world they had made it. Sitting now in the shadow of the famous Hollywood sign, Olsen told himself he too had made it.

It was all very quiet as he sat there in the beautiful, soil-enriched hills. The famous letters stared back at him. He smiled.

Suddenly, distant and faraway voices drifted through his consciousness. Words from the past and present floated through his mind.

"You'll never make it, kid. Why don't you just quit? No street punk from a boarding house ever amounted to nuthin, so just give it up…"

"A ventriloquist…? Man, you must be crazy. A man talking to puppets? It's weird. It's dumb. Don't do it, kid. Take a regular job…like a gas station attendant, or an electrician. Take the easy path…"

Then, within his animated mind, he heard the voice of his new friend, Suzy Dando.

"Believe in yourself, Roddy, and you can achieve anything."

He smiled gingerly. Focusing on the Hollywood sign, as if drawn to it by some quasi-religious super power, he nodded to himself.

"Anything," he whispered. "Anything."

A group of comics were stood around comparing material as Corky rounded the corner of the building and entered Studio 16. The famed studio was the home of The Comedy Club, ATV's legendary Saturday night stand-up show.

Corky, now appearing as usual without his face paint but maintaining his clown attire of yellow and black suit with pink tie, shook his head in awe as he entered the backstage platform, where he could glimpse the theatre beyond.

The four comics all stopped talking and stared at him. At the head of the group was Larry Lassiter, a large, well-built man with slicked back blond hair and reddish skin. As Corky wandered over, he held his arms aloft and smiled broadly.

"Corky the Clown," he cried. "At last you join us in the comedy corner."

Corky nodded uncomfortably. The four others were at least 25 years younger than him. He studied Lassiter and frowned.

"You're, er, you're performing with us next show, right?"

Lassiter bawled with laughter. He came across as the loudest drinker at the party kind of guy. "You bet I am, Cork. Greatest honour of my life." He grasped Corky's hand with both of his and shook it wildly. "I'm so glad you stopped by. I want you to meet the cream of ATV's comedy talent." He introduced his confederates. "Smiley Daniels, Jojo Capone and Billy Race. Boys, say hello to a legend in the field. The world's most talented circus man. Corky the Clown."

The three others looked less impressed, and each just about managed a nod and half-smile.

Corky looked them over, suddenly feeling very old and out of touch.

"So," said Daniels with a cocky air, "the circus, huh? I didn't know them things was still about. The only tents we get around here are at campsites and Indian reservations."

The others laughed. "Yeah," Capone added, "and the last clown I saw was distracting broncos at a rodeo."

More laughter. Corky nodded thoughtfully, squinting at the younger men. He looked down at his yellow suit and pink tie. Then thought of his bowler hat up top. The young TV comedy men wore business suits. Looked more like accountants than showmen.

He finally cracked his best clown smile. "Hey, what is this? A kindergarten? I was looking for The Comedy Club. Are any of your parents around please? I need directions."

Lassiter roared with delight, clapping his hands, as his three companions nodded in some form of respect for the man in the loud suit.

"That's the spirit, Corky. You show em." Displaying a great degree of confidence, he placed an arm around the clown and led him away from the stage, and the three comics. "Don't listen to them jaybirds," he said angrily, "they don't respect true talent. Raw talent. What you got."

They paced around the backstage area, passing dressing room doors. Corky turned to the younger man. "You...you like me?"

"Corky," he bellowed, "you set a blazing trail for guys like me. I grew up in Sacramento. The South Side Project. The only comedy I ever knew was every summer, when Klondike's Circus came to town. And I could go with my Uncle Jim and see you. Corky. And the clowns. All those clowns. We would take in three shows. Sometimes Frisco and Fresno too. It was beautiful. I turned to comedy, to show business, because of you and your guys."

Corky smiled at him, still looking about in awe. "Well, that's terrific, son. I am glad I could be of service to you, er..."

"Larry. Larry Lassiter. I'm on right after you in the show, man. When I was offered a place on the original show by Shapiro earlier this year, I said I'd be honoured to open for you and your clowns. But now the executives at ATV want me to follow you. You know what I told em?" He winked at the clown. "I told 'em no one follows Corky the Clown. His gaff is electrifying. The juggling, the unicycle, the human cannon, the humour. Oh man..." He looked about ready to explode.

Corky grabbed his hand and held it tight. "It's OK, Larry." He looked into the comedian's eyes and saw nothing but genuine delight and awe. "And thank you. Thank you, son, for making an old man feel important. You know a lot of folks consider clowning a dying art form. You've made me think twice about that."

Lassiter shrugged. "What can I tell you, Corky? You're the greatest!"

He slapped his arm back around the older man's frame and led him back towards the stage.

Jenny Cross sat in the apartment she had been allocated in the block behind the studios and reached for a brown paper bag that was sat on a coffee table.

She was wearing a robe having just enjoyed a shower. Her blonde hair was wet and clung to her, while her skin was reddish and moist. Pulling the robe tightly against her, she collapsed into the couch in the centre of the small living room and pulled at the paper bag.

A bottle of Christie's vodka emerged from the brown paper. She looked at it glumly, before hastily unfastening the lid and taking a long, deliberate pull. As she gulped the clear liquid down, she felt her senses come back to life, her reflexes tingle slightly.

She put the bottle, lid still removed, on the arm of the couch and stood up. Catching her reflection in a wall mirror next to a dresser, she visibly shuddered at what she saw.

It was as if she had aged ten years in a week. Her eyes were bloodshot, and surrounded by puffy bags that hung like drapes. Her skin was pale and full of lines, while her lips looked cracked and without colour.

She was awoken from her sudden hypnosis by a rap at the door. She shook slightly and tightened her robe.

"Who is it?"

"Telegram for Miss Jenny Cross," said a youthful, high-pitched voice.

She crossed the room, and opened the door onto its chain. A boy of no more than 19 dressed in a mailman's outfit stood there awkwardly. His eyes enlarged when he saw the woman in the robe.

Jenny saw the envelope in his hand and snatched at it before slamming the door closed again.

"Your telegram, Miss," the boy said to the closed door.

She ripped the envelope open and read the message, her eyes widening in fear and anticipation with each word she devoured. She stood there in the apartment and re-read the message.

IN LIGHT OF NEW SCHEDULE, NEW MEETING PLACE. FARLEY'S FAIRGROUND. BEHIND CANDY FLOSS STALL. FRIDAY. 11PM. DO NOT BE LATE. M

She scrunched the small piece of yellow paper into a ball and tossed it shakily into a bin.

Eyes wide with fear, she crumpled into the couch, and reached for the bottle.

An almighty kerfuffle was breaking out among the various patrons and staff who had gathered at the Hillside Cafe that night.

The 24/7 coffee shop and diner was the unofficial hangout for runners, extras and just about anyone else who wanted the company within the sprawling ATV lot.

On this particular night, members of the Klondike's Circus troupe had descended upon the popular cafe and were getting acquainted with some of the regulars, many of whom appeared in one sense or another on ATV's programming.

The colourful chatting and buying of drinks had just been interrupted by the most unusual and unexpected of sounds.

As the buzz of chitchat died down, the diner's string of patrons seemed to cock their ears all at once. There could be no mistake. The noise was the clatter of horse hooves.

The mystery was quickly dissolved as every pair of eyes in the joint turned to the batwing doors at the entrance. A beautiful palomino horse reared its long head through the doors, with its rider ducking his head and neck under the arched doorway and entering the cafe on horseback.

Everyone in the diner stopped and stared, including waitresses and bar staff.

Then, as if on cue, a cheer sounded across the floor and everyone clapped and whistled as the newcomer and his horse pranced into the cafe.

Jason Lash looked every inch the rhinestone cowboy superstar. Decked out in white and gold silk shirt, slacks and cowpoke leathers, he wore a giant silver Stetson and red neckerchief. His tanned, all-American facial features and sandy blond hair all contributed to the look of a Hollywood superstar, which he was.

With a loud cackle, Lash manoeuvred his horse towards the serving bar and called out to the manager, stood just beyond. "Hey, Pauly, how about two beers? One for me and one for Goldie?"

Everybody laughed. The cafe's patrons all gathered round the cowboy star, offering handshakes and well wishes. He was used to being the centre of attention, and expected no less than the apparent admiration lavished upon him.

From amidst the straggle of fans, Gino Shapiro emerged, smiling widely. He pushed his way through the mob until he was next to the horse and Lash could see him. The two men shook hands enthusiastically, Lash looking down at him with a big grin.

"Shapiro! You son of a bitch! You made it. This is actually happening! Yeehaw!"

The crowd cheered at the uttering of the catchphrase.

Shapiro patted the horse lovingly and looked up into the million dollar looks of Lash. "Of course," he said, "I said you had a place on our show in Los Angeles and, dammit amigo, I meant it."

The horse backtracked slightly, and Lash wobbled in the saddle as he maintained his control and balance in the front of the diner. "Yeah," he snorted, looking at the cafe patrons gathered all around, "but you never said anything about TV. About Central Studio. Hell, I just read about this here circus in Spotlight magazine. Everyone's talkin' bout it. Why, I thought we'd be strutting our stuff in a tent in a field someplace."

Shapiro smiled, enjoying the moment. "Plans change, cowboy. We just got upgraded. Now you can do your act for millions watching at home."

Lash scoffed as he grabbed the reins of his prancing horse. "Hell, I do that every day now, pardner. My last movie grossed in the mills. Everyone knows my name these days. I've got movie executives lined up at my ranch wanting to sign me up. Movies, TV serials, commercials, records, radio. They all want a piece of me and Goldie here." He looked down at Shapiro awkwardly. "But a deal is a deal, pardner. I said I'd do your circus, and...well, here I am. I ain't never gunna let down my fans. Especially all the little Lashers out there."

Shapiro nodded slowly, admiring the fine horse whose reins he had gathered up. "Well, who knows, amigo. This could end up being your biggest show yet." He eyed the cowboy seriously. "We've got a week of rehearsals lined up. Starting tomorrow."

Lash roared with laughter and readjusted his hat. "Rehearsals? I don't need any stinking rehearsals, flyboy. Just put me on the stage and let me at the fans." He looked down, suddenly panicking. "I'm at the top of the bill for this rodeo, right?"

Shapiro laughed mockingly. "Jason, my old campesino, you're just going to have to wait and see."

Lash glared at him. Then, in a well-practised stint, took off his hat and cried out a "Yeehaw" before digging his spurs into the horse's side until it performed a textbook hind-legged pose. With a mighty neigh, Goldie the palomino charged out the batwing doors, with Lash ducking frantically as they soared out the doorway and into the night.

With their exit, another cheer emanated around the diner as everyone stared wide-eyed after the cowboy star. Shapiro looked at the still swinging doors in dismay, then went back to the girl he had been chatting to before the loud, unexpected interruption.

Heavy Brown was idly wandering around the ATV lot, casually studying the warehouses and studio buildings on either side of the pathway.

As he strolled in the moonlight, he smiled at the thought of the many different places the circus had taken him. They had played to some mighty crowds up and down the West Coast and, before Klondike had formed his own stable, in major showgrounds across America.

But there had never been anything like this. Hollywood. TV land. And then, one week later, a show inside a casino in Las Vegas.

It felt surreal. Heavy chuckled aimlessly as he shuffled along the gravelled pathway and entered the giant structure that held Central Studio, where all the action would take place in a few short days.

As he moved through the foyer, he halted at an unexpected sight on the wall. It was a poster for the TV special, must have been drawn up earlier that day.

He ambled across the reception area to the far wall and examined the large, glitzy poster. He was impressed. The pictures had been superimposed onto the paper using technology far above anything he had ever encountered.

The tagline at the top screamed: ATV PRODUCTIONS AND KLONDIKE'S CIRCUS PROUDLY PRESENT... A TELEVISION SPECTACULAR BEYOND YOUR IMAGINATION!

Beneath the tag was a painting of inside a big top, showing the colourful tent and the crowd in the bleachers. Superimposed into the painting were head and shoulders shots of Gino Shapiro, Corky the Clown and Roddy Olsen, all just under a shot of the cowboy, Jason Lash, riding his horse towards the camera.

The text alongside the headshots read: A GALAXY OF STARS! A UNIVERSE OF FUN! IT'S ANOTHER WORLD AS TV MEETS CIRCUS, LIVE ON ATV!

Heavy smirked slightly as he noted the picture of Lash was twice the size of those of the Klondike performers. He read the smaller text beneath the pictures.

"Gino Shapiro, Debonair King of the Air... Corky, the World's Greatest Clown... Roddy Olsen, the Puppetmaster; Suzy Dando, Songstress Supreme... Gargantua, the Human Blob... Goliath, the World's Tallest Performer... Percy Pringle and His Dancing Dwarves... PLUS...

"Special guests... Jason Lash, Hollywood's No 1 Cowboy... Linda Schneider, TV Chat Show Queen...and ATV's own Larry Lassiter, Stand-up Star.

"ALSO APPEARING... The King of Comedy, Steve Irving."

The main headline was at the bottom: CIRCUS OF THE STARS. It was followed by the TV syndication details.

Heavy stared at the huge poster for some time. He frowned. This season, everything had changed. From what they had started out with, for their show to evolve into this, a TV spectacular, was inconceivable to him. He had to hand it to Klondike for coming up with such a bold scheme to save their season, throwing broadcast rights into the ring, but something still did not feel right to Heavy.

He thought of the performers left out. Amanda. Cathy. Both phased out due to the controversy over animals in the train crash. The elephants and monkeys. What would become of them now? He thought, of course, of Emile Rance. Where could he be? Did his lions survive? Then there were the Rough Riders and their team of horses. He shook his head. Too many questions. It felt like everyone had become so entranced and excited by the relocation to Los Angeles, no one had spared a thought for the others.

As he stood there studying the poster, a soft voice woke him from his meditation.

"Whoever saw this coming?"

He turned and was surprised to find Richie Plum stood behind him, dressed unusually in plaid shirt and jeans. He too gaped at the poster.

Heavy nodded. "Yeah. I was just thinking the same thing, pal. How did we end up running a TV special out here..."

Plum wandered over until he stood next to Heavy. They both admired the artwork of the poster in the quiet of the foyer.

"I've got to tell you," Plum began, "this whole thing has been the adventure of a lifetime for me. Never in my wildest dreams did I think joining a circus would be this much fun. I know we've had dark days, and we've had bright days. But the whole experience has been the making of me, Henry."

Heavy grunted slightly. "Well, er, I guess that's the effect the circus has on a man. They say it's in the sawdust."

Plum nodded. "It sure is." He eyed Heavy awkwardly, then looked back at the great poster. "I...er, I don't want to leave. Not now. Not after all we've been through together. I... I want to stay in the circus. Helping you and Kal and, hopefully, Lacey too. I'll do the books. The finances. Whatever needs doing. I want to sign up for next season. And every season thereafter." He looked downwards, as if in disgust. "I don't want to go back to Addison's cubicle office in Frisco now. Not now that I've seen all this." He looked up triumphantly, his pink cheeks almost shining in the dim lighting. "I'm a circus man now. Yes I am!"

Heavy chuckled, throwing an arm good-naturedly around the smaller man's shoulders. "Richie," he barked, "the transformation I've seen in you these past weeks has been something else. Hell, you're right. You are a circus man. This is where you belong now."

Plum smiled with glee, suddenly feeling like a child again. "You think...you think I can stay on after this season? Help the planning for next year? And all that..."

"Don't let's get ahead of ourselves," Heavy said sternly. "We might not even have us a 'next season' right now. It all depends on Kal's latest gamble." He pointed up at the poster above. "It all depends on LA and Vegas. If they are hits, we are in the green. Selling those broadcast rights has kept us going and kept Addison happy, but if we're gunna get bigger and better, we have to be a smash. With the live audience. The TV audience. And, of course, the studio big shots. Then, the word will spread further than ever before. And we could be America's biggest circus!"

Plum gaped at him, bewildered. "The possibilities could be endless."

Heavy winked at him. "Indeed. But, anyway, we need you to concentrate on the books, Richie. Just stay cool and enjoy the ride." With that, he clamped his arm onto Plum's shoulder and guided the smaller man towards the glass doors at the far end of the foyer.

"Now," he began, "there's something you desperately need to know, son. And I'm going to teach you right now. Up in my room."

Plum looked confused as they walked. "And what's that?"

Heavy faced him. "How to play poker. That's the most important factor in any circus tour."

He laughed over-enthusiastically as they left the building.

The following morning, an executive meeting was called in the main conference room of ATV's headquarters.

Located on the top floor, the long, plush boardroom was decorated with a huge shiny mahogany table and a fluffy green carpet, with leather-bound chairs on either side and a slightly bigger, throne-like seat at the head. Beyond, the obligatory floor-to-ceiling window showcased an impressive view of the luscious Hollywood Hills outside.

To Klondike, who arrived early and took his seat at the nearside of the great table, it was like stepping into another world. The world of the boardroom, where big-time deals are brokered and contracts ripped up or renewed; where careers are decided and stars are born.

Dressed in his tanned suit, he had taken Lacey with him, figuring she was more used and suited to such grand meetings. For her part, Lacey was dressed in a silver business suit with her hair tied back, and had brought with her a leather display case of Klondike's Circus press cuttings and promotional materials.

Daryl Addison had arrived next. The banker had made the short trip from San Francisco by helicopter and now sat next to Klondike. The two had exchanged updates upon Addison's arrival in the conference room, but had managed to keep their excitement and anticipation neatly sealed.

Claude Hershey had come in from Las Vegas, backed up by one of his attorneys. He was a giant bull of a man, with a huge head and neck, his receding hairline swept back with gel.

Next to him at the table was Bob Brewer, ATV's head of programming, and next to him was Steve Irving, who carried a sense of authority with him as he greeted everyone gathered in the top-floor room.

But the throne at the head of the table was saved for Samuel Spearman, president of the network, an immaculately groomed, yet inconspicuous little man with short dark hair and pale skin.

It was Spearman who had called the executive meeting, and it was only right he kicked things off after keeping his guests waiting for several moments before taking his place before them.

"All right, all right," he said in a surprisingly soft voice, having eased himself into his seat and taken stock of everyone at the table. "Thank you all for coming. Mr Hershey, we thank you for coming all the way from Vegas and are honoured to have you."

The big man nodded solemnly, chain-smoking his way through a pack of Luckys. Everyone stared at Spearman, who spoke in a dull, somewhat machine-like monotone.

"All right, so Circus of the Stars airs on Saturday week. I agreed to it after an impressive pitch from our very own Mr Irving, who has purchased the broadcast rights for all Klondike's Circus footage for ATV until…well, until someone else buys it off us, I guess." He eyed Irving shrewdly, and nodded. "So we got us two shows. Los Angeles and Las Vegas. I've been through your scripts and storyboards, Mr Irving…" he suddenly eyed Klondike at the end of the table, "and I've studied your circus, my dear Mr Klondike. You've done good work, guys, but you got to understand… I'm the president of this network. What I say runs, runs. That's how this works. You've all got something rolling on this, I know that, but none of you has as much rolling on it as I do. I have to answer to the board of directors. I have to attract investment into the network. A risky move like this…broadcasting a live circus show…could blow it all outta the water." He studied Klondike with what looked like masked contempt. "So, there are ground rules, Klondike. I call the shots. Ultimately. Irving has the plans, but I OK everything. Do you follow?"

Every head turned down the table towards the circus master. Klondike grinned, eyeing each pair of eyes humorously. "Aye aye, sir," he said calmly.

Spearman seemed to growl at the remark. "The idea to put Jason Lash on second to last. It stinks. Lash is one of the highest grossing western stars in Hollywood. This Shapiro of yours…he is nobody. We end with the star name. That's Lash. He will do his roping and horse act as the finale."

Irving interjected. "With respect, sir, I don't think that will work. The trapeze act is the finale of any circus show. What Shapiro does defies logic…as well as gravity. It leaves the audience speechless. Simply put…no one can follow it."

The network president chewed it over. He glanced idly at Brewer. "What you say, Bob?"

Brewer, a skinny, youthful figure in shirt and tie, nodded. "I'm afraid I agree with Steve, sir. It's difficult to see beyond that format. It doesn't mean Lash is anything less of a star than Shapiro."

Klondike waded in. "It's a tried and tested formula, Mr Spearman. The trapeze is the finale of the circus. It's how the show works."

Spearman snorted and glared at him. It was pretty clear to everyone present he wasn't sold on the circus idea, and that he held Klondike and his crew in contempt. "It may work in the desert plains and the county fairs, son. This is Hollywood. The pinnacle of show business. We have a tried and tested formula here, too. And it says the star name closes the show."

Irving held up his hands. "OK, sir, but as it stands at the moment, Shapiro closes. We can alter the line-up if need be. But you asked me to put together a script, and that's what I've done."

Brewer held his breath at the brave challenge to the network's Mr Big. It was a sign of how much ATV valued the comedian that he could stand up to Spearman like that.

Finally, after an uneasy silence, the diminutive man at the head of the table nodded. "Right," he muttered. He looked around suspiciously, as if sensing a conspiracy. Then, he casually extracted a black pipe from his blazer pocket and lit up, sending great clouds of ash-like smoke into the boardroom's canopy. "OK, OK," he muttered moodily, glancing down at his notes. Then, he stared at Klondike again. "They tell me you stubbed out your animal acts. That's the heart of your show ripped out. How do you compensate?"

Klondike cocked an eyebrow. "An unfortunate affair, Mr Spearman. But, you've given us an hour of airtime. We have plenty to fill it in. Our touring show was two hours long, after all."

The network president scowled again, looking down at a sheet of paper. "Oh? What…with the so-called Showcase Revue? A giant fat man. A tall man. Some dwarves prancing around like ballet dancers. That's it, huh?"

Klondike finally cracked a little. Despite the high stakes, and the fact everything was riding on the television special, he frowned back down the table. "It's been a smash hit season so far. Is…is there a problem?"

"Yeah!" Spearman barked, his pipe dangling in the corner of his mouth. "I say that train crash has killed your show, Klondike. With the animal controversy, these rumours of a saboteur in the ranks, the injury to this Shapiro's brother, the lost revenue from your cancelled shows. Sounds like we're bailing you out. We gave you 50 grand for those broadcasting rights. And for what? The surviving ranks of a train wreck!"

It was Addison who spoke next, to the shock of all present. "Why, people could have been killed in that crash!"

"Cool it, banker," Spearman snarled, eyes still locked on Klondike. "If I want advice from you, it will be about an investment account. Now," he removed his pipe and jabbed it in the direction of Klondike. "I've agreed to bankroll you, son, and give you Saturday night air time. That's prime real estate out here, boy. What I want to know is…what am I really getting?"

Klondike smiled good-naturedly. "A show like no other, sir. The circus world meets the TV world. Big top performers, Hollywood stars, TV personalities and, of course, some carnival attractions. TV viewers love variety…just look at Steve's ratings. Well, this is variety at its very core. A bit of everything. All encompassed into a one-hour spectacular."

Spearman nodded slightly. "It's a good pitch. But, last I heard, the circus was on its way out. People prefer movies. The theatre. Drive-ins. Comedy clubs."

Lacey finally made her move, her soft feminine voice making everyone at the table turn her way in a kind of shock. "With respect, Mr Spearman," she said, "I have a raft of press articles that may beg to differ. And not just from local rags. National magazines and news syndicates, all praising our work and offering top reviews."

With her usual cat-like elegance, she rose from her seat and walked calmly to the head of the meeting, standing before Spearman purposefully and dropping the display case of cuttings onto the table in front of him. He smiled up at her, suddenly looking hypnotised.

"And who might you be, sweetheart?" he whispered.

"Lacey Tanner," she said sweetly, innocently, "public relations consultant to Klondike's Circus. And sweet I may be…until, of course, it comes to getting my client publicity. Then, well, I come off about as sweet as a bulldog. But, as I'm sure you're aware, Mr Spearman, when it comes to business, we all don one's mask of persuasion."

Spearman smiled up at her, enchanted. "Indeed, we do, Miss Tanner. I thank you for the documents."

Klondike watched the whole thing, spellbound. Lacey had an uncanny knack of getting them out of a tight spot. He had lost count of the amount of times her judgement and social skills had saved them. Now, she was working her magic on the head of ATV.

"I'm sure you'll agree, Mr Spearman," she said as she walked back to her seat, "the circus is very much alive and well. And breaking box office records, too."

Spearman watched her walk back down the room. "Well, er, I sure am glad to hear that, Miss Tanner." He chewed on his pipe awkwardly, flustered, to the surprise of Irving and Brewer. Then, he came back on track, addressing Irving.

"Now," he barked, "what's this about some fresh-faced kid ventriloquist acting as host? On OUR show! Come on. I wanted you to host, Steve. You can be the face of this."

Irving shook his head. "You haven't seen Olsen perform, sir. I... I have never seen a vent like him. And I've had plenty on my show. This kid is something else. His voice manipulation skills are extraordinary. At the show in Frisco I saw, he did a skit without any of his puppets. Just him and his bare hand. It was otherworldly. The audience lapped it up. Who would have thought it?"

Spearman looked at him blankly. "Right. But he's not a name, is he? You seem better suited to host, Steve. The viewers will relate to that. You introduce acts every night on your show."

"With respect, sir," Irving shot back, "the way Olsen does it, with his puppets interacting with the performers and joining in, it is the making of the show. It's a winning blend. He has to be host."

Spearman growled again, fiddling with his pipe irritably. "Where did this damn kid come from?"

Klondike answered. "It was an incredible thing. He turned up at the winter camp one day. Outta nowhere. Asked for an audition. We gave it to him. And, well, despite a few reservations about the nature of his act, me and my staff were blown away by his talent. We signed him up. Then, on just our second show of the season, we promoted him to host. The response since has been...well, like nothing we have ever known, if I'm honest."

Spearman glared at him down the table. "Explain."

It was Lacey who answered, in an enthusiastic flutter. "Why, the people go crazy for him. Every town we arrive in, there are teenagers, children, families all waiting to see him. We sell posters of Roddy with his puppets, signed pictures. There are interview requests sent to me almost every day from news outlets across the west coast. Everybody wants a piece of the puppetmaster and his little pals."

Spearman stared at her. "Who is he? Elvis?"

Lacey laughed, a hauty, charming cackle. "He is to us. A charming, beautiful boy."

Spearman nodded weakly. "And all this hysteria…in just four months. And he just waltzed into your…your winter camp. Just like that."

Klondike grinned. "They call him the kid from nowhere."

Spearman glared at him, before turning again to Irving. "Jesus, Steve. I hope you're right about this."

"Well," Irving began, "I saw the show in Frisco and I've had reports from the others. I reckon we're gunna give everyone a show to remember."

"All right," the president said in finality. "So, we got LA covered. Which brings us to the second part of our venture. The Golden Dune. Las Vegas. And our good friend Mr Hershey here."

Hershey, who had sat back, smoking, for the entire meeting, his attorney seated in a folding chair behind him, finally leant forward.

"On behalf of the Dune and my associates," the big man spluttered, "I want to thank you, Mr Spearman and Mr Irving, and all at ATV, for agreeing to film the show at my casino. This was already a once-in-a-lifetime venture for me, the chance to do something really different and get the punters in. But now, with the show being aired live on ATV, this has become something else entirely. My casino will get national coverage. Sponsorship. Endorsements. And a Saturday night show!" He clapped his hands together gaily. "Dammit, I haven't been this excited in a long time."

Spearman looked at him queerly. "You, er, don't have any reservations about this Klondike's Circus performing in your casino?"

"Reservations!" Hershey practically exploded. "Listen, pal, I've been dealing with Kal and his troupe of performing magic men for years now. He used to do shows at my ranch in Arizona. And I sponsored his last Vegas show at the Hoover Memorial Park. If Kal says it's a winner, it's a winner in my book. I can't wait."

"So," Spearman said sceptically, "the big top is going to be joined to the front of the casino? In the parking lot?"

"You bet!" Hershey picked up a large sheet of paper, that showed an artist's impression of the joining together of the circus tent and the casino's main entrance. He spoke with a cigarette planted in the corner of his mouth. "Now, Kal just spoke about two worlds coming together. Well, look at this, pal. THREE worlds coming together. TV, circus and casino. All in my Golden Dune. There's going to be more action going down that night than any punter can shake a stick at. We're all in it together."

Spearman seemed strangely unmoved by Hershey's enthusiasm. "I see," he uttered dryly. He looked again at Irving. "Well, Steve. You've given us the outline for these two shows. I've said my piece. I get final say on all this. But, well…" he paused, looking at each face gazing up at him expectantly. "It seems we're good to go. But just remember this." He glared at Irving yet again. "It's on your head, Steve. This is your baby. I hope you know what you're doing." With that, he grasped the leather display case Lacey had deposited, stood, huffed, and left the room via the anteroom behind him, from which he had entered.

His exit was so swift, no one had time to try and say anything else. As the door closed, they all stared at each other.

Klondike immediately addressed Irving. "Jesus, Steve, you've really gone out on a limb for us here. I had no idea. How can I ever repay you?"

The cocky comedian looked ill at ease, for once. "Let's just say I believe in your show," he said quietly, still looking at the door Spearman had exited. He turned back to Klondike. "Now, I've done my end of the bargain, cowboy. Next, you and your 'magic men' have to fulfil yours."

Klondike turned and looked at Lacey and Addison either side of him. "You hear that, folks. The gauntlet has been laid."

Hershey cackled, lighting up his latest cigarette. "Just give us a show we can all be proud of, Kal."

Klondike smiled mesmerically. "I'll give a show the world can be proud of."

Chapter 22

It was getting late and Roddy Olsen was seated in the living room of his temporary flat in the studio block, going through various ATV brochures and promotional materials.

As he sat there transfixed, he was stirred by a light rapping at the door.

He leapt up from the couch, crossed the room and opened the door.

There stood Suzy Dando, dressed in her pyjamas with a thick shoal draped over her tiny frame.

He chuckled. "Can't sleep either, huh?"

She gazed up at him dreamily. "Who can sleep at a time like this?"

"I guess you're right. Come on in."

She scampered into the dimly lit room, threw herself onto the couch and sat with her legs tucked into her, as if she had been living in the flat for years.

Olsen closed the door and hovered over her. "I can't offer you much, I'm afraid. Southern lemonade, the usual."

"I'm fine," she said, nestling into the corner of the couch. "I, er, I just needed the company. This is all so weird. Being here. Hollywood. ATV. In these flats. It's all happened so quick. Now we're here, going out live on national TV. Oh my…my head is spinning."

He looked at her. She looked more a child than ever, he thought. Her beautiful brown hair was tied back neatly, and her cosmetic-less face looked youthful and innocent. He smiled. "Yes, it has been a bit like that, hasn't it? Since the train crash." He collapsed into an armchair opposite. "A whirlwind. The whole thing."

Suzy stared at him, wide eyed. "The whole season…the whole season has been a whirlwind for you, Roddy. Ever since you showed up at camp that day. When you came up to me and introduced yourself. With that." She pointed at his giant signature suitcase, propped up in the corner of the room. "Then Mr

Klondike offered you a place with us. Then you became the announcer. Then…then you became a star."

She idly picked up a poster of Olsen that had been lying on a coffee table. It showed Olsen in his signature silver waistcoat, holding Rusty Fox, Napoleon and Tony Tan all together. The background was a stars and stripes motif design. She looked up. "Remember that first day in my trailer? Our little chat? Everything you ever wanted to achieve…you've done it here with our circus. You're a performer. A headliner. And now this… TV. A national audience. You made it, Roddy."

"Correction," he said casually. "We made it, Suzy. We all won this gig on the back of our talents. Now you have a TV audience too. Everyone can hear your beautiful, sweet voice in their living rooms. You will be singing to the nation."

She laughed airily. "What a thought." Her mood turned serious as she eyed Olsen, in admiration and a touch of apprehension. "This is a big responsibility for you, Roddy. Mr Klondike has put it all on the line for this show. ATV have made a big gamble. We…we all know there's a lot of pressure on you, Roddy. You're like the face of the show now. You're our host. You connect all the acts. It's…it's a lot of pressure for one so young."

Olsen smiled happily. "Hell, Suzy, you know I thrive on it. The more riding on it, the better. I want to perform at Madison Square Garden. On Broadway. This…a TV special on ATV, this is a dream come true. I just can't wait." He nodded at her. "And when I join you on your float at the grand finale for the song, you'll know that we've both made it. That we're both stars."

She shook her head. "You're a saint, Roddy. You're too nice. Please…please promise me that fame won't ever change you."

He laughed. "Fame? Saturday could be a disaster for all we know. I might stink the place out."

Suzy cocked an eyebrow. "I think we all know that's not going to happen, Roddy."

Olsen shrugged. "Yeah, well, I'll be doing everything I can and giving it my all. We've got the guys in TV land to impress, after all."

She studied him, smiling. "Do you think the world can fall in love with Rusty and his pals?"

There was a brief silence, and then the voice of Rusty Fox somehow emanated from the suitcase in the corner of the room. "Sure they will, Miss Dando, sure they will. I'm a star. People lurrrve me!"

She laughed ecstatically. "Roddy," she cried, "you're just too much."

On the following Friday, the entire Klondike's Circus troupe took part in a final dress rehearsal ahead of the first TV special.

The test was run as an exact rendition of what would happen the following evening, with even Steve Irving, Jason Lash, Larry Lassiter and Linda Schneider on hand to fill their roles.

Everyone gathered at Central Studio's main stage, and the show played out before a virtually empty auditorium, with just a small handful of executives on hand to witness the preview performance.

Klondike stood watching eagerly at the stage door. He was less than impressed to be surrounded by a crowd of interested onlookers. As had become tradition, Heavy, Lacey and Plum all stood beside him. But they had been joined by Addison, who had never left the studio lot all week, such was his excitement, as well as Claude Hershey, Bob Brewer, Nicky Shapiro and, for a fleeting moment, even Samuel Spearman, who seemed to stray from his seat in an executive directors' box above the stage to the backstage area, and then back again.

To all intents and purposes, the rehearsal had gone without a hitch. Klondike led the applause at the conclusion, and then called all of his crew into a backstage props room.

It was a tight fit. Everyone crowded in, with Klondike stood at the front end of the small space. He looked around eagerly, taking in the sea of shiny, expectant faces.

Again, Heavy, Lacey and Plum all stood beside him, with the talent spread out in a semi-circle before them. Irving and the newly contracted players had gone their separate ways after the rehearsal. Gathered together now was purely the circus folk. Or what was left of them.

Klondike gazed at his team. There was Gino Shapiro, in his fireball orange jumpsuit, chest still heaving after he closed the rehearsal with his routine. Jenny Cross was next to him in her orange leotard, looking somewhat pale and sickly, but still somehow glamorous. Corky the Clown was there, in his classic yellow and brown suit, pink tie and bowler hat. His ensemble of clowns nestled just behind him, all wearing tweed suits of differing loud colours. Roddy Olsen was there, in his silver waistcoat and purple pants. Suzy Dando, having just completed her latest rendition of 'Can You Feel the Magic Tonight?' hovered excitedly, wearing her sparkling white cocktail dress. Gargantua, Goliath, Percy Pringle, his dwarf dancers and Rumpy Stiltskin all crowded round too, giving the group an otherworldly look, as if this strange group of brightly dressed performers, of all shapes and sizes, had just crash landed onto this planet from another dimension.

Klondike smiled as he looked the troupe over. He caught Addison entering the room at the back and nodded at him. The banker stood by the door, arms folded.

"OK, folks," Klondike began, standing before the group. He took a deep breath. "Tomorrow is showtime. Our biggest show yet. Maybe our biggest ever. Tomorrow and next week in Vegas…there's not a lot between them. This…this is our time, people, our time to shine. The grandest stage of all. Opportunities like this, Saturday night airtime, can come about once in a lifetime. That is why we have to grasp it and give it all we got. Like I know you all will. I know we've had a tough time this season…the train crash is something we will never get over. I want you all to remember our friends we left behind. Amanda. Cathy. Emile. The great Emile. He's out there somewhere, and we can only believe he is with us. Yes, we have seen darkness this season. But, dammit, we got through it, we regrouped and now we have this opportunity. This, this chance to show the world what we are made of! And I want you all to know, you deserve it. Each and every one of you. I am proud of you all."

He studied the faces all staring at him and thought for a moment. He chuckled slightly as he gazed around the prop room. "Y'know, I initially joined the circus at 14 years old. As a roustabout. Ran away from the orphanage where they kept me and joined up with my hero at the time. Eric Ribbeck. Back then, his show was called Ribbeck's American Circus. He was just starting out as a young, ambitious entrepreneur. I can still remember as a young boy being mesmerised by the scale and sheer wonder of it all. Just to be involved, to be in that big top under those bright lights, it meant everything to me. And I knew then I had experienced my calling. Just like you all have in the years since. I remember the trapeze high-flyers in their silver stage suits. The clowns, riding bareback and diving onto the backs of ponies. The elephants. Lions, tigers, grizzly bears, swooping falcons. It was like a zoo on rails. How I loved it."

He paused, lost in nostalgia as the group all watched him. He picked up again. "The war brought that to an end. But I knew where I was headed once I was home from Europe. After life in the marines, I was driven to perform. Old Eric gave me that platform, as his sharpshooter and knife thrower. Cowboy Kal. I became a star myself. Then I became something more. Like an A-game quarterback moving upstairs, I became a player-coach. And then I found my true love." His eyes took on a loving, almost hypnotic look. "Running a circus. My circus. The most beautiful life in the world. Finding and nurturing talent. Coming across all of you. And turning you into stars. The new stars. The next generation. And you can all feel the magic I felt. As a performer."

He paused again, pleased to find everyone hanging on his every word. Even Addison at the back looked entranced. "This is a blessed and privileged life, ladies and gentlemen. You're circus folk, dammit, and there isn't anything finer on this planet, you ask me. When you stand under those bright lights, with the crowds all around you, encompassing you, there is no greater feeling in existence. The bright colours of the big top, the rolling of the circus train, the crowds racing to meet you at each stop, the buzz of the midway. It's all there…you get to feel it, breathe it, even. And then you realise…you realise you're free. Free to be what you want. Alive. Soaring higher than the people and worlds that have inhibited you. Because you're a star of the big top. A sensation of the ages. And the people will love you for it.

"Now, folks, we have the show of our lives tomorrow. I want you to feel it…feel free and alive. And soar higher than you ever dreamed. Enjoy it, above all, but feel yourself at the peak of your powers. Because that's where you are right now. All of you. And now, the world is going to know about it. Because the world is watching."

He stepped forward, resting his foot on an old milk crate. "So fly, reach for the stars. And then you will know how it feels…how it feels to be immortal!"

An almighty cheer went up among the group at the conclusion of Klondike's epic speech. Hands were raised in the air in celebration, the dwarves all danced among themselves, and Goliath even hoisted two of the clowns onto his immense shoulders.

Next to Klondike at the front, Lacey wept unashamedly, while Heavy patted his old friend on the back. "That was like General Patten before the siege of Naples," he cackled. "I never knew motivational speeches were your line, Kal."

Klondike grinned, watching over his troupe as they all talked excitedly and made their way to the door. "And they don't even need it, Heavy," he whispered. "Look at them. A fine group we have assembled this season."

Heavy nodded. "The best. I might even start calling them 'the Immortals'."

They laughed. Then, Lacey stepped forward and gave Klondike a big hug.

"Well said, Kalvin, well said," she gushed. She watched the performers leaving the old prop room. Wiping away a tear, she called out to them. "Knock 'em dead, folks, knock 'em dead."

Plum and Lacey duly followed the performers outside, and were quickly replaced by Addison, who had made his way to the front of the room.

"Stirring stuff, Kal," he said half-heartedly. Addison still wasn't entirely sold on the TV idea, and worried incessantly about failure and the show becoming a laughing stock...and financial failure. He had stayed at the studios all week, fretting and going over figures.

Klondike eyed him coolly. "It's a grand stage, Daryl. They need a grand send-off."

The banker nodded. "Man management. The sign of any good leader. All right, I applaud you, Kal. You know how to lead this team. And they look up to you, all right." He watched the last of the group leave the room, then turned back to Klondike. "I just hope there is a Klondike's Circus after tomorrow."

"What the hell is that supposed to mean?"

Addison looked at him shrewdly. "It means something like this, a TV special, can elevate us to the pinnacle of show business. Or it could ruin us...turn us into a national embarrassment fit for county fairs and back alley bordellos. We will live or die by this Kal, mark my words. Yes, you have saved this season by selling those broadcast rights. I take my hat off to you for that, sir. But where does it leave us for next season? For the future? I just don't know."

Heavy glared at him. "Are you kidding? This show is going to be a smash. People will go crazy for Gino, Roddy, Corky and the showcase guys, not to mention Jason Lash and Steve Irving. This show will be the making of us."

Addison looked thoughtful, turning around to look at yet another poster for the TV special that was posted on a wall behind them. He eyed the big top colours on the poster, the glitzy headings, and the sea of stars splashed on the page.

"I hope you're right, Brown. Because this is big time. And if you want my firm's support and backing in the future, we need success. This TV gamble has ensured you met the profit line this year. But if it all fails, the circus is dead in the water. In pieces. With a lot of missing parts. Not the least, your beloved train." He leaned towards Klondike. "I'm routing for you, Kal. But it's all a gamble. We need high viewership, positive reactions and strong reviews."

Klondike huffed and shook his head. He glanced from Addison up to the poster behind them. "You said we will live or die by this, Daryl. I disagree." He smiled his trademark crooked grin. "I say we will be reincarnated tomorrow. We will not just live. We will live to live again."

With that, he headed for the door, with Heavy at his side. Addison watched them go, then nodded thoughtfully. "May God go with you," he whispered.

Chapter 23
Circus of the Stars. Los Angeles. Penultimate Show

"Ladies and gentlemen..."

The ATV stage announcer's booming call brought the audience to attention. Everyone seated in the large auditorium turned their focus to the stage at the front. Its floor had been coated with sawdust, and a giant red and blue circus-style tarpaulin had been draped at the back, giving the stage a rounded feel.

The cameras were rolling, the lights were shining and the several thousand spectators within the famed Central Studio building were ready for the main event.

The announcer continued. "ATV, in association with sponsors The Golden Dune Casino, Millbank's Cigarettes and Grand Milkshakes, is proud to present Circus of the Stars! And now, here is your host...the puppetmaster, Roddy Olsen!"

An enthusiastic applause broke out as Olsen strutted onto the empty stage. He was dressed in his silver waistcoat and purple pants, and held Rusty Fox by his side.

At the stage door, next to the sound booth, Klondike watched nervously. For once, he stood alone, with Lacey, Heavy and Plum all seated in the third row of the theatre. He studied the youngster walking out in front of the large audience. Olsen suddenly looked very small in front of the wall of spectators, though he had performed to much larger crowds on the road with the circus. It was all the TV equipment, Klondike decided, that made his star ventriloquist look out of sorts. To either side of the performing area, there was an overwhelming collection of shiny cameras, boom mics and amplifiers. With a deep breath, Klondike watched.

"Good evening," Olsen cried, waving to the audience. "Good evening and thank you for joining us for Circus of the Stars. My name is Roddy Olsen and—"

Right on cue, Rusty interrupted: "Roddy, Roddy, Roddy. My dear boy. No one cares who you are. We all know all these people are here to see me. Rusty Fox. Teen idol. Singing sensation."

Olsen looked down at him. "Rusty, what have I told you about interrupting?"

"I don't know. I was too busy looking cool."

Olsen sighed. "Ladies and gentlemen, may I introduce my dear friend Rusty Fox. I must apologise for his bad manners."

"Hey, put a sock in it, Roddy. Without me, you're nothing. I'm the star of the show."

Olsen laughed. "Well, we'll let these good people be the judge of that. So, Rusty, you must be pretty excited. Here we are, in Hollywood."

"You betcha! This is where a teen idol like me belongs. I'm the world's most famous fox…now I want to meet all the chics!"

The audience laughed good-naturedly. "Y'know," Olsen said to the puppet, "we've got a huge show tonight. Jason Lash is here…"

"Lash!" Rusty squealed. "Why, I taught that cowboy everything he knows!" "What?"

"Sure I did. Just listen…" With that, Rusty broke out into a rendition of one of Lash's best-known country songs, The Lonesome Trail. The audience cheered as he sang.

"OK, OK," said Olsen. "So you can sing. What else can you do?"

This was one of his standard routines. "I do impersonations," said the puppet. "Look, here's my impersonation of the so-called king of comedy, Steve Irving."

The fox puppet bent low and grabbed its foot with its mouth, holding it there for comedic effect.

"Next," the puppet continued, "my impression of chat show queen Linda Schneider." He then proceeded to slowly fall over backwards.

"And, finally, here is the king of Hollywood, Donald F Kalchuk." Right on cue, Rusty put his foot in his mouth and fell over backwards.

Cheers and applause broke out across the theatre. Klondike smiled pensively. *Thank god,* he thought, *they were digging it.* He waited anxiously for the climax of Olsen's opening salvo. Between them, Klondike and Olsen had decided to hit the audience with his famed Rock Island Mine routine during his second segment. For his first close, they were trying something new that Heavy had suggested.

"Thank you, thank you," Rusty was saying to the audience.

"All right," Olsen cut in, "not bad, Rusty. Now…" he addressed the camera again. "I would like to introduce our opening act of the show. He —"

"Woh," Rusty snapped. "I thought I was introducing the acts for this!"

"Er, no, Rust. You're here to help me."

"What! They told me I was the host."

"No, Rust. That's my job. I introduce the acts and —"

"No, I introduce the acts!"

The two bickered back and forth, Olsen utilising his remarkable voice throwing skills to make it sound like the two were talking over each other, at the same time. It was a phenomenal trick, with the ventriloquist going head to head with his puppet. The audience sat awestruck, many open mouthed at the magical action.

Finally, Olsen removed a wad of sticky tape from his pocket, ripped a piece off with his teeth and placed it over the mischievous fox's mouth. Then, Rusty continued to make noises, with Olsen dropping his tone to make it sound like a muffled grunting. The audience applauded his genius.

He held up a hand. "Phew! At last," he cried, "now I can host again. And now, ladies and gentlemen…" he halted as Rusty emitted a loud muffled moan from under the tape. "It is my pleasure to introduce a true circus legend. The world's greatest clown, and the fastest juggler on earth. The one and only… Corky the Clown!"

Applause broke out across the studio floor, but quickly turned to gasps as Corky emerged, in his trademark clown suit, but hobbling across the stage, supported by a crutch, and with his right arm in a sling. Everything turned silent.

"Corky…" Olsen stammered nervously. "What…what happened?"

The clown shook his head sadly. He addressed the crowd. "I'm sorry, folks. I… I can't perform for you tonight. I have a serious case."

"What serious case?" asked Olsen.

A grin covered the clown's face-painted skin. "A case of…clownitus!"

With that, Corky's traditional circus music broke out and the veteran performer tossed the crutch away and performed a daring forward somersault, before ripping off the sling and hurling it into the audience, who cheered in surprise.

"You see, kid," Corky said to Olsen, "I still got it!" With that, he somehow produced a trademark custard pie from within his jacket and slammed it into the youngster's face. On his arm, Rusty cackled underneath the sticky tape. Corky glared at the puppet, before producing another pie and pushing it into Rusty's tiny head.

One of his assistant clowns then came out with the customary unicycle, and Corky went to work on his act. Mounting the cycle, he pedalled furiously in a large circle across the studio floor as another clown hurled six juggling pins at him one after another. Taking them all in his grip, Corky began his quick-fast juggling act, while spinning around on the cycle.

The crowd applauded slowly, as if not overly impressed.

After several minutes of juggling, Corky was handed the firesticks; tall cinders of Claywood that had been set alight. Now, he juggled four in what slowly began to resemble one giant ball of fire, still whizzing around on the cycle. In the background, an electric piano soundtrack accompanied the daring feats.

Then, in one sudden movement, Corky extinguished the fire sticks by pushing each into his mouth and pulling them out, quelling the fire, to the shock of the theatregoers.

Barely pausing for breath, the veteran clown pushed his hands onto the saddle of his cycle and performed a handstand as the cycle continued to roll along. He then thrust his hands onto the peddles and began driving the device with his arms, while remaining vertically straight and upside down.

After a few laps, he eased to a halt, disembarked and bowed to the warm applause.

The announcer's voice suddenly sounded. "And now, ladies and gentlemen, the piece de resistance. Corky the Clown will perform his famed human cannonball act."

Right on cue, the circus's giant black and red cannon was wheeled out while, at the opposite end of the stage, a giant net was affixed to the support standings.

Corky waved to the crowd, before donning a comical pair of aviator goggles. Then, he mounted a red ladder that led to the mouth of the giant cannon and lowered himself into the barrel, feet first. As his head disappeared inside, an audible gasp reverberated around Central Studio as everyone took in the surreal sight.

The cannon was lit by one of the clowns, and an almighty bang exploded at the base. In an instant, Corky was sent rocketing out of the mighty device, and careened towards the net at the far end of the theatre. With his arms tight against his torso and his legs straight, the clown looked like a human dart as he flew through the air and smashed into the net, eventually rolling down and landing in a heap upon the crash mat below.

As the audience roared its approval, many within trying to figure out how it was all possible, Corky struggled to his feet, gave a wave and then bowed elegantly. Removing his top hat as he bowed, the flimsy headwear suddenly caught alight, only for Corky to quash the fire by clapping his hand into the hat, giving the viewers at home one last smile and wink at the camera. He bowed again as the applause ran out.

Behind him, Olsen and Rusty had reappeared, the pie mix rinsed from their faces.

"Let's hear it for Corky the Clown!" Olsen cried. He was carrying a large black case in his free left hand, which he placed on the stage floor.

As the applause died down, it was Rusty the fox puppet who spoke next.

"OK, folks, now you're in for a real treat. I am now going to perform one of my favourite songs for you all. You all know it. It's called Rock Island Mine."

Backstage, Klondike could only smile. He hoped the ventriloquist's perennial crowd-pleaser would be a hit here in TV land, as it had been on the road.

"Woh, woh, hold it," said Olsen nervously. "You know how it is with that song, Rust. It's fast. Very fast. You, er, you won't be able to sing that quickly."

"Oh, I think I will."

"How?"

"You're just going to have to work harder, Roddy."

As the crowd laughed, a new voice emerged; a muffled tone coming from the case beside them.

"Hold it, hold it. Let me out, god damn it!"

Olsen looked at Rusty, then back at the box. "Uh-oh. You woke him up."

Rusty shook his head. "This isn't going to go down well."

The muffled box-voice barked again. "I said let me out. And that's an order!"

Olsen duly bent down, opened up the case, and produced Napoleon, dressed as ever in his standard military fatigues.

"Ladies and gentlemen," said Olsen, "may I introduce my other good friend, United States Army's favourite GI, we call him Napoleon."

Faint applause and laughter followed as the ventriloquist hoisted the new puppet onto his left arm, before the army character bellowed: "Attention!"

Olsen continued. "Napoleon, what are you doing here tonight?"

"Why, you slimy maggot," said the elderly man figure with the white hair, "what do you think I'm doing here? I need to save you, the people in TV land and all the maggots out there in the theatre. The fox is gunna sing. I have to stop him before it's too late."

"You can't stop me, old man," Rusty shot across, as Olsen placed the two puppets on either side of him, looking from one to the other.

"Silence, dummy!"

"Dummy!" Rusty laughed. "We're both dummies!"

Laughter filled the studio. "Listen," Olsen began. "If Rusty wants to sing, and Napoleon wants it stopped, I have an idea. Why don't we all sing?"

"What's the song?" Napoleon said warily. "America The Beautiful? Amazing Grace?"

"Er, Rock Island Mine," said Olsen.

Napoleon's eyes narrowed. "That's the fast one, right?"

Rusty giggled. "Oh yeah!"

Napoleon squinted at Olsen and nodded. "All right, just try and keep up, maggot."

And then the music sounded. Olsen played out his most celebrated stint, as he sang along with his two puppet creations, swapping voices as the song grew quicker and quicker.

At the end of the mini-performance, the audience were on their feet, cheering wildly at the extraordinary display of voice manipulation. Olsen and his two puppets bowed, and the stage announcer's voice sounded again.

"Ladies and gentlemen, please welcome the host of ATV's Cabaret Hour, the incomparable Linda Schneider."

The applause continued as Linda Schneider, a tall, rotund woman with shining, wax-like dark skin and a black beehive hairdo, waltzed onto the stage, dressed in a beautiful dark green evening gown. She approached Olsen and congratulated him, before shaking hands with Rusty and Napoleon.

"Oh my," she gasped into the microphone. "Well, it doesn't get much better than that, folks. I always said Hollywood was full of dummies. I never knew there were such talented ones knocking around."

She took the mic in her hand and strode around the stage with the air and grace of an experienced performer.

"Now, when they asked me to appear in a circus, I told them there were only two types of gals who appeared in circuses. Bearded ladies and knife thrower's assistants. I said I'm neither. They still wanted me. So I told them I ain't growing no beard and if they want me to be pinned to a wheel having knives thrown at me, I'll throw them to the lions." She looked into the camera and winked. "No clowning."

The audience gently laughed at her soft patter. Backstage, Klondike looked on ruefully, nodding to himself. It was a special guest appearance from an established star, and looked it. *Still, she had a loyal fan base,* he thought, *and they would probably tune in just to see her.*

"So I told the executives at ATV I'd happily introduce another act. Said I'd welcome in something that's close to my heart. Something I can relate to." She paused, staring disdainfully around. "So they gave me the freak show!"

More laughs. "No, seriously," she said, "it is my privilege to introduce to you all a band of performers unlike anything you've ever seen. They are a key part of Klondike's Circus. They come in all shapes and sizes, with all manner of skills and talents. And, ladies and gentlemen, we call them… The Showcase Revue…"

With that, dramatic waltz music was heard on the theatre's sound system and the human blob, Gargantua, appeared on stage. The beastly giant raced across the theatre floor before exploding into his repertoire of cartwheels, finishing his run with a forward roll. Turning, he then performed a textbook handstand.

Hearty applause followed, as Gargantua executed a series of jumps, stretching his legs and touching his toes.

Then, following a loud drum roll, out came Goliath. Holding his arms aloft and roaring at the audience, he then grabbed a hold of his right leg before pulling it up and behind his neck, grinning at the shocked faces in the auditorium.

Within seconds, out came Percy Pringle and the dwarves, who performed their running leap routine, with each one diving at Goliath and landing on different parts of his body. When all the dwarves aside from Pringle were settled within the giant's immense frame, Pringle pulled a tiny ukulele from an inside pocket and began playing 'Yankee Doodle', to which Goliath began dancing a jig, with the dwarves all clinging to him.

Even Klondike couldn't help but laugh as he watched the maddening ensemble bouncing around the stage floor.

Gargantua then re-emerged and picked Pringle up onto his wide shoulders, before all of the troupe walked in a circle, Pringle playing his instrument faster and faster.

Then, just when the unusual collection of bodies couldn't get more extreme, out on stage popped Rumpy Stiltskin, bouncing up and down on his massive six-foot stilts and using them as pogo sticks. He breezed between the two giants, before one of the dwarves daringly flung himself through mid-air and landed on Rumpy's shoulders. Rumpy bounced to the edge of the stage and deposited the dwarf onto a soft mat, before heading back to Goliath and collecting another of the clinging figures, before escorting them to the mat.

He repeated the trick until all of Pringle's dwarves were standing at the edge of the stage.

There then came another slow drumroll, and the spotlight fell on Rumpy alone. The ultra-agile stilt-walker bounced along several times before performing a flying somersault of his own, his stilts spinning round as he flew headfirst through the air.

This gravity-defying act drew another hearty round of applause, and marked the finale of the newly named Showcase Revue. Gargantua, Goliath, Percy and his gang and Rumpy Stiltskin all bowed and waved their appreciation at the delighted patrons before them.

The stage announcer's voice then returned overhead. "Ladies and gentlemen, please welcome ATV's rising star of comedy, Larry Lassiter."

The cheers for the Showcase performers were still ringing out as Lassiter, dressed in a sharp grey suit, meandered onto the stage.

"Let's hear it for the carnival club!" he wailed as he held an arm out towards the departing troupe. "Gee," he said, turning to the audience. "What a band of freaks. I mean, woh! Have you ever seen anything like it? Personally speaking, I don't see it. They're all a bunch of oddities to me, straight out of a freak show in —"

Unbeknown to Lassiter, Goliath had walked back onto the stage and paced menacingly towards the comedian who was now insulting him and his friends. The giant continued, unseen by Lassiter, until he was directly behind him. Then, with a roar of anger, Goliath spun the smaller man around, placed hands on his belt and throat, and picked him up effortlessly over his head, holding him aloft in the air like a doll. The audience cheered in shock and surprise. The giant then performed push-ups with Lassiter, hoisting him up and down, while the fast-talking comedian pleaded for mercy.

Finally, Goliath gently dropped Lassiter to the floor, before storming off in mock aggression and waving to the cheering patrons.

Lassiter acted giddy, unsteady on his feet, before propping himself up on the microphone stand. "Gee whizz," he mumbled, "take me back to the days of Fred Fargo, the dancing drunk."

He straightened up and offered a smile. "Folks," he began, "I'm here to talk to you about clowns. Clowns, the livelihood and backbone of any good circus. In the foreground, the background and, of course, centre stage, every circus needs its clowns…"

An eerie, gospel-like tune played overhead on the speakers. With that, one of the Klondike's Circus clowns emerged onto the sawdust, riding a unicycle and juggling six tennis balls. He was followed by another, who wandered onstage frantically pulling bright handkerchiefs from his sleeve in a never-ending motion. Then came another clown, this one creating animal shapes with large balloons. A fourth clown then emerged, this one dressed in a mock fireman's uniform and spraying the others with water from a toy hose.

"Wow," Lassiter exclaimed as he watched the group around him. "You guys are great! Say, do you think I've got what it takes to be a clown?"

Suddenly, the clowns all stopped their respective acts and stared at him. The audience giggled. Then, the foursome pounced on the comedian, each one fiddling with a different part of his body. In seconds, they spun Lassiter around, and he faced the crowd again. Only now, his face was painted white, with a red plastic button nose and eye make-up, and he wore a red bowler hat and giant pink kipper tie. He glared at the cameras.

"My god," he cried, "I'm a clown!"

With that, he bounded onto the shoulders of the lead clown, who then mounted his unicycle and rode around the stage in a wide circle. As Lassiter expertly perched upon the clown's shoulders, he was thrown a bundle of the bright handkerchiefs, which he wore around his neck, before the third clown to enter threw him a balloon. Concentrating as he steadied himself on the shoulders of the cycling clown, the comedian quickly made a dog shape with the inflatable, to impressed applause. Then, fittingly, as he held the balloon aloft, the fireman clown sprayed him with the hose, and he clung blindly to the figure beneath him. The two wheeled slowly towards a backstage door, and disappeared from view. Seconds later, a recording of a loud clattering of pots and pans smashing to the ground filled the speakers. The gag drew cheers and happy applause. As the cheers rang out, the remaining three clowns formed a human wheel – by grabbing each other's ankles and curving their bodies – and gently rolled off stage in yet another surreal sight.

As cheers and clapping rang out in Central Studio, Roddy Olsen returned to the stage, this time carrying just Napoleon.

"Well, how about that?" said Olsen, impressed.

"Harumph!" Napoleon grunted, eyeing the stage door. "That kid Lassiter is nothing but a second rate punk! You know what would straighten him out?"

Olsen rolled his eyes. "A stint in the US Army?"

Napoleon sneered at him. "Wise guy, eh? You know something, Olsen, you ain't that clever. Hell, you put your hand up other guy's behinds for a living!"

"Napoleon!" Olsen cried. "This is a family show. We don't talk like that. Children are watching."

"Kids! Why, they oughta be heading to the nearest enlistment camp. Get 'em in young, that's what old Ike used to say."

Olsen glared at him. "Er, Napoleon, where did you actually serve in the Army?"

"World War Two, you chump." He bowed his head. "But they wouldn't let me storm the beaches at Normandy."

"Why not?"

"They said I was too small, too soft, and couldn't go anywhere unaccompanied."

"They had a point."

"Shut your puke hole, maggot!" Napoleon glared at him. "Now, who is next on stage in this so-called Circus of Stars?"

"I am!"

The crowd cheered in surprised delight and every head turned as Steve Irving made his way down the theatre aisle from the back of the studio building, walking past the seated audience members and up onto the stage as thunderous applause broke out.

Irving climbed a few short steps onto the stage floor and shook hands with Olsen.

"Wow!" Olsen cried. "Ladies and gentlemen…it's the king of comedy, Steve Irving!"

Irving acknowledged the applause, before staring at the puppet on Olsen's arm, who had just barked out: "Steve who? I never heard of ya, kid. Now, move along, we got some real stars to bring out."

Irving grinned good-naturedly. "So, Napoleon," he said in his practised stage manner. "I heard the Army is full of dummies. I didn't expect to see an actual real one here tonight."

Napoleon sneered. "And I was told there were some top-class comedians here tonight. I'm still waiting to see one…"

Irving chuckled. "Y'know what, I'm gunna shut you up for good, you old rascal." With that, he put his hand in Olsen's pants' pocket and produced the wad of sticky tape from earlier, breaking off a small piece.

Napoleon panicked. "You can't silence me! I'm the voice of the US Army!"

Irving smiled smugly. "Want a bet?"

With that, he made to place the tape over the puppet's mouth, but actually put it over Olsen's lips. The crowd laughed loudly.

"There," Irving said happily, dusting off his hands and moving away with the microphone.

But, as Olsen made muffled gasps under the tape, Napoleon's voice echoed across the theatre again: "You can't silence me, Irving! I'm the voice of America!"

Shocked laughter filled the auditorium at the trick, as Olsen made a mockery of trying to haul the puppet off stage as it shrieked again.

Irving waited for the applause to die down, before continuing with his monologue, his hand gently resting on the mic stand.

"Well, I've seen it all now, folks. A man who can make anything talk. Even when he himself can't. Oh my." He straightened his tie and looked at the crowd before him. "Folks, I want to thank you all for joining us tonight and for supporting ATV and the circus. We've seen some incredible acts here and now…now you've got me!"

He grabbed the mic and strutted across the stage. "It's been my privilege to be here as part of this special. Me and Klondike's Circus go back a long way. Kal Klondike asked me personally to perform here. Well, he said if I didn't he'd feed me to Gargantua!" He smiled at the giggling. "I said to him, I want to be at the top of the show. Apparently, that's on Goliath's shoulders! No, seriously, I said I want to be the star of the show, no fooling. I was told that was a toss-up between me and a small fox. Hmm, I said. I had to wonder what kind of show I was getting myself into. But I said to the management, I said I would be happy to appear, have a few laughs, and that's that. One thing I don't want is to get tied up in all this…"

From out of nowhere, a lasso appeared and encircled Irving's tiny frame.

"What the…" said the diminutive comedian. Then, a wailing "Yee-hah" filled the studio and, after a sudden clapping of hooves, Jason Lash burst onto the theatre floor, riding his horse Goldie and laughing hysterically. The western star was dressed in a white rhinestone-themed outfit, with leather straps and a magnificent silver Stetson. He held the soft end of the lasso and rode slowly to Irving, before dropping the rest of the thick rope beside the startled comedian.

The audience erupted with loud applause, many standing, as Lash performed a hind-leg salute on Goldie and held his Stetson aloft, smiling broadly at the acclaim.

"Howdy pardners!" the cowboy bawled. "Thank you so much." He glanced sideways at Irving. "Enough talk, pilgrim! These people wanna see a show. And, dammit, we're gunna give 'em all one. Yee-hah!"

With that, he left Irving tied up in the lasso and dug his spurs into Goldie. The great golden palomino took off at a gallop around the stage.

Irving made a comedic show of unwrapping himself from the lasso, before diving out of the way as Lash came riding towards him in an ever-increasing circle.

Now it was Lash's turn to soak up the limelight. And he did just that.

A country and western theme boomed over the speakers as Lash rode Goldie round and round the stage, getting faster with each pass. He ran through his repertoire of riding tricks. First, he lifted his legs in the air and performed a headstand on the saddle as Goldie galloped. He then slipped himself under the horse by grabbing a hold of each stirrup and hanging blindly alongside the mount's swinging legs.

Lash then expertly performed 'leapfrog' vaults, hurling himself from side to side over the saddle while holding the handgrips.

Finally, Goldie slowed his pace and performed another hind-leg salute, as Lash waved his hat and screamed wildly at the audience.

As the applause died down, Lash dismounted and a stagehand appeared to lead Goldie away, handing the brightly dressed cowboy another large lasso.

The western star now went through his roping tricks. First, the spun the lasso into a wide arc, drawing a large circle of rope that seemed to dance in the air. With minimum effort, he hopped back and forth through the circle, as it began to decrease in size. With his final jump, the circle's diameter was barely three feet, but still Lash soared through it.

Waving at the cheers from all around, he next spun out a large circle of rope and let it encircle his frame, spinning like a hoop around his body, rising from his knees to his head as he expertly guided it upwards.

Guiding the lasso to a standstill, he then collected it up and held it aloft, to more applause. Then, with a comedic turn of face, he placed his hand over his eyes as if staring into the distance. He whistled loudly, spun the lasso over his head and hurled it into an area backstage. Then, with a grin, he pulled it in. As more of the rope appeared to the audience, it suddenly became apparent that he had ensnared Linda Schneider with it, the end of the lasso encircling her slender waist. As he pulled her closer, she made a play of demonstrating loudly at the behaviour. Then, as he pulled her all across the stage until she stood next to him, he placed a kiss on her cheek. Linda pretended to be entranced as he delicately pulled the lasso off, before gesturing to something backstage.

Then, Goldie trotted onto the stage and stood beside the couple. As Lash got down on one knee to kiss her hand, she suddenly mounted the horse and clung to it as it trotted away, waving mischievously to the crowd.

Alone on the stage, Lash looked on forlornly. A stagehand appeared, handing him a guitar. Strumming the instrument softly, Lash then slowly broke into one of his hit country and western songs, The One That Got Away.

At the conclusion, he smiled warmly, Linda, Irving and Goldie returned, and they all stood happily as the audience applauded.

Everyone's attention then turned to the far side of the stage, where Olsen appeared with Tony Tan, dressed as ever in his tuxedo.

"Ladies and gentlemen," Olsen began jovially, holding up his free hand, "may I introduce to you a legend of cabaret entertainment. Las Vegas's most renowned lounge lizard. The king of crooners… Tony Tan!"

The tuxedo-clad puppet nodded at the amused applause. "Thank you. I just wanna start by saying, er, by saying…"

Olsen glared at him. "Tony! Are you drunk?"

Tan looked back at him. "Well, what of it? I just came off three bookings at the Desert Inn and I gotta play this crowd next. How am I supposed to keep up?"

Olsen shook his head. "Tony, I told you about scotch."

Tan stared giddily into the camera. "Folks, if your picture at home is a little blurry, don't worry about it, it's the same for me."

The crowd laughed good-naturedly. "Now, Tony," Olsen began, "we are here to introduce a very special act. You remember that, right?"

Tan straightened. "Of course! The flyer. The one who does his thing up there." He turned to Olsen. "And you know what that means?"

Olsen nodded grimly. "Of course. Your favourite song."

"You bet!" With that, music aired through the overhead loudspeakers and Tan launched into his rendition of the Frank Sinatra hit High Hopes.

As he reached the song's climax, the applause began. Olsen held up a hand and began the next introduction.

"Ladies and gentlemen, prepare to be astonished as Klondike's Circus presents to you the most daring, breathtaking act of trapeze artistry in the world. Presenting first, the queen of the skies, the enchanting Jenny Cross. And on centre ring, the master high-flyer…love him, cheer him, never forget him…it's the debonair king of the air, the one and only… Gino Shapiro!"

The crowd cheered heartily again, as Shapiro and Jenny strode out grandly, wearing their trademark fireball orange attire. Olsen, and indeed Tan, both nodded to the flyers before shimmering backstage.

Ropes fell from above to the stage floor and, in a flash, the duo heaved themselves up, soaring towards the studio ceiling high above.

As they ascended some 60 feet into the air, they pulled themselves from the ropes onto their respective rings. From there, as every eye in the auditorium gazed upwards, they began to swing back and forth.

The standard routine had been tweaked for this performance. Shapiro, who had been swinging wildly, hung by his hands only and propelled himself onto the side turret, which had been affixed to the edge of the building days earlier.

Jenny wrapped her knees over her ring and fell back, swinging upside down in the support position, arms outstretched. With a cry, Shapiro dived off the turret onto his ring, performed a textbook 360 swing, and propelled himself towards Jenny, who caught his hands and swayed him back and forth once before hurling him onto the turret at the opposite end of the building.

The audience cheered, their 'oohs' and 'aahs' echoing across the stage as Shapiro flew back and forth. He completed the same routine in reverse. Then, on his third pass, he executed a double somersault between his ring and Jenny's, before she swung him up onto the support turret. For his return trip, he substituted a double somersault for a scrunch-sault, clasping his knees with his arms, and vaulted back across the air.

Arriving at the turret again, he held his arms aloft and soaked up the applause. With nothing but a 60-foot drop and the empty stage below, the act was, as always, an incredible sight.

Jenny then performed her standard ring act, swinging herself over and over before hanging by her legs, fishing out a cosmetics bag from her leotard and applying make-up to her face. As the crowd laughed, Shapiro dived onto his ring, stretched himself, holding on with his hands, before spinning over several times with stunning velocity. Letting go of his bar suddenly, his body flew into the air like a dart. He held his arms out wide and performed a helicopter fall as he dropped the 12 feet or so back to his ring, which he somehow landed on in a sitting position.

Vaulting back to his turret, Shapiro then performed the classic double loop, swaying over to Jenny, who carried him back and forth several times at great speed, before releasing him. He spun high into the air, and spun his body around twice in mid-air, before guiding his frame to the far side, landing on the support beam with cat-like grace and agility.

The two trapeze artists waved jubilantly as cheers filled the studio building.

Then, the announcer's voice boomed overhead again.

"And now...the master trapeze artist, Gino Shapiro, will perform the ultimate feat of gravity defiance and grace...the high wire."

Shapiro slipped down his re-laid support rope to get prepared for his customary finishing act. The high wire had been set up far below, with the plastic-coated lead wire stretching out ten metres between two giant plastic platforms, raised, for this performance, 30 feet off the ground.

As Shapiro slid down to the platform nearest the audience, the customary drum roll began. The master showman, Gino took his time, rubbing a small pot of salt into his stockinged feet and staring silently at the wire.

Then, with a theatrical flourish, he let his arms fall out wide and slowly mounted the narrowest of bridges. Looking nowhere but straight-ahead at the opposite platform, he carefully but confidently crept across the wire, his arms stiff as support beams as they extended either side of him, his steps coming in short, almost balletic movements.

As the audience held its collective breath, the entire auditorium silent as a crypt, Shapiro crept to the opposite end of the wire, then paused. With a sudden, alarming motion, he flung himself almost upside down and executed a perfect cartwheel to see himself over the threshold and across the final two yards of the wire. With a theatrical flourish, he flipped himself onto the far platform, regained himself, and stood mightily; the eyes of everyone in the entire building bulging at the sight of his acrobatics.

After a second of stunned silence, a raucous standing ovation followed, with every audience member on their feet cheering the incredible feats of the master trapeze maestro. True to form, Shapiro stood gallantly on the platform, arms raised aloft, waving cheerfully and blowing kisses to the adoring audience.

It was a stunning ovation, and lasted almost 60 seconds.

At the side of the stage, Klondike laughed spasmodically, relief his overwhelming emotion. Standing there gaping at the stage, he didn't even know what he was chuckling at, but could not control himself. He fist pumped his hand and then joined in the applause, clapping enthusiastically as Shapiro mounted the ladder that would finally reunite him with terra firma.

As Shapiro hit the deck at last, a collection of stagehands steered the platforms and stage equipment away. Then, in an instant, the stage announcer's voice returned one final time.

"Ladies and gentlemen, we hope you've enjoyed Circus of the Stars. Thank you so much for joining us. Now, we present to you the renowned Klondike's Circus tradition of the grand finale. Here to sing us out, songstress supreme Suzy Dando!"

The applause had been virtually constant since Shapiro's stunning cartwheel, and it merely continued in one long thunderous ovation. It could be argued that many in the theatre barely noticed little Suzy as she wandered on stage in her shining white cocktail dress. Looking like a child chorister, Suzy paced to the microphone stand and picked up the mic, slightly unnerved by the wall of noise before her.

Then, the familiar tune sounded on the overhead speakers, and, acquiring her almost startling ability to summon such a high voice, she sang.

'Can You Feel the Magic Tonight?' had rarely sounded better, the acoustics on the sound stage amplifying her sweet voice perfectly.

As she belted out the familiar lyrics, the grand finale swung into action. For this TV special, instead of trucks carrying carnival floats featuring the performers, Irving had pitched an idea that they use convertible Cadillacs. The shiny cars would be driven by men dressed in chauffeur outfits and the performers would stand in the back. The idea came from parades afforded to sports stars returning from championship games.

The first silver Cadillac rumbled slowly on stage, curving around in a circle. Behind the chauffeur between the seats stood Corky and his three clown pals, along with Larry Lassiter, all waving enthusiastically to the cheering crowd. For good measure, Corky slapped a custard pie into Lassiter's face as the camera zoomed in on the performers.

The next Cadillac was red and followed 30 seconds later. Standing in the back this time were Gargantua, Goliath and Rumpy Stiltskin, still on his stilts.

Following behind was a green Cadillac, carrying Percy Pringle and his dancing dwarves. The troupe took it in turns to stand on each other's shoulders as the car slowly rumbled across the stage in front of the audience.

Next up was a purple convertible, with Roddy Olsen standing in the back with, incredibly, Rusty Fox on one arm, Napoleon on the other and Tony Tan standing on his own in the far corner. As this car approached, Suzy herself moved towards it, mic in hand, and hopped up over the doors and onto the middle seats, next to Olsen and his puppets. She stood in the centre of the elongated vehicle and continued singing with Olsen, along with Rusty, Napoleon and Tony, all seemingly joining in, Suzy placing the mic in front of each for a line of the song.

The audience's applause at the appearance of Olsen was thunderous, a point not lost on the ATV executives watching.

The Cadillac rolled by, and all eyes switched to the next one in the procession, a gold car featuring Steve Irving and Linda Schneider, with Jason Lash riding his horse alongside. All waved grandly to the cheering crowd, before Lash acrobatically stood on his stirrups and jumped daringly into the back of the car, landing on his feet on the back bench seat and taking Linda in his arms, to the delight of the watching patrons.

Then, as the brightly lit cars all rolled slowly around the stage in a giant circle, an orange Cadillac slid onto the arena floor, and the cheers grew again. There stood Gino Shapiro and Jenny Cross, in their fireball orange jumpsuits, alongside a third man with his arm in a sling, unknown to many present but recognisable to friends of the show as Nicky, who wore a suit. Nicky held Gino's arm aloft and they all soaked up the applause and acclaim. The shiny, expensive ensemble of Cadillacs continued creeping around in their circle onstage, as Suzy's voice reached a crescendo for the climax of the song. As she finished, the music died down and the stage announcer's voice suddenly sounded: "And it's a wrap."

That signalled the end of the broadcast, and the cameras finally stopped rolling, while, high above, several lights blinked out, giving the stage a darkened, budgeted look.

The cars levelled out in their convoy and made for a giant stage exit at the very rear of the backstage area, slowly rolling off the arena floor and across a tiled promenade, falling slowly out of sight.

The applause slowly died down as the caravan of cars disappeared from view. Many in the seats remained for long afterwards, staring dumbly at the stage as if trying to comprehend what they had just witnessed.

Within minutes, an army of stagehands had assembled on the deck and in the back areas, all going about their business in a quiet, efficient manner.

Klondike walked almost in a daze across the backstage floor, watching the shiny Cadillacs as they reached the exit. He shook his head in wonder, taking in the expensive TV equipment and fancy stage effects all around him.

Suddenly, Addison came racing across the stage, joining him as he walked towards the rear. The banker had rarely looked so animated.

"Kal!" he cried. "Kal! You did it, Kal. You did it!"

Klondike looked in shock at the exasperated Addison before pointing down the backstage corridor to the exiting Cadillacs.

"No, Daryl," he said calmly, "they did. They did it all."

Addison nodded, his face flushed with excitement. "They have saved us! My god…that was incredible." He looked back at the rapidly emptying auditorium. "Did you see that reaction? They loved it."

Klondike looked down at the smaller man. "And you, Daryl? What did you think?"

Addison stammered slightly, eyes wide. "I thought…" he began, looking back at the stage. "Hell, I thought it was the most incredible spectacle I ever saw!"

Klondike raised his eyebrows. "Jesus. I'll take that, partner."

Addison uncharacteristically burst into laughter – as with Klondike, the relief was palpable. He offered his hand and, as Klondike took it, suddenly embraced him in a warm and unexpected hug. Losing all of his customary business-like poise, the older man threw his arm around Klondike and led him towards the exit, past teams of scurrying backstage workers and executives. Everyone seemed to be buzzing.

"And I'll drink to that," Addison said. "Come on, let's celebrate!"

Chapter 24

Roddy Olsen stood in his dressing room, wiping a cold, wet flannel across his face as he gazed at himself in the mirror.

The novelty of the giant personal room, complete with fully stocked fridge and a shower, had not worn off on him, and he still found himself gazing about idly as he wound down after the show.

He removed his silver waistcoat and carefully hung it on the back of the dresser chair. He stared at his beautiful white satin shirt and loud purple pants as he surveyed himself in the huge mirror. The past few days had felt like some kind of outer body experience, and he struggled to comprehend what it all meant to him.

He could still hear excited backstage workers, officials and even the occasional patron outside as they buzzed about, still on a high of their own after the show, which had ended barely ten minutes ago.

As he patted the flannel around his eyes, he jumped at the sound of a knock at the dressing room door. He was about to call a greeting when the door burst open and Gino Shapiro, of all people, waded in. He was still dressed in his orange jumpsuit and wore a white towel around his neck, his face and neck drenched in sweat from his performance.

The two men stared at each other. Shapiro cocked his head and sniffed as he gently eased the door closed, eyeing the luxurious room suspiciously.

Olsen frowned. "I think you've got the wrong room, pal."

"Puppetman!" Shapiro greeted with a grin. "Look at you in your five-star dressing room."

Olsen turned back to the mirror. "Don't you mean 'dollmaker'?"

Shapiro eased himself into the room, gently perching on the edge of the dresser and looking Olsen over with a mixture of pride and humour. His eyes twinkled and Olsen felt himself involuntarily stiffen.

"Come on," the trapeze ace said in a soft tone, "don't be like that. I come in peace. No more hostility or poor talk. Did you see what we all did out there? Did you see, eh boy? They loved us...just as we all knew they would. We should all be proud." He patted his towel against his chest, exposed by the low cut of his outfit. "You ask me, I say the chairman has done it! He has saved the circus." He looked the pensive Olsen over. "You should be happy, kid."

Olsen shook his head. "Listen, Shapiro, you've made it clear time and again throughout this tour what you think of me. You've dismissed my act on every stop, in front of everyone. I don't care what you think. Why don't you do us both a favour and...and get the hell out of here."

Shapiro surprised him by laughing softly, his eyes still alive. "Such fire in an amigo so young." He shook his head sadly, then suddenly turned serious, standing opposite the younger man. "OK, Olsen, OK. I tell you what I come here for. And you remember, I come to you. That's not how this works...normally. But here I am...in your dressing room. I come to give you this, amigo..." Solemnly, like a gallant knight from days gone by, Shapiro extended his arm and offered Olsen his hand.

Olsen stared at it, as if it was some kind of grotesque alien form. He hesitated.

"Take it," Shapiro uttered forcefully.

Finally, as if in slow motion, Olsen grasped his hand and shook it. The two men stared at each other pensively. Neither flinched for a moment.

Then, Olsen snatched his hand away and wiped at it with the flannel.

"There," Shapiro was saying softly, "was that so hard, amigo?" He sat down on the edge of the dresser again. "You deserve that. My respect. I grant it you. You know, it's not every day I come to another act and offer them my—"

"For Christ sakes!" Olsen suddenly snapped, tired of the patter. "What is this all about, Shapiro? What do you want with me?"

Shapiro gazed at him queerly, then nodded slowly. "OK, OK. I get to the point." Now he eyed the youngster with a steely resolve, his voice dropping to a conspirational whisper. "You don't need me to tell you, kid. Ours were the largest cheers out there tonight. The people...they love us. Just like on the road. But now in TV town." He licked his lips, eyeing the dressing room door. "We could be good together, you and me. You want to know what I want. OK, I tell you. A pact. You and me. To stay together. Wherever the road takes us. I get offered movies, TV... I take you with me. As a support act. You get offered shows, maybe in Vegas or Reno or wherever, you take me too. We form a package. You understand, boy?"

Olsen stared at him in dismay. "Are you crazy? What…what are you saying? How can you even consider such a move? What about Mr Klondike?"

Shapiro stood up angrily. "You don't think I consider the chairman?" he spat out. "How dare you! Kal is like a brother to me. Sometimes, a father. He would be the key to all this. Kal would be our manager. It would be as it is now. We would still be in the circus, of course. But I'm talking about the off-season. The extra work we all need. What do you plan to do all winter, Olsen? Sit in that holding camp up north? Pah! You can get yourself gigs, all over the country. I can help. The chairman too. I just need to know… I just need to know you're with me." He looked Olsen over with assertiveness locked in his gaze.

Olsen looked down, and shrugged noncommittally. He fiddled with his hands. "I don't know what to think," he said quietly. "I guess… I guess I hadn't planned that far ahead. Winter! Gee…this has all been such a whirlwind. I guess I don't want it to end."

"You have to plan ahead," Shapiro urged gently, "and I can help you." He thought quickly, studying the younger man; the confident body armour seemed to have slipped. He moved toward him. "You and me…we were the stars out there, Olsen. Yes, I admit I have given you a lot of bad mouth. Dismissed your act. But tonight, out there on the TV stage, you were a true star. This I know. I was wrong about you. I admit, yes." He placed a hand on Olsen's shoulder. "You have a big future in this business, my boy."

Olsen shook his head, unsteady and strangely on edge under the older man's gaze. "I appreciate it." He forced the words out. "To be honest, I haven't thought too much about the future. I can't see beyond the Golden Dune next week."

At that moment, the dressing room door burst open and Suzy Dando came bolting in, still wearing her beautiful white cocktail dress and clinging to a bottle of champagne. "Roddy, oh Roddy, I've found you, you…"

Her words trailed off as she noticed Shapiro, with his hand on Olsen's shoulder. She froze, holding the bottle before her like a time bomb.

"What! What is he doing here?" she gasped.

Olsen stared at her awkwardly, but Shapiro laughed cheerfully, slapping him on the back and heading for the door.

"It's OK, sweetheart," he said, smiling at Suzy as he hastily retreated, "I was just giving our superstar here a few tips on how to handle fame. Hell, he sure needs them now, and I should know." He stroked Suzy's arm as he made for the doorway. "Well done, darling girl. You were great tonight." He turned to Olsen again. "Think about what I said, superstar." Then, he was gone.

Suzy closed the door nervously, and wandered over to Olsen. She placed the bottle on the dresser and gave him a quick hug. Then she glanced back at the door, holding onto his arm.

"What was that all about?"

"I think," Olsen began, still confused. "I think the great Gino Shapiro is...scared of me!"

A mighty cheer erupted as Klondike opened the door to his temporary office in the main ATV headquarters building.

He waltzed in, an unlit, heavily chewed cigar hanging from the corner of his mouth, and smiled grandly.

Lacey was holding aloft a bottle of champagne and popped the cork as he entered, before dancing across the room, throwing her arms around him and holding him tight in a forceful hug. Richie and Heavy were both behind her sitting at the desk, cheering and clapping as he entered.

Klondike returned Lacey's hug and held up a hand in celebration. Behind him, a still over-animated Addison skipped in, and began clapping spontaneously.

"Kalvin baby, that was a sensation," Lacey was gushing. "You did it! What a show! It will be a smash. I just know it."

"The lady speaks sense," Heavy muttered, manoeuvring himself across the office to pat his old friend on the back. "I was hooked. And I knew what was coming next. Everything went without a hitch." He eyed Klondike wistfully. "We knocked 'em dead, old buddy."

"We sure as hell did," Klondike spat out, the cigar hanging limply from his mouth.

Plum shook hands with the circus master. "Congratulations, Kal," he said simply, smiling widely. "We're all proud of you."

They all stood in a circle around Klondike, while Addison screeched, "That's the spirit!" and took the bottle from Lacey and began pouring the fizzy liquid into some glasses lined up on the desk. The others stared in shock; none had ever seen the stoic banker so excited.

Lacey kept a hand on Klondike's shoulder. Delicately, she removed his ever-present fedora hat and threw it like a frisbee onto a leather couch. "Get ready for a publicity monsoon," she purred. "I bet all the stations and all the papers in Hollywood will be on the buzzer before long. All will want to interview our stars…and, of course, the man behind it all." She nodded at him appreciatively.

He finally pulled the limp, wet cigar from his mouth. "We're all happy. But let's wait and see what those Nielsen ratings make of our show. That's what we're answering to after all."

Heavy eyed him speculatively. "That's true, Kal, but we can have peace of mind. We did everything in our power to make this a hit. None of us could do more. This was our…our…"

"Our zenith." Plum finished the sentence as he sat behind the desk and took a glass.

"Indeed," Lacey murmured, still smiling mischievously. She took a glass of champagne and fell back onto the couch as if flopping around in her living room at home. Grandly, she threw her arm into the air. "Who would've thought we'd make it here? In Hollywood! After all we've been through." She raised her glass. "Here's to all at Klondike's Circus."

They all joined in the toast. Klondike smiled at the public relations specialist as he sipped his drink. "Here's to the class of '58. Including my new backroom team." He nodded to Lacey and Plum.

"This is incredible," Addison was saying, pouring himself a second glass. He stared at the pictures on the office wall, posters advertising ATV's latest hit shows. "Look at how far we've come. Where we were a few weeks ago. The train wreck. You guys holed up in that backwater town. And now…now this! A television spectacular. THAT show." He seemed to pant slightly. "Think of the offers that might come in! From all over the country. Jesus!" He eyed Klondike squarely, his face full of respect and admiration, a look the circus master had never seen in his banker and principal investor. "Kal," he said quietly, "I… I'm sorry I ever doubted you. I should have known. You always have an ace up your sleeve. Even in the face of disaster. This TV idea of yours was inspired. And it has saved us." He slowly offered his hand and gulped. "Put it there, partner."

Klondike laughed aloud. "You said it, Daryl. I told you to stick with me!"

The two shook hands warmly, before everyone in the office laughed.

After a few drinks in the makeshift office, Klondike excused himself and made a quick tour of the ATV building. He checked in with the props department and the sound technicians and made sure everyone was happy.

Then, he returned to the Central Studio complex and made a point of visiting ever dressing room in the backstage quarters. He shook the hand of every performer and offered a few words of praise and admiration, before moving on to the next room. After visiting Shapiro, Corky, Olsen, Suzy, Gargantua, Goliath, Percy Pringle and his troupe and Rumpy Stiltskin, he called in on Linda Schneider and Larry Lassiter, who happily accepted his appreciation. He found Jason Lash at a private VIP bar on the first floor, and managed to shake his hand while the cowboy star waxed lyrical with a few of the girls from the typing pool.

Then, he headed for Steve Irving's dressing room, at the far end of the VIP lounging area. He knocked once and simply waded in.

Irving was sprawled on a long, fluffy sofa, sipping a martini and smoking a cheroot. His show tuxedo already looked worn and faded. He looked up tiredly as Klondike entered.

"There he is," he said in an exasperated tone as Klondike waded in. "The man who made me put my neck on the line." He sipped his drink.

Klondike nodded and made for a small wet bar, hastily pouring himself a scotch. He didn't mince his words. "I can't thank you enough, Steve. For going along with it all. All for old time's sake." He stared at the comedian seriously. "You may have saved us, my friend. And I won't forget it."

Irving rested his head on the back of the sofa and cackled. "Don't mention it, cowboy. It was like you said, this was a mutually beneficial agreement. I knew it would be. If the Nielsens are as hot as that studio audience back there, we will have a winner. And I'll be the ATV golden boy. All over again."

Klondike grinned. "Nice work if you can get it."

"You bet," Irving murmured. "And this could just be the beginning. Just remember our arrangement... I want Shapiro, Olsen and Corky on my show. Soon!"

"A deal is a deal."

Irving eyed him curiously. "So what happens now, hot shot?"

Klondike downed the contents of his glass and wandered about the room. "Well, I have a meeting with Spearman tomorrow morning. We will discuss what's going to happen in Vegas, I guess. I'm sure he'll have plenty of feedback to give me after tonight."

"Spearman," Irving said weakly, appearing on the verge of sleep. "That old sucker. He's never happy. He wants Lash on board for the whole nine yards. Just do your thing, Kal."

"That's all I ever do," Klondike muttered, eyeing his host. He hesitated. "Can I ask you a question, Steve?"

"Shoot."

"Why are you so tired?"

Irving laughed sheepishly, rolling about slightly on the couch. He slurped at his martini. "Because it's all so god damn exhausting! Out here."

Klondike nodded. "Why not return to circus life? The open road and all."

"Hell, maybe it would do me good." Irving looked about him, puzzled. He seemed lost in thought. "Say, Kal, whatever happened to our old boss? Ribbeck. You think he'll contact us after this?"

Klondike visibly shuddered, grimacing slightly. "Old Eric. Don't worry about him. He's out there somewhere. This TV special of ours could change everything. Even his feelings towards us." He smiled ruefully. "I'm sure he'll make an appearance somewhere down the trail."

Farley's Fairground Park lay dormant and lifeless at the late hour, only the dim moonlight casting a ray of light upon the now still dodgems and Ferris wheels.

The site looked like an abandoned play park in the eerie night-time, with its stalls and shooting galleries left to fend for themselves, as if someone had hit a fire alarm and led a mass evacuation.

The fairground was just yards from the Clearview Beach, and a gentle sea breeze drifted across the park. All was silent, as the light of the half-moon offered glimpses of the many attractions on offer in the daytime.

Suddenly, a tall, lean woman appeared from behind a parked caravan and slowly, cautiously crept through the fairground.

Jenny Cross gulped heavily, as if waiting for a wraith to ambush her out of the darkness. She used the moonlight to guide her through the centre of the fairground, eyes wide and staring into the gloomy path before her. She was dressed in her giant black cloak, and hugged it tightly around her. Stumbling forward, she continued to look.

There. She saw it. Candy floss. 99 cents a stick. The stall was designed to resemble an old Indian teepee, and looked about as abandoned as the rest of the fairground. She rushed towards the flimsy structure and then stood, waiting. Her face looked pale and gaunt, her breath coming in short, sharp gasps. All was silent.

"My compliments, Miss Cross. You were excellent on stage this evening."

She leapt up on the spot at the unexpected rasping voice behind her, which permeated the night-time air like a bolt of lightning. Trying to calm herself, she turned and realised he had been standing inside the stall itself. Then, a small wooden door shot open and the ghostly figure emerged into the night.

She stiffened, as she always did on seeing him for the first time. He wore his usual get-up – dark green trench coat, grey fedora and dark slacks. As always, the collar of his coat was tucked up, obscuring much of his face. In the darkness all around, it was impossible to see much anyway. There was something new this time – he held a rolled up booklet of some kind. Staring idly, she realised it was a programme from that evening's show.

"You…you were there?" she whispered.

"I am always there. Watching. You just never know it."

She stammered, breathing almost convulsively. He stood just three yards away from her, and she suddenly felt petrified. Her whole body shook.

"My god!" she blurted, surprising herself. "The train crash. You could've killed us all. Nicky got his arm broke. The circus animals needed surgery. Everything was just crazy."

He seemed to growl at her. "You knew what this was when you signed on. Don't try and get sentimental on me now."

Suddenly, she cracked. She shook her head and the tears came rapidly. "I want out!" she blurted. "This…this is all too much. How can you expect me to perform under this pressure?"

He took a step toward her. "I don't expect you to perform, Miss Cross. I expect you to do what I tell you. That's how this works, remember? You do what I say, and I bankroll your new life." He let the words linger, and she slowly caught sight of a pair of bright blue eyes burning through the darkness between his coat collar and the down-turned tip of his hat. "Your new life. Palm Springs. You remember now, eh?"

She slowly shook her head, drying her eyes under his mesmerising, but strangely absent, gaze. "I don't know what more I can do," she said simply.

The figure grunted. "Don't give me that, woman. We both know what comes next."

She froze, staring at him with wild, frightened eyes. "No!" she blurted. "No. Not that. How can you think such a thing?"

"The big one," the mysterious figure said coldly. He seemed to stare out at the ocean, seemingly lost in a world of his own making. "When I set out to strategically dismantle Kal Klondike, I wanted to do it piece by piece. But each piece would be more dramatic, more painful for him, than the last. So his world would eventually disintegrate, bit by bit. That way, his demise would be so much more painful, more drawn-out, than if I had merely killed him, like I could have done so many times. No, this way he goes down like a condemned forest, tree by tree. And the only way to do that is by dismantling what he loves most…his beloved circus. He has lost his train, that should have been a mortal blow. Now he thinks this TV business has saved him. Well, he's wrong. I can hurt him further, and this time by taking down his most prized possession…the great Gino Shapiro."

She stared at him in horror. "You're crazy! I don't know what or who you really are, but you're a lunatic. I should go to the police right now and end it all."

"But, of course, you won't," the figure said conversationally, still looking out to sea. "Because you're as up to your neck in this as I am. We are partners."

Jenny pulled at her hair in despair, his chest pounding as she thought frantically.

The mysterious figure continued. "Klondike destroyed my life once. Long ago. From what I can tell, he almost did the same to you. This is all merely pay back. You want him to suffer just as much as I do. That's why we came together. As one. Admit it…you want him to suffer." He took a step toward her, and she saw again a glimpse of the horrific scar tissue covering his face and neck. "And so it's time for the next stage."

She studied him almost morbidly, lost in the horror of it all. "Who are you?" she said.

"That's a question we'd all like answered!"

They both turned, startled by the new voice that had come from the nearby dodgems track. Jenny glared at Mercer, who for the first time since she had met him seemed alarmed and panic-stricken. Grasping at his trench coat, he moved forward and stared into the darkness all around.

"Who goes there?" he hissed.

His reply was surprisingly genial. "Well, all things considered, I suppose you'd say a friend."

An elderly man with thick white hair wearing a long blue overcoat emerged from the darkness, shadowed by a younger man in a leather windbreaker.

Jenny studied the newcomer in the gloom, then gasped in shock. "Ribbeck!" she cried.

"One and the same," said Eric Ribbeck, as he wandered casually toward them, having appeared out of nowhere. Luca Marconi walked a pace behind him, looking menacing and keeping one hand in his jacket pocket.

Mercer paced backwards, rattled and agitated, like a cornered bobcat.

"You're a long way from home, old timer," he rasped. "This is a private meeting. Move on and you'll come to no harm."

"What harm have you got in mind?" snarled Marconi, puffing his chest out and removing his hand from his pocket to reveal what looked like a knuckle-duster.

Mercer seemed to hiss like a snake. "What do you want?" he said impatiently.

Ribbeck stopped walking when he was directly in front of Jenny and Mercer. He lit a cigarette slowly, deliberately, then studied the figure in the trench coat.

"Answers." He blew smoke into the night air, still studying the man. "You're the one behind everything that's gone bad for Klondike. The saboteur, as we called you. You had Miss Cross here on board, but you called the shots." He took a tentative step towards Mercer, his eyes widening as he took in the man's terrible complexion and facial disfigurement. "Like she said…who are you?"

Mercer stopped fidgeting and looked at Ribbeck directly. The night suddenly felt very quiet. "All you need to know," he said in his slow, rasping tone, "is that we were close once, just like you were with him. But he betrayed me. Cost me everything. Then, something happened, and I found myself, finally, in a position to strike back." He cocked his head. "Any of this sound familiar, Ribbeck?"

The older man coughed slightly. "That yahoo Klondike is a competitor, a rival. Once we were partners. We went our separate ways. I aim to stay one step ahead of him. It's become something of an annual duel. In the circus world, I'm number one. But Klondike…well, let's say he is the only one that worries me? Why? Simple. Because I trained him."

Mercer stood perfectly still. "Then why don't you let me get on with what I have to do? I'm going to cripple Klondike's Circus. For good. When I'm done, it won't exist anymore. Klondike will be finished. You'll benefit as much as anyone."

Ribbeck seemed to nod slightly, toying with his cigarette. "I guess I'd like to know just who my benefactor really is."

Jenny suddenly came back to life, unable to watch the surreal exchange any longer. "For Christ sakes, stop this nonsense. You're both as mad as each other. Let's just end this charade and get back to town. Please!"

Marconi suddenly approached her. "Cool it, peaches," he said in a queer, gruff voice. "Let the men do their talking."

She studied him in shock. "Hey, I know you!" she blurted.

"You'll get to know me real well if you don't put a sock in it," Marconi said, standing over her threateningly.

Ribbeck had ignored the whole exchange, and was studying the mysterious man in the trench coat. He nodded slightly. "I think I know who you are. Klondike mentioned you a few times. Way back. He...he thought you were dead."

Mercer seemed to chuckle. "So does everybody." This time, it was he who took a step forwards. The two men took stock of each other in the eerie moonlight. "Now, what I want to know is this...are you going to join me?"

Ribbeck baulked. He idly tossed his cigarette into the soil. "I don't know what you have in mind, or what this is all about. But...but I want no part in it." He shook his head, then glared at the other man. "My grand plan is to control the world's greatest circus. That means buying out the contracts for Shapiro, Olsen and just about anyone else Klondike unearths. I want them! After watching that TV show of his tonight, my ambition burns even stronger. Find a way to get those performers under my big top and, hell, then we may have a deal."

Mercer shook his head, almost sadly. "That's not a deal I want to entertain, old-timer."

Ribbeck made to turn. "Then, in that case, there is no deal, boy. You're wrong, we don't want the same things. Not at all." He looked his quarry over with sudden disdain. "I don't know what you have in mind, you sorry-looking son of a bitch, but there's an old saying. Don't spin the wheel without all your bets covered. If you're gunna spin, you sure as hell better know what you're doing." He took one last look at the man in the shadows, almost in disgust. "What the hell happened to you anyway?"

Mercer looked up, and the others all felt a slight chill as the man's collar slipped slightly and revealed more of his facial scarring. "Something bad...long ago. It made me, somehow, more than just a man. If you cross me, you'll find out just how much more."

Ribbeck stared at him, then smirked and nodded at Marconi. "Horse manure!" He turned to leave the fairground, Marconi moving away from Jenny and following obediently. She heard the old man muttering as the duo left the fairground, "the son of a bitch is crazy…"

Then, sobbing slightly, she turned back to Mercer and shivered. "Now what?" she blurted.

The scarred figure looked her over coolly, as if there had never been any interruption. "Like I said. The next stage. Do it. In Vegas. Like we talked about."

With that, he extracted a large envelope from inside his trench coat and hurled it into the turf before her. "Consider that your next down payment towards Palm Springs."

She looked quickly down at the package, then back up at the man.

But, already, his ominous form was blending into the eerie shadows beyond, and he was gone again. It was as if she had been visited by a ghostly apparition.

With an almighty gasp, Jenny dropped to her knees and grabbed at the envelope.

Tucking it into an inside pocket, she shuddered convulsively and stared up at the moon.

"God help me."

Chapter 25

HATS OFF TO A STAR-STUDDED SPECTACULAR!

By George Rowbanks, Los Angeles Tribune

The circus. An old-fashioned entertainment performed in a tent by wandering gypsies, featuring such lurid acts as clowns, bearded ladies, acrobats and the kind generally known as freaks. Right?

An emphatic no.

ATV's spectacular Circus of the Stars, broadcast on Saturday night, turned many people's idea of a big top show, mine included, on its head with this incredible one-hour extravaganza.

There was something for everyone: comedy, high-flying thrills and spills, glamour, traditional circus fare and, of course, the kind generally known as freaks – they make for interesting viewing, what can I say.

The bold TV special was the brainchild of ATV executives, comedy star Steve Irving and circus impresario Kal Klondike, whose circus formed the centrepiece of the show. Sprinkled into Klondike's established and popular format like shards of cotton candy were some meaty special guest appearances from Irving himself, Western star Jason Lash, TV diva Linda Schneider and comic Larry Lassiter.

The show ran off like a variety special, with each act offering something fresh and original, and the guest stars a nice diversion.

There can be no debate, the circus acts made for incredible television. Trapeze artist Gino Shapiro took most of the plaudits for his high-flying acts of derring do, which climaxed with a mesmerising high wire walk in which he performed a cartwheel. Corky the Clown provided traditional circus fun with his juggling and unicycle riding, not to mention being fired from a (fake) cannon. And then there was the freak show, again featuring some jaw-dropping feats, as the human blob Gargantua and the 'world's tallest man' Goliath played to the crowd.

One of the show's winning hands was its host, rising star ventriloquist Roddy Olsen, who performed between each act with puppet pals Rusty Fox, Napoleon and Tony Tan. Displaying astonishing and original voice throwing skills and bringing his creations, almost literally, to life, young Olsen would seem to have a big future in show business. His mastery of ventriloquism is a work of genius.

All in all, Circus of the Stars was a thrill-ride from start to finish, and a wonderful addition to ATV's tired and trusted Saturday night line-up.

So, move over Ed Sullivan and Jerry Mahoney, variety has a new home. And it's called ATV.

"Klondike, you son of a bitch!"

Samuel Spearman muttered the greeting with a queer smile as he sat sprawled behind his mahogany desk in his executive office on the top floor of the ATV building.

Klondike squinted at him moodily as he entered the huge room, looking around edgily at the fine carpeting, plush artwork adorning the walls and, of course, the immense view of the Hollywood hills lurking behind the floor to ceiling windows.

He took a deep breath as he wandered in. "Hell of a greeting, Mr Spearman."

The network boss surveyed him shrewdly, his ever-present black pipe rooted in the corner of his mouth. "Hell, I just don't know what to make of you, son." He motioned Klondike into a leather armchair facing him. Then, he laughed out loud; an odd, condescending laugh. "You, the circus master. You and Irving come to me with this crazy idea of a circus TV show. We run with it and then, god almighty, it turns out to be a smash hit."

Klondike leant forward, excited. "A hit? But the Nielsen ratings don't come out until —"

"I don't need no stinking Nielsens to tell me what's a hit. There were a thousand paying schmucks in that studio audience. I saw their faces, son. They ate it up like hungry dogs. And so will the viewers at home. I got my station manager asking me when we can show a re-run. A god damn re-run!" He studied Klondike curiously, chewing on the pipe stem. Suddenly, he looked uncomfortable. "I gotta hand it you, Klondike. I know a hit when I see it and, well, that…that show of yours was a hit."

Klondike stared back impassively. "Well, thank you," he said coolly. "Glad to hear it."

Spearman nodded. "You lived up to your end of the bargain, Klondike. And, so, I intend to live up to my end. You'll get everything Irving promised you. And, of course, we'll get you, your team and all your equipment to Las Vegas. All part of the deal."

Despite his distaste for the man, Klondike smiled. "Thank you, sir."

Spearman grunted, shuffling some papers on his desk. "Not at all. I'm sending our best technicians to Vegas. We're going to transform that casino tent, or whatever the hell it is, into something real special."

"And so Las Vegas," Klondike said smoothly. "What are your thoughts?"

"Thoughts?" Spearman spat the word out. "Keep everything the same as last night. Same show, new location."

"The format won't change. Obviously, the material will be altered to fit in with the Vegas crowd. Besides, you wouldn't want the same show twice on TV."

"Just keep the line-up in the same order and rotation."

Klondike frowned. "What about the guests stars? Linda, Lassiter, and Lash?"

Spearman didn't pause for breath. "Will all be waiting for you when we roll on the Saturday. Irving will travel with you tomorrow."

Klondike was astonished. "Lash is coming to Vegas? Are you sure?"

"You're god damn right I'm sure."

"But he has Hollywood commitments."

Spearman growled, removing his pipe and jabbing it in Klondike's direction. "Now, you listen to me, circus man. Lash is beholden to ATV. I got dirt on him up to my armpits. And without ATV, he wouldn't be worth a dime. He'll be with you on the Vegas show, don't you worry."

Klondike nodded, almost in wonder. "Jesus... I had no idea. OK, so we'll stick with the Hollywood format. Everyone loved it."

Spearman smiled. His fleshy, pale face and black, thinning hair gave him the look of a cellar hermit, much less a top executive. He stared at his visitor for several moments. "Just remember what you promised Irving. We want all your guys on his show. Kinda like a regular thing."

Klondike nodded. "Done. That will benefit all of us."

The ATV boss shifted in his throne-like chair. "Take care in Vegas, Klondike. I've seen a lot of shows, and a lot of performers, come unstuck out there. It's another world. Not everybody takes to it."

Klondike made to stand. "What can possibly go wrong?"

The two men shook hands and Klondike left the grand office.

"Just repeat the trick from last night," Spearman said as he left.

And so Klondike's Circus rolled on to the Nevada desert, and Sin City itself, Las Vegas.

As promised, ATV trucks transported everything, with the studio bus again transporting all personnel. Except, that is, for Klondike and Heavy, who again brought up the rear of the circus convoy in Klondike's jeep.

The crossing from LA to Vegas took six hours.

The caravan of studio trucks crawled through the desert plains until it finally landed at the edge of town, rolling past dwellings and new-builds until it crossed into the downtown area and then, triumphantly, onto the Strip.

At that time, Las Vegas was every inch the boomtown, completely unrecognisable from 30 years earlier, when Bugsy Siegel had opened the Flamingo in a barren desert oasis, surrounded by little more than sand and cactus.

Now, building developments were everywhere; every businessman and tycoon on the West Coast wanted a share in a casino, and they were sprouting up almost too fast for any support staff to be shipped in to furnish them.

The circus folk looked on in wonder as the bus rolled down the Strip, the sun glinting off the asphalt to give off a mighty glare in the blazing midday sun.

The casinos stood monolith-like all around, like giant outcroppings on a sea of barren rock. They went past them all: The Desert Inn, The Sands, The Monte Cristo, Nero's Palace, The Wild West, The Sundown.

Then, finally, towards the southern end of the Strip, the bus pulled into the Golden Dune, a giant, gold-painted building that sat way back from the road itself, with a gigantic parking lot and escalator walkway leading into the casino itself.

Everyone gaped in awe as they saw the all-new circus tent sitting aside the great building. Like the casino, it was all gold and appeared, as promised, to be joined onto the main building itself. The far end of the new-look big top was attached to the side of the casino, and what had previously been a fire exit had been opened up to allow casino-goers access to the circus floor, via a ticketing turnstile. Non-paying patrons could watch the show from the side of the gaming floor, though there wouldn't be room for many. If you wanted to see this new attraction, you needed a ticket…and this was proving to be the hottest ticket in town.

The circus tent was indeed a breathtaking sight, in its resplendent gold. It had taken over half of the parking lot, and bled out almost onto the Strip itself.

As Klondike pulled his jeep into the grounds, he was delighted to see the circus promoted on a traditional white Las Vegas advertising bill outside the casino entrance. It read:

Saturday – For one night only…

Klondike's Circus and ATV presents 'Circus of the Stars: Live in Las Vegas'

Showing at the Golden Dune Big Top

Klondike grinned and looked across at Heavy beside him.

"Well, look at that, old buddy. Our own Vegas bill."

Heavy shook his head, the sweat pouring down his face as he spluttered slightly. "I never thought I'd see it, Kal. Let's take a picture of this!"

They both laughed as Klondike drove towards the VIP parking area. "I want to see the inside," he drawled excitedly.

Everything was set.

The circus tent was erected perfectly across the tarmac, with specially selected sawdust already scattered across the grounds. It would be impossible, once inside, for anyone to know that they were walking on what had previously been parking slots.

Giant stacks of bleachers had been set up in a great circle, with aisles every 15 seats and a wooden wall at the very front to separate the seats from the circus floor. A traditional tent flap at the back gave access to an array of backstage trailers and sound stages. And, of course, at the far end, the casino floor beckoned, the bright lights of the slots enticing and entrancing as they glimmered in the distance beyond.

As Klondike and his team gently walked across the all-new arena floor, every pair of eyes stared in wonder at the hastily renovated big top. Not only was it the grandest and most elegant looking circus venue any of them had ever seen, no one could believe how quickly it had all been set up – and at what expense.

Klondike, Heavy and Plum wandered wraith-like across the sawdust, staring out beyond the giant flap at the trailers beyond.

"This is incredible," Plum was saying. "How did they know we'd want all this? And who on earth fitted the bill?"

Klondike grinned knowingly. "This is Vegas, Richie," he said in awe. "Nothing is too much here. And Hershey has worked with us for years. He knows this business almost as well as any of us." He walked to the edge of the tent and gently rubbed the velvet gold material. "What I don't get," he mused, "is how did they get this up and running so fast? We're all set here. Hershey has transformed his casino to accommodate us."

Heavy smiled. "Like the ATV guys, he must really believe in us."

Addison walked across the floor, appraising the great tent and nodding in approval. "These casino guys have gone all out, that's for sure," he said. He pointed beyond the flap towards the trailers. "ATV have supplied all the technicians and the extras. Those trailers are in a private compound housing staff quarters. You'll find dressing rooms for everyone back there."

"Outstanding." Klondike stepped outside and eyed up the trailers. "This is the way to do a show. No doubt."

Lacey was walking slowly around the circus floor with Suzy. Both stared up at the seemingly endless rows of bleachers.

"It's all so wonderful," Suzy said, gushing. "To think, a few weeks back, we were holed up in that hotel, thinking we were finished. That it was all over. And now…now this! We sure have a lot to be thankful for, Miss Tanner."

Lacey smiled wisely. "We certainly do, darling girl. A Las Vegas audience. There's nothing like it in show business." She waved an arm around grandly. "Just look at all this. Claude Hershey has given us this…this golden big top, as a gift. A gift for us all to express ourselves in. For you, young lady, to shine in."

Suzy beamed. "I can't wait."

Lacey nodded. "I know." She looked back and forth, in awe. Everything was so immense. "Y'know, I've seen plenty of shows in Vegas down the years. But this town has never seen anything quite like this. A live circus. Attached to the casino floor. This tent! Our array of acts. We're going to shake the desert up, I just know it."

They walked on across the sawdust in the direction of the flap.

Gino, Nicky and Jenny were all stood in the very centre of the circus floor, all three staring straight up at the tent's canopy.

"Well, I'll feel a lot better after you've checked all the ropes and harnesses later, Gino," Nicky was saying, a sports coat covering his sling. He had a worried look as he eyed the trapeze get-up hanging limply from the roofing unit high above.

Gino, dressed in a fashionable tracksuit, grinned like a hyena. "Relax," he mused. "These guys out here know what they're doing. A rig is a rig. Same anywhere in the world." He noted his brother's concern and placed an arm around him. "Don't worry, dear Nicky, I check later in practice."

He gazed up again, arching his neck to get a good look. Then, his eyes swept around the bleachers encircling them. "My boy, just picture it. All the Vegas people out here in the audience. The TV crew filming it all. Every big shot in Vegas up there, in their seats. It's just too much. First, we have Hollywood, now this! We owe the chairman big time, my friends. He has turned the circus into the height of show business bravadas!"

He laughed haughtily to himself, as if in a trance. Then, with a sudden frown, he turned and noticed Jenny stood next to him, staring towards the casino entrance as if she had seen a ghost.

"Jenny girl," he whispered. "What the hell? Would you snap out of it? What...what the hell is wrong with you?"

She turned, and the brothers were momentarily aghast at her pale complexion and tired, weary features. She looked as though she had not slept in days.

"I... I'm sorry," she blurted in a queer voice. "I guess I haven't quite been myself since...since the train crash."

Gino looked at her, reaching for her hand. She refused it and took a step back.

"Darling, you look sick," he said softly. "Are you not sleeping?"

She trembled, folding and unfolding her arms around her frame. "I... I am OK. I'm sleeping. Just...it was the crash. What happened to the animals? To you, Nicky...to everyone. We could have been killed."

Gino frowned, taking a step towards her. "There is something more, no. Tell Gino, mamacita. Is okay..."

"No!" she rasped as he reached for her. "I just need rest. That's all."

"You need a doctor?" Nicky asked.

"No!" She turned frantically, and began walking in a frenzy towards the casino entrance. "I'm fine. Just let me look around a little, huh."

"Jenny!" Gino called. "Tell me this...this will not affect your performance?"

She stopped, turned and looked at him directly. "It will not affect my performance. You have my word."

Gino nodded. "Then go. Enjoy the casino."

271

He watched her slope off, then turned back to Nicky. "I just don't know about this dame, Nicky," he muttered. They watched her go. "She is like a…what do they say? A zombie. She must be sick."

Nicky leant closer. "I'll tell you her problem. Drink! I can even smell it on her."

Gino looked at him, then back at her. Then, a strange look crept over his bronzed features.

"What?" Nicky said.

"I dunno," Gino whispered vaguely. He frowned in puzzlement. "She just said about the train crash. That night. I remember now. She was so worried…worried about you, Nicky. She fled our carriage, she went looking for you, boy. I had said you were up front, in the observation carriage. Just before we were derailed." He looked across the circus floor, towards where Jenny now walked. She was near the newly created casino entrance now. "It's strange," Gino whispered. "Almost as if she…"

He looked at Nicky, back at the disappearing sight of Jenny, then up at Nicky again. "Bah!" he wheezed, rubbing at his ever-aching shoulder again. "I need a drink."

He trudged off, leaving a bewildered Nicky all alone in the centre of the floor.

Meanwhile, Corky and Olsen were wandering around the perimeter of the great arena, taking in the enormity of it all as casino staff hustled past, taking equipment to all areas of the newly created 'Golden Dune Big Top'.

Corky chuckled as he threw an arm around Olsen's frame. "I bet you never thought you'd perform in a place like this, eh Roddy? Look at this tent!"

Olsen could not stop staring. Dressed in a T-shirt and shorts, he looked like a juvenile who had skipped class. With his wide-eyed stare and half-smile, he looked every inch an innocent outsider, thrust into the limelight. He swallowed hard.

"Just incredible," he muttered. "This will be the greatest night of my life!"

Corky laughed again, guiding the youngster along and patting him lightly on the shoulder. "That's the spirit, kid. And, remember, it's all going out on national TV too."

Olsen grinned. "It's all too much."

The ageing clown, who looked nothing of the sort at that moment, in his loose fitting sweater and jogging bottoms, nodded. "I gotta hand it to you,

Roddy," he began in a wise tone. "Everything you've accomplished here, since you joined up. The people love you, kid. I love you. You're the future here, son."

"And you're a legend," Olsen cut in.

Corky smiled, still holding the younger man. "That may be true in some quarters. But for me, this TV special is about having one more day in the sun. A swan song, maybe. I can't go on forever." He straightened up as they walked slowly along. "But you...you are the future. And you have a great future in this business, Rod. Trust me, I should know." He turned slightly and eyed the ventriloquist coolly. "But, alas, it may take you to bigger and brighter places than this."

Olsen's eyes widened, and he threw a hand around the all-new big top. "What the hell could possibly be bigger and brighter than this, Corky?"

The veteran clown smiled and nodded politely. "That's the spirit, kid," he whispered.

They continued walking, and eventually joined up with Klondike and the others at the flap.

Everyone started talking at once. An excited hubbub engulfed the group – everyone was fascinated about the new setting. Wild gesticulations and exclamations followed as the group conversed.

Then, out of nowhere, Jim McCabe appeared from outside, walking through the flap with a satisfied grin.

Klondike stared at the short, brawny road manager. He had forgotten all about him in all the excitement. He moved towards him and shook hands.

"McCabe!" he barked. "Jesus. What the hell happened to you? You made it?"

McCabe nodded greetings to the ensemble in the tent, then addressed Klondike in a business-like manner. "You bet I did. Those ATV teamsters tried to hustle me and my boys out of the way in LA, said it was their gig to get the equipment here in those big fancy trucks. Well...let's just say we reached a compromise." He looked back at the trailers outside. "Everything's here, Kal. All our stuff. Plus some additions from ATV. We even managed to set up the midway out front."

Klondike nodded excitedly. "I saw. Excellent work, Jim."

McCabe half-smiled, adjusting his ever-present porkpie hat. "Well, me and my boys – or, at least, what's left of us – went to work, doing what we do best."

Klondike frowned. "How many roustabouts do you have left?"

McCabe shook his head. "Six. A measly six sons-a-bitches. We lost more in LA. God only knows what happened to them. You know these guys…drifters, roughnecks, ham and eggers. They go wherever they smell a quick buck. They got so spooked by the train wreck." He shook his head. "I dunno. I just dunno anymore."

Heavy spoke up. "Are your six men in it for the haul?"

"Sure. They came down with me this morning. Anderson, Beekes, Maguire, Selenzy, Cahill and Marconi."

Klondike and Heavy glanced at each other and nodded. Everyone settled down as they all looked about them in the circus tent. Even McCabe seemed entranced as he entered and gazed about.

"Well," Klondike finally announced. "We've all got our own rooms here, folks. We're in one of the most expensive casinos on the Las Vegas Strip. There's slots, poker, Blackjack, craps, a sports book…the fun is endless. And we've all got wages burning a hole in our pockets after the LA show. So…all I can say is, knock yourselves out. Show time is in four days!"

With that, the whole group went their separate ways, with most heading towards the novelty of the casino entrance.

An excited atmosphere permeated the movements, and everyone seemed to have a spring in their step.

Gino Shapiro waltzed across the casino floor like an A-list Hollywood celebrity.

Dressed now in a tanned shirt with black slacks, with several medallions hanging grandly around his amply displayed chest, he soaked up the glances and whisperings that accompanied his every step as he moved across the packed gaming floor.

Stopping occasionally to give autographs and to have a polite word with the gamblers – and even a photograph or two – Gino happily wandered around the gaudy carpeting, the bright lights of the slots and endless neon tubing causing him to squint.

The front end of the main casino floor was covered with a seemingly endless haul of one-armed bandits, coin slots and various other games of chance. Thrown into the mix were various games such as the wheel of fortune, roulette table, a faro booth and a keno station. Then, separated from the slots domain by a restaurant and bar area, the big-shot card tables then took over the far end of the gaming floor. There were 22 blackjack and 14 poker tables, with baccarat, gant and hearts also played on single tables. The mass of green baize was almost blinding, much like the neon lighting effects that seemed to run across everything.

As he walked along the floor, looking somewhat bemused at the assembled mass of gamblers from across the country, he shook his head. The only sounds he could hear were the clinging of coins and the ker-chung of the slot machines.

Finally, he reached a large side door with the words TOPSIDE BAR. BY INVITATION ONLY emblazoned on a tile attached to it. He nodded at a large security guard, who hastily opened it up.

Inside was a world of peace and tranquillity, compared to the jungle he left behind as the great door closed.

A huge, modern bar made of oak and with the obligatory run of neon lights attached to the deck, ran across the length of the far wall. A tuxedo-clad bartender stood to attention behind. There were two other people in the whole joint – Jason Lash and a showgirl, who looked like she had just walked off the set of Folies Bergere.

Gino smiled as he approached the pair at the bar, taking a stool next to Lash.

The western star, dressed in a beige suit with Stetson, was engrossed in conversation with the elaborately dressed woman, who had a hand on his thigh.

Gino ordered his customary sarsaparilla. When the barman stared at him in confusion, he settled for a Scotch and soda water.

"Gino, you made it," Lash said, sounding slightly worse for wear. "Welcome to Sin City."

Gino nodded in reply and smiled at the woman.

Lash made the introductions. "Gino Shapiro, debonair king of the air, best trapeze artist in the world...meet Gilda Hayworth, actress and dancer, current star of Dazzling Destiny, which is now playing at the Golden Theatre."

Gino shook the offered hand. Then he turned to Lash.

"How long you been here?"

Lash scoffed, twiddling his hat in his hand. "At the bar? About three hours. In Vegas? I rolled in last night. Spearman sent me down in his car."

Gino shook his head. "Special delivery, huh?"

"Something like that, pardner."

"Listen," Gino began, sipping his drink, "I wanted you to know I'm very happy you are back with us for this show, Lash. Having you here makes this feel bigger than ever."

"Oh, I'm back," Lash muttered. He looked at the sea of empty glasses before him ruefully. "Performing under you, pardner. On YOUR show." He picked up a random shot glass and downed a pinkish liquid. "Giving you guys extra viewers."

Gino frowned. Behind Lash, Gilda seemed to have lost interest and had signalled the barman. "Why do you do it?" he asked Lash.

"Why?" the cowboy said vaguely, miserably. "I'm beholden to that son of a bitch Spearman, that's why! It's what he wants."

"What's that you say, amigo? Beholden how?"

Lash laughed bitterly. "One too many broads. Let's just call it that. Spearman has too much on me. If he went public...well, I can't..." he let the sentence hang. Then he drank some more.

Gino nodded. Now he understood. He raised his glass. "To broads."

Lash met his toast, knocked back a tequila, then steadied himself on his stool.

"Say," he bellowed loudly, "speaking ah broads, that girl partner of yours was in here earlier."

Gino glared at him. "Jenny?"

"Yeah, right, Jenny. Looked terrible. She was knocking back highballs. All alone in here, she was. When I first came in, I came on over, took my seat, but, I'll be damned, she didn't wanna know me. Even after that show we all did in LA together." He leaned in close to Gino. "A strange dame, that one Gino. Hell, she looked like she just got outta rehab."

Gino nodded thoughtfully. He rubbed a hand through his oily, jet-black hair. "You're not wrong, amigo."

Lash continued hazily. "I remember when I saw you guys in Frisco that time, what, two years ago. She was smoking, man. A blonde bombshell, all right. I couldn't keep my eyes off her."

Gino stared vacantly. He noticed Gilda had disappeared. "What can I tell you? Times change. People change. She hasn't been right all tour."

"What's her story?"

Gino flinched slightly. "Ha! She used to be with the chairman."

Lash stared at him. "Klondike?"

"You bet. They were an item. For a whole season. He called it off. No one ever asks him about it."

"Jesus!" Lash exclaimed. He lit a cigarette and blew a waft of smoke towards the mirrored ceiling above. "Man, what a hornets' nest this circus of yours is." He studied his old friend once again. "Do you trust her, Gino?"

Shapiro glared at him. He looked at his glass, across to the barman, then back at Jason Lash. His brown eyes were like stone. "Of course."

"Read 'em and weep, boys. Full house!"

A roar of agitated annoyance, mingled with a touch of respect, fired up from the poker table as Heavy claimed yet another hand in what was turning into a very frustrating night for his rival players.

Claude Hershey studied Heavy's face-up cards with a look of bewilderment, then smiled at him in wonder. "God damn, Heavy," he murmured, a giant cigar clamped firmly in his mouth. "You play one mean game of stud."

The brawny man grinned back at him. "You bet."

Next to him, Klondike chuckled. "Always been the same, Claude. You take on Heavy Brown at stud, you gotta bring your A-game."

Klondike and Heavy had been invited to Mr Hershey's very own 'executive game', played in a back room at the rear of the main casino floor. The hushed grotto was peaceful and secluded, away from the maddening hubbub of the gaming action all around them. Soft lighting lit up the small room, and tuxedo-clad waiters came and went with drinks, cigarettes and snacks from the kitchen. A giant cabinet in the corner stocked enough gaming chips to last several decades.

Along with Hershey himself, also present at the game were his attorney, Brian Chambers, and one of his many 'whales', an old oil baron named Clayton Harper.

As Heavy gleefully collected his chips, Hershey nodded to the shooter to deal the next hand.

"I never knew you boys were so hot on the baize," he said conversationally. "Hell, I host an executive game most nights back here. Clayton here tends to clean up most the time. We get some real high rollers. Some players from the world series even." He eyed Klondike and Heavy with a twinkle in his eye. "You boys ought to try a hand in that. You could win you's a fortune."

Klondike and Heavy glanced at each other and smiled politely.

277

It was difficult not to be intimidated in the Dune owner's private poker grotto. A suited bodyguard stood by the door, a slight bulge under his armpit showing he was armed. Another man, more muscle, patrolled the corridor outside, occasionally entering briefly to check on security.

Klondike had known Hershey for years, but this was the first time he had ever been invited into his inner sanctum for the 'executive'. He felt like he was the casino boss's new best friend. The big man was so confident the circus would be a success, and it bled right off his frame.

Hershey swept us his new hand as a fresh deal hit the table.

"But, then again," he muttered, chewing on his massive cigar, "I reckon you boys are gunna be minted in the circus business. After LA. After this."

Klondike eyed his cards, deposited a chip into the pot, and nodded. "It would take an army to haul me away from the circus business. Finest business in the world, you ask me."

"Listen…" it was Chambers, the lawyer, who spoke next, shocking everyone having kept quiet for most of the game. "We are all a little, er, concerned about this so-called devil drop that Mr Shapiro is performing." He stared at Klondike, looking afraid. Then, his eyes narrowed. "Is it true…he will fall all that way through mid-air?"

All eyes turned to Klondike around the big table. The circus boss was impassive. "Damn straight."

"My god," Chambers muttered nervously. He folded his cards, barely even looking at them. "You have to understand, Mr Klondike. From a legal perspective, this is crazy. Why, he might be killed out there! Live on TV. Imagine what that would do for us, the Dune, for your circus! You'd be finished!"

Klondike maintained his steely gaze. "Well, you don't know Gino. He's the best. He won't screw it up."

"He better not," Harper spoke up. "If he does, it's curtains. Your boys will be scraping his remains off that imitation sawdust out there."

A stony silence engulfed the poker table. Klondike frowned at Clayton Harper, then threw three chips onto the baize. "Forget about it. Gino says it will work, so it will work. I raise by 30."

At the head of the table, Hershey cackled good-naturedly. "Hell of a boy, that Latino. Hell of a boy. I still remember when you all first came out here all those years ago. That Shapiro…boy, what a babe magnet. He had cocktail girls queuing up to meet him. You remember, Kal?"

Klondike smiled as the players saw the next bet. "Sure I remember."

Chambers suddenly spoke again. "He may be all of those things, but he's taking a massive risk with this stunt, fellas. He could die out there! Doesn't anybody care?"

Klondike bit down hard on the fine edge of a fresh cigar. "That's the nature of the circus, mister. There is always risk. That's why we're a sell-out."

Hershey laughed boisterously again, enjoying the exchange. "That's my boy, cowboy Kal. Always talking tough."

An eerie silence slowly engulfed the poker table, until it was shattered as Heavy laid down his cards.

"Four tens! Just gimme all your chips, boys!"

Lacey Tanner and Daryl Addison were seated at the bar in one of The Golden Dune's cocktail lounges. It was very late and they had discussed plenty.

Despite being almost midnight, gamblers were everywhere on the gaming floor behind them. The bar, however, was strangely sparse, with just a few tired hangers-on clinging to the counter.

"You deserve a medal, Lacey," Addison was saying as he surveyed his umpteenth glass of cognac. "Kal said as much. What you've done for the circus these past months. It's a transformation, and you played a large part in that. Kal can't speak highly enough of you and Richie. It just vindicates my decision to send you out here."

Lacey nodded slowly, gazing as if hypnotised at her own glass of wine. She was dressed immaculately in a black trouser suit, and her beautiful violet eyes were wide and thoughtful. "It's funny," she mused. "What the circus has done to me. This lifestyle. These wonderful people. The crowds we play to. I… I can't describe it. The talent we have… Gino, Roddy, Corky, Suzy, the showcase guys. Now, the TV specials. Steve Irving and all." She shook her head, waking from her reprieve. "It's indescribable." She sipped her wine. "Make that, otherworldly."

Addison laughed, lurching on his bar stool. "Richie feels the same."

Lacey twitched. "Of course he does. For the first time in little Richie's life, he is on an adventure. Before now, everything was always mapped out for him. Now, he doesn't know what each dawn will bring."

Addison nodded gamely. "It's a commendable lifestyle." He sipped at his drink and gave her a long stare. "So," he finally blurted. "Have you given any thought on when you're coming back? To Addison and Lee. To Frisco."

Lacey shuddered nervously, and ran a hand through her shiny red hair. She eyed him, then turned away.

Addison stiffened. "What is it, Lacey?"

She took a deep breath. "I might not be coming back, Daryl."

"What? What do you mean?"

She looked about, shifting on her bar stool. She shook her head and then glared at him. "Haven't you figured it out yet?"

He stared at her. "The circus? This? You…you want to stay on?"

She smiled weakly. "Like I keep telling you, Daryl, this whole experience has changed me. No, transformed me…on an emotional and spiritual level. And, let's face it, I'm good at it. I've generated more publicity for Klondike's Circus than, well, than it has ever known. And, what's more, I like it. I enjoy it. It makes me feel good."

Addison gaped at her, confused and bewildered and, ultimately, deflated. He grabbed at her hand. "Listen, Lacey, my dear, this has been a good summer but, dammit, you don't belong here. You're a publicist. Not a travelling saleslady. You belong in Hollywood, in Burbank, on Broadway. You have smash hit shows to work on."

She eyed him dismissively. "Circus of the Stars on ATV is the most successful show I've ever worked on. And, I might add, the most fun."

Addison nodded rapidly, holding up a hand. "All right, all right," he snapped. "I get it. I get this. But, well, I don't want to lose you, Lacey. You're the best in the business at what you do."

She suddenly took his hand in both of her own, and looked deep into his eyes, making him blush and burst into a cold sweat. "But, don't you see, Daryl. This isn't the end. It's the beginning. We will all be in this together. Addison and Lee will still back the circus, just like before. Only now, it will – hopefully – be your biggest money-maker. And you'll have me on the inside. Everyone will benefit."

The older banker squirmed in his bar stool, and looked her over, several thoughts gnawing at his mind. "You'll work full-time as the publicist? Jesus! Have you discussed this with Kal?"

She smiled beautifully. "I don't need to."

Addison frowned. His mind raced. "What's going on here?"

Lacey looked about her gaily, and took a long sip of wine, extravagantly flourishing the glass with her hands. "Kalvin..." she breathed. "How do I describe it? We have this...this... I guess we have natural chemistry as business partners. We seem to have stumbled onto new ideas in unison, almost as if we're connected somehow. It's a strange, magical phenomenon. He has been my teacher out here on the road. And I've lapped up everything he has shown me. And vice versa. Look at how media savvy he is now. We've taught each other in a way. And, I have to be honest, Daryl, it has led me to produce some of my best work. Because I believe in the circus. I believe in Kal Klondike."

Addison stared at her in shock. "I'm happy for you," he grunted. He looked about the bar dumbly. Then, he focused on Lacey again. Finally, he smiled. "This whole experience has really got you, hasn't it?"

She batted her eyelids demurely. "Oh yes." She looked at him excitedly. "The first time Roddy Olsen walked into the holding camp in Santa Cruz. His audition. It was something else, Daryl. I knew, I just knew, we had something special on our hands. A star was born. Right there in that old marquee. And he had come in off the street. A drifter. The kid from nowhere."

Addison nodded. "An incredible story, that kid."

"Just being there, signing him up, watching him flourish. I can't tell you..."

The older banker smiled gamely and nodded slowly. "Good for you, Lacey. Good for you."

She smiled back merrily. "And now this show, here in Vegas. What a fitting climax to the season. I still can't believe how Kal pulled it all off."

Addison shook his head. He had lost count of how many days he had been away from his office in Frisco since deciding, in alarm, to ride along with the circus. *It does grow on you,* he thought idly. *No wonder so many folks go for it.*

He ordered another cognac. "Well, this will be a show like no other. Gino and his devil drop will make sure of that."

She looked at him. "On Saturday night, the devil will be dressed in flaming orange, and will fly through the air like no other."

They both laughed.

It was the night before the big show, and the great gold circus tent was quiet and foreboding at this late hour.

The only noise and, indeed, pool of light came from the curious entranceway into the casino, far away on the left-hand side of the arena floor.

The thousands of bleacher seats could be seen through the shadows, all around, and the sawdust looked like molten ash on the deck below.

Gino Shapiro crept across the floor silently, like a wraith in the night. He was gazing upwards, as if hypnotised, staring intently at the tent's ceiling, his eyes looking like they might pop from the sockets at any moment.

He was dressed in a thick white fur coat, and wandered along with his arms out wide.

His gaze was fixed upon the little-seen roofing ring, hanging from a beam at the very top and centre of the big top's shell. It looked the same as any other trapeze ring. Only this one was planted on the very ceiling, not halfway or three-quarters of the way up.

Shapiro half-smiled, cocking his head as he stared insanely at the ring, all that way above him.

"Tomorrow we dance, old friend," he whispered to the empty arena, eyes locked on the roofing ring. "Do not let me down."

Then, as if someone had pressed a switch, he turned and stormed off, heading to the flap, and his temporary trailer outside.

Chapter 26

Final Show. Circus of the Stars. Las Vegas

The big top was filled to capacity a whole half hour before showtime.

Most spectators were gaping upwards, their heads slanted at an uncomfortable angle, as they studied the sheer immensity of the tent they found themselves in.

With its shiny gold sheen, the newly constructed circus arena felt like the inside of a giant money pit. A fitting sensation for the Las Vegas show.

Row after row of excited attendees spread out across the endless blocks of bleachers, as waistcoat-clad pit girls flogged candyfloss, ice cream and hot dogs in the aisles.

An electrifying pulse seemed to ripple through the crowd, with all the chatter fast and excitable. The build-up to this circus spectacular had whipped the city's punters into a frenzy, and everyone wanted to see what the fuss was all about.

Eric Ribbeck took his seat in the centre of the left-hand grandstand, accompanied by Veronica Hunslett. He was dressed in a business suit, and noticed a few glances come his way as he settled in, just behind the circus's VIP seating area.

"I'll be damned if I ever saw anything like this," he muttered acidly, as he took in the scope of the mighty gold tent. "Look at this thing. I feel like I'm in a god damn spaceship."

Veronica nodded, her usual poker face showing little emotion. "It would seem our friend Klondike has stumbled onto a gold mine out here. This is a massive audience."

"And live on TV," Ribbeck added dryly. He shook his head, studying the glossy programme he had bought moments earlier at a kiosk. "That son of a bitch. Last month, the yahoo was on his knees after the train crash. Now…he has all this."

"Just how did he do it, Eric?"

Ribbeck snarled like an animal. He seemed to have aged ten years in the last few weeks, Veronica thought. "He has all the key ingredients," the older man continued. "Contacts. Knowledge. Flair. IOUs. And, most important of all, luck. Even when he's down, he's on his way up."

Veronica studied the crowds, the excited faces, young and old, all around. "This is some finale for their season."

"I can see that," Ribbeck snorted. "Our final show is next month in Beaumont, Washington. A show field outside a polo ground." He looked around in disgust. "We need some Vegas big shots in our pocket. Without question."

As he studied the interior of the tent, marvelling at its construction, his eyes suddenly fell on Luca Marconi, who was standing at the front of the grandstand, staring straight at him. Marconi was dressed in the standard roustabout attire of lumberjack shirt and jeans, and was holding a spanner.

Ribbeck nodded at him. The younger man subtly replied with a barely noticeable nod of his own. Then, he turned and vaulted over the hoardings and onto the sawdust.

Ribbeck smirked, then began looking over the crowd behind him.

Suddenly, he froze all over.

There he was. Two rows up, and about 12 seats along from him. Green trench coat and fedora. The mystery man was sat right there, watching and waiting, just like he was. Yet again, it was impossible to make out his facial features, only a cold pair of eyes that stared out emotionlessly at the extravagant fare before him.

Ribbeck turned away before the man could see him. Had he noticed him? It was impossible to tell. There was something about seeing the figure sat there in his trench coat that made Ribbeck feel shivery and nauseous. What was he doing? He tried not to think about it.

He thought about telling Veronica about the mystery man's presence just behind them. But then, he thought better of it and instead tried to concentrate on the show that was about to commence.

His ageing green eyes locked onto the tent flap straight ahead of him, and he gazed at the group of roustabouts and backstage casino staff who were rushing around, completing final, last-minute tasks.

He squinted across the circus floor, trying to get a glimpse of the man, his former partner turned adversary. It had been several years since the two of them had met, face to face. He felt nervous, and oddly excited.

Klondike had upped the ante with LA and now this. He had to respond in kind. And he wanted Klondike's star attractions. Bad.

He waited for Klondike to show himself at the flap.

The newly constructed backstage area comprised of a large walkway and fenced-off area in the Golden Dune's gardens, where the circus trailers were scattered randomly in the shadow of the great tent. The midway had been constructed out front, and the circus stars' preparation area and dressing rooms were neatly tucked away out back.

The trailers had been trucked in from the ATV lot, and were large and luxurious. They sat there baking in the evening Nevada sun, as everyone braced themselves for another huge evening of circus enlightenment.

Klondike, Heavy and Plum were wandering about the trailers like stressed-out wedding planners that had lost a bridegroom.

They went from trailer to trailer, checking in on everyone. The scenes they found in each of the mobiles were a delight. Gargantua was tucking into hamburgers and fries, despite being due on in less than an hour. Percy Pringle and his crew were sat about in a circle in their trailer, singing old gospel medleys. Suzy was doing breathing exercises when they checked in on her. And Corky was giving a motivational speech to the showcase clowns in the largest trailer at the back of the compound.

When they checked in on Gino Shapiro, they found the flyer chatting casually to Nicky and Jenny.

"You guys all good?" Klondike asked, poking his head through the narrow door. He grinned. Gino and Jenny made an astonishing sight, all decked out in their orange jumpsuits.

Gino smiled coolly. "All present and correct, my chairman. I am just, ah, trying to soothe Jenny girl. She worry about the big drop later."

Jenny looked up at him as he placed an arm on her shoulder. She looked dazzling in her multi-coloured make-up and seemed to have caught some much-needed sun on her cheeks. "It's just," she whispered, "it's just there's nothing I can do for that jump. I'll be helpless."

Klondike spoke up. "Don't worry. Gino's been working up to this moment his whole life."

She looked at him in the doorway, and seemed to scowl. Then, she softened. "I guess so."

"Of course," Gino said grandly. "The world is watching. And the great Gino Shapiro will not disappoint."

Klondike grinned down at Heavy and Plum, stood just outside. "That's the spirit," he drawled, "go get 'em."

He climbed down onto the grass and led the way to the trailer next door. Knocking once, he pushed the door open. Inside, he found Lacey Tanner perched on the dresser, chatting excitedly to Roddy Olsen.

"Oh, sorry," Klondike said awkwardly at the door. "I didn't mean to interrupt. I'm just doing my rounds. You OK, kid?"

Lacey beamed. She was in her circus attire now, a beautiful golden and green cocktail dress. "It's all right, Kalvin. I was just telling our boy here how proud we all are of him."

"Right," Klondike blurted. He studied Olsen. "This is the grandest stage in all of Vegas, kid. And tonight you get to own it. Are you ready?"

Olsen smiled confidently. "You better believe it, Mr Klondike."

Lacey threw her head back and laughed aloud. "As sure of himself as he always was. Just like when we first met. When we got you that contract. Do you remember that day, Kal?"

Klondike nodded knowingly. "Yes, I remember. And we all have a lot to thank you for, Lacey. You championed young Roddy here from day one. And we'll never forget it. The circus owes you. Always."

Olsen looked up at the glamorous PR specialist perched before him. "No one owes you more than me, Miss Tanner. And the same goes for you, Mr Klondike. And you two, Mr Brown and Mr Plum," he called to the others just outside the door. "You guys have made me. And I won't ever let you down."

Lacey stared at him, a mixture of pride and admiration filling her beautiful features. She patted him on the shoulder, then winked at Klondike. She had been right behind the kid from the first minute. He smiled knowingly.

"Good luck, kid!" he boomed, before exiting the trailer. As he left, he saw Lacey pull Olsen's trademark silver waistcoat from a bag.

The next stop was what the circus folks had dubbed the 'VIP tent'. It belonged to Steve Irving, but his fellow Hollywood dwellers Linda Schneider, Jason Lash and even Larry Lassiter had set up camp inside. The four seemed to have found a mutual interest – Hollywood gossip.

When Klondike peeked inside the trailer door, Linda was sat in a high chair, dressed in a robe, her hair and make-up being attended to by a young girl. Lash and Irving stood before her, drinking Scotch and smoking, both enchanted by the TV star's endless stories. By contrast, Lassiter sat on a couch, reading a magazine.

All four greeted Klondike enthusiastically as he looked in on them. After a few pleasantries, Klondike looked at the half empty whiskey bottle perched on the folding tabletop.

"Just take it easy with that stuff," he drawled as he left. They all laughed at him. He shook his head. *Hollywood folk,* he thought to himself.

He joined Heavy and Plum back in the gardens and the three strolled around casually, looking up at the tent and watching as paying spectators queued around the other side of the great behemoth beside the casino.

"To think," Heavy said quietly, as all three gazed at the crowd of people beside the gold tent. "We have ended up here. With all this. Shows in Hollywood and Vegas. Two TV specials. After all we've been through. One of these days I'm gunna wake up, boys."

Klondike grinned as he took a last look at the trailers. "One thing's for sure. It's been a season none of us will ever forget."

Plum looked agitated. "There's one thing we've all overlooked, though."

They stared at the smaller man, who had paused behind them.

"Our saboteur."

He said the word deliberately, dramatically. "There's no way of knowing if our friend is going to strike again. Sure, it all went quiet after the train crash and Munson. But…" he paused for effect. "We still don't know what happened on the road. And if there is a saboteur, he could still be out there. And we've forgotten about him."

Klondike shook his head. "Forgotten is the wrong word, Richie. The simple fact of the matter is, none of us can do anything unless this mystery person shows themselves. All we can do is plan and prepare our shows and do our jobs as best we can. Then deal with whatever gets thrown at us."

Heavy spoke next. "I think the train crash was the big deal for whoever was behind it. What could be worse than that?"

"We don't know who we're dealing with," Plum said seriously. "And if it's one of our own who has betrayed us…they can strike again at any time."

Klondike removed his hat and ran a hand through his thick, dark hair. He thought of everything that had happened this season. The investment deal with Addison. The arrivals of Lacey Tanner and Richie Plum. The discovery of Roddy

Olsen. The lion attack. The negative press. The sell-out shows. The disaster of the train crash. And then the salvation of Los Angeles and this extravaganza in Las Vegas.

He thought of everyone. Addison. Jenny. Ribbeck. Irving. Spearman. It seemed everyone had some form of vested interest in his circus. How times had changed, he thought ruefully.

Then, with a slap on the shoulder of Heavy Brown, he motioned towards the flap, his showtime headquarters. "Come on, boys," he said. "Let's get this circus started."

The Las Vegas show was almost a direct re-run of Los Angeles.

Various geographical references were changed in the dialogue, and several jokes were directed at Golden Dune owner Claude Hershey but, on the whole, the fare was hugely similar to the previous show.

The audience reaction was also of a similar calibre.

The Vegas crowd cheered enthusiastically at Roddy Olsen's opening routine.

Corky followed with his individual display and was warmly greeted.

The celebrity acts, featuring Larry Lassiter, Steve Irving, Linda Schneider and Jason Lash, also went down a storm.

The showcase revue was met with gasps of astonishment and several stunned silences.

Olsen's stream of sketches with Rusty Fox, Napoleon and Tony Tan brought the house down once again.

To Klondike, watching as ever at the flap, the whole thing felt like a repeat showing of the LA extravaganza…only this time played out in this huge gold tent.

Lacey, Plum and Heavy were with him at the flap, all three exchanging excited looks and exclamations each time the vibrant audience cheered.

As Olsen and Tony Tan began their duet of High Hopes, Klondike felt an icy hand run down his back. This was it. The showstopper. He turned to the outside and watched, fear and desire his overwhelming sensations.

Here they came. Gino Shapiro and Jenny Cross. A duo of flyers in flaming orange.

Both theatrically acknowledged the wild cheers thundering from the rafters, as the backstage announcer made the usual introductions.

"…the one, the only…the debonair king of the air… Gino Shapiro!"

The tall ropes fell from above and Gino and Jenny hurtled upwards like jungle cats.

Reaching their rings high above, the crowd held its collective breath.

The steady applause duly followed as the pair of flyers swept through the air, back and forth, their usual opening routine as spectacular as anything any of the paying patrons had ever seen on the strip.

Then Gino broke into his triple roll routine and standing falling drop, while a grinning Jenny performed her balancing act while applying make-up.

Every head in the giant big top was angled upwards, the ground forgotten, as the trapeze artists wowed all below. The usual gasps and cries bled up from the audience.

The pair completed several more of their somersaulting leaps.

Then, as a drumroll sounded, Gino descended his tall rope for the tightrope walk below.

His usual closer, this time the daring walk was a support act. Ever the showman, Gino took his time manoeuvring across, keeping the fans on the edges of their seats. Klondike knew, could see, that his star man's mind was focused.

Gino completed the tightrope walk with the now customary cartwheel. This time he acknowledged the cheering crowd with just a wave and blown kiss. Then, staring upwards, to the very top, he hauled himself up the fall rope. As he pulled himself up, closing in on Jenny high above, he winked at her. She looked away. He thought he saw tears in her eyes. No matter. Nothing could distract him now.

Klondike gulped heavily on the ground, and nodded at Lacey and Heavy. No words were needed. Only the announcer's voice could be heard as the curiously enchanted crowd watched the tiny blip of orange above them as it hurtled higher and higher into the dome of the tent's summit.

"And now, ladies and gentlemen, for the first time in Las Vegas history, The Golden Dune is honoured to present to you now…the most dangerous, death-defying act ever seen in the circus. Behold…as Gino Shapiro performs the dastardly, the delirious, the devastating…devil drop!"

A pulse-like applause broke out across the tent. Then, pure and unbroken silence.

The quiet was almost eerie, as thousands of spectators, every set of eyes in the place, and more at the entrance to the casino – who desperately tried to crane their necks into the tent – watched the tiny figure in orange, now perched alongside the ceiling.

Gino let go of the rope at last and positioned himself on the roof ring. He looked nowhere but straight down, at a spot 12 yards to the right of where Jenny perched in her ring far below.

With maximum concentration, he turned his breathing into a rhythm and gently began rocking back and forth.

He watched Jenny, some 30 feet below him, as she held the centre ring, awaiting his signal. She stared straight upwards, watching and waiting.

What Gino, or anyone else in the arena, could not see were the streams of tears running down her cheeks, smearing her cosmetics. She tried not to tremble, but felt herself shaking.

It seemed impossible. For the first time in all their years together, she was praying Gino would fail. But for purely selfish reasons. So she herself would not have to complete the most horrific act imaginable. She had no choice, she knew that now, but there was every chance she would be saved from her infernal duty. If only the unthinkable would happen…and Gino Shapiro missed his ring.

She whimpered as she locked her gaze onto his frame above her.

The otherworldly silence that gripped the big top was broken by an audio recording of a slow drum roll. This was it.

The crowd remained emphatically silent.

On the ground, Klondike felt a wave of cold sweat wash over his face and neck, as if he had been showered with a handful of water. He felt Lacey's hand suddenly grab a hold of his from behind. It was shaking.

He sensed rather than saw the entire cast of Klondike's Circus slowly gathering behind him outside the flap entrance. All heads were locked upwards. Several tried to say something.

But none of it seemed to resonate with him. All he could do was watch the drama in the heavens.

Then, it happened.

Gino gave a nod. Jenny released the centre ring. The ring swung out into the centre of the tent. It seemed to grace the air in slow motion. But it picked up speed as it flew towards the centre.

Then, from what seemed the top of the world, Gino took a step forwards into nothingness. His body hurtled downwards, straight as an arrow, as he plummeted through the air. His arms and legs remained straight, his body looking like an orange side of timber, as he plummeted down towards the sawdust floor far below.

A cacophony of screams and wild gasps filled the circus tent. Thousands of patrons were witnessing what looked like certain suicide.

The ring had come to the end of its swing and was coming back towards Jenny. As it gently flew back, Gino's soaring frame shot past it. Two hands appeared from the speeding orange blur and, suddenly, he was clinging onto the ring, as it jerked sideways and bucked like a wild bronco.

He made it.

The whole stunt had lasted three seconds. To all watching, it had felt like an eternity. But now it was over, and Gino Shapiro was safe and well and back attached to a trapeze ring.

He careened wildly through the air for several moments, clinging to the lifeline of the ring, then pulled himself into a sitting position as it began to settle. He threw his head back in triumph, then looked across at Jenny. She glared at him, but he was too enthused and over-stimulated to notice. He yelled out a congratulatory word to her, then stood on the ring to soak up the adulation of everyone in the tent.

The crowd erupted into joyous applause, cheering and screaming at what they had just witnessed. The sudden explosion of noise sounded all the more emphatic after the prolonged silence that had preceded it.

Gino stood there, swinging gently on the ring, one arm raised aloft in triumph. He blew kisses to all corners of the big top, wearing the largest of smiles. He was breathing heavily, his face and body caked in sweat, but already his mind was whirling. This stunt, witnessed by one of the biggest crowds in Vegas history, would set him apart from all other flyers…on a pedestal all of his own.

Down at the flap, Klondike and all the others applauded happily. All looked up in wonder at the man in orange waving to the fans. Nicky appeared at the head of the crowd at the flap, and Heavy put an arm around him in celebration.

Klondike continued clapping, until he was forced to stop as Lacey embraced him in a tight hug. She looked up at him. Her eyes were alive with a strange, unnatural excitement. "Thank you," she whispered.

He looked down at her, cuddling her frame. "For what?"

"For this. This thrill ride."

They both looked up again as Gino bowed theatrically on the centre ring.

The applause finally began to die away. Gino built up momentum on the ring, still nodding his thanks at the audience all around. All that was left was to vault over to Jenny, who would catch him and propel him onto her tall rope. Then he was done for the summer.

He leant back as the centre ring swung backwards, drove his weight against it again, swept back and then prepared to launch himself towards Jenny.

Jenny had gotten into position, hanging upside down with her legs supporting her, ready for a standard catch and throw.

With the audience still dazzled by the devil drop, Gino took another breath and threw himself off the ring. He dived through the air towards Jenny's waiting hands, and spread his arms out for the receive.

Then, he saw something horrifying.

As he flew towards his partner, he saw her mouth one word at him. "No."

He was two yards away from her waiting grasp when the truly unthinkable happened. She moved her arms in.

It was a subtle motion. From any distance, it would have looked like an accident. An honest mistake in handling. But to Gino, there was no mistake. She meant to kill him.

That thought struck him as he flew past her, under her, their hands missing by inches as she pulled hers away at the very moment they were due to join his as one.

It sounded like every female in the tent screamed at once. A chorus of anguish. Everyone in the audience now stood, gaping in horror at the falling trapeze artist.

Gino did not panic. With the ground racing up towards him, he pulled his knees into his chest, threw himself into a wild somersault, and spread his arms out wide in a gliding motion. The unreal stunt brought him a few yards extra and, as he plummeted like a stone to the sawdust below, he held his arms out front like an Olympic diver, desperately searching for Jenny's tall rope. He fell at an angle, diagonally, and saw the rope play out before him as he descended insanely.

The ground came up to meet him. He turned in mid-air onto his back, and his right arm grasped something firm. His hand clung to the rope like a rivet. His right shoulder popped and felt like it had come straight out of the socket. Turning, letting his body droop vertically, he clasped the tall rope with both hands above his head. He hung there limply, shaking like a leaf.

Then, he looked down. The sawdust floor was right there, about three yards beneath his feet.

The relief was indescribable. He just let himself hang there, clinging to the rope like a sloth. He slowly regained his senses. The crowd was on its feet again, cheering in a crazed, almost angry, manner. He swayed back and forth on the rope.

Klondike, Lacey and the others were racing across the circus floor. Everyone connected to the circus seemed to be heading right for him. He watched them curiously.

Klondike was wild as he sprinted across the sawdust. "Jesus Christ!" he stammered. Only Nicky, despite having his arm in a sling, was able to keep up. Both were ashen-faced as they made for the tall rope on the far side of the tent.

Gino watched them in a daze. Then, with sudden, chilling clarity, he looked up. Eighty yards above, Jenny was gazing down at him, still swinging gently on her ring. She was crying. Everyone could see that.

Then, as the focus of all watching slowly switched to her, she began to swing back and forth and, in a sudden cat-like move, threw herself onto the tall rope.

At the bottom, Gino shook his head and regained his senses. He stared at the woman perched at the other end of the rope he clung to. Suddenly, his face transformed into a savage, monster-like apparition.

"You bitch!" he screamed savagely. "You do this to me! You try to kill me! God damn you, I… I will…"

With that, he hauled himself up the rope, hand over hand, flying up like a possessed entity. His shoulder screamed, his vision was blurred, but he could not help himself.

As Klondike and Nicky reached the bottom of the rope, Gino was suddenly gone, rising 20 feet up in seconds.

"Gino! No!" Klondike roared. His mind raced. He could not explain what had happened, but suspected it was no accident. A grim picture of what was truly going in within his circus was forming at the back of his mind, dawning on him slowly, but he pushed away such thoughts for the moment. He clasped the bottom of the rope and glared up at the two figures, now barely 30 yards apart, and moving higher with each second.

"Come back, brother," Nicky shouted as he looked up worriedly. It was no use.

By this point, the audience was in a frenzy. Many roared their disbelief, and many more simply sat there gaping at the unreal spectacle before them. Insanely, a whole number of circus-goers thought this was all part of the show, and lapped it up with gusto.

Elsewhere, a team of casino security guards and several uniformed police officers stormed onto the circus floor, all racing to the centre of the stage.

Pandemonium suddenly reigned all across the great gold tent. In seconds, the sawdust was populated by all sorts. Roustabouts fanned in all directions, and patrons tried to scale the guardrail and vault onto the circus floor.

But almost everyone's attention was focused on the drama high above.

Klondike, Lacey and Heavy all gaped in despair as they stared up at the rapidly ascending pair in orange. "Gino!" Lacey screamed.

Gino was lunging up the rope, seemingly one-handed, closing in on Jenny with each painful second.

Jenny had now reached the roof ring, and was curiously manoeuvring herself into a sitting position. No one knew what she was planning. Then, she suddenly threw her weight forwards and slammed her fist through the top of the tent, making a small hole. Grabbing frantically at it with both hands, she began tearing a larger gap in the shiny gold ceiling. Sat precariously on the ring in the tent's centre, she leant back and pulled her arms taut, enlarging the hole.

"Jesus!" Heavy whispered in shock. "She's trying to climb out. Where...where can she go?"

"It's suicide," Lacey stammered, hand over her mouth. "Someone stop her!"

Klondike stared in stunned silence at the lady in orange directly above him. He looked around in despair, desperately thinking.

Jenny had formed a hole in the tent's rooftop. She leant back again, ready to propel herself through, when suddenly she slipped straight off the roof ring and fell backwards, her flailing hands missing the seat as she tumbled off.

Another chorus of screams filled the by-now frenzied circus crowd. Everyone watched as the beautiful female flyer in the bright leotard fell gracefully through the air, like a stone, not a single limb moving. She didn't cry for help, or scream in terror. She just fell. Down and down.

And straight onto a large red canvas. She seemed to bounce into the plastic material and was thrown 20 feet back into the air. She bounced again on landing, and finally settled. A group of police officers and security staff had quickly, and wisely, assembled the safety mat once the danger had become evident. A group of six men had held it up above their heads, waiting for disaster. It later became apparent that the folded tarpaulin had been put in a first aid chest near the casino entrance after a safety check by officials employed by McAllister, Hershey's lawyer.

Everyone quickly surrounded the large red mat, as Jenny sat there, dazed and confused and in a state. Her face was red, and tears flowed maddeningly as her blonde hair clung to her skin. She shrieked repeatedly, shaking spasmodically.

Up above, Gino slowly descended the tall rope, but now appeared in a great deal of pain and waited while support staff rapidly erected a mobile scaffold to collect him. He looked down at his partner with ice-cold eyes as he clung desperately to the rope with one hand.

The police had now joined Jenny on the safety mat, after lowering it to the deck. One immediately turned her around and withdrew a pair of handcuffs from his belt.

"Jenny!" Nicky screamed as he tried to approach her. The police had formed a ring around her now, and no one could touch her. "Jenny! Why you do it? Why?"

She shuddered convulsively as the police manhandled her, shaking her head and sobbing wildly. Then, out of nowhere, she stared into the audience beyond and her eyes suddenly blazed with recognition. People were everywhere, on the circus floor, racing for the exits, trying to escape this madhouse. But Jenny had seen something.

"There!" she screamed in a blood-curdling roar. She pointed into the bleachers. "There he is! It was him! He made me do it! He did this!"

Everyone stared into the audience. Police, security, Klondike and his crew, Nicky, even Gino above them.

Klondike felt a queer feeling as he watched a man in a green trench coat, wearing a fedora hat, scrambling up the stairway as if out of breath. He needed no further invitation. With a mighty jolt, he sprinted across the sawdust and leapt over the gangway bars. Heavy tried to keep up just behind.

With a cry of defiance, Klondike bounded up the steps four at a time, closing in on the trench coat. He pushed past shocked circus-goers, those who hadn't already deserted the tent, and felt a wave of fear and tension rush over him as he abandoned everything in search of the truth.

Then he was on him. Klondike tackled the man from behind, sending him crashing into the wooden steps. Shocked, the stranger turned on his back and kicked Klondike in the jaw with all the force of an angry mule.

Klondike reeled from the blow, but managed to grab the man's ankle as he made to stand again. The two tumbled over, rolling down a few steps, before Klondike grabbed the man's collar and threw him onto his back.

Staring down at him, he froze all over. He was looking at a ghost.

"Drago!" he whispered in a strange, eerie tone. He looked down, aghast at what he saw. The man was a hideous, disfigured mess. Without the hat to hide his face, it was possible to glimpse the mass of scar tissue and severe burns across his face and neck. His hair had seemingly been scorched clean off. And his eyes were bloodshot and resting in hollow craters. But there was no mistake. Klondike recognised instantly a face he had long ago forgotten. A man, he thought, dead. Max Drago. His old drill sergeant in the Marines before World War II. A psychopathic maniac he had helped court martial.

As he leant on top of his adversary, stunned into motionless, Klondike lost all focus and the man arched a powerful uppercut into his cheekbone.

Klondike flipped over backwards. The man stood triumphantly and sneered down at his fallen rival. Then, suddenly, he pulled a revolver from his coat.

He lined the gun up on a sprawled Klondike and smiled down at him sadistically. "See you in hell, Terry Calder."

He gripped the trigger. Then there was a mighty whooshing sound and his body seemed to plunge forward like a fallen redwood. Heavy, who had approached from behind, had cracked him over the skull with a fencepost.

Max Drago fell motionless on top of Klondike, the revolver falling harmlessly onto the steps.

Klondike closed his eyes in relief. When he opened them, half the world seemed to be gazing down at him.

Heavy, Lacey, Plum, Corky, Olsen, Nicky, Suzy, even several roustabouts. They were all there. A small circle had formed around him as he lay among the bleachers.

Heavy grabbed his shoulder. "You OK, boss?"

Klondike gasped. "I am. Thanks to you, old buddy."

Lacey was in his arms instantly. "Oh, Kalvin, thank god." She held his head in her hands for a moment, then stared in shock at the unconscious man next to them. "Who is that?"

Klondike shook his head, still stunned. "Max Drago. I thought he was dead. Everyone did." He studied the prone form for a moment, still shocked and uneasy at the revelation. "Looks like he survived the fire he had supposedly perished in."

Lacey frowned as the crowd all began talking at once. "From the file? The Marines? The one you got court martialled?"

Klondike nodded weakly. "The same. Alive all this time. Looks like he carried a grudge for all these years."

Heavy gripped Klondike's hand and hauled him to his feet in one motion. "Kal," he exclaimed, "what the hell is going on?"

Klondike looked at his oldest friend, then at Lacey and the others. Everyone looked startled. None of it seemed to make any sense to any of them.

But to Klondike, a picture of what was going on was slowly forming in his mind. He rubbed at his jaw, cursing, then gazed in a dreamlike fashion at the shambolic state of the circus floor before him. His circus.

Red-coated security men seemed to be everywhere. Police too. A hoard of over-excited spectators were running around the floor, for no apparent reason. The giant red safety canvas sat forgotten on the sawdust. There, to the side of it, several police officers were escorting Jenny away. She was looking straight downwards.

The scaffolding in the tent's centre was now at full height, and a couple of labourers were gently helping Gino from the tall rope. The trapeze artist collapsed onto the top of the structure, then sat up and looked about giddily. His eyes caught those of Klondike in the stands. Both men nodded grimly.

Then, suddenly, a large, elder man in a black suit was in front of Klondike, blocking his view.

"Detective Stevens, LVPD," he barked. "You Klondike?"

"You bet."

"We need you downtown, son. Someone needs to explain this mess."

Klondike turned and pointed at the prone figure of Max Drago on the steps behind him.

"That's your man, Detective," he announced. "That son of a bitch has left a trail of destruction in the wake of my circus. I'd be interested to hear his story."

Stevens frowned at him. "You're in no position to give orders, Klondike. This whole...horror show is on your shoulders. You're all coming down to the precinct."

The detective glanced at Lacey in her cocktail dress, Olsen in his shiny silver waistcoat, and Corky in his clown attire.

"Jesus," he muttered, "they told me there'd be trouble with the circus in town."

Klondike held up a hand. "I'll explain everything, sir. Just, please, cuff that man before he wakes and runs. It'll all become clear."

Stevens shook his head. "OK, OK. I want some answers though, dammit." He motioned to two uniformed officers, who hauled the unconscious Drago to his feet and applied handcuffs.

Klondike studied the man's face as he was held upright. "I just can't believe it."

"I'll come to the station with you, Kal," Lacey said quickly.

"We don't need a Fremont Street showgirl down there, ma'am," Stevens said, "I need my men to concentrate on their work, not gawk at you."

Lacey pouted moodily at him. Heavy took her arm. "I'll go with Kal."

"Me too," put in Plum, who looked like he had witnessed the second coming of Christ, such was the look of wild exasperation on his cherubic face.

Then, Stevens led the way back down the steps towards the sawdust.

As they walked uneasily down the stairway, Lacey whispered to Klondike: "Oh my god. I've got about a hundred questions."

Klondike grimaced. "There's only one I want answered right now."

"And what's that?"

He gulped heavily. "Please tell me all that didn't go out on live television?"

Chapter 27

"Don't worry, Kal. In live broadcasting, there is a rule called the 30-second time delay."

Steve Irving said the words calmly, defusing a potentially frenzied situation.

Klondike glared at Irving from across the room, then gazed at Samuel Spearman, who nodded silently.

"So what does that mean?" he snapped.

"It means," Spearman said, interjecting, "that your boy Shapiro's near-death fall after that bitch missed him up there is now the greatest circus stunt in history. And it was the climax of your show. Not the devil drop. But the, ah, death drop."

Klondike stared at him. "What?"

"We made it work," Irving said smoothly, pacing the large room. "With the 30-second delay, anything is possible. Our cameramen recorded everything. But we were able to cut as soon as Gino grabbed the rope near the ground. Then, before the pandemonium broke out, we stopped filming the circus and cut to shots of the crowd cheering. Then, we slowly rolled the end credits and stopped the broadcast a little early. Obviously, the Cadillac float parade wasn't going to happen, so we closed a few minutes ahead of schedule and rolled a few extra commercials before the Saturday night movie."

Spearman cleared his throat. "It was not the ending we had in mind. But, hell, in the circumstances, I don't think anyone can complain. Ultimately, we just put out on film one of the greatest stunts the world has ever seen. Gino getting to that rope...man, I still can't believe what I saw."

Klondike glared at him. "It wasn't a stunt, dammit. He was almost killed."

Spearman held up a hand. "That will be our secret, Klondike. There's nothing anyone can do now. The show has gone out. The movie is airing now. It's all over."

Irving placed a comforting hand on Klondike's shoulder. "It's OK, Kal. We did what we had to do." He took a sip from a Martini he was nursing. His tone changed. "Why did she do it, Kal?"

Klondike ran a hand through his hair. Then, as if deflated, he sank into an armchair in the corner. He suddenly felt very tired.

He had gone to the police station with Detective Stevens and his entourage immediately after the show. He'd overseen Drago getting placed in a cell.

Stevens had begun questioning him, but soon cooled off after a seemingly never-ending parade of witnesses described what had gone down under the big top. Spectators, roustabouts, performers, even fellow cops, all gathered at the detective's office within the precinct building downtown. Everyone wanted to share their story, and Stevens soon realised he had his two prime suspects behind bars in Jenny and Drago.

He allowed Klondike and his crew to return to the Golden Dune, on the condition Klondike returned to the precinct the following morning for a thorough debriefing on the night's crazy events.

Klondike had tried to check in with everyone. He returned to the Dune in time to see Gino on a stretcher being taken into an ambulance. The flyer reported that he had dislocated his shoulder. The medics said he was also suffering shock. Klondike vowed to visit him in hospital later that night. Nicky accompanied his brother in the ambulance.

But, despite the surreal turn of events, Klondike's priority had to be the show, and its television broadcast. He sought out Irving backstage, and the two were soon summoned by Spearman, who had requisitioned Claude Hershey's casual office on the first floor.

Spearman had been present in the audience that night. He was still trying to piece together what exactly had gone wrong.

Now, Klondike sat in the armchair in the large, open office, both hands over his face.

"It was some kind of revenge," he said weakly. "Jenny has had it in for me. Ever since I broke it off with her. I just never understood quite how fierce her feelings were."

"And that gimp with the burnt-out face?" Spearman growled, pipe in mouth. "He put her up to it?"

Klondike nodded slowly. "Another unhappy figure from my past." He looked idly around the office. Framed pieces of casino memorabilia adorned the walls. "I'm still trying to put it all together."

Irving perched on the end of the desk. "Why let Shapiro fall to his death?"

Klondike winced. "Again, revenge. Gino is my most prized possession. The star of the show. Kill him and…well, how do we recover from that?"

Spearman nodded aggressively, taking it all in. "So the broad and the gimp. They were the ones behind all the trouble? The train crash? That lion incident? The negative press?"

Klondike looked up, pale and perplexed. "It would appear so."

Spearman shook his large head. "Jesus Christ."

Irving tried to soften the mood. "Woe betide all who leave a woman scorned."

The three of them remained silent for several moments. Then, with a huff, Klondike stood. "I gotta get outta here."

Irving moved towards him. "What are you going to do now?"

He looked at him. "Well, if you boys are sure the broadcast is all OK, I got to check up on everybody."

He made for the door, shaking slightly.

"Relax, Klondike," Spearman called after him. "I know that was all a little rough. But, look at it like this. After tonight, and after LA, you're now in charge of the most successful circus in America. Everyone's gunna want a piece of you. Including ATV. Klondike's Circus is now a box office blockbuster."

Klondike half-turned and looked at the two TV men soberly. "Yeah, well, right now it sure doesn't feel that way."

Then he left.

Gino Shapiro lay half asleep in a private room at the hospital.

Like his brother, he now had his right arm in a sling, and looked pale and withdrawn.

When Klondike entered the small single room, he found Nicky seated next to the bed, the two brothers conversing quietly in either Italian or Mexican. He never could tell.

The pair looked like identical twins now, with their white slings across their chests.

Klondike eased himself in, placing a hand on Nicky's shoulder as he leant over the bed.

"How you holding up, partner?"

Gino gazed at him vacantly. He was shaking ever so slightly. He was dressed in red hospital pyjamas, his bedsheets pulled down. Ever the showman, he forced a grin. "I'm alive."

Klondike smiled back. "You sure are. The greatest flyer in the world. You sure as hell proved that tonight." He tried to laugh, but suddenly felt very weak and tired. He looked downwards. "I'm sorry, Gino."

"Why? For what?"

Klondike stared at him. His bronzed features seemed ashen and somehow hardened. "This all happened on my watch. It's my responsibility." He paused, and guilt consumed him. "And...it's all my fault, Gino."

Gino and Nicky stared at one another. Then Gino said: "What talk is this? It's Jenny's fault, amigo. It was her who let me fall." He stared at the white ceiling. "Why she do it, chairman?"

Klondike leaned closer. "Well, that's just it, Gino." He gulped heavily. "She did it to get to me. To destroy me. This all happened because of me."

Gino turned his head on the pillow. "What? But it was me she tried to kill."

Klondike smiled dreamily. "What am I without you?"

Nicky spoke up. "This is because you dumped her, no?"

Klondike shook his head. "That...and she was misled. By the devil himself. I'm due at the police station tomorrow. We're gunna piece the whole thing together. But, yeah, her hatred for me was clearly an issue."

Gino gazed at him. There were tears in his eyes. "That stupid, mixed-up broad. I took her in. Gave her everything. All my secrets, to her were shared. She was my partner. And this..." he suddenly looked savage. "This! This is how she repays me! God damn her to hell." Then he leant back and closed his eyes. He whispered: "She try to kill me, chairman. I can still see her tucking her arms in on the ring. Santa Maria...she crazy."

Klondike nodded. "The cops will tell us more. But, I want you both to know... I'm sorry. For everything, dammit."

He looked at them. At their slings. This had not been a vintage year for the Shapiro brothers. Despite the devil drop. And the so-called death drop. He stood tall. "They tell me you'll be outta here tomorrow. I'll see you back at the casino."

Gino looked up at him. He smiled. "Is OK, chairman," he said softly. "It will be all right." He studied the circus master curiously from his hospital bed. "I want you to know, performing for you has been the greatest thrill of my life. This changes nothing. We still a team. Always. That crazy broad ain't gunna screw this all up. I still want to be the best. And I want to be the best under a Klondike big top."

Klondike walked to the door and grinned. "That's more like it. And don't worry, you're the best in the world all right after tonight. Just wait till you see tomorrow's papers!"

He left the brothers grinning together.

"Max Drago. Aka David Mercer. Aka the mystery man. I want you to know, it was all him. He's the one who's been stalking you all season. He confessed to everything this morning. Seems to think it'll get him a lighter sentence. Hell, it's gunna be a long time till that sorry-looking son of a bitch sees daylight."

Detective Stevens delivered the stinging indictment as he slumped, exhausted, behind his desk at the precinct.

Klondike, Heavy and Plum all sat on office chairs, spellbound as the detective gave a summary of what he had learnt. He had interrogated both Jenny and the man known as Mercer over the course of the night. He had seemingly pieced together quite a dramatic story.

Klondike just sat there, gaping in shock. "But," he whispered, "but Max Drago was killed in an explosion in Brazil. Back in 48, I heard. Several of my old Army buddies were there at the funeral. How is it he was alive all this time? And then to suddenly appear now…like this. What the hell is going on, Detective?"

Stevens looked at him moodily. He was wearing a short-sleeve shirt, and his gun sat idly in a shoulder holster. He drank from a giant paper cup full of black coffee and dragged on a cigarette.

"A plan!" he spat out. "Drago, or Mercer, spent years planning this gig. Here's what happened…" he drained the cup and stubbed out the smoke, before looking over his three visitors with bloodshot eyes. "Max Drago was certified dead in 1948. In an explosion in an ammunition warehouse in Brazil, just like you heard, Klondike. There was a funeral in his hometown, Denver, and even a cremation. However…" he paused for effect. "Max Drago survived the explosion. He walked from the burning warehouse. Disfigured for life, his body covered in burns and rotting flesh.

"And so began a new life for this no-good sucker. He had been living as a mercenary after his Army discharge. Doing jobs for guerrilla groups and underground gangs for years. He hadn't enjoyed the life. So he did what anybody would do in his situation. Presumed dead. Certified dead. He started over. Began a new life. David Mercer was his new identity. He became a professional gambler, then a handicapper for various Mob outfits in New York and Los Angeles. Even here, in Las Vegas."

Plum looked as animated as ever down in the police precinct. "How do you just reinvent yourself like that?" he cried.

Stevens huffed. "It's easy, if you have a plan. Drago wanted a piece of Syndicate action. He was a good gambler, and knew he could make a score. And that's, apparently, what he did. Things started picking up for him. Fancy house in Carmel. Vacations in Miami.

"But, of course, wherever he went, he was considered a freak. A scarred, hideous monster. Even his employers avoided face-to-face meetings. His disfigurement began to send him spiralling into insanity. Despite the money he was making, he was a tortured soul. He started thinking about how he had come to be a freak, a gimp. How was it he had been in that warehouse in Brazil? What had led him down that sordid path?"

Stevens glared at Klondike now, eyes widening. "The answer, Klondike, is you!" He lit another cigarette, snarling slightly. "You! It was you who had got him court martialled and booted out the Army. A once promising career as a top brass military man ruined. Wrecked. All because one of his recruits had complained. That, in his eyes, was where it all started to go wrong. After his Army career ended, his life took a nasty turn. And that eventually led to his disfigurement and his disgrace."

"Come off it, Detective!" Klondike suddenly blurted. "That's his story. Max Drago was a disgrace to the United States Marines. He almost killed half of his platoon through rough treatment. Hell, he used to run me and my pals down with a fire hose every single morning. He locked me in an underground cell for three straight days with no food or water. The man is scum and deserved all he got."

Stevens exhaled gently. "That may be so, sport. But I'm talking about his side of things. You wonder why he had a vendetta against you. I think it all adds up pretty smart."

304

"The girl," Heavy said in a dreamlike voice. The big man was still struggling to make sense of any of it. "How did she fit into all this? We took Jenny in as one of our own. Kal and Gino gave her everything."

"So I heard," Stevens said with a sardonic glance at Klondike. He sat up straight. "Jenny Cross was his outlet. A perfect inside man. Or woman, in this case. He heard about what happened between you and Jenny, Klondike, and saw an opening. This is how shysters work, boys. They wait. They seek an opening. They exploit. Drago realised what was going on. He heard, somehow, about your history with Jenny. He tracked her down to a Los Angeles bar last winter. Then he got the full story. Heard how she HATED you, and everything you stand for. She was, to him, the perfect insider within your circus." He looked at the men glumly. "Then, he went to work. Like a private detective, he put together a file on her. Before long, he knew everything. And so...he knew what buttons to press."

Klondike was transfixed by now. "Go on, Detective."

"It appears Jenny wanted out of the circus. But couldn't afford it. And knew no other way of making a living. Drago threw money at her. For information. Then, he promised to set her up in Palm Springs with a new life. Beautiful condo on the beach. Easy money working twice a week as a cocktail girl at Mob-backed card games outta town. It was all so easy. And if that wasn't enough..." He paused for effect, and suddenly looked disgusted.

"What?" Heavy barked.

Klondike understood. "He threatened her."

Stevens nodded grimly. "Damn straight. It seems Jenny became so afraid of this guy, she was completely in his power. She did everything he said. He kept giving her parcels of money. The whole thing must've seemed like a fair deal in her warped mind. But, of course, it just got more and more out of hand."

"Jesus!" Klondike said. He shuddered. "What exactly was their deal?"

"Drago gave her money. And instructions. Each time they met. She said she never saw his face properly. They always met at dark places, in the shadows. And she had to keep her distance." He shook his head. "So the deal was, she had to sabotage your circus. Bit by bit. Each act was more costly to you and your crew. It was like Drago wanted to destroy you piece by piece, stage by stage. So he used Jenny and his newspaper buddy, Sidney Hackett, to get you. First, there was the press conference. Hackett told the world about your big surprise, the devil drop. She had fed him that. Then, there was the escaped lion. The negative press from Hackett after your shows. The big one was supposed to be the train wreck —"

"Don't tell me she was behind that!" Klondike raged.

"No, that was all Drago. He bought that destabiliser thing at an old railroad auction. But, of course, even that derailment could not stop your circus. So, as we all know, the dastardly duo then resorted to murder, and trying to kill Shapiro on the trapeze rings. Again, they failed. Thank god."

A grim silence engulfed the small office. Klondike looked at Heavy and Plum sadly. All were lost for words.

It was Plum who broke the quiet. "So, Jenny was the saboteur all along?"

Stevens nodded. "That's right, son. You boys knew you had a Judas within your camp. It was the pretty lady all the time."

Klondike rubbed his eyes. "I think I'm gunna throw up." He eyed the detective firmly. "I had no idea her hatred of me was that strong. That it could lead her to all that."

Stevens took a deep breath and went to refill his coffee cup from a pot on a corner desk. "Women like Miss Cross..." he said weakly. "They go through life looking for a result. Look at her. Born into care. Hoboken, New Jersey. Grew up an outsider. No schooling. Her gymnastics was a way out. Took her outta the old neighbourhood. Made her a circus star. For years, she grafted. Living on the road. No kind of life. She spent her days waiting for a result...something she could put all her hopes and dreams on." He stared at Klondike from across the office. "That was you, Klondike. When she began a relationship with Mr Kalvin Klondike, circus owner extraordinaire, all her worries evaporated. She would be Mrs Klondike. There would never be another worry in her now blissful life. Being with you was that result she had been working for all her life. All those tough times were now forgotten. She had bagged herself a circus owner. A boss." He padded around the small room, coffee in hand. "Alas, when you broke it off, it was just too much for her to bear. She went from being madly in love with you to...well, wanting to see you slowly bleed to death. And that is why she hooked up with Drago."

Klondike was just staring at the detective. He felt like he couldn't take any more. He shook his head. "God, I had no idea she felt like that."

"How could you? You were too busy running your circus. And looking out for your people. You're not to blame. Sometimes, boyfriends and girlfriends just don't work out. We all know that. But Miss Cross... She had never really experienced love before. It consumed her in every way. The fallout after broke her."

Heavy suddenly leapt up, aghast at what he was hearing. "For Christ sakes!" he roared. "The damage that stupid broad has caused. All cos Kal broke it off with her! What the hell is that? She could have gotten us all killed in the train crash. Did she think of that?"

Stevens drank his coffee. "It would appear not."

Plum said: "What charges are you holding these two on, sir?"

"Jenny Cross will be nailed with attempted murder and, depending on what the field boys come up with regarding the train wreck, possible accessory to murder. For Drago, conspiracy to commit murder."

"Mass murder!" Heavy cried.

Stevens glared at him. "The courthouse boys will decide that, large pants."

Klondike finally stood, looking pale and withdrawn. "Can I see her?" he said quietly.

"Absolutely not. No visitors. We still don't know what to do with her. Or, for that matter, what we're allowed to do. She is mentally unstable. A psychiatrist is coming to do an evaluation at 12."

Heavy swore. "I hope they lock her up in the nuthouse."

Stevens looked vague. "It's been known to happen. We can't just let her loose. God only knows what might happen."

Klondike stiffened. "Is she…suicidal?"

"That's for the fancy shrink to decide."

Everyone just stood there, lost in their own thoughts for several moments.

Finally, Stevens said: "Well, Klondike, on behalf of the people of Las Vegas, thank you so much for bringing your once in a lifetime circus to town. Me and the boys down here at the precinct will sure as hell never forget it. If you're seeing Mr Hershey again, please ask him to tear that god damn golden monstrosity outside his casino down. It's blocking out the sunlight."

Klondike stared at him, squinting long and hard. Stevens returned the look. The two men stared each other down for 30 seconds. Then, finally, Klondike nodded and delicately offered his hand.

"Thank you for your work, Detective Stevens. I'm truly sorry about all this. It is my responsibility. And I accept that. I'll be at the Golden Dune for the next few days if you need me. Anytime."

Stevens seemed to soften, taking the offered hand. "I appreciate it, Klondike. And, er, I'll be in touch. You boys take care now."

With that, Klondike, Heavy and Plum exited the police station.

In the baking hot parking lot outside, they all quietly walked towards Klondike's jeep. The morning heat was sweltering.

Heavy looked crestfallen. "Jesus. What a turn of events. I don't know what to say, Kal."

Plum was a sweaty, reddened mess. He pulled at his shirt collar. "And where do we go from here? What do we do now, Kal?"

Klondike reached his beloved jeep and placed a hand on the outer frame. He took a deep breath. "Hell, we regroup. The season's over. And it was one hell of a wild one." He climbed behind the wheel and looked up at his companions. "I don't know about you boys, but I could use a drink. Make that...50 drinks!"

Chapter 28

The great gold tent looked barren and bereft of life now.

The small hole in the roof that Jenny had made with her hands allowed a hazy ray of sunlight to shine down onto the sawdust below, and this created an eerie scene of daylight muscling in on gloom.

The rows of bleachers were deserted and forgotten. Even the litter from the previous night's show still clustered the walkways and stairwells. In all the chaos, nothing had been cleaned or taken away. It was as if the big tent had been abandoned.

It was also strangely quiet. The entrance to the casino floor had been crudely boarded up with sheets of timber. The scene of some of the most shocking events to ever befall a circus was now off-limits to patrons.

Klondike crept across the sawdust in a dreamlike state. It was always a surreal experience to glimpse an empty big top. Especially this one, the big gold blockbuster. And particularly after a show like last night.

He wandered around uneasily, as if awaiting further mishaps to emerge. Looking up at the empty seats all around, he visualised the cheering fans, the joyous applause, and the endless laughter.

Then he heard the screams. The panic. The shock. The stunned silence. He sensed again the bedlam.

It had all happened right here.

He looked back at the flap, where he had witnessed everything, just like always. He had never seen a show quite like that.

He shook his head as he walked. It was a terrible shame. Last night had been another smash hit. Before the madness began.

Roddy Olsen's skits had generated his by-now customary wild applause.

Corky and his clowns had got the laughs. The showcase boys had stunned everyone yet again. And the circus's celebrity guests had impressed.

Then, there was Gino Shapiro and his devil drop. No one would ever forget that. Or what followed. It was hard to believe the ATV guys had made that all part of the show.

He stood near the centre of the arena floor, looking about sadly. Last night would haunt him forever. None who had been involved – performers, spectators or staff – were going to find it easy to just move on.

With a huff, he looked up at the roof ring high above, and squinted into the protruding sunlight flashing through the hole in the tent.

"Like something out of a movie, wasn't it?"

The cold, hard voice from behind made him jump. It shook him out of his reverie entirely, such was his shock. He did not need to turn around to know who it was. So he didn't.

"Hello, Eric."

He heard that patronising, Southern cackle he would always remember. He could picture the sneer. The smug smile.

"Looks like you stoked up quite the hornets' nest, boy. But, then again, you always did have a flair for the dramatic."

Finally, Klondike turned.

Eric Ribbeck was standing at the flap, dressed in a dark brown western suit with necktie and shiny boots. He had aged dramatically in the five or six years since they had last met face to face. Klondike looked over his old rival's thick white hair and aged, line-ridden face as he slowly waltzed back to the tent entrance.

Ribbeck lit a thin cigarillo and watched him, smiling, as he stood leaning against the guardrail by the grandstand.

As Klondike approached, he moved forward. Finally, the two men faced each other, standing just three yards apart.

Klondike took a deep breath. "You were here, weren't you?"

Ribbeck screwed up his leathery old face. "Quite a trapeze act, boy. Having a flyer try to kill her partner. Damned if I ever saw anything like it." He looked up at the roof ring, squinting through the sunrays. "But, from what I heard, you're going to get away with it. Seems the TV people have made it all part of the show. So Gino nearly falling to his death is now the world's greatest ever circus stunt. Pah! I call it attempted murder."

Klondike stood still, ready for anything. "The poor, mixed-up kid. She didn't know what she was doing."

"Oh?" Ribbeck looked surprised, casually blowing out smoke as he glanced idly around the big top. "I heard she did it to get to you, junior. After how you treated her. Too bad. She'll probably end up in an asylum somewhere now. Banging on padded walls for the rest of her miserable life."

"What do you want?" Klondike suddenly rasped.

Ribbeck's eyes enlarged. He placed the cigarillo back in his mouth. "Answers."

"Answers to what?"

"Who was he?"

Klondike sighed. He nodded to himself. "Max Drago."

Ribbeck chewed it over. "Hmm, the man who almost killed you. Before the fighting even began."

"That's right."

Ribbeck began circling him, walking in slow, small steps. "You know I bumped into him. Back in LA."

"What?"

"I didn't know his identity, of course. I couldn't quite figure out who he was, or where he fitted in to everything. I remembered that yahoo Drago you used to go on about. Seemed to fit. He told me he had a long-term vendetta against you. Probably blamed you for his mule face."

Klondike took a step forward threateningly. "Drago approached you?"

"Not quite. I, er, came upon the knowledge that he was stalking your circus. It was obvious someone was out to get you. After all that rustling on the road. We came across one another after your LA show."

Klondike glared at the older man. "What in hell happened?"

Ribbeck chuckled. "Hell, he wanted me to join him. I said no. Hell no. I don't want any part in anything underhand."

"Spare me your poor mouth, Eric! Why the hell didn't you tell me what was going on?"

Ribbeck's eyes flared. "How in the name of Texas was I to know what he was planning? Murder? I had no idea, boy, and that's God's honest truth. He just told me he wanted to wreck your circus. Hell, I imagined he'd steal some popcorn or something. Maybe cause a power cut."

Klondike was shaking his head. "You're full of garbage. I don't believe a word."

"That's your privilege, junior. I didn't want to get involved. And that's the end of it." He eyed Klondike teasingly, still pacing slowly round in a circle. "Besides, I know everything that's going on in your operation. I have my eyes and ears. Why would I need him?"

Klondike smiled back. "You mean your man... Marconi, right?"

Ribbeck's confident posture deflated slightly. He frowned. "You knew?"

"Sure. McCabe figured it out. Somehow, he just didn't figure as a West Coast roustabout. What with his swarthy skin, slick black hair and fancy clothes? The boys soon fingered him. Thing was...he was a good worker, and helped us out when we were short on men. I guess I should thank you, Eric."

Ribbeck shuddered. "Don't mention it," he hissed.

Suddenly, Klondike was angry. "Why the hell do you bother with all this, Eric?"

"What's that?"

Klondike moved a step closer. He frowned, showing his contempt for the man. "How much are you worth? A million?"

Ribbeck chuckled. "Oh my goodness, yes."

"So why? Why do you even bother at all? Running your circus. Travelling coast to coast. Sticking your nose in. Fighting me every season. What's it all worth?"

Ribbeck glared at him, twiddling the cigarillo. "You know why, Kalvin. All too well. I told you long ago. And you're exactly the same."

Klondike shook his head. "You've got sawdust in your heart..."

"It never lets you go." Ribbeck looked around whimsically. "You know that. Now, more than ever. We're the same, you and I. We know how it feels to run a big top. The grandest feeling there is. Nothing like it in this world, boy. I told you how I felt, long time ago. And I knew you felt the same. It just took running your own outfit for you to realise. Now...now, you get it all right."

Klondike was smiling now, a thousand notions running through his mind. Questions and answers he hadn't thought of in years.

"Eric..." he muttered, "were you ever young?"

Ribbeck cackled again. "Oh yes. And just like you. I wanted to be number one. As you know, that was accomplished long ago. But...things that have happened along the way. They..." The older man seemed to weaken, suddenly looking ill at ease and vulnerable. "They strengthened my desire. Made me forget about my life outside the circus. Family, friends, everything. All lopped into the garbage. All I want is to run America's greatest circus. That's it, boy."

Klondike grinned, folding his arms. "Next season should be interesting. Maybe this time Klondike's Circus will take over as number one. We've got a huge fan base now thanks to our sell-out runs and the TV deals."

Ribbeck stood there looking him over. He nodded. At long last, he cut to the chase. No more small talk. Only business.

"I'd like to buy out the contracts for Gino Shapiro and Roddy Olsen. What kinda figures you looking for, junior?"

Klondike laughed out loud and clapped his hands. "Just like that, huh?" He met the man's eyes. "No way, Eric. That's not up for negotiation."

Ribbeck's eyes seemed to inflame slightly. "No negotiations? Dammit all, boy, I could make you rich. Think of all the things you could do with a fresh haul of green. A new train for one thing!"

"None of that matters," Klondike said. "Gino and Roddy are not for sale. We're tying them down to new, long-term contracts right now. They're mine, Eric. They perform under my big top."

Ribbeck nodded slowly. "A wise move, boy."

"You had Gino once before. You never should have let him go."

"Maybe you're right, junior. It didn't feel like a big thing at the time. He was my support act to Dirk Tempest. But now, in the spotlight with your outfit...he has risen to the stratosphere of our business."

Klondike nodded glumly. "I guess that concludes our business."

Ribbeck smiled smugly. "I want those two under my big top, Kalvin. And, you well know, when I want something...usually, I find a way to get it."

"Is that a threat?"

Ribbeck hurled his cigarillo stub into the sawdust and turned to leave. "No," he barked, walking slowly through the flap. "It's a prophecy."

With that, the old circus master crept away. Away from Klondike. From the big top. The big confrontation was over.

Klondike stared vacantly at the spot he had just relinquished. The whole exchange had felt like a surreal dream.

With a huff, he exited the tent.

"Well, boys, I think the best thing we can do after last night is somehow put it all behind us."

Suzy Dando brought a tray of steaming coffee cups over from her kitchenette and laid it onto the dining table, where Roddy Olsen and Corky were seated, chatting idly. Suzy's trailer felt warm and stifling, but all three were glad of the coffee after a largely sleepless night.

Corky, still dressed in his clown suit, minus the tie, sipped at his mug. "I still can't believe it. Jenny did all that just to get back at the boss."

"Awful timing," said Olsen. "That was our biggest show yet. She left that crowd in dismay."

"Some show," Suzy replied bluntly. "I didn't even get on! And nobody even cares!"

Olsen and Corky looked at her. The clown spoke quietly. "I think there are other factors troubling folks, my girl."

Suzy's usual mask of innocence returned. She looked down. "Of course. I'm sorry. It's just...it was one weird night."

"That crazy, mixed-up kid," Corky whispered.

"Well, thank god Gino survived," said Suzy. "I don't know how...that manoeuvre he did in mid-air was unbelievable. But, he made it." She laughed softly. "He even made that look good!"

"And half the crowd bought it as part of the show," Corky added. "Makes it all the better."

The three drank their coffee at the small round table in the far corner of the trailer. An uneasy silence slowly engulfed the long, narrow enclosure.

"So," Suzy said at last, forcing a touch of enthusiasm. She gazed at Olsen with her large blue eyes, batting her eyelids. "What are your plans for the off-season, Roddy?"

Olsen shrugged. "Hell, I don't know. I haven't ever had no off-season before. I guess I'll try and get some gigs going in LA and Frisco. Comedy clubs. Holiday parks, maybe. Thanks to the circus, people know me now."

"No, no, no," Corky said in disgust. "No, Roddy. To hell with all that. Get TV work. That's where you belong. Hollywood and Vegas. Come on, son, I'll help you. Your profile is huge right now."

Olsen whistled. "TV work? Hell, that isn't easy to come by, Corky."

"Of course it is, son. You've just been the star of back-to-back Saturday night network specials. You're hot stuff right now. Speak to Steve Irving. He will broker it. Trust me. Kal will tell ya the same."

Suzy nodded approvingly. "Come on, Roddy. You can do it."

Olsen smiled beautifully. "OK. I'll seek out Irving. A guest spot on one of his shows would be a dream come true."

Corky nodded. "It's coming true."

"Just be back at Santa Cruz by spring," Suzy put in with a grin.

Olsen laughed. Then, he turned to the clown. "How about you, Corky? Are you going to be on TV again?"

"Hell, no," said Corky, fiddling with one of his multi-coloured handkerchiefs. "I've got a few assignments lined up with Kal. Talent scouting. We're looking to bring in some new clowns and comics for the circus. Kinda to make up for the loss of the animal acts." He leant forward. "Got a live one lined up next month. I'm off to Hawaii to see a young clown who's ripping up the circus circuit out there."

"How interesting," Suzy mused. She looked around her trailer sadly. "Well, as for me, I'll be doing my usual off-season tour of duty. A month of church groups and gospel choirs, then the Christmas shows with the Brogan family in Burbank. They will be on the radio if you care to listen. Then a few months of nothing much, and before you know it I'll be back at the winter camp in Santa Cruz, ready to do it all again."

Corky was gazing into his coffee cup. "Next season will be huge for us. After this…" He looked at Olsen seriously. "You will be a massive part of that, Roddy. Come back next year refreshed and ready for action. Keep working. Refining. Fine-tuning. Your act is everything."

Olsen baulked. "Hell, you're the star, Corky. A circus legend. Where would Klondike's Circus be without its star clown?"

Corky smiled slightly. "I just hope I'm not going to end up being a referee between you and Gino, like back in Munson."

The youngster shook his head. "We're all on the same team. Despite what he says. Besides…he's got other things on his mind after last night."

"I think that's true for all of us!"

They all turned and stared at the open doorway, where Klondike had wandered in, with Lacey at his heels. The duo looked like they were hitting the beach, in shorts and baggy T-shirts.

"Mr Klondike!" Suzy screeched. She ran over to him and embraced him in a child-like hug.

He patted her softly. "Hey, Suzy, what's wrong?"

She looked up at him. "I'm sorry. It's just last night was…was…"

"We know," Lacey put in. She took the girl in her arms and comforted her gently.

Klondike breezed in and shook hands with Corky and Olsen. "Well boys, we're here for a few days at least. Everyone is in shock still. Hell, I don't even know which way to head. But I also want to hear what the cops plan to do with Drago and Jenny. Claude Hershey has kindly allowed us the use of these trailers, so, well...what can I say? Let's all take it easy for a while."

Suzy was wide-eyed and tingling. "How are we going to get everything back to Santa Cruz?"

Klondike looked at her weakly, glancing at Lacey for support. "Well, I'll be talking to Addison about that. But, if I figure right, after the two TV specials and the figures they've likely drawn in, we've got a helluva lot of green coming our way. Big bucks! All being well, we're not going to need to worry about transportation for, well, some time."

"Jesus!" Corky rattled from the table. "If that's all true, Kal, we need to get some big deals in the pipeline. Big cities. And nationwide. Come on! This is our big chance! We've got to move with it."

Klondike smiled at him like a wizened cat. "Don't you worry about that, Corky."

Lacey crept over lithely. "What Kalvin means," she breathed, "is that we've already made inroads into next season. I've, er, made some calls. I, we, think that...with a little work behind the scenes and the right investment, including from ATV, next season could be our biggest yet!"

Corky roared his delight, before honking an old air horn he had in his pocket. The others laughed.

"But," Klondike interjected, "we still need to clear the air here. What happened last night was unprecedented. Hell, Gino isn't even outta the damn hospital yet." He looked at each of the faces staring back at him. "But, for now, I want you guys to know... I'm proud of each and every one of you. In these two TV specials, you all hit it outta the park. Somehow, it all came together. The TV project, the tent in Vegas, the two final shows. Hell, there's never been a season like it. Probably never will be again, I know that. We went from despair to the height of show business in Hollywood and out here. The madness from last night shouldn't take anything away from that. We did our jobs, and we were a success."

He touched Suzy on the shoulder and patted Corky's back. Then, he looked at Olsen almost mesmerically.

"And you, Roddy," he whispered, almost in awe. "You have changed everything for the circus. And we'll never forget it. Talk about a breakout star. I still can't believe how you flourished. None of us can."

Olsen smiled, slightly embarrassed. "Roll on next season, boss."

Klondike smiled back. "Damn straight."

Lacey grinned at them all like a Cheshire cat. With a theatrical flourish of her arm, she exclaimed: "To next season!" She looked at each of them. "Well done to each and every one of you. Now, let's get ready to hit the big time next year. You're stars, all of you. And don't ever forget it."

Everyone smiled widely, and for a moment the madness of the previous evening and Shapiro's near-death fall evaporated.

Lacey turned to Klondike, a mischievous look dominating her beautiful features. "Now, Kalvin. I believe you said something yesterday about a cocktail at the deluxe bar."

Klondike laughed and raised his hat to the others. "You bet. So long, folks. Enjoy yourselves. Just be ready when we move out."

With that, the duo exited the trailer. Olsen, Corky and Suzy all stared at each other.

"Well, what do you make of that?" Suzy whispered.

Corky chuckled. "I'll tell ya, girl. There goes the greatest partnership the circus world has ever seen."

Olsen looked out a side window, suddenly overcome with emotion. "And two people who changed my life forever."

They walked tenderly across the parking lot and into the Golden Dune's gardens, situated at the rear of the casino. This area was covered in shade, a nice break from the relentless heat of the Nevada desert sun.

They made their way across a finely cut lawn, then paused briefly to look at the Dune's renowned fountain display. Tiny jets of water rocketed out of a small reservoir at interlapping intervals. Then, every few minutes, a giant fountain of water erupted from deep within the pool, sending sheets of water skywards.

It was an arresting sight, and they slowed their pace to a crawl as they passed.

"How come you never married?"

Lacey's direct question caught him on the hop. They both laughed awkwardly.

"Married?" he blurted in surprise. "Hell, who would want to marry into a lifestyle like this?" He studied the water shoots. "Not exactly a settled down existence. On the road six months a year. Spending the other six either holed up in a winter camp or travelling across the country looking for talent. Who would want a piece of that?"

She smiled demurely. "You'd be surprised."

He laughed again. "Well, you sure as hell took to it, Lacey. But I don't know why." He looked at her. She was almost unrecognisable in a T-shirt and shorts. The glamorous professional was gone. She now resembled a California beach girl. He continued: "How about you, Lacey? Why is it you haven't tied the knot yet?"

She shook her head. "The cycle of a modern-day career woman. I have dedicated my life to getting ahead as a public relations consultant. My career was everything to me. Every time I went on a date with a fella, he was aghast when he realised I earned triple what he does. Something like that kind of kills the traditional male role of provider and protector. Things just kinda…fizzle out."

He nodded. "I can get that."

"I guess in a lot of relationships, you have to look beyond your work. Explore mutual interests and hobbies. Embrace life itself."

Klondike grunted. "I never met a gal yet who liked all that I like. Poker, western movies, wrestling matches."

She smiled sweetly. "You're one of a kind, Kalvin."

They walked on quietly for several minutes, the silence growing more awkward by the second. Finally, Klondike said: "So…have you made up your mind yet?"

"About what?"

He smirked. "Come off it, lady. We both know what we're talking about here. Let's just cut to the chase."

She nodded coolly. "You're right." She stopped, turned and studied the magnificence of the fountains before them. "I told you how I feel in LA. Nothing has changed, Kal. I mean it."

Klondike grinned like a jaybird. "Why do I want to hold my hat up and cry, 'yee-haw'?"

She laughed. "Because it's what you wanted."

"Damn right!"

"What we both wanted."

He grabbed at her elbow excitedly. "So you're really gunna stay on? For next season?"

She smiled brightly, shaking a little. "Of course I am, Kal Klondike, you big oath, you! I can't wait. My god! Look at me!"

"And you've told Addison? And the bankers?"

"Ha! Days ago. They think I'm crazy. A lost little girl. Swept up by a road trip and some bright lights."

Klondike chuckled. "Hell, that's how we all got started."

She hopped back and forth, as excited as he was. "Well, it certainly changed my life."

"And what about your work in the movies? In Hollywood and Broadway?"

"For the love of God, Kal," she barked playfully, "look at what WE have just put together. It's like I told Addison…these last two shows with ATV have been bigger than anything I ever worked on. In Hollywood, Broadway or, hell, Timbucktoo!"

Klondike was beside himself now, laughing and grinning emphatically. Although, he later admitted, the overwhelming emotion he felt was one of relief.

He grabbed her arms. "I bet you never thought you'd see the bright lights of Hollywood when you agreed to join the circus!"

She smiled up at him. "You're right about that. I was prepared for months of hard living. Out of a suitcase. I didn't pack a single gala dress."

He suddenly released her, a look of panic setting in his craggy features. "How we going to do this though, Lacey? You need to sign a contract. We got to get you on my payroll."

She waved her hand. "Don't worry. All in good time, my dear Kalvin. I still work in association with Addison. And, believe me, he wants in on your circus more than ever after all this. Why, you could soon become his biggest money-maker. Why not? The way things are going…" she paused, leaning against a railing in front of the pristine reservoir. "We'll come to an arrangement. Me, you and Addison. Richie too. We're all in this together. There are no corporate wars here. We all want success."

Klondike joined her at the railing, his jaw set in stone. "And you're going to get it! Next season will be our best ever. We got some new acts to find to replace everyone that left this year. That's a lot of talent. But a helluva lot of green has been freed up for next year with our old friends off the payroll. So, this is a huge opportunity. Hell, we've got to create a new show!"

Lacey looked at him and rolled back her head. "I can't wait, Kal baby."

He leaned over the railing, folding his arms. "So, er, that brings me back to my early point. One of my many earlier points."

She raised an inquisitive eyebrow at him as they stood in the sunshine.

"What can I ever do to thank you…thank you for all this? You've gone above and beyond the call of duty with your work for us, Lacey. I want to show my appreciation."

She gazed at him tentatively, then grinned mischievously. Suddenly, she looked like a teenage girl. A cheerleader chatting to a quarterback. "Well, there's only one thing I can think of."

She let the silence linger, before adding: "A date."

Klondike hesitated, feeling awkward. "What…with me?"

She rolled her eyes. "No, with Gary Cooper! Of course with you, you big ape!"

He laughed, scratching the stubble on his chin. "OK, but, er…it's, well, it's been a little while since I dated anyone."

"I know, Kal."

"I'll have to think about what and where we…"

"It's simple, tough guy. We're not playing poker. We're not going to watch a western. And we're not going to see any of that accursed wrestling you love so much."

He nodded dumbly. "What would you like to do, Lacey?"

She exhaled loudly. "In this heat…" she looked at him shrewdly. "Let's go ice skating."

He baulked. "Ice skating! Hell, I ain't never done no ice skating before."

"It's easy. You just need the perfect instructor."

With that, Lacey linked her arm in his and gently led the way towards the sun-kissed Las Vegas Strip. And whatever lay beyond.

DEATH-DEFYING CIRCUS STAR IS STRIP SENSATION

By Billy Cassidy, Las Vegas Star

Legendary trapeze artist Gino Shapiro left circus patrons enraptured in shock last night after performing the most enthralling stunt ever seen in a big top.

The Mexican/Italian sensation was surely close to death after producing a stunning 'death fall' of close to 60 feet, his act causing audience members to cover their eyes and scream their disbelief.

Shapiro, 42, made to swing into trapeze partner Jenny Cross's arms. But the duo performed a daring 'missed landing' – something possibly never before seen in circus history – before Shapiro plummeted like a stone towards the arena floor.

There seemed no way of saving himself, but the enigmatic showman manoeuvred himself in mid-air with a wild somersault and then somehow propelled his flailing body to the 'tall rope' lying idle close by.

An almighty sigh of relief was universal throughout the audience, almost as loud as the applause that followed it.

As if that wasn't enough, Miss Cross then fell even further, from the very roof of the circus tent, dropping all the way to the bottom, where a safety net was waiting.

However, the lady's fall appeared very choreographed and safe. Shapiro's dramatic dive of destiny was anything but. Indeed, almost all watching thought that a terrible mistake had been made and that he would fall to his death. What a showman!

Incredibly, moments earlier Shapiro had performed his advertised main attraction, the rarely seen devil drop. That stunt involved the great man falling in a standing vertical drop a good 20 feet from his roof ring to the centre ring, which he grasped as he thundered past.

The fact he then offered an encore of what I have called the death drop just shows what an incredible entertainer this Shapiro is.

He now surely stands as the most celebrated performer in today's circus world.

Although Klondike's Circus features an interesting array of performers and side acts, this feat of showmanship and death defiance will never be forgotten by anyone who witnessed it.

Please come and visit Vegas again next year, Mr Shapiro.

Epilogue

The desert plain was barren and deserted. Just a few rocky outcroppings scattered here and there, like liners in a vast ocean.

The relentless sun created a dreary, almost mystical feel, as the endless fields of sand rolled out to eternity.

This was no place for humanity to exist. Yet a lone figure, dressed like a vagabond in scattered rags, lurched across the desert, struggling to put one foot in front of the other as he waded unsteadily towards a pile of boulders turned white by the sun.

The man looked like he had spent weeks in the wilderness. His scraggly red beard and wavy, unkept hair were matted to his face by sweat. His skin was red, raw and covered in callouses. Only the eyes, green and stinging with intent, showed any real sign of life as he crept forward, seemingly oblivious to the inhospitable conditions he found himself in.

He was following tracks of some sort, his eyes rarely leaving the trail in the sand before him.

He finally reached the great mound of boulders. Studying the tracks in the dusty sand below, his eyes widened and he finally stopped walking.

With a loud exhalation, he looked about, his eyes shifting wildly about the rocks. Then, he stopped dead and stared at a fixed spot.

Tears probed the blazing green eyes.

Slowly, mournfully, he made himself walk forwards, to a point just off the centre of the rocks. Then, he stopped again. He held his head.

Before him was an ungodly sight, plucked straight from a horror story.

There before him sat a wild-looking, unworldly beast. Its golden fur was matted and burnt, with clumps of it missing, revealing pink flesh. The monster sat there, its mouth and neck covered in dried blood.

It was perched over what could only be the carcass of another such animal. This one was lying flat on its back, its insides having been removed and eaten by the other. It was a grotesque sight, with the bloodied corpse of the fallen beast looking like a mound of flesh and gore, while the first monster devoured what was left, feasting on its brethren.

Emile Rance stood staring at the horrendous sight, entranced by the horrors he had uncovered.

The first beast seemed to recognise him, and stopped grilling over the corpse, standing to attention. Its face was caked in blood and covered in welts and sores. But something was definitely there. Understanding. Appreciation.

Rance glared at the animal. Suddenly feeling enlivened and reactivated, having previously been close to death, he studied the live and the dead.

Then he spoke, addressing the first beast in a hoarse, quivering tone.

"Fear not, brave Cassius. This is not your fault. The blame lies with another. Now, reunited, we shall be as one once more. And, together, we shall seek what is rightfully ours."

His eyes met those of the giant lion and both man and beast seemed to connect. He whispered the word with a chilling clarity, that seemed to break the bitter silence all around them.

"Vengeance."